THE FIFTH

He tried to tell her not to look back, but the glimmer of hope in her face was so pathetic that he could not add to her hurt. He put his arm around her and they walked into the hall where John's things lay on the bench. He reached into the box and drew out the peculiarly carved jade. He slipped the thin cord of leather around Mei Shau's neck and pressed it to her warm flesh where it lay like a stigma.

"Wear it to keep me in your thoughts," he said gently. "I would wish we had never met if it would spare us the pain of parting."

Her eyes were haunted. "It is better to suffer pain than never to have known your love," she whispered. "I will wear it until you return to me. My life is yours forever."

"Don't say that—don't believe it." Guilt filled him.

She touched a finger to his lips to silence him. Her smile was serene as she kissed him with a tenderness beyond her own suffering.

Her lips were cool and dry, bled of passion by the reality of their parting. Cold weariness filled his chest.

"Go now," he said gently.

She touched the jade amulet around her neck and lovingly pressed it between her breasts.

THE FIFTH JADE OF HEAVEN

Marilyn Granbeck

Hamlyn Paperbacks

A Hamlyn Paperback

Published by Arrow Books Limited
17-21 Conway Street, London W1P 6JD

A division of the Hutchinson Publishing Group

London Melbourne Sydney Auckland
Johannesburg and agencies throughout
the world

First published in Great Britain
by Hamlyn Paperbacks 1984

© Marilyn Granbeck 1982

Printed and bound in Great Britain by
Anchor Brendon Limited, Tiptree, Essex

ISBN 0 09 934220 0

To Morrice . . .
with very special love, and very
special memories of Hong Kong

Things that are done, it is needless
to speak about . . . things that are past,
it is needless to blame.

CONFUCIUS

PROLOGUE

In the brackish noonday heat a lone figure walked slowly along the path near the wall of Military Headquarters. Nearby a leafy parasol tree spread a green fan over the hillside, and clusters of creamy blossoms fluttered in the errant, whispering breeze. The monotonous thrum of *tacuas* pierced the hot silence.

Shadows played across Mei Shau's oval face as she watched the soldier step from the path and open the gate of the last bungalow. He vanished behind the thick hedge screening the house from its neighbors. She swallowed her bitter disappointment. It was unusual for foreigners to be about in the midday heat. The bungalows were shuttered against the glaring sun and the heavy humidity. How long would she have to wait?

On Garden Road, St. John's Church stood bathed in the shimmering light. Mei Shau had never known Hong Kong without the presence of the foreign devils and their stark temples, yet the nearness of St. John's disturbed her. It was too sharp a reminder of the wide sea between East and West, of the universe that separated her culture from William's.

She shivered as though a cloud had passed over the sun. No river flowed so wide that it could not be bridged. Her love was stronger than a thousand saplings bound together, and more flexible than a single branch. When she was with William, there were no differences...they were one. She loved him with a sacredness that filled her with awe more powerful than the wrath of the gods who dwelled in the mountains, sea, and sky. It was as if for seventeen years she had been only the faint outline of a person, waiting for a skilled artist's brush to add the details that gave her breath. William had created the masterpiece, had brought her to life from the flat canvas of existence. And he'd taught her to savor passion, to give herself completely to him, and take in return all he had to give.

She glanced along the path as a dog wriggled through a hedge and limped across the road. There was no other sign of life, but the stranger had entered William's house. She dared not enter while he was there. She whispered a silent prayer to the heavens that he would leave soon. Time vanished like wispy smoke when she was with William, and this delay was agony.

She let her gaze linger on the other houses along the row. Behind drawn shutters, the foreign women were resting after their morning strolls or visits for tea. They exhausted themselves with chatter as meaningless as the clatter of bamboo stalks in the monsoon wind. They gathered like colorful insects on the small promontory where the footpath ended at Kennedy Road. "Scandal Point," William said the men called it. There, wagging tongues exchanged secrets and blackened reputations. Jennie—the name rolled across her thoughts like a painful burr—had devoured gossip there like a child with sweet rice cakes.

But Jennie was not here . . . there was only William.

She squinted under her wide straw hat. The gate she was observing opened, and the soldier came out. She watched him cross the roadway and enter the place of the soldiers. Quickly she lifted her basket and settled the bamboo straps across her shoulders. Bowing her head like a dutiful coolie, she hurried down the dusty walkway behind the bungalows facing Queen's Road. The first time she'd visited the house she had made the mistake of approaching from the front, climbing the stairs from the road to the verandah, and pulling the bell beside the carved teakwood door. A woman had answered. The lady of the house. Jennie. Mrs. Adams. In a tone one would use with a disobedient dog, William's wife had ordered Mei Shau to go around to the back and give the laundry to the *amah*. The front door was not to be used by *Chinese*. She had made the word an ugly sound, as though her pale skin made her superior to all Chinese, whether they were descendants of prosperous families or of peasants who waded in the rice fields.

Later, when Mei Shau met William, she knew he was as different from his wife as jade is from gravel. Gentle, kind, loving William. She quickened her steps until she reached the bungalow and slipped into the cool green yard. Only the swifts winging across the afternoon sky witnessed her clandestine meetings with William.

As she climbed the steps, the rear door opened as if William had been watching for her. He pulled her inside and gathered her in his arms. The basket slipped from her shoulders and thudded to the floor, spilling the carefully wrapped parcels into a heap. William's breath fluttered at her face and his lips claimed hers hungrily. Her pulse became a soaring wind as she was engulfed by his eagerness and passion. His stature dwarfed her, but she was safe in his strong arms. Safe and loved. He was part of her and she of him. They were one.

She trembled as his hand moved across the flesh beneath her *san*. He cupped one tiny breast as though it were the dearest treasure in his world. The strong rhythm of his heartbeat was in tune with hers.

"You're late," he murmured, unfastening the straw hat so that he could stroke her gleaming ebony hair. His smile was tender and eager.

"I saw the soldier enter."

A shadow crossed his face and the light was snuffed out of his eyes. Mei Shau touched his cheek and looked at him solemnly. He looked so sad that her heart ached.

He sighed heavily and sank onto the narrow bench near the door. She dropped to her knees and pressed his hand in hers, waiting. He drew a labored breath and sighed again. It was like the sound of a winter wind on a desolate mountain peak. Mei Shau's heart trembled.

"The soldier brought news from Shanghai that my brother has been killed."

The burden on Mei Shau's heart lightened. William's brother was a soldier in the distant international city of Shanghai, part of a world she did not know. Her father and brothers scorned the presence of foreigners in the Celestial Empire and vowed that the Nationalists would drive them out, but she knew nothing of politics or war. She knew only love.

William lifted a box from the bench. "John's personal effects. The soldier brought them." He lifted the lid and fingered a worn wallet, a sepia photograph of a woman, a few papers, army identification tags, and a small, flat, carved piece of jade on a narrow thong of leather. He let the items fall through his fingers. "It's damned little to show for a man's lifetime."

"His soul travels to heaven. His loved ones will aid its journey."

He smiled wanly. "You Chinese have an answer for everything," he said, not unkindly. He squeezed her hand and pushed the box aside as he rose from the bench. He took her in his arms again.

"It's not as if John didn't know the risk he faced," he said, more to himself than to Mei Shau. "Every soldier knows it."

She encouraged him with a smile. She knew nothing of soldiering or of why the English and Americans fought on Chinese soil. Shanghai was many days distant; she cared only because William was sad. She wanted to hold him close and dispel his grief, to bring back the smile to his lips and the light to his eyes. She knew only that their time together was passing rapidly and could never be recaptured. She stroked the soft hollow at the back of his neck and pressed her slim body against his hard planes.

He gazed at her. "You're good medicine," he said gently. "It's been an eternity since yesterday...." He bent to her lips and kissed her tenderly, then passionately. She trembled against him as her desire surged, clinging to him and giving her mouth completely to his kisses. He lifted her from her feet as if she weighed no more than a feather and carried her down the dusky hall to the bedroom. Mei Shau had never glimpsed the drawing room since that first terrible day Jennie had answered the front door. It was an unpleasant place where Jennie's image still dwelled, and Mei Shau refused to look upon it even though Jennie was gone. Mei Shau preferred the cool, dark bedroom where she knew only William.

Smiling, he lowered her to the four-poster bed where the mosquito netting was knotted back and the coverlet turned down. She unfastened her *san*. Desire filled William's eyes as his gaze caressed her breasts and slim waist. Quickly, he peeled off his encumbering shirt and trousers. Naked, he knelt to remove her loose-fitting black trousers and flat sandals. Each touch of his fingers made her tremble with desire. She loved him so.... Smiling, he traced the roundness of her hip, the sweep of her slim thigh, and the firmness of her calf. He lifted one of her delicate feet to his lips and outlined each toe with his tongue. Her foot was so tiny that it might have been bound in her infancy, but its perfection told him that was impossible. Mei Shau shivered deliciously and felt a warm wetness between her thighs. She threaded her fingers into William's dark curls as though they were spun silk. She needed to touch him, to hold him, to fulfill the promise of their togetherness. She had to drive away the specter of Jennie, and of his brother's death. This moment belonged only to them.

She envisioned his entry into the temple of her body, and a new surge of moisture readied her. She encouraged him, spreading her thighs to let him inhale the musky scent of her desire. When he pressed his face against her dark-veiled mound, her breath escaped like a caged bird set free. Her breasts surged, the nipples erect, as his tongue darted into her secret places. She wanted . . . she knew. . . .

She stretched like a waking cat as his lips trailed up her body, then put her arms around William and saw her reflection stare back at her from the deep pools of his eyes. She was drawn deeper, swirling and sucked into those bottomless pools as his erection parted the curtains of her desire. Then they were a merging tide, swept together helplessly, rising, ebbing, then cresting to a shuddering peak. Afterward the sea whispered an eternal lullaby.

Mei Shau cradled William's head against her shoulder. In the two months they'd been lovers, she'd become finely tuned to his needs. She wanted to prolong his pleasure with loving embraces and the delicate touch of her hands and mouth, but sometimes he was like a man gone too long without food, unable to resist gorging. But then in the wake of his engulfing pleasure, he was content to let her rouse him a second time.

Her fingertips sought the throbbing heartbeat of his throat. He stirred and smiled without opening his eyes. Each crevice and contour of his face was as familiar to her as her breath. Each plane of his body was a source of wonder and joy. Smiling secretly, she slid her hand to his flat, hard belly. He opened his eyes and drew a sharp breath.

Startled, she gazed at him questioningly. She rarely pressed him to reveal inner thoughts she found so hard to understand, but he looked so alarmed that she blurted out, "What is it, William?"

He drew away and rose from the bed, then stood staring into the glass above the washstand. Frightened, she followed him and stood with her arms twined about him, studying his reflection. His tanned brow furrowed like a terraced field.

"Do I not please you, my love?"

"Christ!" He caught her in his arms savagely as though he would devour her.

For a moment, her world was right again, but he pulled away unexpectedly. Snatching up a red silk robe, he strode toward the door. She ran after him. She'd never seen him angry except for the silent rage that had gripped him when he'd felt compelled to apologize for the way Jennie had treated her. But there was raw anger in his every motion now as he opened the door at the end of the hall and strode out. Mutely she followed him as he headed for the strange foreign bathhouse that had been erected under a tent behind the scullery. The grass was hot under her bare feet, and the sun washed her body with its merciless heat. Her fear grew as he stepped inside the flapping enclosure of the tent. They often shared the shower water over their bodies in the afterglow of their lovemaking, but she hesitated to join him now. His back was to her without welcome, and his jaw was a hard line as he lathered himself with jasmine-scented soap.

She'd never before observed a foreigner's response to death. Was this William's grief over his brother? Why did he not release the devil by weeping and beating his breast? She would grieve with him, and they would frighten away the evil spirits that tried to capture his brother's immortality. When she could stand his silence no longer, she stepped hesitantly into the hot cubicle and again encircled him with her arms. Unmindful of the cascading tepid water, she leaned her cheek against his damp back and let her hands search out the source of his manhood, cupping and gently massaging the parts of his body that gave her so much pleasure.

William sighed and cursed himself for his silence. He'd intended to tell her as soon as she arrived, but the news of his brother's death had preempted his own worries. And then his desire and need for Mei Shau had overwhelmed him. *Coward,* he berated himself silently. *Tell her now, she has to know. . . .* But her hands, already working their magic, robbed him of courage. He raised his face to the sporadic spray so that the water beat at his eyes and filled his mouth. *Tell her. . . .* Her nipples were diamond points against his back, her belly a warm cushion for his buttocks. *Tell her. . . .*

Again the moment for talking passed. He swung about and covered her mouth with kisses as she surged against him. Lifting her, he brought her to his hardness. She guided him expertly. His pulse thundered as her body enveloped him, welcomed him, claimed him.

For a long time afterward, they stood like statues of lovers entwined under gently falling rain. He would be leaving part of himself, he realized. For a moment, pain wrenched his chest. Leaving her seemed impossible . . . but he knew he would go. He'd always known.

Back in the cool bedroom, William watched Mei Shau dress. A great weight had settled on his heart again as he realized time was running out. How serene she looked, at peace with herself and the world. He searched for words.

"Mei Shau, I . . ."

She smiled and tipped her head like an inquisitive sparrow. "My love . . . ?" Her velvet, trusting gaze caressed him.

He drew a sharp breath. "I'm leaving tomorrow."

The smile stayed stitched to her face like the thread of a silk tapestry, but her fingers paused at the drawstring of her trousers.

"Your brother's funeral?"

He shook his head and covered his eyes with his hand, unable to look at her. "I'm being sent home. My work is done." He'd known for almost a week. The knowledge had been crucifying him, but he'd been unable to tell her. He tried to convince himself he could vanish, that he owed her no explanation, no lingering good-byes. During the months since she'd first come to him, he'd been careful not to mention "love." There was no denying his physical attraction to her; she was stronger than the powerful drugs the Chinese favored, and he was as addicted to her as any man could be to opium. But in spite of his tender feelings, he'd avoided promises he could not keep, and Mei Shau hadn't wanted to admit there was no future for them; she had been too happy living in the present. He'd been happy, too. Damn. "I leave in the morning." The words were wrenched from him.

The light went out of her eyes. She was so still he could not detect her breathing. She was like a wounded doe waiting for the second bullet to end its misery.

He stuffed his shirt into his trousers with jerky motions. "I won't see you again. I have to spend the night aboard ship. We sail before dawn."

In the silence, he could hear the moaning of his heart. He'd never made any promises, he reminded himself. They'd known it had to end this way.

"Have I not loved you enough?" she said at last. "Do I not please you?"

"Of course!" He gripped her shoulders and she did not flinch under the pressure. Her eyes were downcast and her face pale. "It's been perfect, you know it has! But I have to go *home*. We always knew I'd have to leave someday." He raised her head. "We both knew," he said as gently as he could.

Her eyes filled with agonized tears. Her lips quivered as she looked away again. "You will come back...."

"Mei Shau, Mei Shau!" He folded her into his arms and buried his face in her damp hair that smelled of sunshine and jasmine. "I should have told you sooner," he whispered, trying to still her trembling.

After an eternity, she looked up, her eyes still shimmering with tears. "I could not have endured the pain. It is better this way." Her voice was so faint he barely heard the words. "I will wait for you."

He shook his head despondently as he traced the line of her cheek and brushed away a silver tracery of tears. These few months had been so wondrous, they seemed destined to go on forever. But there was no forever for their kind of love. He had a wife in California; his life was there. There was no place in it for Mei Shau. He'd known that from the start. With the approach of summer, Jennie had refused to stay in Hong Kong until his work was finished. "I'll go home and have the house ready when you come," she'd said. "It's been a terrible year for me here, Will. Don't ask me to endure another summer. Not now when I'm carrying a baby."

So she'd gone, and he'd stayed, and he'd found Mei Shau. Now he had to go too, but part of his heart would stay with the beautiful Chinese girl forever. Just as his brother's body would forever be interred in foreign soil. John had known the danger of soldiering in a country on the brink of revolution, but William had been oblivious to everything but his fascination and desire for the Oriental girl. It had been a different kind of danger but it was ending as tragically. He tried to tell Mei Shau he would not come back, but the glimmer of hope in her face was so pathetic that he could not add to her hurt. He put his arm around her and they walked into the hall where John's things lay on the bench. He reached into the box and drew out the peculiarly carved jade. He slipped the thin cord of leather around Mei Shau's neck and pressed it to her warm flesh where it lay like a stigma.

"Wear it to keep me in your thoughts," he said gently. "I would wish we had never met if it would spare us the pain of parting."

Her eyes were haunted. "It is better to suffer pain than never to have known your love," she whispered. "I will wear it until you return to me. My life is yours forever."

"Don't say that—don't believe it." Guilt filled him.

She touched a finger to his lips to silence him. Her smile was serene as she kissed him with a tenderness beyond her own suffering.

Her lips were cool and dry, bled of passion by the reality of their parting. Cold weariness filled his chest.

"Go now," he said gently.

She touched the jade amulet around her neck and lovingly pressed it between her breasts.

In time she would accept the truth, he told himself. If it was easier for her now to believe he would come back, it was a small deception for him to play. He watched her settle the straw hat over her ebony hair and stack the laundry neatly on the bench before she shouldered the basket. He went with her to the door but did not take her in his arms again. It would only prolong the pain for both of them. Sadly, he watched her descend the narrow steps and start along the path. He closed the door so he would not see her go out of his life forever.

1

Summer exploded on Paris with a lushness that dazzled Arisa's senses. After several weeks of intermittent rain, sunshine spilled onto the streets and gilded the shop window with its discreet lettering, *Galerie Saint-Gerons*. The fragrance of flowers wafted on the warm breeze coming through the open doors, swirling through the thickly carpeted rooms, feathering over the displays of freshly dusted antiques. On an ornate Louis XIV settee, Eduoard gestured animatedly as he chatted with Madame Taix.

"It is the perfect piece for the dining room."

"I simply can't visualize it, Eduoard. So bold!"

"Exactly what the room cries out for!" He spread an expressive hand toward the baroque Italian showcase replete with dancing gilt cupids and flamboyant carved scrollwork. "It will be a focal point to soothe the eye and please the spirit. And a perfect display for your exquisite Sevres!" He closed his eyes as though envisioning the fine porcelain behind the glass doors of the cabinet.

"It's not large enough to hold the service."

"No, no, no!" he said in an astonished tone. Arisa hid a smile as she arranged a small bunch of violets in a scale blue Worcester mug.

"Only the choice pieces," Eduoard explained. "Set apart so they can be fully appreciated."

The slender woman with blue-gray hair sighed, still studying the cabinet as though trying to bring the picture into focus.

"I will come personally to arrange the monteith . . . the *bleu de roi* vase . . . the pomade jars. Perhaps one or two plates. Perfect. Yes, and if it does not fill you with awe . . ." He fluttered a hand. "We shall take it back, of course. I could not bear you to be unhappy."

Madame Taix sighed again.

"We shall deliver it tomorrow," Eduoard said decisively, sealing the bargain with a dry kiss on the woman's leathery hand. "I guarantee you will be delighted—wait and see!"

The soft tinkle of the phone punctuated his promise. Arisa moved to lift the receiver as Eduoard escorted Madame Taix to the door and gave her last-minute assurances.

"Galerie Saint-Gerons," she said quietly. She'd cultivated a low tone in keeping with the subdued elegance of the *galerie*. Eduoard was the only one permitted to speak much above a whisper.

"Mademoiselle Travish, *s'il vous plaît*," said the voice on the other end.

"Yes, operator, speaking."

"An overseas call . . . one moment." The lines clicked and hummed, and a distant, distinctly American voice said, "Your party is on the line. Go ahead, please."

"Miss Travish?"

Again Arisa said, "Yes." The voice was male, brusque, and totally unfamiliar.

"This is Justin Forbes—of Darwin, Forbes and Benson."

He seemed to expect her to recognize the name. With a touch of impatience, she asked, "What can I do for you, Mr. Forbes?" She mentally reviewed the few contacts she had with American antique dealers, but she couldn't recall a Forbes.

"I have been trying to reach you for several days."

"I was away." Three days at Cannes with Eduoard . . . a get-away weekend to "put things back in perspective." She glanced at his profile outlined against the brittle sunshine. He still didn't want to accept her decision.

"The concierge refused to divulge your whereabouts. I left an urgent message to have you return my call."

She hadn't been to the apartment yet. "What can I do for you, Mr. Forbes?"

"Ah, Miss Travish, I regret breaking the news like this. . . ."

"What news, Mr. Forbes?" Would he ever get to the point.

"Your father . . . my client . . . died last Saturday."

She held the phone numbly. Her father dead . . . She felt an emptiness in her breast where there should have been pain. The breeze took on a sudden chill and she hugged her arms across her body as a child would.

"Miss Travish? I'm sorry to break the news so abruptly. You do understand?"

"I understand, Mr. Forbes." Did she? "Naturally I'm upset. I had no idea—"

"We're delaying the funeral until your arrival. And there are other matters that must be attended to. Are you familiar with the terms of your father's will?"

"No." She hardly knew him. As a child she'd shared with him the special intimacy of father and daughter, but over the years he'd become a stranger. No, that wasn't fair, she told herself. He hadn't done it alone. She'd estranged herself from him. Her exile had been her choice, not his.

Forbes was talking again. "There are ramifications, of course, but essentially your father has left the business to you, Miss Travish."

She was jolted out of dull shock. "To me?"

"A small percentage goes to your brother, and he receives other considerations. The details are better left until we can discuss them fully. How soon can you be in Los Angeles?"

She smiled mechanically at a stiff, blond customer who had paused to inspect an intaglio engraving. She waited until the woman moved away. A young clerk went to close the doors at a signal from Eduoard, who was annoyed by the ruffling breeze and the noise of traffic.

"I'm not sure, Mr. Forbes. A few days perhaps." She hadn't been back to California since her precipitous departure eight years ago. She'd kept in touch with her father and had seen him several times when he'd been in London or Paris. The meetings had been strained for both of them. "How did it happen?" she asked Forbes.

The lawyer hesitated as though exerting effort to move his thoughts away from the business he wanted to discuss. "A heart attack."

"Was he alone?" It seemed important that he hadn't met death without someone near.

"Ah, yes, I believe so."

Pain began to seep through her numbness. Her father had wanted her to return ever since her graduation from Cambridge, but she'd put him off with vague promises and excuses. Instead, she built a life for herself in London and Paris and let ties wither to a tenuous thread.

"Perhaps you'll be good enough to phone me as soon as you're back. My office is on Wilshire at Beverly Glen." He gave the address.

The conversation seemed at an end. Belatedly, she thought to ask about the house. It, too, had passed to her at her father's death—for as long as she wanted it. When it was sold, half of the proceeds would go to her brother Quentin.

She cradled the phone. Elliot Travish—dead. She'd go back, of course. Guilt twinged her conscience. She should have visited. It would have pleased her father, even if she hadn't stayed. He'd always talked about the shop as though she were part of it, describing particularly lovely pieces of jade or porcelain as though she'd known exactly where he'd placed them. Occasionally he'd mentioned his trips to Hong Kong, but she never pressed for details. Hong Kong was even further in her locked past . . . a closed book.

She saw her reflection in an eighteenth-century mirror as she went to look for Eduoard. The color had drained from her cheeks. Still, she felt only an edge of grief, and the realization compounded her guilt. No tears . . . her lavender eyes were clear and bright, all the more so because of the pallor of her face. She pinched her cheeks and forced a smile as Eduoard came from the alcove, his face weary in an unguarded moment.

"If she doesn't like that damned Cucci when I get it up there, I'll kill her," he said.

"I doubt that," Arisa commented dryly.

"Then I'll kill myself. My God, what a whiner she is. One would think she was spending her last five thousand dollars instead of dear old papa Taix's pocket change."

"Eduoard . . ."

"Every time she spends a franc I have to hold her hand and nurse her like an infant."

"Eduoard, I have to go to the States."

He was about to say something, but bit off the words and stared at her. "To the *United States*?"

"Don't make it sound like Outer Mongolia," she said wearily. "Yes, the United States. Los Angeles, to be exact."

"But you hate Los Angeles!"

"My father died," she said flatly. Why didn't she feel grief or pain—anything but the horrible numbness that was squeezing her into a hard, tight ball.

Eduoard's eyes rounded and his hands were still. He was suddenly Edward Simon, the man he kept disguised under the cloak of Eduoard Saint-Gerons. "I'm sorry, Arisa, truly sorry. I know you were fond of him in spite of the distance you kept between you."

She looked at him in surprise. Was he merely trying to

placate her with sympathetic words? Eduoard took her arm and drew her through the alcove to his office. He installed her in a comfortable suede armchair that offered no illusion of being an antique. The office was strictly reserved for rare moments when he escaped from the pretenses of the shop. He poured wine into two crystal glasses and brought one to her.

"It'll help, babe. Want to talk about it?"

"There's nothing to say. A lawyer called me—just now. My father died on Saturday. They couldn't find me until today. The funeral . . . legal things . . . I have to go back."

"I'll arrange the ticket," he said gently. "Would you like me to drive you home and help you pack?"

She shook her head and managed a smile. "No, I'm all right."

He smiled. "You always are, *cherie*. How long will you be gone? There's no rush, I'll get someone to fill in. Take as long as you need."

She sighed. "I won't be coming back to the *galerie*, Eduoard. It's the perfect time to make the split."

"Because of our quarrel? Don't be silly, Arisa. We're still friends. We always will be. This isn't the time to—"

"Please." They'd been over this too many times. It wasn't just the end of the love affair. She was tired of what the *galerie* stood for, the catering to money rather than a love of art. Eduoard had long ago lost any respect he had for the antiques he dealt in. They'd become sausages or rounds of cheese that had to be pushed out of stock before they ripened too well. Profit margins and the bottom line were all that counted.

"Drink your wine," he said gently, bending to kiss the crown of her golden hair. "I won't mention it again. You have enough to occupy your thoughts. There'll be plenty of time to discuss it when you come back."

She let it rest there. She'd already told him about her dream of buying a tiny gallery away from the chic glitter of the Place de la Concorde. Small, intimate, devoted to the connoisseur . . . She'd taken a small option on it, in fact.

She sipped the wine.

"Call me from Los Angeles?" he asked, sitting on the edge of his desk and regarding her solemnly. "I want to know you're all right."

"Of course I'm all right—and I'll go on being all right. The lawyer's call was a shock. Dad hadn't even been ill. Somehow,

I never really thought about his dying. It was as if my mother's going was the end, you know? Death had done its thing and that was it. My father..." She sighed and shook her head. "I'm babbling."

"It's therapeutic."

"I really must go." She set aside the glass and got to her feet. Eduoard took her in his arms.

"I'll miss you, darling." He brushed her lips gently, hoping for a response, but she was unyielding in his arms. Finally he let his arm fall to her waist and walked with her to the door.

"I'll stop by this evening with your ticket."

"No, please. I'll pick it up here in the morning. There's so much to do."

"You're sure?" His eyes caressed her.

"Positive." She stood on tiptoes to kiss him. "You're really very nice," she said. "Thank you."

She had another shock waiting for her when she reached the apartment. There was the concierge's note about returning the overseas call, and there was a letter addressed in her father's careless, hurried hand. A voice from the grave. She forced the foolish, macabre thought away. She got a letter from her father every month with the allowance check he sent. He always scrawled a line or two—news or questions or bits of trade gossip.

She tore open the envelope and pulled out the check and a folded letterhead. Taped to one corner was a small key. She read the note quickly.

Dear Arisa:
I was planning to be in Paris by this time but it looks like I'll have to give up the idea for a few months. I came across something I want to look into. Hang on to this key for me? Good girl. I'll pick it up when I see you in the fall.
                                          Love,
                                          Dad

She peeled back the tape and weighed the key in her hand. It was thin and flat, like the kind used for a post office or safe deposit box. Something he intended to take care of when he came to Paris. But now he never would.

She dropped it into her jewelry box and went in search of the concierge to get her suitcase from the storage room.

The savor of a city is as unique as a fingerprint. Silvery mist homogenizes London's Victorian essence and the dull rumble of the twentieth century. The fragrance of spring and Gauloises is Paris, cantankerous and irritable one moment, irresistable and lighthearted the next. Hong Kong is an incongruous medley of skyscrapers, narrow laddered streets, supersonic jets, and red-sailed junks. Los Angeles is sun and sand and smog, the casual life shouldering against the brittle glamour of the tinsel industry that is its pulse.

If London is a grande dame, Paris an irresistable lover, and Hong Kong an irrepressible Auntie Mame, Los Angeles can only be considered a wayward child. And despite sulky fits, unpredictability, and transgressions of commission and omission, it has a winsome charm that assures forgiveness and love from Angelinos.

A blanket of heat wrapped around Arisa as she emerged from the International Flight terminal. She'd never considered herself an Angelino, but she couldn't deny a sense of coming home. The motionless palms along the airport circle were taller than she recalled, and her memory had magnified the congestion of traffic, which was actually no worse than Picadilly Circus or the Boul Miche. The pressurized dryness of the jet had parched her throat, and it burned now as she inhaled the smog, which was *exactly* as she remembered it.

Behind her, the porter maneuvered a handcart with her luggage. "Taxis over here, Miss."

As she started after him, a tall, dark-haired man blocked her way. She tried to move past, but he touched her arm possessively.

"Arisa Travish?"

She frowned, caught by surprise and uncertainty. She hadn't kept in touch with anyone but her father in the years she'd been gone.

"I'm Carter Montaigne," he said, "your father's partner. I intended to meet you at the gate but I was detained."

The porter halted at the curb and looked at her inquiringly. She hesitated. Her father had no partner. She'd never heard of Carter Montaigne and never seen him before. Before she could answer, he signaled the porter.

"Put the bags in the gray Mercedes." He indicated a silver 240 SL parked in the white zone a few car-lengths back. The porter began to wheel the cart in that direction.

"Just a minute," she said angrily as the tall man began to steer her toward the car. She jerked her arm free. "Porter, put my bags in a taxi."

The porter sighed and began to retrace his steps as he raised a hand at the line of waiting cabs.

With a touch of impatience, the man who called himself Carter Montaigne said, "I appreciate your caution, but I am who I claim to be, and I drove here for the express purpose of meeting you. I've already apologized for being late." He gave her a saccharin smile. "Now tell the porter you don't want a cab, and I'll drive you home."

Her nostrils flared. "I'm not in the habit of allowing myself to be picked up by strangers, Mr. Montaigne. Try your wiles on someone else." She spun away with a toss of her blond hair across the shoulders of her beige linen traveling suit. The sky-cap had her bags piled in a cab and was holding the door open. She handed him a folded bill and climbed in. Behind her, she heard Carter Montaigne's exclamation of disgust, but when she glanced around, he was already striding away.

She gave the driver the address on North Wetherly and sank against the warm cushion. Incredible! The man had evaluated her hesitation as confusion and branded her a tourist—a lonely female who might respond to a friendly overture in a strange place by someone pretending to know her father. That was the giveaway, of course. Her father had never mentioned anyone named Montaigne. And he had no partner. Of course her father knew hundreds of people she didn't, but it was unlikely any of them even knew she was here. She'd cabled the lawyer—no one else.

Friend or whatever, Montaigne deserved what he got. His imperious manner might impress some women but it irritated her. She knew a dozen men like him—charming, clever, and chauvinistic by accident of birth. Men who considered women pretty ornaments to give them pleasure.

He was clever, she had to credit him that. Some women would be taken in by his proprietary air. He was a man accustomed to having women melt at the crook of his finger; clearly he didn't expect his authority to be questioned.

The cab slowed to a crawl at the northbound cloverleaf to the San Diego Freeway. A twinge of panic, long forgotten,

crept along Arisa's spine. She closed her eyes as her breath
caught, but they flew open as a fiery image of the crash that
had claimed her mother's life scorched her memory. She
gripped the armrest with shaking fingers as she forced herself
to glance at the merging traffic and the flashing lanes of cars.
It had been eight years . . . it was over . . . done. The steady
whine of the passing cars became a roar. She concentrated on
the yellow curve of the cab's hood until the traffic was an off-
focus blur. She wouldn't panic. She'd come to terms long ago
with the horrible guilt she'd suffered over her mother's death.
In the months following the accident, she'd buried herself in
self-pity and refused to take up the threads of life. Finally her
father had sent her abroad to school, and gradually she had
returned to the world of the living.

But never to Los Angeles.

She closed her eyes. All during the flight she'd tried to put
in order the problems that faced her. The first was attending
to whatever had to be done here. Forbes said there were legal
matters—a will, taxes. Then there was the shop. Travish Imports was a thriving business. Over the past twelve years her
father had built it into one of the leading antique shops in the
city. And now it was hers, according to Justin Forbes. Hers.
She could do with it what she pleased. She'd weighed the pros
and cons on a dozen different judgment scales during the past
twenty-four hours, and she had come to the conclusion that the
most sensible thing to do was sell it. She wasn't equipped to
run a business of that magnitude, even if she would consider
living in Los Angeles. There would be bookkeeping, inven-
tories, pricing—all on a much larger scale than she was accustomed to at the *galerie*. Travish Imports required a skilled
hand at the helm, and an expertise in Oriental artwork that she
didn't have. Chinese art had always been her father's only love.
The fascination began when they'd lived in Hong Kong, and
it had carried over to a new career after they'd moved to California in 1967. Travish Imports dealt solely with top-grade
works of art from the Far East; its reputation had been firmly
established by Elliot Travish's personal knowledge and hon-
esty.

She'd given only fleeting thought to her brother. Quentin
wouldn't give a damn one way or the other, as long as he got
whatever money was coming to him—a percentage of the profit
if she kept the shop, his share of the net if she sold. He'd never

been the least bit interested in the shop.

The cab moved onto the off-ramp at Wilshire Boulevard. Arisa's tension eased as they left the freeway and moved fitfully along the wide, busy street toward Beverly Hills. She should have cabled Quentin, but she felt no guilt. He'd delegated breaking the news of Elliot's death to Forbes; he hadn't even bothered with condolences. Despite their blood tie, he'd always been a stranger. Like her mother, she'd long ago learned to live without expecting anything of him. She wondered what "considerations" he'd gotten in their father's will to offset the minor interest he received in the business. Even Elliot had not been close to him, though he had always stayed in touch. At times, she suspected her father's regard for Quentin was based entirely on the mysterious bond to one's first-born. His son. It was ironic that Quentin should be cut adrift now. Or was he? Forbes hadn't indicated the size of Elliot's estate. Perhaps Travish Imports was only a small part of it.

The cab turned on Wetherly Drive and slowed as the driver peered at the numbers.

"It's the one with the red door," Arisa told him. By the time the cabbie pulled to the curb, she'd extracted the key her father had insisted she keep. She asked the driver to carry in her bags, then tipped him handsomely.

The house was not large by Beverly Hills standards, but its well-kept stucco and wood facade never went out of fashion. The door had been one of Elliot's extravagances. It was beautifully carved teak, burnished to a soft, gleaming cinnabar color. He'd bought it in derelict form at a small shop on Wellington Street in Hong Kong, then spent months restoring its beauty. He'd always called it his Peak door. Arisa had only vague memories of one like it in the Hong Kong home they'd been forced to flee in 1967.

As she stepped inside, she realized that nothing had changed. It was like going back eight years. Every piece of furniture was exactly the same and in the same place. Her mother had decorated the house carefully when they'd finally been able to afford the move from the tiny Valley bungalow. She'd chosen fine Oriental antiques to complement the modern, comfortable pieces. Two low sofas and brass tables formed a conversation center in front of the fireplace. A handcarved K'eng seat with its movable, shortlegged table between red velvet cushions, and two bold Chinese armchairs flanking a

high tea table, formed an "L" around a magnificent sculpted
Oriental rug, vibrant with rich reds and blues and a central
golden peacock. Traditional bookcases and occasional tables
took on an Oriental flavor, being decorated with wooden figurines, a white jade Ming tree, a Foo dog in bright blue porcelain, and a *sancai* elephant boldly splashed with green, yellow, and aubergine glazes. On the mantle, a T'ang horse
surveyed the room with baleful eyes; on the walls, an original
Chinnery, a scroll done in Phoenix and Dragon calligraphy,
and a modern oil of a crane in flight completed the blend of
East and West.

Everything was spotless; not a speck of dust drifted in the
shaft of sunlight spilling in through the tall window beside the
fireplace. Out of habit, Arisa crossed to draw the parchment
screen that served as a window shade. Her mother had always
protected the rug and furniture; the afternoon drawing of the
shades was a ritual. Judging from the immaculate condition of
the room, Arisa realized her father had never abandoned the
practice. Strange, she'd never thought in terms of her father
loving the house, only the shop. But he'd taken perfect care
of everything since she and her mother had gone out of his
life—almost as though he were awaiting their return. Arisa ran
an experimental finger across the top of the mantle. Obviously
a housekeeper had stayed on after his death.

Even in Europe, she'd heard about the soaring values of
real estate in southern California. The house would bring a
good price. She didn't like to think of disposing of the things
her mother had chosen, but she was sure it wouldn't pay to
ship them to Paris, except for a few of the choice pieces. Still,
she might buy an apartment or house. When the small *galerie*
she would purchase in Paris flourished, she would need a
permanent home. Time enough to consider all the aspects when
the *galerie* was hers. Smiling, she gathered up her suitcases
and struggled up the stairs.

Like the living room, her bedroom looked as if she'd left
for school that morning instead of for France eight years ago.
She'd selected the off-white wallpaper with delicately twined
willow branches when she was a high school freshman. The
Peking opium bed was a reproduction of a nineteenth-century
piece; its ornate lines were softened by a mattress cover and
pillows done in quilted cotton to match the wallpaper. On the
overshelf, a beautiful lacquer vase stood beside an empty coke

bottle sprouting a spray of pipe cleaners that were tagged with rock concert tickets. She smiled, remembering the youthful passions that had crowded her life. Thank heaven her taste in music had matured. She shook her head as she looked at a Grateful Dead poster pinned to the wall. Her mother had taken it down when she'd discovered it. In defiance, Arisa had used her lunch money to buy another, then refused to eat even when her mother relented and made restitution. It had been one of Arisa's frequent attempts at declaring her independence. Deep down, her tastes were similar to her mother's, but at sixteen she had refused to admit it.

She put her clothes away in the closet and bureau, then carried the empty suitcases to the hall closet. Downstairs, she dialed Quentin's office only to be told he was out for the day. She left a message, then called Forbes and set up an appointment for the following morning. With these essentials out of the way, she took a leisurely shower in the blue-tiled bathroom and dressed in a comfortable yellow shirtwaist dress and matching sandals. Forbes hadn't mentioned a car, but she found a set of keys on the pegged rack beside the back door. The Oldsmobile Cutlass was one she'd never seen. She coaxed the engine to life on the second try, pressed the overhead garage-door opener, and backed onto the street. A breeze had risen and the air felt deceptively cooler. It was warm for June. The preview of a hot summer? She recalled how her mother often bemoaned the desert dryness of the Basin, forgetting how she'd once complained as bitterly of Hong Kong's oppressive summer humidity. Was anyone ever satisfied with life, Arisa wondered. Was she? Perhaps not fully—not yet.

She drove leisurely along Wilshire, refreshing her memory by the familiar landmarks and noting with surprise the amount of new construction. Not long ago, she'd read an article in which the writer observed that it was impossible to make anything in Los Angeles look one hundred years old. Buildings had the look of perennial youth, sometimes shabby and unkempt, but never exhibiting the maturity of centuries that distinguished the grand cities of Europe. She thought longingly of Paris. She already missed it.

She turned north on Camden and crept fitfully through the mid-afternoon shoppers. The block off Rodeo had become as crowded as its famous neighbor, with an array of elegant shops, boutiques, and restaurants, many of which she'd never seen.

At Little Santa Monica, she swung into the parking strip and found a space just vacated by a champagne-colored Porsche. When she opened her purse, she realized she had no change. Annoyed, she was about to go in search of some at a nearby store when she suddenly recalled her father's habit of keeping an emergency stash. She felt along the underside of the dashboard and found a small magnetized box, which clattered rewardingly as she pulled it free.

There was an excitement in the air of Beverly Hills that the rest of the city lacked. Smartly dressed women walked with graceful stride, their high heels melodic on the pavement, changing tempo with a pause to inspect shop windows. Beyond acres of plate glass, shoppers handled merchandise and extolled or disdained its worth while polite, bored clerks stood by patiently. Jeweled fingers explored racks of summer garments with careless ennui.

She stopped short as she recognized the familiar window of her father's shop. She hadn't realized she'd come that far already, but there was no mistaking the striking, simple display that was Travish's hallmark. The show window contained only three items artfully arranged against black velvet: an exquisite rectangular white jade vase on a high, splayed foot, and carved with dragons and designs of *t'ao t'ieh*, bosses and whorls; a *blanc de chine* figure of the goddess Kuan Yin with child, elegant in flowing, uncluttered lines; and slightly behind. a glazed imperial *San ts'ai* porcelain plate. The artistically simple taste bespoke appreciation of each piece.

As Arisa entered the shop, a brass pagoda bell tinkled. The noise of the street vanished and she was wrapped in a cocoon of elegance. Though clerks glanced up, none left their posts at the various sections of the store. Travish's was an unhurried place for shopping or browsing, and customers were quietly seduced into a buying mood. Clerks were trained to encourage and lure, never to pressure. The merchandise had undoubtedly changed a dozen times over, but there was a feeling of enduring familiarity. In a square earthenware pot near the door, a gnarled bonsai spread delicate leafy arms. Near one wall, a low bench offered an invitation to sit and view a richly embroidered silk tapestry hung at eye level. An expanse of pale jade-colored carpet drew the eye to the rear display area set apart on a dais surrounded by a mahogany railing that was supported by carved white ballustrades. Polished limewood and glass showcases were highlighted by recessed lighting. They were uncluttered; the few pieces on each shelf were reflected by a mirrored back glass so that they could be studied individually for best effect— ivory and jade carvings, antique porcelain, bronze, carved lacquer, and silk paintings.

Above the spacious display floor, a loft ran across the rear of the building. With its rich paneling and decorative mirrors, it blended so unobtrusively with the decor that only the staircase gracefully curving up to it betrayed its existence. Glancing up, Arisa recognized the one-way glass that disguised the offices. Her father's, the largest, was at the right near the staircase that led from the main floor. Deline Armitage, as store manager, commanded the one next to it. The smaller two at the other end were occupied by a secretary and an accountant. Or at least they once had been. Arisa wondered what changes would be made now.

She realized with surprise that the shop had been enlarged. An adjoining store had been incorporated so that Travish Imports now occupied a huge square. She was impressed. Her father had come a long way from the small, crowded store he'd first opened on Melrose Avenue.

Her sandals sank into the plush carpet as she stepped onto the dais and wandered slowly among the displays. She paused to study a jade belthook. One of the clerks, a slim Oriental girl in a blue silk *cheongsam* that exposed several inches of smooth nyloned thigh, glided over to her.

"It's Han Dynasty," she said in a cultured, friendly tone.

"It's beautiful," Arisa said honestly. The jade glowed as though a moonbeam had been trapped inside the stone.

"Would you like to look at it more closely?"

"Please."

The girl unlocked the case, picked up the piece with delicate hands, and presented it to Arisa. It was warm and smooth, and the perfect carving was still distinct after almost two thousand years. Studying its incredible beauty, Arisa felt a stir of reverence for the culture that had produced it.

She was aware of a subtle tension in the girl beside her and turned to see an older woman approaching. Handing back the belthook, Arisa went to meet Deline. The woman moved with an inherent Oriental grace that Western women could never emulate. She was dressed in an embroidered silk *cheongsam* that would have made her figure enviable in a woman half her age. Her unlined face was flawless. She inclined her head with a warm smile.

"Arisa, how good it is to see you."

Arisa clasped the outstretched hands. "It's been a very long time, Deline. You haven't changed a bit."

Deline smiled. "But you have. You have grown into a lovely young woman."

Arisa returned an appreciative smile. Even though she'd known Deline more than half her life, the woman was still an enigma. Elliot Travish knew her as a capable, efficient worker who was his right hand, if not his lifeblood, in the business. Raised in the Orient, she had an intimate knowledge of her art heritage. She was as familiar with a Fukien funerary vase or a Ming stemcup as she was with the Chinese characters that signified her name. And for eleven years, she'd shared this knowledge with Elliot as he'd built his importing business. She'd helped design the shop in Beverly Hills and kept it running smoothly. Customers were impressed with her charm and expertise without realizing they were being subtly persuaded to make purchases they hadn't planned.

Now, as ever, this facet of Deline was clearly in evidence. But Melisande Travish, Arisa's mother, had sensed a different side to the woman. Arisa had always been aware of the tension in her mother's face whenever the two met or Deline's name came up. No woman could completely accept another—especially a bright, attractive one—who spent eight to twelve hours working at her husband's side, but the resentment resulted from more than petty jealousy on her mother's part, Arisa was sure. Hostility bordering on hatred glinted through the facade of Melisande's politeness. She never talked about Deline, even casually. It was one of the dark areas of her mother's feelings that was better left unexplored. Arisa's loyalty to her mother had always overridden any she might have formed with Deline.

"Your father was proud of the beautiful woman you've become." A tiny crease momentarily marred the perfection of Deline's face. "I share your grief. If there's anything I can do. . . ."

"Thank you." Arisa felt a twinge of guilt realizing Deline actually had known her father better than she. Smiling, she glanced around the shop. "I'd forgotten how beautiful this place is. Is business good?"

"Excellent," Deline murmured.

Arisa looked around—pleased. Her gaze came to rest on a bamboo brushrest carved in the form of a narcissus.

"Eighteenth century, isn't it?"

Deline nodded. "Your father bought it on his' last trip to Hong Kong. He'd be pleased that you recognize it."

Arisa's knowledge of Oriental artwork was miniscule in comparison with Deline's, but she was delighted at being able to unlock her memory bank so readily. She stepped toward another showcase where a Cromwellian silver porringer and several excellent pieces of English pewter and porcelain were displayed. She looked at Deline questioningly.

"Since when has Travish Imports carried European merchandise?"

Deline's eyes were unreadable. She tilted her head and made a graceful gesture toward the stairway. "I was just about to make tea. Will you join me?"

Ancient Chinese custom—tea first, then talk. Arisa followed the petite woman to the loft and was ushered into the second office. It might have been a bit of China transported *in toto* to its present spot. It had been redone since Arisa last saw it, and was more exquisite than the room that had always impressed her as an exotic haven. The walls were done in a textured silk as fine as rice paper. The color gave an illusion of transparency, and the subtle shadings seemed to move behind it like shadows. All the wood in the office was deep-hued limewood, neither brown nor red but both. It gleamed like a polished table in candlelight. Deline's desk was an Oriental antique. Arisa had seen a similar one at Christie's but couldn't place the period. It was inlaid with gold and mother of pearl, and the sides were magnificently carved in bas-relief. In the center of the room, a low table was surrounded by three formal Oriental tea chairs, their heavy lines softened by vermillion cushions.

"Please sit," Deline said. She disappeared behind a silk screen. A moment later, Arisa heard the kettle being filled and the soft clink of china. Deline returned with a red lacquered tray holding parchment-thin Chinese teacups of lustrous pearly green china. She set it down, seated herself across from Arisa, and folded her hands in her lap, fingers to palm, like an Oriental princess posing for a portrait.

Unaccountably, Arisa felt a touch of annoyance. So far,

Deline had completely ignored her question, and seemed prepared to continue doing so. Arisa forced the issue. "I'd like
to know about the European pieces," she said directly.

Deline seemed to sigh, though she made no sound. Only
her lips moved. "For almost a year," she said, answering the
question put to her earlier.

Arisa's brows arched. Her father hadn't written anything
about it. Strange. . . .

The kettle hissed and Deline escaped behind the screen.
When she returned with the brewing pot, she set it on the tray
and resumed her pose. Her gaze touched Arisa's face and
seemed to see beyond the flesh.

"Tell me about it," Arisa said with a hint of sharpness. Did
she have to pry every sentence from the woman? "My father
must have had a complete change of heart to abandon his
devotion to the Orient."

Frowning, Deline lifted the lid of the teapot and judged the
aroma. Satisfied, she filled two cups and set one in front of
Arisa. At last she said, "It was more a matter of expediency
than preference. Not that he hadn't been interested in Europe
before. He saw so many beautiful things on his trips . . . he had
always thought it might be an area of expansion."

"Just like that?" Arisa snapped her fingers silently. She
couldn't believe her father had suddenly been captivated by
antiques he'd been exposed to all his life in other galleries. He
appreciated the craftsmanship well enough, and the value, but
he'd always claimed a man should choose a sphere and stay
within it.

"It was not a hasty decision."

"But why, for heaven's sake, did he choose it at all?" She
was impatient with Deline's refusal to be direct. As manager
of the shop and her father's friend, Deline was perfectly aware
of whatever reasons or excuses her father had given.

Evasively, Deline countered with a question. "Have you
spoken with your father's lawyer?"

"Only by phone, in France. I have an appointment to see
him tomorrow. Why?"

"It would be best if you discuss the matter with him first."

"*What* matter?" Would she never get a straight answer?
"Are the reasons for my father's decision some huge secret?"
She made no attempt to hide her annoyance.

"Perhaps I can answer your question, Miss Travish."

She had not heard the door open, and she turned to find herself looking into the angry eyes of the man who had accosted her at the airport. Her mouth opened, then snapped shut as she whirled to stare at Deline. No surprise registered on Deline's serene face. It was almost as though she had been expecting him—waiting for him.

He crossed the office in two easy strides and settled himself in the red-cushioned chair next to Arisa.

"Arisa, this is Carter Montaigne, your father's partner," Deline said.

"Miss Travish and I have already met," he said dryly. "I trust you had a pleasant cab ride?"

"Very." She set down the teacup to hide the trembling of her hand.

Before she could recover from her surprise, Montaigne went on. "Travish and Montaigne," he emphasized his name significantly, "have been in the European antique market for eleven months. The suggestion came from me that we join our talents, and the merger has been as successful as I predicted."

He sounded so smug that Arisa's temper flared. "Is it true, Deline?" she demanded.

Deline did not look up from the cup which had suddenly riveted her attention. "Yes. Your father has known Carter for several years. His reputation is not exaggerated."

Arisa racked her memory for the name, but she was sure she had never heard it before. Still, she could not dispute what was being forced on her as fact.

"I see." She turned an icy gaze on Montaigne. "I refuse to apologize for what occurred at the airport, Mr. Montaigne. Under the circumstances, you're fortunate I didn't call the police and have you thrown in jail!" She was smarting at his arrogance and wanted nothing more than to slap him down. She was still shaken by the news that he was part of the business Forbes had led her to believe was hers.

The amused expression on his face remained as his eyes hardened. "For offering you a ride? You would have made a bigger fool of yourself."

Her cheeks flamed as she tightened her lips.

"But what's done is done," he said condescendingly. "Now, there are a number of business matters we must discuss. Forbes can acquaint you with the details of the partnership your father and I drew up. Basically, I own thirty percent. As executor of

your father's will, I have the responsibility of seeing that the
shop runs smoothly until the estate is probated. You can be
sure I'll do so, since I have a personal interest as well as a
financial one. Quite frankly, Arisa..." She bristled at his familiar use of her name. "I am willing to buy out your interest.
You have no business experience, and I'm sure you have little
interest in changing your life-style. Your father was resigned
to your decision to live in Europe. If you prefer the purchase
to be set up over a period of years, you can have an income
that should keep you nicely. We can't tie it all up until after
probate, but Forbes can draw up a binding contract if you and
I agree on terms."

Arisa listened with swelling rage. His arrogance was in-
sufferable. Her temper exploded. "I have no intention of turning
over my father's business to you!" she said hotly. "I'm not a
child to be told what I must or must not do!"

His eyes flickered with surprise. For the first time since
she'd met him, he seemed taken aback, but only for an instant.
The cool disdain returned almost immediately. "I'm not suggesting charity but a sensible economic move. You can't ac-
tively participate in a business you know nothing about. You'd
handicap both of us. If you want to remain a stockholder..."

"The *major* stockholder, Mr. Montaigne," she reminded
him spitefully. A tick of irritation at the corner of his mouth
showed her barb had struck vulnerable flesh. She had con-
trolling interest whether he liked it or not, and there was little
he could do about it without her cooperation. And he'd damn
well whistle for that. He should have thought twice before he
displayed his arrogance so openly. She gave only a momentary
thought to the hasty words that had put all her plans in jeopardy.
They were not irrevocable. Time enough to agree to Montaigne's offer when he'd had time to worry a bit. And regret
his bold manners.

Carter realized he'd taken a wrong tack. Elliot had warned
him how stubborn Arisa was, but he'd also made her seem a
bit flighty and interested only in her own pleasure. Somehow,
Carter hadn't expected the temper. Now he'd have to pour oil
on the waters he'd troubled. He was certain her original plan
had been to sell and that she was taking this stand only because
he'd ruffled her feathers.

"It might be better to let it go for now," he said. "I'm sorry
I plunged in so quickly. You haven't had time to recover from

your trip. Shall we save the discussion for another time?"

"If you think I can be persuaded to change my mind, you may have a long wait," she said sweetly.

He smiled. "We won't get anywhere by snapping at each other. A truce?" He arched a black brow questioningly.

The tension in the room was uncomfortable. Arisa realized Deline was watching her with a curious expression. Were there innuendos she had missed? Deline had been hesitant to mention Montaigne before he came on the scene. Were they friends or enemies? It was impossible to say, judging from Deline's manner, but Arisa sensed a strong undercurrent.

She gave Montaigne a careless smile, neither yielding nor defensive. "If there's no great secret about it, I'd like to know more about this expansion into the European market. My father was devoted to Oriental art. What made him change his mind?"

Deline glanced at Carter, and for an instant Arisa thought there was a small ripple of pain in the unfathomable almond eyes. Deline was more an expert on the Oriental than Elliot had been; it must have been a blow when he decided to expand elsewhere.

Carter leaned forward as Deline filled the teacup for him. "Your father was never unfaithful to that love, but he saw a chance to acquire a steady clientele in other areas as well. Most decorators today vary motifs. A merger of European and Oriental has become very popular. Many excellent pieces from the East can be found in the finest homes and collections. It's traceable to the early trade of the East India companies in Canton. Even though Europeans were mainly interested in silk and tea, they recognized the quality of Chinese porcelain and brought a lot of it back with them, not to mention jade and other intrinsically valuable pieces. There's as much Oriental work on the continent as in America. I'm sure you've observed that in your travels. There's a great deal of Eastern influence in some of the later periods of France and England." He paused, realizing he was getting far afield. With a quick smile, he addressed himself to her question again. "Your father realized he couldn't afford to ignore the trend if he wanted to compete with the bigger shops. The cash flow generated by an expansion would profit the Oriental business as well. That was his primary concern."

Arisa regarded him curiously. He was couching his words as though she were not capable of understanding the concept.

"Exactly what are you saying?" she demanded.

"Our partnership was a financially sound move for your father," he said bluntly. "The company was in distress. Your father had no capital to buy merchandise he needed. He approached me about investing because we'd been friends a long time. I proposed the partnership, since I was looking for an opportunity. Expansion into the European markets was one of my conditions."

She listened with growing wariness. He was saying that her father had been in financial trouble. She couldn't buy that. Her father had never hinted at anything but complete success, and her allowance checks had never been so much as a day late or a penny short. The business had been growing steadily for years with only normal fluctuations caused by the national economy. If there had been financial strain, what had brought it on? Or was Montaigne fabricating the story to salve his conscience about insinuating himself into a profitable venture? She glanced at Deline, who was sitting as motionless as one of the jade carvings in the shop. Surely she'd come to Elliot Travish's defense if Montaigne was blatantly lying. Arisa realized how little she knew about her father's business. It would be foolhardy to challenge Montaigne.

"I see," she said.

Montaigne went on. "I assumed your father had told you about our partnership. You can verify what I say with Justin Forbes, your father's lawyer. He's handling the estate. Have you contacted him yet?"

"I have an appointment with him in the morning."

"Then let's postpone any further discussion until you've talked with him." He set down his cup and rose. "Now if you'll excuse me, I have work to do." With a glance at Deline, he added, "Help Arisa with anything she needs." Then to Arisa, "I presume the funeral will be this week?"

"I'll have to talk to Quentin."

The mention of her brother's name brought a curious glint to Carter's eyes. Had they met head on?

Carter nodded. "Deline will keep me posted." He turned to leave, then paused at the door. For the first time, Arisa saw a touch of gentleness in his expression. "I'm sorry about your father. We were friends." Then the door whispered shut behind him. For a moment, his tall figure was outlined against the soft lights of the shop as he walked past the one-way glass. Then he was gone without a sound to suggest whether he'd entered her father's office or descended the stairs.

Was it her imagination or was Deline relieved that he'd left? Deline smiled pleasantly. "Have you been at the house? Was everything in order?"

"Perfect, thank you."

The Eurasian woman nodded. "I asked the cleaning woman to stay on until you had a chance to settle in. You can make other arrangements if you prefer."

"I wouldn't know where to begin. If the woman is capable, I see no reason to change. Thank you for taking care of things so admirably. I know how much my father relied on you. I'll do the same if it isn't too much of an imposition."

Deline gave her a warm smile. "Anything at all, please call on me. About the funeral . . .?"

Arisa felt the weight of the unpleasant decision. "Have you talked to Quentin?"

"He was in earlier. He's been awaiting your arrival to discuss arrangements. May I suggest a quiet service and burial at Forest Lawn?"

It seemed sensible. Her father wouldn't want an exhibition of grief. They'd never discussed it, but he'd refused to have a showy funeral when Melisande died. Grief was a private thing. She nodded at Deline's suggestion. She'd discuss the matter with Quentin but knew her brother would prefer that the responsibility lie elsewhere. Quentin was not one to take on unpleasant tasks. The stirring uneasiness that had filled Arisa since her arrival in L.A. settled into guilt as she realized how little she knew of the circumstances of her father's death. Deline had been close to him for years, with the genuine warmth of friendship. Arisa framed a tentative question.

"How did it happen? Was he ill or was it . . ." Quick? Was a last heartbeat an eternity or a fraction of time? Death could be mercifully quick for the dying, but it could be agonizingly slow torture for those left behind. Like when her mother . . .

Deline's face clouded. "He'd been ill," she said softly. "No one knew. He never complained, but he did not take care of himself. The . . . end came quickly. He was just gone. When he did not call or come in one morning, I . . ."

Arisa rose and put a comforting hand on the woman's shoulder. So it was Deline who had faced the reality of discovering the horrible truth. Her father *had* suffered and died alone. Tears pricked at her eyelids. For the first time since Forbes' call, grief penetrated her shock. She fumbled for a tissue and dabbed at her eyes.

"Thank you, Deline. I'm glad he had you as a friend." Deline bowed her head. "Will you have dinner with me tonight?" Arisa asked suddenly. She wanted to know Deline better, to learn about the father she had ignored for so long.

Deline sighed and folded her hand over Arisa's warmly. "I'm sorry. I have an engagement, but another time soon." When she looked up, her smile was serene.

"I'll count on it," Arisa said.

YEAR OF THE RAT

Hong Kong, November 1924

She knew long before there was any outward sign to betray the growing life in her belly. Her heart whispered a lovesong to William across the undulating sea. A lovesong: Child of love, our child, William, beloved William. A lament: Hear the murmur of the tiny new life within the walls of my body. Come . . . know with me the joy of our firstborn. Return and replenish my spirit.

Her spirit sang from first cock crow until darkness crept through the webbed streets of the city. Even in sleep her dreams murmured the never-ending song. Dreams of William—his arms, his lips, his body. She woke with her hands pressed over her ripening breasts and the small bulge of her belly, and she sang her silent song to the darkness. William would return. The song would reach his heart. He would know and he would return.

At her father's laundry, she worked diligently to belie the aching tiredness that became part of her. She bowed obediently to her father when he ordered her to deliver heavy loads to foreign houses. She ran along Sun Street and up and down the steep roads of the foreign sector. As atonement for her desire to pause in the shade of a red pine or a sweet gum and savour her heartsong, sweat dripped down her cheeks and between the new hardness of her breasts. When she recalled sweet thoughts of the tent shower she'd shared with William, her steps quickened. She bent so that her sweat-dampened *san* would not outline her secret.

Summer dwindled into the welcome coolness of autumn. When the wind danced in the leaves and played a melody in the tall grass of the hillsides, she felt the first flutter of the life she carried. William would come soon. Her aching exhaustion would vanish then. He would rub the taut skin of her abdomen and the soft place at her back beneath her breathing bones. When they were together once more, the days of waiting would pass on swift wings.

'Aw jung-yee nay, her mind and body and spirit sang. *I love you, sweet William.*

Alone in the shop one day, she leaned against the wall, her eyes closed as she waited for her father to finish the petticoats and shirtwaists he was ironing for the English general's lady. They had to be delivered before dark. From the back room where big tubs stood and steam hissed from the irons, Mei Shau heard her father muttering. She closed her mind to his denunciation of the cursed foreigners who broke his back and raised blisters on his calloused hands. She could not curse the foreigners. William was one of them, and so was their child. As though the thought had reached the baby, it stirred restlessly and kicked at its prison. She placed her hand to it lovingly and let out a sigh that said all the words she could not speak.

"Are you all right?"

The English voice startled her and she sprang up. For one dizzy moment, she thought William had come for her! Her mouth opened but then closed quickly as she saw a corpulent woman with iron-gray hair.

"Are you all right?" the woman asked again.

Mei Shau nodded dumbly. She realized her hand was still talking to her child, and she dropped it quickly. The woman frowned.

"I've some uniforms to be laundered. Tell your father I need them before noon tomorrow." She stared at Mei Shau. "You understand English?"

Another nod.

"Deliver them to the hospital. Miss Abigail. He knows."

Mei Shau again moved her head mutely. The woman gave her a curious glance just as I Fong emerged from the beaded doorway.

"Ah, there you are, I Fong. Laundry, I need it quickly."

I Fong smiled as though he had never cursed a foreign devil. "Do quick," he promised. He set down a basket and snapped his fingers at his daughter. She bent to lift the heavy load and escape as quickly as possible.

The iron-haired woman stabbed a finger toward Mei Shau. "She shouldn't be carrying heavy baskets like that in her condition." When I Fong smiled and bowed again, words poured heedlessly from her devil tongue. "It's dangerous for the baby. I don't suppose you're seeing that she gets a proper diet, either—plenty of fruits and vegetables and milk. It's a wonder your women survive childbirth the way you treat them like pack animals." She peered at I Fong, who was digesting the English words slowly, then patted her own fat belly in its tight stays. "Dangerous for the baby." She shook her head and her eyes appealed to the English god who dwelled in the empire above the rooftops. "A miracle of God's infinite wisdom, assuming he bothers with Chinese," she said. "Mind you, the uniforms must be at the hospital before noon." She marched out.

Mei Shau saw the surprise on her father's face turn to rage as she tried to slip past him. He grabbed her so violently that the basket was flung from her grip. She bowed her head as his hand struck hard across her skull. The basket bounced and rolled. Neatly stacked laundry spilled like an avalanche of snow on the wood floor. He struck her again and again, blows that were powerful with his silent fury. His face twisted into an ugly mask. When she fell to her knees, he grabbed up the bamboo cane he used to climb the steep stairs and rained blows across her cowering body. Pain coursed through her in a hot river until she could no longer tell from where it came. His feet kicked and bit into her flesh, and though some of the pain must surely have been transmitted to his bones through his soft slippers, his fury drove him relentlessly. At last he stood heaving mighty breaths that shattered the silence.

"Dog vomit! Stink pig! Worthless sow!" Contempt filled him and he kicked her again, wearily now that his energy was spent. With a large surge, he raised a foot and sent her spinning.

She was terrified as he breathed dragonlike above her, the bamboo cane shaking helplessly in his hand.

In a furious burst of Chinese, he demanded to know why she had lived to bring disgrace upon the family. "A girl. Female offspring of a dog! You repay my generosity for not killing you as you emerged from your mother's belly by bringing shame to the house of Leong! I could have gotten a good price for you as a slave if I hadn't listened to your mother's entreaties to allow her one daughter to comfort her when our three sons were grown! Aiii, you have repaid the debt by becoming a prostitute! I will kill you now!"

He raised the cane again, but it fell with a bee's sting on her pain-wracked shoulders. He kicked feebly, then sat down abruptly, his breath wheezing in his tired chest.

His screaming had caused passersby to peer into the shop.

It had also brought her mother flying down the rickety steps from their rooms above.

"My husband—*aiii!*" She glanced at the cowering Mei Shau and quickly bent to pick up the spilled laundry. She brushed at the garments, clucking when she saw that two petticoats were hopelessly smudged. "They must be done again," she lamented. She rose, clutching the starched cottons. Her dark hair was touched with brush strokes of white, and her face sagged in a million wrinkles. Though middle-aged, she was already ancient. She backed to the safety of the beaded archway as she saw the expression on her husband's face.

He whirled on her. "You knew. A mother knows these things, yet you said nothing to me?" he demanded. "Have I not been a good husband? Have I not provided for you and our sons? Have I not demeaned myself in this city of foreign devils because you feared the warlords of our village?" He spat the words venomously, lashing with his tongue now that his physical energy had ebbed. "Whore! Sow! Filthy dog shit! Take her out of my sight!" He pointed with his chin at Mei Shau as though she were not fit for his glance. "Hide her from my eyes until I gather the strength to plunge a knife into her belly and cut away her disgrace!"

Her mother hastily put the spoiled laundry aside and crouched over Mei Shau. Taking her arms, she dragged her to her feet. Mei Shau's body screamed under her bloodied *san*, but she held back her terrified sobs. She licked away the salty blood at the corner of her mouth as her mother pulled her from the room. Once out of I Fong's sight, her mother's touch gentled and her eyes filled with compassion behind her fear. She was trembling as badly as her beaten daughter.

Each step was agony. Tears scalded the welts on Mei Shau's face where her father's cane had struck. But her belly was untouched. She had shielded the child from her father's wrath. The knowledge gave her strength to struggle up the stairs and fall upon her pallet.

Her mother undressed her as she would a child, crooning and rocking in comfort and misery. From a high window where a shaft of light found its way between the closely packed buildings, she took an aloe plant and broke off two spiny leaves. Gently she rubbed the soothing balm on Mei Shau's welts and cuts.

"My daughter . . . my daughter . . ." She rocked and shook

her head in despair. "I can no longer protect you from your father's wrath. What have you done, what have you done, child of my womb?"

Mei Shau sobbed and let the tears fall for the first time. "I have done nothing. I have loved. It cannot be wrong to love."

Her mother's face drew into a pitiful mask. "*Aiii*, who is this miserable son who has led you to shame? What house is also disgraced by the weakness of a man?"

Mei Shau cried out blindly. "William is not weak. He loves me!"

Her mother recoiled as if struck. All too late Mei Shau realized she had spoken the name that had been silent in her heart.

"A foreigner?" Her mother sagged as though her spine had been cut away. She sobbed into her hands.

Mei Shau touched her. "He loves me, and I love him. He will take care of me and our child. My father need never look upon my face again."

Her mother's head jerked up. "Where is this *William?* Tell me so I may beg him to come for you quickly before your father carries out his promise to end your life." Her fingers clawed at Mei Shau's arm, begging.

A sob burst from Mei Shau's lips as she fell back upon the pallet. Frightened, her mother soothed her until she could speak again. Haltingly, Mei Shau told how she'd met William and loved him and how he'd gone away. "But he will come back—soon." It was a plaintive cry from her wounded heart and body.

Her mother wept silent tears of pity and anguish. Her husband's hatred of foreigners ran deep. He would surely kill Mei Shau if he discovered the truth; even a mother's love could not prevent it. Had not I Fong pledged to drive foreign devils from his homeland? *Aiii*, he would snuff out his daughter's life for the glory of patriotism. *Aiii!*

She made tea thick with white chrysanthemums and sat beside Mei Shau until she swallowed it. Then she drew up the coverlet and left her alone.

Mei Shau drifted into troubled sleep, where she wandered helplessly through the Ten Courts of Hell. Her father drove her on with wicked lashes from his bamboo cane, shouting obscenities and trying to claw the child from her belly. The Gods of the Court screamed as they demanded her traitor's heart be cut out, her liar's tongue forever severed. She stumbled and fell under their lashes and gleaming knives. In the distance, the God of the Tenth Court waited to mete out Mei Shau's final punishment. In the hot, smoky haze from the fiery pits, she saw William beckoning to her. She stretched out her hands, begging him to help her climb from the torturous place, but the flames engulfed William as she was dragged back by her father's hands. Weeping, she plunged into the darkness of damnation.

After a very long time, shadows merged and began to swirl about her. She opened her eyes slowly. A cold, dusky haze filled the room. Voices came through the gloom, from the other side of the door, and she realized she was no longer dreaming.

"She has shamed the house of Leong with her bastard child."

"Send her away but spare her life." That was her mother, weeping.

"And the bastard who would forever disgrace the name of Leong?"

"Mei Shau must live with her shame. It is a more fitting punishment than death."

Drawn into darkness again by fever, Mei Shau dreamed that her child had been born and they had spirited it away so that she would never cast her eyes upon it. She cried out, and her hand sought the reassuring mound of William's child until she dropped back to sleep again.

When she woke, a single oil lamp flickered in the cold room. She cowered from the shadows, and clutched the jade William had placed around her neck. Her mother spoke softly.

"Dress now. You are to journey north to the village of our people. Elder Brother Lei Tong will take you." She placed a hand on Mei Shau's brow and found it cool. She drew back the coverlet and helped her daughter rise. When Mei Shau resisted, she scowled. "There is no time to waste in foolish stubbornness. Each moment gives your father time to take back the promise he has given so reluctantly. Hurry."

Mei Shau spied the bundle of clothes her mother had packed. Tears filled her eyes. "I cannot go." If she left Hong Kong, how would William find her?

Roughly, her mother forced her up. "Your life is spared. Do not speak foolish words. It is better to live than never to hear the cry of your child—the American's child." The words were a stinging burr on her mother's tongue, as though it pained her to speak them. But beyond the heartache in her eyes, there was compassion and a bond that only women could share.

"Quickly now. Lei Tong comes for you before the sun climbs."

As Mei Shau began to dress, her mother brought a length of soft cotton to bind her belly. "Winter winds bite the north country. Your journey is long." In whispered tones, she related the plan. Mei Shau and Lei Tong would journey by train to the province of Anhwei. Mei Shau's brother had agreed to escort her since he was on his way to join the Kuomintang army and fight for People's Rule. From Nanking, Mei Shau and Lei Tong would travel by cart or foot to the village where Third Cousin Lo Bun lived. Lo Bun's wife was dead; he would be glad to have a woman tend his house. If Mei Shau brought forth a son, Lo Bun would be glad to have strong hands to help in the fields, even a boy tainted by the blood of the foreigners. If the child was female, Lo Bun would have the right to sell her as he would a daughter of his own.

"Hurry . . . no time to be lost . . . it is decided. . . ."

Mei Shau moved like a puppet whose master has grown weary of working the strings. Her mother had won her a chance at life. To refuse now would seal her doom, and her child would never be born. She would do as she was commanded . . . and she would wait for a chance to escape Lo Bun. She would return to Hong Kong to find William.

The train followed a single track through the hills and valleys like a weary ox. Mei Shau ached from the hard wooden bench and the jostling motion. She was numb with cold and despair. Lei Tong treated her like a pig he'd been commissioned to transport; he had not spoken to her except for his occasional demands for wine or rice from the basket their mother had prepared for the journey. He spent the hours talking with the other men of the glorious Kuomintang that was ridding China of its oppressors. The country was in the throes of giving birth to a republic—*Min-chu—Min-ch'uan—Min-sheng!* People's rule—People's authority—People's livelihood! The Manchu Dynasty would be overthrown. The penetration of foreigners would be driven back. The great revolution was at hand.

Lei Tong told his fellow travelers only that he was taking his sister to her village before he joined a military unit in

Shanghai. Like his father, Lei Tong would prefer his sister to be dead and her name blotted from memory in the Leong family. His father must be senile to let his senses be addled by a woman's tears. His mother had sworn to do her own and Mei Shau's work in the laundry if Mei Shau's life was spared. As if an old woman could keep such a vow! Her frail body would collapse under the weight of the heavy laundry baskets and fall in the street like an overheated horse at Happy Valley Racetrack. Pah! Sniveling females! Their only worth was to bear strong sons to carry on the name of Leong, not half-American bastards like the one growing inside Mei Shau's belly. He glowered at his sister huddled in the corner. *Aiii,* the gods would not be pleased with such a travesty. A curse would forever be on their house. Perhaps the shock of seeing an ugly half-American bastard crawl from Mei Shau's womb would anger them so that they would strike down both mother and child.

He found solace only in the fact that the journey gave him the opportunity to drink wine and talk about the coming revolution. A young military cadet from the academy at Whampoa had boarded at Canton. His knowledge of guns and plans for the Kuomintang's push to overthrow the Chinese warlords and the foreigners alike filled Lei Tong with zeal. Perhaps he would go to Canton instead of Shanghai, to join the Union of Youth, like the cadet. They were pledged not to retreat but to die fighting if need be for their cause.

Lei Tong's imagination fired to white heat. His education had been limited by his family's poverty. Though he knew he could not compete with the elite students accepted into the academy, he would find a way to join their force, as a foot soldier if necessary.

Mei Shau barely heard the boisterous men. The journey had stretched into an eternity. The baby in her belly protested vigorously, kicking and flailing as Mei Shau was pitched this way and that by the rocking motion and sharp jolts of the coach. She shivered in the rush of cold air that whistled through the ill-fitting windows and made the car a cavern of grime and noise. Her eyes stung; she had long ago given up trying to keep her face and hands clean of cinders and dust.

The train was behind schedule, having tarried at stations much longer than intended as the men scrambled down to the platform to listen to the latest news from Canton and Shanghai, where workers were being organized to support a mass military movement into the provinces. Chiang Kai-shek had returned from Moscow, where he had placated the Russians about his refusal to allow them to control the Academy, yet he kept their support and weapons and retained his presidency of the Academy. Sun Yat-sen's death had strengthened the appeal to the nationalist spirit to fight the threat to China's survival.

The train slowed, and Mei Shau opened her eyes to peer out the dusty glass. They were leaving the flat, terraced rice fields to climb a mountain pass. The hills turned blue-gray in the afternoon dusk, like the face of a sorrowful lover hidden by the mist. She'd lost track of time as the miles slowly fell behind. It would soon be night, the fourth spent on the miserable train. How glad she would be to quit the train even for an ox cart. Perhaps there would be sweet-smelling hay where she could rest and plan her escape. Listening to the talk of the men, she knew with dread certainty that Lo Bun would share her brother's hatred of her and the child. The baby's life would be snuffed out before it wailed its first cry.

She sighed softly and shifted her weight to ease her cramped muscles. Suddenly, the train lurched and the wheels screamed on the rails. She was flung forward and clutched the bench to keep from pitching across the car into the knot of men. Stunned, she tried to figure out what was happening. Half drunk, the men had been slouched with their feet propped on a small wooden chest. A wine bottle had splintered, spraying them with a shower of glass and wine dregs. Now curses rent the air as the men disentangled themselves. Sen, the young cadet, pushed away someone who'd fallen atop him on the dirty floor. He stumbled to his feet, but another lurch sent him sprawling. He howled indignantly.

Lei Tong shook his head and pulled himself to a window to peer out. The train had halted. He rubbed the sleeve of his padded jacket on the glass as flickering lights danced on the hillside. Suddenly, a deafening explosion rocked the air. Lei Tong leaped back, but he was pushed forward again as the others crowded to the window.

Mei Shau tested her limbs gingerly. Her head roared with the wild clamor but gradually she became aware of shouting voices and thundering horses' hooves.

"What is it?" one of the men demanded.

"Are they military?"

"No, there's been an accident."

Another thunderous boom sounded so close that Mei Shau clapped her hands over her ears.

"Gunfire!" Sen pushed away and raced to the end of the car. With a surge, he yanked back the bar that fastened the door and pulled it open. Drawing a pistol from his belt, he vanished into the darkness between the two cars.

A volley of shots rang outside amid the most incredible noise of men and horses Mei Shau had ever heard. Frightened, she cowered in a corner as her brother and some of the other men ran for the door.

"Thieves!"

"Bandits!"

"Some warlord bent on lining his pockets with more coins than he's been able to steal from the peasants!"

One elderly passenger hesitated as he watched the others crowd through the door to follow the cadet. More shots rang out; splinters of wood exploded close to Mei Shau. The old man dived under a bench and shrank into the shadows. Mei Shau was too frightened to move. Beyond the shattered window, torchlight leaped eerily as a line of horsemen raced by. There was an exchange of shots near the end of the car where her brother and the others had gone. Mei Shau trembled. They had only the cadet's gun against the heavily armed bandits outside. The horses made a wide circle as the riders prepared to retrace their line. As a new burst of firing exploded like a string of firecrackers, the men stumbled over each other in their haste to return to safety. Sen paused to fire another shot, then pushed past Lei Tong.

"Tear up the benches!" he shouted. "Barricade the windows!" The others obeyed, eager to leave decisions to the military man. Lei Tong's face glowed and his eyes glittered as a rider went by the window. Acrid smoke from burning tar and gunpowder drifted into the car.

"Grab that!"

"We'll hold off the bandit pigs. Did you see the engine?"

"It's derailed," Sen said ominously. "We stand to fight or die."

The bandits were no longer in sight, but the sound of their guns exploded along the length of the train. The glow of the torches moved toward the engine. Sen smashed away splinters of glass at a window and leaned out. Lei Tong howled and fell back.

Mei Shau saw a dark stain spread across her brother's jacket. Unmindful of her own safety, she crawled over to him but he pushed her aside roughly. She slunk back past the whimpering old man under the bench who had covered his eyes and ears. She huddled, her back pressed against the rough wood, her knees wrapped in her arms to protect the child.

Outside, a dull glow lighted the sky and sent a pall of smoke upward. "The wood car is afire," Sen shouted, leaning again from the window. A rapid volley made him jerk back. He fell to his knees as two horsemen galloped by, spraying the car with bullets.

Without warning, the door behind Mei Shau crashed open. She stifled a scream. A bandit in a heavy coat crisscrossed by bandoliers of ammunition filled the doorway. He held a pistol in one hand while with the other he steadied his aim. As he pulled the trigger, the explosion roared in Mei Shau's ears. Sen was flung back, hovering a moment, then falling across Lei Tong on the floor. In the dim light, the scene was like a shadow play on a dull screen. The other passengers quickly raised their hands to show they were unarmed and backed away from the fallen men. The bandit's heavy boots shook the car as he advanced. He was close enough so that Mei Shau smelled the grease and filth of his clothes. With his gun aimed to keep the cowering men at bay, the bandit kicked the cadet and rolled him over. Sen's eyes stared blankly; the stench of his evacuated bowels made the bandit snort in disgust.

Free of the dead weight, Lei Tong's gaze fixed on the bandit with a grimace of pain and maniacal fury. The bandit flicked him a glance, seeming to dismiss him. He turned away but spun back abruptly and crashed a heavy boot on Lei Tong's hand. Mei Shau heard his bones snap. Her brother gasped and tried to raise his injured hand, but the bandit's foot came down again. Lei Tong's elbow broke like a dry reed under the wheel of an ox cart. When an anguished wail escaped his lips, the bandit threw back his head and laughed. Then he stooped to pick up the cadet's pistol which Lei Tong had been reaching for. Slipping it under the bandolier across his wide chest, the warlord bandit grabbed Lei Tong's coat and dragged him to his feet. Lei Tong moaned. Blood dripped from the bullet wound in his shoulder, and his arm hung useless in its sleeve. He swayed but the bandit held him upright.

"You would shoot me?" He raised the pistol to Lei Tong's ear, then lowered it with an ugly laugh. "Lead would pass through your empty skull without touching anything." The bandit spat in his face.

Lei Tong tried to imitate the gesture of contempt, but he was too weak to force spittle past his lips. It dribbled down his chin. The bandit snorted. "You drool like a fat sow. Your bravery vanishes in the wind." He blew a puff of fetid breath in Lei Tong's face. "Gone, ho? Where is your courage now, fool?" He raised the gun speculatively, touching the tip of the barrel to Lei Tong's chin, his chest, and finally to a point below the jacket where Lei Tong's trousers met. Lei Tong cringed in spite of himself and went taut with terror. The bandit laughed again.

Still laughing, he pulled the trigger.

Mei Shau's scream mingled with the echoes of the gunshot and her brother's screams of agony. He doubled, clutching his exposed genitals where the impact had torn away his trousers. Blood ran down his legs and dripped from his sodden clothing to puddle the floor.

Laughing, the bandit flung him into his own filth. He turned the gun on the others and ordered one man to search for valuables. Quaking, the man obeyed. The rest were so terrified that they eagerly dumped the contents of their pockets. Several stripped off jewelry and added it to the pile.

When he had everything, the bandit stuffed his pockets and moved toward the door. Mei Shau's glassy gaze was still on her brother. She had not made a sound since her one agonized scream, but the bandit was as aware of her presence as he was of the stench of blood and death in the car. He stopped in front of her and stared, then yanked her up. With an appraising glance at her slim body, he shoved her out the door in front of him.

Stumbling, Mei Shau was thrust down the steps. The fire in the wood car was a lusty blaze; fingers of flame reached into the darkening sky. She could see bandits riding in slow circles around the train while some of their number raided the other cars. They had unhitched the rear cars so that the conflagration would not spread too rapidly and rob them of their booty.

The bandit dragged her into the darkness where they were out of sight of his fellow raiders. Pausing only long enough to shove his pistol into his belt, he undid his voluminous trousers and threw Mei Shau to the ground. With a harsh ripping sound, her *koo* fell away from her naked flesh. He knelt between her pale legs, thrusting and groping at the tender joining of her thighs. Grunting, he mounted her, driving his swollen organ into her depths, lunging, thrusting, growling as his excitement soared. She felt his unbearable heat inside her where only William had ever entered. She struggled but was powerless under his weight. The bandolier tortured her breasts and scraped her swollen belly. She gagged at his stench and turned her face away as he bore down in the throes of lust. His hot poison filled her as he grunted like an animal until he was sated.

He scrambled to his feet, thrusting his shriveled organ back into his baggy trousers. Without another glance at her, he strode away.

She scarcely dared breathe as his footsteps crunched away. When at last she heard him mount his horse and ride off, she crouched on her knees and vomited. A long time later, she managed to get to her feet and piece together her torn *koo* to conceal her nakedness. The train was silent except for the crackle of the flames and the keening wails of those who had lost their paltry possessions.

Slowly, she began to walk down the tracks, away from the train.

2

Arisa's interview with Justin Forbes was cool and impersonal. Everything Carter Montaigne had said was true; he owned thirty percent of Travish–Montaigne outright, and a clause in his agreement with Elliot gave him first refusal on the disposition of any stock. That her father had retained reciprocal rights on the partnership stock was little comfort. Forbes showed her a financial statement that revealed a gradual but formidable decline in profits over the past five years, with the most recent balance sheet indicating the heavy losses Montaigne had delicately labeled "distress." The business had been on the verge of bankruptcy. She didn't have to be an expert bookkeeper to see that expenses had heavily outweighed the shop's income. When she questioned the lawyer, he promised to have a complete profit and loss statement drawn up for her.

He had some advice as well. "Mr. Montaigne has discussed his desire to buy your stock. I think it would be a wise move on your part, Miss Travish. The business is surviving this temporary setback with Montaigne at the helm, but it will be some time before you can realize any profit on your inheritance. He's willing to begin payment now even though closure must be delayed until after probate."

"How long will that take, Mr. Forbes?"

"Barring any claims against the estate, six months, perhaps eight or nine. I'll do everything I can to facilitate matters. In the meantime, Montaigne will be able to bring the company out of its slump." He leaned back and looked at her over rimless half-glasses that spanned the wide bridge of his square face. He said in an avuncular tone, "You would be hard-pressed to find a fairer offer. Your brother is willing to sell as quickly as possible. He sees the advantage of a quick profit."

"What percentage of stock does he get?"

"Five."

Not enough to give Montaigne any edge. And not enough to whet Quentin's appetite to stay in. She asked Forbes about the other considerations that went to Quentin.

"Half the net from the sale of the house when you decide to sell. A small portfolio of stocks and bonds he handled for your father. Most of the assets assigned to him have already been paid over a period of years. Your father made several generous investments in your brother's brokerage business in lieu of an inheritance."

"I see."

Forbes closed the folder spread on his desk. "Have you decided on the funeral arrangements?"

She'd spoken to the mortuary people earlier. The service and interment would be held the following day.

Forbes nodded. "I shall be there, naturally. Perhaps there'll be a few minutes afterward when the four of us can discuss our next step."

"I don't think I'm ready to sell, Mr. Forbes. I'll make up my mind after I see the statement you're preparing, but it would be unfair to encourage Carter Montaigne to think that the matter is settled."

The lawyer peered owlishly over his glasses. "I've neither encouraged nor discouraged him, Miss Travish. My advice comes from genuine concern with the affairs that have passed to you on your father's death. I've handled your father's legal matters for ten years."

"And very capably, I'm sure." Arisa stood to go. She wasn't certain if it was Forbes himself she was annoyed by or the fact that he seemed to side with Montaigne. She was being foolish in not further exploring Montaigne's offer. The money would free her to go back to Paris and buy the small gallery she'd been dreaming of.

Why wasn't she leaping at the chance?

Quentin returned her call shortly before noon without any apologies for the delay. "It's been a long time, Arisa. Sorry it's such a sad event that finally brings you back, but these things have to be expected when people get older. What was he—sixty-three, sixty-four? Hardly a young man anymore, though he liked to think he could keep the pace he always had."

A host of resentments filled Arisa at her brother's cold dismissal of the life of the man who'd sired them. Neither of them had established an ideal relationship with their father, but

Quentin might at least have shown some inkling of regret or
comparsion. No, not Quentin. He'd been more like a distant
cousin than a brother. She rarely thought of him as part of the
family. She'd been six years old when he left Hong Kong for
his undergraduate work at Stanford. He'd never come home
for a visit, not while he was in school, or later when he began
working for a large brokerage firm in Los Angeles, or even a
few years later when he attained the success of his own office
in Beverly Hills. Quentin was Quentin's man, totally and sufficiently, with no portion to mete out to family or friends.

She steered the conversation to an innocuous channel, telling
him the arrangements she'd made for the funeral service.

He had no criticism or comment except to add, "I asked
Deline to arrange something at the house afterward. It'll give
us time to talk." Before she knew it, he'd said good-bye and
hung up.

Furious, she slammed down the receiver. Why was it he
could always push the wrong buttons! It would never occur to
him to ask her before he made plans. The ordeal of a macabre
post-mortem made her shudder. After her mother's death, people had streamed into the house to stand about with long faces
that were no comfort to the deceased's family. Their condolences and capsule memories of Melisande smiling and alive
only emphasized the cold finality of her death for teenaged
Arisa—who'd been driving the car that cost her mother her
life. Arisa had finally fled to her room to escape the voices
and memories.

No matter what Quentin had arranged, she'd make sure
nothing like that happened again.

Quentin pushed aside thoughts of Arisa as he put down the
phone. It was a nuisance having her back, but he had more
important things on his mind, things that had to be handled
today if he was going to make it to the funeral tomorrow. He
went through the small stack of pink message slips his secretary
had placed on his desk. He separated one from the rest and
pinned it to the desk blotter with a golden ruler that had his
name engraved in bold letters.

He'd been trying, without luck, to get to Gerald Paxton for
weeks, and now Paxton was calling him. He licked his lips
nervously and knuckled his mustache. Paxton wasn't calling

to pass the time of day. He'd already as much as told Quentin there wasn't any room for him in the new project California Planners was handling. Quentin had caught wind of the deal when he was investigating investment possibilities for several of his clients. It could have been one of those things that slipped by most people without their giving it a second glance and later, when it proved out, made them say, "Damn, I heard about that when it was in the planning stage and I thought nothing would come of it. I really blew it."

Some people. But Quentin's instincts had been alerted immediately. The name Paxton rang a bell, and he checked it out. Gerald Paxton had been in charge of some of the biggest coups in California real estate since the sixties. He'd been responsible for some of the most outstanding hotels and shopping centers in southern California, though always from behind the scenes. Paxton was the man with the ideas, and each one pure gold.

The Tahoe scheme was the sweetest Quentin had ever come across, a multimillion-dollar resort that would surpass anything ever built. California Planners had six hundred acres of prime Tahoe lakeshore and a concept that was revolutionary. The resort complex would combine the features of the finest hotels with elegant resort facilities; in addition, there would be an adjacent shopping center—not a hotel arcade but a major shopping mall, with a first-run theater, bowling alleys, roller rink, shops, even a major department store, all a minute's easy stroll through a climate-controlled skyway. It would attract vacationers from all over the country, maybe even the world. It had the potential of rivaling Disneyland as a California attraction.

Quentin had delved into the plans and the groundwork that had been laid. California Planners had already had the land surveyed and acquired the permits. Construction would start in the spring. And there'd been another fascinating bit of information uncovered: the zoning commission at Tahoe was bending under pressure from the environmentalists to put a moratorium on building. There was a damned good chance that no more commercial permits would be issued within a mile of the lake. The new complex would not only be the best—it would be the last. Sew up the market.

He squared the pink message slip and picked up the phone, pressing the button for his private outside line. He cleared his throat while he listened to the ring.

"Good afternoon, California Planners."

"Gerald Paxton, please. This is Quentin Travish returning his call."

"One moment, Mr. Travish."

A few seconds later Paxton was on the line. "Hello, Travish. Good of you to call back."

"I was out of the office, sorry to be so long." He realized he couldn't grovel with a man like Paxton. He stiffened his tone. "What can I do for you, Mr. Paxton?"

"Are you still interested in our Tahoe project, Mr. Travish?"

Quentin's palms began to sweat. "I'd shelved it after our last conversation, Mr. Paxton. You led me to believe you were not open to outside investors." He knuckled his mustache nervously.

"That was true at the time, but the picture has changed. Your name came up at a recent stockholders meeting. One of our investors spoke very highly of you."

Quentin was so astounded he stared at the phone as if it had bitten him. When he found his voice, he said, "Who might that be, Mr. Paxton?"

Paxton laughed. "I don't think it's necessary to bandy names about, Mr. Travish. The purpose of the stockholders meeting was to discuss an opening that came up in our investors' packet. One of our people would like to draw back in favor of other pressing commitments, and we'd like to accommodate him. Our investors agree they'll pick up the slack if you're not interested, but it was suggested I present the opportunity to you. From time to time we have projects that are open to new investors. This might be a start."

A foot in the door with the Tahoe deal and the possibility of bigger things in the future! Quentin licked his lips. "What kind of investment are we talking about, Mr. Paxton?"

"Fifty thousand. Twenty thousand cash, the balance in thirty days. It's a small slice, but as I say . . ."

"I understand," Quentin said quickly. Even one-hundredth of the Tahoe resort would bring him millions! "I'm interested. I appreciate your thinking of me. And the recommendation by your investor—thank him for me, please."

"I take it that's a 'yes'?"

"It is. I'll have my accountant write a check. Perhaps we could have lunch?"

"I'm tied up this week . . ."

"Some time soon. I know how busy you are."

"Never too busy to talk with my people, Travish. Welcome aboard. I'll have the girls get the paperwork underway. As soon as we have your check, we'll give you a call so you can come in and sign."

"Fine. Thank you, Paxton."

When he'd hung up, he sat squeezing his palms together. His excitement had overbalanced everything else while he was talking to Paxton, but now the euphoria was beginning to give way to cold practicality. When he'd talked to Paxton before, he'd been sure of being able to borrow the money from Elliot. When Elliot died suddenly, he'd shifted his hopes to the share of the old man's estate. It had been a cold shock to find out that his father hadn't divided up his assets equally between his son and daughter. It had been even more of a shock to discover Elliot had taken every precaution to see that his will could not be broken. There was documentation of Elliot's claim that Quentin had received more than the value of Arisa's stock over a period of years—"Loans" which were written off at Elliot's death. So he got a lousy five percent of stock that would take years to show a profit. Even if he sold it to Montaigne, it wouldn't get him more than a couple of thousand.

No wonder he'd shelved all thoughts of pursuing the Tahoe deal. But here it was being dropped in his lap. All he had to do was come up with fifty grand. He massaged his fingers.

Where?

There wasn't time to play the commodity market. He had to come up with quick cash. He should have taken decisive action right from the start, but how was he to know Paxton would come through with an offer?

He swiveled his chair to look up at the ticker tape as it flashed symbols and numbers. GM 53⅛ . . . IBM 63¼ . . . MMM 57⅜ . . . He scanned the tape in search of something significant. The answer had to be there somewhere. . . . His eyes searched the tape relentlessly until he finally found what he was looking for. His chair moved forward as he leaned over to verify the notation. CNT 25½ . . . Conoct had traded at 25½—moved up three for the day. Reaching to the file cabinet, he pulled the Holderbein folder from the drawer and opened it.

There it was—20,000 shares of Conoct. He dried his palms on his sleeves. Conoct had been Quentin's wonder stock right from the start. A winner. It had put him into the big producer category as a broker two years ago, when he put customers into it with the first public offering at \$4.25 a share. Now Conoct was going to give him the \$20,000 he needed immediately. He'd find a way to get the rest before the thirty days was up.

He glanced through the Holderbein folder. Halsey Holderbein was one customer who'd bought Conoct in the original offering. Quentin had been his broker for some time and had performed well for him, but it was the Conoct stock that had really gained Holderbein's confidence. Now Quentin wasn't just another broker—he was the man who'd put Holderbein into the high six-figure range in his investment portfolio and kept him there. Holderbein's confidence had grown to the point where he gave Quentin power of attorney to trade his stock without consulting him first. And with Holderbein out of the country right now, the timing was perfect. The television producer was in Saudi Arabia doing a series on political and social changes in the suddenly oil-rich emerging nation. The trip would keep him away for some time, and, greedy little bastard that he was, Holderbein had opened a checking account with \$15,000 so that Quentin could write checks for any "hot" stocks that might come along. Always covering his bets.

Well, that would be the excuse to use if he needed one. With the Conoct up three points today, he'd tell Holderbein the stock had been sold before the move had started. Hell, \$22.50 a share was damned good profit, considering he'd bought it at 4¼. No, Holderbein was more likely to ask why he'd sold it at all. The stock had been moving up in price but the trading had been relatively weak. The price had gone down for a while, though, when the market opened this morning, and the last time Conoct had risen to this price, plenty of people had sold. It could be argued there was resistance at these prices. Sure. He'd sold half of Holderbein's 20,000 shares because he thought it best to take some profits in view of what looked like internal weakness in the stock. Half the people in the market would buy that—why not Holderbein?

Anything else? If he was going through with this, he had to be damned sure he thought through every detail. He couldn't think of any other questions Holderbein might raise, and there'd be no problem transferring the stock, since he had power of attorney. Now all he had to do was find a buyer. He had several clients who'd jump in on Conoct, but there was only one who could come up with that kind of money on short notice. He reached over and pulled out another file, then picked up the phone as he scanned the page for the number. After he'd talked to a succession of receptionists and secretaries, Evan Reynolds answered.

"Quentin Travish, Evan. I don't like to bother you when you're busy, but something's come up I think you'll be interested in. Remember that stock I mentioned a while ago—Conoct?"

He heard a guarded "Yeah."

"I think I can pick some up for you at a pretty good price."

"How's it acting this morning?" Reynolds sounded bored, but his question indicated interest.

"It's 25⅜ bid and 25½ asked, up 3 on a little over 11,000 shares so far today."

Reynolds paused for a bit and then said, "The last time we talked about Conoct it was around 22 or 23, wasn't it?"

Quentin knew he had his attention now. "I think it was just under 23. It's been acting strong and doesn't show any signs of letting up, and with . . ."

"Don't you think 25½ is a little expensive? I know they got a good balance sheet and their future looks good, but 25½ seems high."

Quentin had gone too far to give up now. "You're right about their balance sheet and their future, Evan. As far as price, what would you say if I could save you $10,000 and get the stock without commissions?"

"I'd have to say I was interested, but I'd want to know how you plan to do it."

The point of no return. Quentin glanced at Holderbein's folder. "One of my customers owns 20,000 shares. He's out of the country right now and needs some money in a hurry. He's given me power of attorney to sell 10,000 shares, but if he sells the Conoct on the market, it's sure to drive the price down. So naturally, he wants to sell privately. Even though it's up to 25½, he'll take 24½ to avoid driving the price down, and he'll pay the commissions the buyer would normally stand."

There was a heavy pause. Quentin knew the dress manufacturer was making some rapid calculations. Finally, he said, "Sounds interesting, Quent, but I'd still have to come up with $245,000. I don't have that kind of cash sitting around idle."

"You've got over $600,000 buying power in your margin

account. You can take the money out of that and still be well above your minimum maintenance requirements."

"Why can't I just buy the Conoct on margin?"

Reynolds was getting defensive. A thin film of sweat formed on Quentin's lip. "My client wants me to wire him the money first thing in the morning. I'll have to deposit the money in his account right away." It was his turn to push a little.

"One other problem," Reynolds said, but the hostility was gone from his tone. "I'm leaving tonight for the fashion show in New York. How you gonna get all this done?"

"No problem, Evan." Quentin smiled and leaned back in the chair. "I'll have the cashier's department issue you a check for $245,000 from your margin account. I'll pick up the stock from the safety deposit box and a copy of the power of attorney so you can send them to the transfer agent to get the stocks registered in your name. You give me a check for $245,000 tonight, and your wife can deposit the other check in the morning."

The short pause that followed seemed like an eternity, but Reynolds finally said, "Okay, but you'll have to be here no later than five-thirty."

"No problem," Quentin assured him again. "It's only a forty-five minute drive from the bank to your place." He glanced at his watch. "I can be at your house by four-fifteen or so."

"Okay."

Elated, Quentin hung up, already thinking about how he would proceed. First there'd have to be a bogus checking account to wash Reynolds' $245,000 check so he could avoid showing that amount in the account Holderbein had opened. He'd write his own check to Holderbein's account for the Conoct at 22½ a share.

By morning, he'd have the check to California Planners covered. He grinned and knuckled his mustache. All in all, a fantastic day's work, he told himself. He slipped the two folders back in the file and left for the cashier's department.

The day began with a gray haze filtering the sun like a pall of smoke. Arisa slipped into a cotton robe and ate breakfast listlessly. It would be impossible to stay cool once the haze burned off, especially on a sun-bruised Burbank hillside. The funeral director had suggested a morning service, and she was thankful now. By noon the heat would be unbearable. She'd checked with Deline to make sure a hundred people hadn't been invited to the house. Deline had reassured her: only the family and a few of her father's close friends and associates were expected. Since there had been no announcement of the funeral arrangements in the newspaper, the service would be small and private as well. A car would pick Arisa up at nine-fifteen.

At eight-thirty, she showered and put on a cool green linen dress with simple lines, narrow white piping being the only detail. She drew her hair up in a loose knot that kept it comfortably off her neck, then fastened a gold and jade pendant around her throat. Surveying herself in the mirror, she knew she looked her best. For her father . . . he'd like it.

When the chimes sounded, she picked up her white linen purse and checked for the house keys as she went down. A sandy-haired young man in a gray suit was on the step.

"I'm Tanner Holmes. Carter asked me to pick you up." At her look of surprise, he grinned boyishly. "If you don't mind, that is. Carter didn't say what I should do if you did mind, but I'm hoping you won't." He shook his head at the complicated sentence he'd uttered. "Well, you get the idea. If you'd rather ride with someone you know, I can call . . ." He flipped his arm to shoot back his coat sleeve and glance at his watch. "Nope, too late. Never make it. Looks like you're stuck with me."

She smiled in spite of herself. He was completely disarming. "Surprise doesn't necessarily denote displeasure, Tanner. I'm grateful."

"Not delighted?" He made a sheepish face, and she smiled again.

"Yes, delighted too. Shall we go?"

Moments later they were seated next to each other in a black Eldorado. He guided it easily along the narrow street, then circled the block to head north on Doheny.

"The car's rented," he said conversationally. "I drive a beat-up Fiat convertible. I hinted to Carter that his Mercedes would be appropriate, but he doesn't take hints readily."

"I prefer this," she said. She was far more relaxed with Tanner Holmes than she would have been with Carter, and surprisingly relieved to have company rather than to drive to the funeral alone. She studied his profile as he concentrated on switching lanes to get around a slow-moving tour bus. Through the green sunscreen windows, she could see the guide talking into a microphone.

"Did you know my father?"

He nodded. "I've done a lot of work for him. We were friends. I sure as hell miss him."

His sincerity took Arisa by surprise. He glanced at her, and his eyes were gentle. "Your father was a great guy, Arisa. He had his ups and downs these past few years, but he was okay."

She smiled. "Thanks, Tanner." It was comforting to know her father had friends. "What kind of work do you do?"

"Restorations and repairs. Your father gave me a break when I was just starting out. I've got my own shop now only because he encouraged and prodded me. I came out of the service with enough scars to make me bitter about everything I'd ever known. It was your old man who showed me life wasn't such a bummer if you went after what you wanted. And if you didn't take it too seriously. He knew how to laugh and enjoy himself."

She'd never thought of her father that way, but she found herself liking the idea. Curious, she asked him about Carter Montaigne.

He shrugged. "He's okay. Your father trusted him. Maybe that was good and maybe it wasn't."

"What does that mean?" she asked, looking at him.

He shrugged again. "Nothing special. Carter knows what he's doing and he sure perked things up in a hurry. I just don't like seeing him move in on something that another man worked hard to build for so long. The partnership was difficult for me to accept, particularly after your father convinced me a man could make it alone, you know."

"Do you think Montaigne took advantage—?"

"I didn't say that. Hell, Carter's a sharp businessman and he's getting results. Your father had let things slide. Maybe Carter was just what he needed. Forget I said anything, huh?"

Arisa wasn't willing to drop the subject yet. "My father was always devoted to his business. My mother used to complain that he never had time for his family. What happened to change all that?"

He was silent for a moment but then said, "He was lonely. The spark went out of his life when you and your mother were gone. He kept hoping you'd come back."

She blushed guiltily and turned to stare out the window so

he wouldn't see. She'd never considered her father's loneliness or needs, only her own. But that couldn't be changed now. Looking back at Tanner, she changed the topic. "How did you become interested in restoration work? Exactly what do you do?"

He concentrated on making the light as they began the climb over Laurel Canyon.

"Natural talent," he said with a grin, his good humor restored. "Talent tempered by a lack of the kind of guts it takes to get anywhere in the art world by painting originals. Your father said I had a lazy hand. Maybe he was right. Anyhow, all my life people have been telling me I had to develop my talent, work at it. I played around a bit, but a couple of years on Uncle Sam's big canvas in the East knocked off the spark. I was just drifting when I ran into your father. We got into an argument right off, about a statue at an auction at Sotheby Parke Bernet."

"You met him at an auction?"

"Before the sale, actually. We were wandering around the showroom down on Beverly and came eye to eye around a figure of a Chinese deity. He asked me if I was going to bid on it. When I said no, he said that was good, because it was a reproduction. That's when the argument started. I knew it was authentic, but he didn't believe it until I pointed out a tiny chip where the piece had been painted and some of the original showed through."

"You saw this at a glance?" She was impressed. There were experts who would hesitate to make a judgment like that without hours of testing.

"Sure. The piece was bronze, I could tell that by the weight. The facial details looked like someone had pressed them out in a cheap mold, but they were actually filled with paint. God knows why anyone would want to cover up a beautiful piece like that, but there are a lot of idiots running around. Somewhere along the line, one of them must have figured he was giving the piece a new lease on life with a clean coat of lacquer. Maybe some bored housewife—whoops . . ." He winked at her and grinned. "I mean some house*person* decided it would fit her color scheme better if it was a pretty shade of blue. Who knows? Anyhow, I told your father if he could get it at anything under two grand, he'd have a hell of a bargain on his hands."

She realized they were on the freeway and she hadn't even

reacted to the whining traffic. They made the lane switch at Vineland that would keep them on the Ventura Freeway. Arisa didn't even flinch when a blue Jag cut in front of them at the last minute. Tanner eased his foot on the accelerator and gave the other driver all the room he needed.

"And?" Arisa demanded.

He gave her another boyish grin. "He made me a deal. If he bought it, it was up to me to restore it so he could sell it as the original."

"Did you?"

"Sure. It took me awhile, but it was worth it. He came off with more than triple his investment. And I came away with enough self-respect to know what I wanted to do with my life. I've been in the business ever since."

They came to the Forest Lawn exit and were sweeping down the long curving drive toward the rolling green vista of the Memorial Park. Tanner drew up close to the chapel to let her out and gave a jaunty salute as he went to park the car.

The haze was bright and thin; it would be gone soon. The heat was already beginning to build. The inside of the chapel was cool, though. Carter Montaigne was standing at the door of the sanctuary.

"Good morning, Arisa," he said quietly. He led her to a front pew. The room was half-filled with people who watched them walk its carpeted length and take seats. Arisa glanced around for Quentin but didn't see him. Then she looked at her watch. Ten minutes were left before the service began. She wished she'd paused a moment at the door to inspect the mourners, but she was too discreet to turn around now and stare. Beside her, Carter was silent.

She looked up at the rosewood coffin and the banks of flowers surrounding it. Who was the man whose body lay encased there? A blend of images filled her thoughts. Which one was he? All. None?

Her earliest memories of him were of a ruddy-faced, laughing man who'd swung her in the air as he'd called her his little "butterfly." Soaring, she watched the world spin as she shrieked with the joy of freedom, secure with her father's strong hands firmly about her waist. A smiling man who claimed her from her Chinese *amah* for a Saturday excursion into the heart of Hong Kong . . . the colorful stalls along Ladder Street, the musky, incense-filled Man Mo Miu, where they'd knelt to shake fortune sticks, the grotesquely flamboyant Tiger Balm Garden, a walla-walla ride across Causeway Bay. Afternoons filled with wonder and laughter. Or the occasional trips to his cluttered office in Prince's Building on Ice House Street, where she'd perched on a high stool while he sketched plans that would become reality and patiently answered every question her childish mind conceived. Architecture. The drawings would become buildings some day. The graceful lines of a pagoda roof or a moon-gate door incorporated into a contemporary building. Stately Georgian lines and gothic arches. A blend of East and West. Like him? No, he didn't have Chinese parents, he told her, but he loved China's ancient culture. Did she know the Chinese were over 4000 years old? Even *amah*? she'd asked. No, *amah's* ancestors, who were gone but whose history would live on in beautiful works of art that had been preserved over the centuries.

When she was four, he'd introduced her to the wonderful inner sanctum of his study at the house on Mount Austin Road. Not even the house *amah* was allowed in that private domain. Nor did her mother ever go there, though Arisa was sure she could have. From a wall cabinet, he'd taken down his treasures. Sitting beside her on the brown leather divan, he'd traced her small chubby fingers over the smooth lines of a bronze censer and the Chinese characters that were pressed in its base. The seal mark of *Yu Tang Ging Wan* showed it was nearly two hundred years old, he'd told her. There was also a rhinoceros-horn cup with delicate patterns of leaves and the fungus *ling chih* carved on its surface. . . . The four-character mark of Ch'ien Lung, he'd told her, and she'd repeated the words solemnly. . . . A gray-green piece of jade carved in the shape of a fish. . . . A silvery-white cicada of pale jade. His collection had been started lovingly after the war that had destroyed so much of China's beautiful culture. Treasures must be preserved, he'd told her. Their beauty would endure forever. She'd nodded with the wisdom of her scant years. He'd smiled and hugged her. Someday his collection would be hers, and she would love and respect it as he did.

The organ music ebbed its last mournful notes and there was a rustle of anticipation. Arisa stole a sidelong glance and saw that Quentin was seated across the aisle. Beside him, there was a flash of yellow and green print, but she couldn't see the woman's face. A minister entered from a curtained doorway and took his place behind the podium.

She barely heard his words. Elliot hadn't been a church-goer, and Arisa knew that the minister had prepared his text from notes he'd been given. Flowery praise to elaborate bare facts. Tribute from a stranger. In her heart, she paid silent homage to the father who'd been a stranger to her as well.

From a curtained arch at the side of the altar, a woman in a gray dress began to sing "Peace in the Valley." When she finished, the minister retreated and the audience began to stir. Carter touched her arm and indicated an exit where cars were waiting to take them to the gravesite. Arisa got to her feet.

She saw that the room had filled. Her gaze swept the crowd—most of the faces were unfamiliar. The woman with Quentin was young and blond and vacantly pretty. Her yellow and green dress set off her hair and tanned complexion but was inappropriate for the occasion. As she rose, she slipped her arm through Quentin's and touched her eyes with a lace hand-kerchief. Arisa noticed that two rows back, Deline Armitage was watching Quentin and his companion with critical aware-ness. Deline was dressed in unrelieved white, elegant despite the simplicity. With a jolt, Arisa recalled that Deline had worn traditional Chinese mourning white at her mother's funeral too. Their gazes met momentarily. Deline bowed her head. Beside her, a middle-aged Oriental man in a dark suit and a carefully knotted tie stared at Arisa. His face was expressionless, and his flat black eyes were shades drawn across any emotion. His gaze didn't waver when she met it. He made Arisa think of the elderly poor Chinese who sat like ancient statues in shop doors of Hong Kong, untouched by life as it passed by.

Tanner Holmes was near the aisle in the rear row. His mouth lifted in a reassuring smile as his gaze caught hers. She lifted her chin slightly to acknowledge it. In the row in front of him, Forbes, the lawyer, looked stiff and pompous as he surveyed the departing family. He seemed to single out Quentin, or perhaps the girl in the yellow and green dress—disdainfully, then let his gaze move on. Like an eagle surveying the territory below his aerie, searching out a target.

Carter touched her arm again and steered her to the side door where a limousine was parked. He helped her in. Behind him, a small knot of people gathered in the shade of the portico. Quentin came forward quickly at a look from Carter. The blond girl was still clinging to his arm, but Carter murmured something and she stopped at the car door. Her face was obscured, but from her stance, Arisa guessed she didn't like what she'd heard. Quentin ducked into the car and settled beside Arisa. Carter closed the door. The car pulled away slowly and another immediately took its place.

"Well, Arisa, I wouldn't have known you," Quentin said. "Eight years have made you a woman." His gaze seemed to encompass her face, her figure, her poise.

He hadn't changed, except for a slight thickening in the body and a small mustache he'd grown. "You're looking good, Quent."

"Tip-top," he agreed readily. "Sorry I couldn't get over to the house, but I've been busier than hell. I'm into something new." He stopped when he saw her impatient look. "I'll tell you about it another time. How's Paris?"

"It was fine when I left it," she said dryly. Why was it she always wanted to get away from him as soon as they began a conversation? He irritated her just by being there. Remembering the comfortable ride and the camaraderie she'd shared with Tanner earlier, she wished he were here now. But the first car was reserved for family. Carter had made that perfectly clear when he intercepted Quentin's companion.

"Who's your friend?"

He looked at her blankly.

"The girl in the green and yellow dress?"

"Oh, Lily. Sorry I didn't introduce you. I planned to, but Carter insisted she'd have to ride in another limo." He didn't look pleased with having been forced to acquiesce.

"Who is she?"

"A friend of Elliot's. She wanted to come along. What could I say?"

"Ever-obliging Quent."

He shrugged, his gaze intent on Arisa's face. "What are you going to do about the shop?"

Her impatience swelled again. "Let's at least get dad buried before we begin carving up his estate, please."

"Touchy, touchy," he said irritably. "Okay, but Forbes is coming to the house later. Let's get a few things settled so I don't have to take more time than I have to away from my office." Piqued, he turned away and sat sulking.

She scowled and studied the scene beyond the car window. All she wanted was for the day to be over. She knew her nerves were on edge, and that she was handling things badly. It would only make everything worse if she got Quentin's dander up. But it was impossible to talk to him without arguing.

The car rolled to a stop in a secluded section of simple headstones. The driver held the door, letting her out first, then coming around to open Quentin's side. Halfway up the hill, a newly opened grave was surrounded by a blanket of artificial turf to disguise the raw wound in the earth. With a start, Arisa recalled being led up the hill on her father's arm at her mother's funeral. She shivered and pushed the image back into the closet of her memory. Quentin glanced at her but did not take her arm.

Chairs had been set up under a green canopy to ward off the sun, which was a white disc flattened on the bleached sky. Arisa found sunglasses in her purse and slipped them on as she took one of the folding chairs. From behind their screen, she watched the others file up the hill. Lily trailed beside Tanner from one of the last cars. In the lead, Deline and the Oriental man were followed by Carter and a strikingly beautiful woman in pale pink. Arisa hadn't noticed the woman in the chapel, and she studied her curiously. She was sure the dress had come from Paris, though she couldn't place the designer. Everything about the woman quietly proclaimed elegance—and money. She was the type who frequented the fashionable spas of Europe or was at home in the lavish party set that Eduoard was addicted to. She walked sedately beside Carter with a proprietary air that made it obvious she was with him. Arisa did not turn as they took seats beside her.

The smell of roses and gardenias and carnations filled the hot air. The minister stood at one side of the draped casket until the group assembled. Arisa focused her attention on the twin headstones bearing her parents' names. Mesmerized, her thoughts could not focus on the mound in Forest Lawn but involuntarily went back in time . . .

Melisande Whitaker Travish was born in Hong Kong and lived there all her life except during the war and the four years in Los Angeles that had ended in her death. Always Hong Kong remained the enticing dream, the alluring past, and the future to which she would return one day. She never gave up that hope, desire—or need. Hong Kong was everything that

Los Angeles was not. Hong Kong was home. She and Arisa would return . . . someday.

Melisande gave birth to Arisa on a humid September morning in the maternity ward of Mathilda Hospital on the Peak. She gazed at her infant daughter with bursting pride and a fierce determination that the child would never know a moment's unhappiness that was in her mother's power to prevent. As soon as they went home from the hospital, she turned Arisa's daily care over to a baby *amah*, as was the custom in the colony; she'd chosen the nurse with the same meticulous care as she had a pediatrician. Lam Liu-chung had a sense of dignity and pride in doing her job well, and like all *amahs*, insisted on doing it her own way. Melisande understood this inborn characteristic of the Oriental servant, and she did not fight it. She gave Liu-chung instructions, knowing they would be carried out, but she never dictated the manner in which they were to be accomplished. When she wanted the baby clothed for an outing, she left the choice of garments to Liu-chung. Her own satisfaction was already guaranteed, because she had selected Arisa's entire wardrobe personally. There was not a nappie, dress, or tiny knit she had not approved. When gifts flooded in after Arisa's birth was announced, Melisande wrote enthusiastic thank-you notes, even though she exchanged many of the gifts for garments more suited to her personal taste. In the case of gifts from distant members of her own family in England, or Elliot's friends in the United States, packages were opened, evaluated, and dispersed immediately to the Christian Children's Fund if they fell short of Melisande's standards.

Melisande never infringed on Liu-chung's duties, but from the beginning she established that certain hours were set aside each day for mother and child to be alone, just as there were specific times when Liu-chung should bathe, feed, or put the baby to bed for a nap. On the rare occasions when Arisa was ill, the *amah* tended her and carried out the doctor's orders. Melisande hovered or sat holding the child while Liu-chung cooled the fever with cloths dipped in pungent herb brew. Despite the formidable language barrier—Liu-chung had only a vague command of English and could neither read nor write Western characters—they communicated by instinct, gestures, and their common bond of love for Arisa. To Melisande, twelve-year-old Quentin was old enough that his life could be entrusted to the Hong Kong International School and the guidance of his father. She and Liu-chung devoted themselves to the golden-haired infant who had blessed the Travish household after so many barren years.

Melisande's indulgences were counterbalanced not only by Liu-chung's practical care but also Elliot's devoted, but firm, hand. Arisa grew into a winsome child with a ready smile and a quick temper—which was an effective tool in getting what she wanted from her mother. By the time she was a toddler, she was rarely denied any pretty thing that caught her fancy. And by the time she was old enough for school, Arisa accepted her parents as separate entities who afforded her different pleasures. She took for granted the private times she spent with each of them, and she accepted the fact that they rarely spent time together as a family. There was an invisible gulf between her parents that neither tried to breech, and that Arisa never questioned.

Another peculiarity of her home life that Arisa simply accepted was that, despite having lived all her life in Hong Kong, Melisande was coolly aloof from the Oriental people. She treated servants with authority that elicited their best work but drew no warmth. She had no friends among the Chinese community, nor did she socialize with wealthy Chinese matrons who lived on the Peak. Although she didn't forbid Arisa Chinese playmates, neither did she encourage the friendships. When she entertained her husband's Oriental business associates, it was with a quiet reserve that passed for shyness, but a hard glint in her eyes made Arisa wonder if hatred lay behind her calm exterior.

Despite this, Melisande held Chinese antiques in high esteem. The house on the Peak was decorated with the finest pieces available from Hong Kong shops and imported from abroad. Yet after the move to California, Melisande refused to set foot in the shop her husband established as a new career. The breech between them became an open rift that was never healed . . .

The minister's voice signaled the commitment of Elliot's body to the grave. Arisa tried to concentrate on his words but they were a meaningless jumble. She glanced at the people standing uncomfortably in the hot sun. Seeing Tanner, she wondered why he hadn't joined them under the canopy. The gaunt Oriental who'd been with Deline had not joined them either. He stood slightly apart from the rest, his eyes hidden behind dark glasses.

She brought her attention back as the minister scooped up a handful of dirt and scattered it over the coffin. A small puff of dust rose like a departing soul. It was quickly claimed by the hot wind and dissipated across the hillside.

Good-bye, Dad....

The last remnants of haze had burned away, and Beverly Hills shimmered in a pool of merciless heat. A caterer's truck was parked in the driveway. When Arisa saw one of the girls from Travish-Montaigne, she realized how efficiently Deline had planned.

The air conditioning hummed softly, and the house was pleasantly cool. Arisa had ridden back with Tanner, rejecting her brother's offer that she accompany him and Lily. Tanner's cheerful banter was subdued, and they made the trip in companionable silence, each with his own thoughts. Arisa escaped upstairs to wash her face and press a cold cloth to her neck for a minute before reapplying a touch of makeup.

Downstairs, she detoured through the dining room and kitchen to see if there was anything she could do, but Deline's contingent of caterers had everything in hand. Two girls in black uniforms were arranging trays of hors d'oeuvres on the dining room table. A large punch bowl and cups were on a silver tray at one end of the sideboard, several decanters of liquor and bottles of mix on the other. In the kitchen, piping hot canapes were being removed from a microwave.

The others were in the living room: Deline, Forbes, Tanner, Quentin, and the impossible girl in the print dress. Near the fireplace, Carter stood talking with the attractive woman in pink. Again, Arisa was aware of the possessiveness in her manner.

Tanner came over to her as she walked in. "Can I get you something to drink? It's a fruit punch, no kick. Or there's hard stuff."

"A light vodka and tonic, thanks."

He winked and vanished toward the dining room. A girl passed with a tray of food, and Arisa accepted a tiny hot quiche. Her brother moved away from Lily and came toward her.

"Forbes says you're not going to sell," he said accusingly.

"That's right. Not yet, anyway," she said. She noticed that Quentin's fleshy face was still handsome, with startling dark eyes under heavy black brows, but that drooping line had begun to form around his mouth, as though he hadn't practiced smiling enough to keep his face firm.

"Why not?" he demanded.

She bristled at the cutting edge in his voice. "I don't think I have to account to you for my decisions."

His mouth tightened and his face flushed slightly. "You'd be a fool to pass up Carter's offer." When she lifted her chin, he said quickly, "Sorry, I'm coming on a little strong. I want what's best for you. I guess I still think of you as baby Arisa." He smiled but his eyes were still cold.

"It seems to be the consensus of opinion around here. First Carter Montaigne, then Forbes, now you. For Dad's friends and family, you all seem eager to toss away everything he worked so hard for." She was angry again. Not only at them, but at herself. Why was she so defensive, so protective of her father's memory? And so ready to postpone her own plans? If she sold the stock to Montaigne, she could be back in Paris within the month and the *galerie* would be hers. She could get on with her own life instead of trying to resurrect her father's.

Quentin puffed like a blowfish. "'Toss away' is a peculiar choice of words. Carter is offering a fair price. He has a great deal of money invested in the business. Without him it would have gone under long ago. Dad really let things go to hell."

She glared. "Maybe I don't like being hit from all sides and told what to do," she said hotly. She'd only been in Los Angeles forty-eight hours and all she'd heard was sell, sell, sell.

"Don't be childish," he snapped. "This is a chance to make a decent profit on something you didn't even own two weeks ago. If you take Carter's offer, I'll invest the money for you. I can get you a hell of a lot better return . . ."

Arisa sighed in exasperation. "Not now, Quent, please. I admit I haven't exactly been a model daughter these past years, but Dad is barely in his grave. Everything's happening too fast. Give me time."

As he tried for a concerned smile, his expression reminded Arisa of a cat waiting for an unwary bird.

"We'll talk again later." He was almost jovial, clapping a hand on her shoulder in an intimate gesture. "Let's have lunch soon."

"Fine, Quent. I'll call you." She slipped past him as Deline came through the hall. Arisa intercepted her. "Thanks for arranging everything, Deline. I'm afraid I never gave it a thought."

"Is everything satisfactory?" Deline looked about with an appraising glance.

"Perfect," Arisa said. She watched Carter, who was talking with Justin Forbes. The lawyer's glance flicked toward Arisa, then away quickly as he realized she'd seen him. Were they discussing her? She seemed to be a popular topic of conversation these days. Forbes or Carter—or both—had talked to Quentin sometime in the past twenty-four hours. The girl who'd been with Quentin was sitting beside Tanner on the white sofa, her legs crossed, exposing her thigh. Arisa couldn't decide if his intent expression was fascination or boredom. She glanced back to Deline. "Do you know the woman Quentin brought along? He says she was a friend of my father's."

Deline's cool gaze touched Lily briefly. "She's been in the shop a few times. She has no business being here."

Arisa looked inquisitively at the Eurasian woman. The sharpness in her tone was surprising. Obviously Deline was displeased by Quentin's lack of discretion.

"Who is she?"

"Lily Taylor. She works in one of the shops on Brighton Way. Your father met her somewhere in the neighborhood." A maid went by with an empty tray. "Excuse me," Deline said quickly, and followed the girl out.

Arisa walked toward the group by the fireplace. Forbes halted in mid-sentence and smiled at her.

"Arisa . . ."

"Don't let me interrupt," she said.

"No, no, we were just chatting, but I do hope you and Quentin and I can have a few minutes later?"

She didn't answer as she turned her gaze toward the blonde. "I don't think we've met."

The woman looked at her coolly with a hint of amusement. "I'm Claire Prigent. Carter and I are old friends." She gave him an amused glance, and he picked up the cue:

"Claire has a decorating studio in Beverly Hills. Your father and I have worked with her for a long time."

"Thank you for coming," Arisa said formally, from the depths of insincerity. She didn't iike Claire and she resented Carter bringing her. *Meow,* she chided herself. "Excuse me, there's another guest I haven't met." She moved away toward the twin sofas where Quentin and Lily sat just as Tanner returned with her drink. She took it and they sat side by side on the opposite sofa.

Lily turned lazily, not bothering to pull down her skirt which hiked several inches up her sleek thigh.

Lily said brightly, "I was just telling Quent how much we're all going to miss your father. He was a great guy. He knew how to enjoy life."

"Did you know him long?"

"About a year, but he was one of those people you feel like you've known all your life. Know what I mean?"

Arisa wasn't sure if Lily was inferring more than a casual relationship, and the thought made her uncomfortable. She wanted to know more. Something about Lily demanded explanation. "Are you in the antique business?"

Lily gave a short barking laugh. "Me? God, no. I don't know a Ming from a Chippendale." She giggled at her joke. "I work at Jana's Boutique."

Arisa recognized the name of a shop near Travish Imports. Travish-Montaigne, she reminded herself wryly, glancing toward Carter.

"You live in Paris?" Lily said.

"Yes." Arisa wondered if Lily was having an affair with Quentin.

"It must be nice to be able to live wherever you want and not have to work for a living. Me, I'm a poor working girl." Lily settled back with the weariness of a truck driver after a cross-country haul. Her breasts heaved with a tremendous sigh.

"I work," Arisa said with annoyance.

"Yeah? I thought . . ." She shrugged her silken shoulders and let the sentence hang.

"Just what did you think?" Arisa asked with as much sweetness as she could muster. Her own conscience had been niggling her badly enough without having a stranger pick up the refrain.

Lily sensed her awkward position and became defensive. "Elliot said you never stayed in one job long enough to know what you wanted."

"Sometimes you have to change jobs in order to find out what you really want," Tanner said, swirling his drink. "It beats putting in a lifetime at something you don't enjoy, and it takes a hell of a lot of self-honesty." He smiled at Arisa. "Your father also said you'd be able to write your own ticket someday. He believed in you."

She thanked him silently with a glance. She hadn't accustomed herself to the fact that her father had discussed her so freely with his friends. It was like dressing in the privacy of your bedroom and suddenly realizing the blinds are open. She suspected, too, that some of Lily's ideas came from Quentin. They sounded like the blanket condemnations he was fond of making. She wished now she'd put her foot down when Quentin told her about this gathering. It was a meaningless gesture.

Arisa and Tanner refused drinks as the maid came by, but Lily took one eagerly. Her pouty mouth worked nervously until she raised the glass. The drink was half gone when she lowered it.

"Well, I can't afford to change jobs just 'cause I don't like one. It costs too damned much to live these days. You know what I pay for a one-bedroom? Three-sixty." She looked around for sympathy. When none was forthcoming, she took another swallow of the drink. "Three-sixty," she repeated, underscoring the number. "Unfurnished." Her voice climbed, and the two men by the fireplace looked around.

"I don't think anyone's interested in your rental problems, Lily," Quentin said uncomfortably.

"Well, they damned well better be," she said in a burst of anger. "My landlord wants his dough sure as clockwork the first of the month. Elliot promised to pay me back by then. What the hell am I supposed to do?" Her blue eyes blinked and she forgot to flutter her lashes.

"Lily . . ." Quentin put out a hand as if to stop her flood of words.

"Don't 'Lily' me," she snapped.

He recoiled in embarrassed silence. Behind him, Justin Forbes cleared his throat and peered owlishly. Lily fastened an angry glare on him.

"You're his lawyer. Okay, isn't it up to you to take care of his debts?" she demanded.

"There's no record . . ." Forbes frowned.

"I don't give a damn about records! I want my money." She was a little bit drunk. The words were spit out like bullets.

"Exactly what is this debt?" Carter Montaigne asked.

"One thousand bucks, that's what it is. He didn't have time to go to the bank, he said. He was taking off on that trip to Hong Kong and needed traveling cash. He promised to pay it back with interest as soon as he got back."

Carter's voice was low and controlled. "When was this?"

"Two weeks ago. Next thing I know Elliot's popped off and no one at the store has time to talk to me. Okay, so everything's turned upside down because poor old Elliot's dead, but enough is enough. Now I want my money—I *need* it."

"Do you have a note?" Forbes said pompously.

"No, I don't *have a note.*" She mimicked the lawyer's sonorous tone and made an ugly face. "Elliot never welshed on a debt in his life. You don't go around asking your friends to sign for favors."

Forbes worked his mouth as if trying to get rid of a bad taste. "I'm afraid that without some documentation, the matter will have to be investigated."

"I told you, I need it now," Lily exploded.

Carter motioned a hand as Forbes started to answer. "I'm sure this can be settled readily, Miss Taylor, but I think the discussion should be postponed to a more appropriate time. Stop by my office tomorrow. Noon, or whatever time you go to lunch."

"One o'clock," Lily said, mollified now that she'd gotten attention.

"I'll expect you." Carter put down his glass and turned to Claire. "Shall we go? I'm sure it's been a long day for Arisa and she'll be glad of some quiet." He threw a meaningful glance at Lily.

An awkward silence filled the room as Claire retrieved her purse from a table and preceded Carter out. She seemed highly amused by the whole incident, and Arisa felt a new wave of resentment. Forbes was still scowling. Quentin had turned a mottled shade of purple. Arisa was seething at Lily's vituperous attack. What in the world had made Quentin bring her here, or to the funeral?

Lily lifted her empty glass toward Quentin, rattling the ice cubes for a refill. Arisa was on her feet instantly.

"You've had enough. It's time to leave," she said flatly. She glared at her brother. "See Lily out, Quent."

Lily sputtered, but Quentin put down his glass and took her arm. "Arisa's right, Lily. We should go."

Lily's lip jutted dangerously. Arisa thought she was going to erupt in another tirade, but she banged her glass on the table and picked up her Gucci purse. Obviously she knew when she was outnumbered. She got to her feet with as much dignity as she could muster, smiled sweetly around the group, then flounced into the hall, Quentin at her heels. A minute later, the front door closed, but not before Lily's parting shot carried back into the room.

"Bitch! Who the hell does she think she is?"

Forbes cleared his throat nervously. "This sort of thing happens," he said. "An opportunist sees a chance to badger a grief-stricken family for a few quick dollars. It's a variation of the old Bible order con. Carter will straighten her out. If she bothers you again, Arisa, I'll have someone from police headquarters throw a scare into her. She'll realize she can't go around trying to intimidate people."

His sudden bravado amused Arisa. He'd been willing enough to abdicate responsibility to Carter a few minutes ago. All at once, Arisa was tired and wanted to escape. Tanner glanced at her and got to his feet.

"You look like you could use another drink. I'll get it." He picked up her glass and vanished into the hall, leaving her alone with Forbes.

He cleared his throat. "I'm sorry we didn't have the opportunity for the discussion I suggested. Perhaps another time would be more appropriate." He reached into an inside coat pocket, drew out a long envelope, and laid it on the table. "There's no need for a formal reading of the will. Your brother already has a copy. I'll leave this one for you." He straightened and glanced around the room as though he might have forgotten something. "I'll check with Carter and Quentin on a convenient time for our discussion after you've had a chance to think about selling your stock. Good day." He took a few steps toward the door, then paused. As an afterthought, he added, "The service was just right. I think your father would have approved." He nodded and went out.

Arisa sank back against the sofa in relief. Lily's outburst had been in the worst taste. Quentin was a fool. Did he know about the supposed debt their father owed Lily?

Tanner returned and handed her the glass. "Vodka and tonic." She nodded gratefully. "Is Deline still here?"

He shook his head. "She left. The girls are cleaning up. I'll keep you company while you have your drink, then I'll get out of your hair too." He folded himself onto the sofa opposite her and took a swallow of the drink he'd fixed for himself. "I get the feeling there's no love lost between you and your brother."

She shrugged, realizing she didn't resent his observation. "I hardly know him. He went away to school when I was just a kid. After we moved to California, we still didn't see much of him. My father kept in touch but that was about it."

"Your father never talked much about him."

"There isn't much to say, I guess. Quentin is just Quentin.

We've all lived with that a long time."

"The black sheep?" Tanner asked with a grin.

She laughed. "Something like that. Any idiot who'd bring someone like Lily to his own father's funeral . . ." She grimaced.

He rubbed the side of his cheek with his glass. "Look, I should probably keep my mouth shut and my nose out of what isn't my business, but something puzzles me. I don't know if it's important, but you ought to know."

She looked at him, frowning.

"Lily said she made the loan to your father because he needed it for a trip to Hong Kong."

Arisa felt a flutter of anticipation.

Tanner shook his head emphatically. "Elliot wasn't planning a trip to Hong Kong or anyplace else two weeks ago."

"How do you know? How can you be sure?" She was eager to believe Lily was lying.

"Because the Hankow collection was in town. Every buyer in L.A. had been waiting months for that baby. Elliot went to the exhibition every day—so did I. He had his eye on a pair of Ming bowls that were mates to some he'd sold a few years back. Beauties. They were from a set used in the Imperial Palace during the fifteenth century. Elliot knew the bidding would be brisk, so he wanted to get an edge by snooping around and know who was in the game. The Mings didn't go on the block until Thursday and Elliot got 'em." He looked up with a pensive expression. "He spent the rest of the week admiring them and patting himself on the back. He could barely pull himself away from the store. He'd have taken them home with him if it hadn't been for the insurance. Believe me, he wasn't thinking about any trip to Hong Kong."

Arisa's eyes glinted. "So Lily is lying."

Tanner raised his eyebrows. "It bears looking into. It's possible Elliot needed the money for something else and gave Lily the first excuse he could come up with."

"That doesn't sound like my father," Arisa said firmly. "Why should he borrow money from a woman he barely knew?"

Tanner sipped his drink. "He could have needed the money for something personal."

"A thousand dollars in cash?"

"He was impulsive. Maybe he saw something he wanted to buy."

"Oh, for heaven's sake, of course anything is possible, but

not very probable. Admittedly my father was in financial trouble a year ago when he was forced to take Carter Montaigne into the business, but the shop is solvent now. He could have written a check that could be covered the next day if his account was short. No, I think Lily is a gold digger trying for a quick payoff. She thinks we'll give her the money just to get rid of her." She snorted. "I don't think she'll get very far with Carter Montaigne. He knows there was no Hong Kong trip, and he'll see through her story. I think Lily will meet her match tomorrow when she walks into Carter's office."

Tanner nodded with a grin. "I think she already has. I'll never forget the expression on her face when you told her to get out. She was ready to tear your eyes out."

Arisa grinned, oddly flattered by Tanner's approval. She sipped her drink and thought again how easy he was to be with.

"I like a woman with spunk and fire," he said.

Embarrassed now, she made light of it. "Actually, I was sick of listening to her, and of my dear brother standing there unwilling to shut her up. He has the sensitivity of a cactus. I don't think I've missed much not knowing him better all these years, even if he is family."

Tanner finished his drink. "I'd better let you get some rest. Hey, look, if there's anything I can do . . ."

"Thanks. You've been a great help already."

He bowed ceremoniously. "Delighted." He fumbled in the pocket of his gray suit, which had acquired a slightly rumpled air, as if it were miscast on him. He came out with a small flat leather case and extracted a card. "My apartment is above the shop. Same number for both. I've got a good ear for listening any time you need one. And I also know the best enchilada place in town. I'd like to take you some night. I can tell by looking at you that you're a connoisseur." He winked outrageously.

"I'd like that," she said, walking with him to the door.

"How about Wednesday? Unless you've already got plans?"

"Wednesday would be fine. Thanks for the ride, Tanner, and for everything."

He grinned. "See you. We'll have to make it early—say six?"

"That's fine."

He signaled thumbs up. "I'd better get this rental pumpkin back. See you Wednesday." He took the steps in a leap and ran down the walk.

YEAR OF THE COW

Hong Kong, March 1925

Mei Shau's swollen body twisted on the straw mat, and she pressed her knuckles to her teeth. Her delicate oval face was bathed in sweat. Her loose robe clung to her body like wet moss. She longed for release from the engulfing agony. Whimpering softly, she tried to think of William's gentle hand soothing her as his child pushed against the confines of her body.

Dreams had sustained her throughout the months of waiting. Since she had walked away from the bloodshed at the train, she'd closed her mind to the horrors of reality and existed only inside herself. Somehow she had made her way back to Hong Kong, mostly on foot, driven by the need to be in the place where William could find her. The journey had taken more than a full passage of the moon; each torturous step had been bearable only because it brought her closer to William. When at last she reached Kowloon, she spent two days on the waterfront before she found an old woman who agreed to ferry her across the harbor. Huddled in the sampan, Mei Shau lifted her face to the raw wind that raked the choppy water. The cold stung her flesh mercilessly. The ancient hag who poled the sampan took pity on her and gave her an oilskin to ward off the spray.

In the city, she lived on the streets, begging or stealing bits of food from venders' stands when she was faint with hunger, and sleeping in doorways with only newspapers to cover her. And when she realized that her deprivation would harm the child, she finally admitted what she already knew: she could not face her ordeal alone. So she waited patiently at the gate of the English hospital until she recognized the plump Miss Abigail who had revealed her secret to I Fong. Mei Shau was so filthy and tattered that the woman started to pass by in disgust, until Mei Shau identified herself in a rapid burst of English. Before the astonished nurse could recover from her surprise, Mei Shau told her story and begged for help—not for herself but the child's sake. She vowed to repay her debt by working at any tasks she could perform. Moved to compassion, Miss Abigail took her home where she warmed, bathed, and fed the pitiful thing Mei Shau had become. She cared for her as she would a child, tending the scabrous sores on Mei Shau's feet, strengthening her frail body until Mei Shau's health returned. They talked, but Mei Shau never mentioned William's name, lest the foreign woman share her family's contempt for her half-Oriental child. Miss Abigail reluctantly promised not to mention Mei Shau's presence to I Fong; his treatment of his daughter angered her so much that she refused to set foot in his shop again. Mei Shau repaid her trust not only by cooking and cleaning but by doing the laundry as well, so there was no need for Miss Abigail to consider visiting her father's shop.

The New Year came. The streets were strung with bunting and lanterns and the air was filled with the incense of joss sticks and the pungent odor of firecrackers. Mei Shau took no part in the festivities except to venture as far as the tiny temple on the Street of Heaven to give thanks for her deliverance, and to whisper the prayer that was always in her heart. So close was William that she envisioned his face in the eddying smoke of the smouldering joss coils, and heard his voice in the ringing gongs.

He still had not come when the first dull pains forecast the arrival of their child a month later. Now in her agony, she wanted to cry out for him to share her pain and the joy that would come when their son emerged from her dark womb and presented his face to the sun. The agony would be forgotten, William would come to them . . . to her and his son.

A black tidal wave gripped her in its swirling current and dragged her into its depths. She gasped as she struggled to free herself, but the wave sucked her under and held her with iron claws. Down . . . down . . . down . . . Pressure roared in her ears like a scream wrenched out in agony. The sound deafened her. She shuddered as the wave renewed its strength and dragged her into a frantic spiral, surrounding her, filling her, and at last spewing her out of the undertow onto the wet, warm sand.

The pain was gone except for a dull ache where the baby had been. She wanted to open her eyes, but they were heavy with salty water. She tried to raise her head as she heard the faint mewing cry of a gull, but she fell back, too exhausted to move. Her drenched body began to cool, bringing a shiver.

The door opened and a draft washed over her.

"Merciful God!" Miss Abigail's voice thundered in the misty dimness.

Mei Shau smiled as the woman's footsteps hurried across the room. It was right, it was good. . . . She was aware of the nurse kneeling beside her, yanking aside the bloody, wet robe and lifting the child. It whimpered. Mei Shau opened her eyes and saw a tiny foot kick as the baby began to wail vigorously. Such healthy lungs. He would be a strapping lad. She raised her hands to welcome him. Miss Abigail shook her head and went to the bureau she had installed in the tiny scullery when she'd made it into a bedroom for Mei Shau. She cradled the squalling infant in one arm while she groped for a swaddling cloth. With deft motions, she wrapped the baby before returning to the pallet. Mei Shau gazed with shining eyes.

"My son," she whispered, holding out her arms to receive the child. Miss Abigail knelt and laid the bundle in her arms. With incredible joy, Mei Shau looked upon the face of her firstborn. So tiny . . . She smiled in wonder. The infant curled one hand over the edge of the swaddling cloth. Its fingers were as delicate as slender stalks of heavenly bamboo. The hand of a scholar . . .

"My son," she whispered. "He will grow to be a man as tall and proud as his father."

Miss Abigail's voice was gentle. "It's a girl, Mei Shau, and she'll grow as brave and proud as her mother."

Mei Shau looked at the woman who had befriended her. "A girl?" she asked, knowing that no false breath escaped the foreign woman's lips.

"A lovely girl." Miss Abigail reached for the coverlet Mei Shau had thrown aside during labor and gently drew it over the mother and child. The vigor returned to her voice. "I'd judge she weighs five pounds and is as perfect as any baby I've ever seen. Now it's time to rest. I'll have you warm and dry in a minute, then I'll tend to the baby. Here, give her to me." She lifted the child from Mei Shau's arms and placed it in the basket they had prepared, settling the infant on the soft, clean linens. The baby mewed softly. Miss Abigail brought dry garments for Mei Shau and slipped her into them, tossing aside the bloodied robe and stripping away the soiled mat to tuck another in place. She secured the edges of the blanket around Mei Shau.

"Snug as a bug," she pronounced. "Sleep now, child, you've earned it." Lifting the basket, she went out and closed the door softly.

Mei Shau lay very still, scarcely daring to breathe. A girl. Not the son she'd vowed to give William, the son that would bring William to her side once more. A girl.

A tear crept from her eye and slid slowly down her cheek. A girl. She wept because she knew she would never see William again.

3

"What right have you got to complain?" Quentin demanded. "How the hell could I know she was going to pull a dumb stunt like that?" A flush spread across his face and he loosened his tie. Just when everything was going smoothly, Deline had to start in on him.

"It was incredibly bad taste to bring her," Deline answered calmly. "Even if she hadn't mentioned the money, she had no place at your father's funeral." She poured the tea and put a green translucent cup in front of him.

God, she'd make tea if California was sliding into the ocean in an earthquake. "I suppose your Chink friend is part of the family," he snorted.

Her eyes were black fire. "Don't ever say that again. I warn you!"

"All right, all right." He held up a placating hand. "I'm sorry about Lily. Let's forget it. She was trying to put the squeeze on me. I thought maybe if I did her that little favor, she'd shut up and handle it through Forbes."

"And now she's seeing Carter. It would be better if this could have been avoided."

"Carter will take care of it one way or the other. He doesn't want probate held up by claims. The faster he can get Arisa to sell, the better."

"She is refusing."

"I know, but she'll change her mind. She's always been stubborn, but she's not stupid."

Deline set down her cup and folded her hands delicately.

"None of this solves your immediate problem, Quentin." She met his gaze. "The only solution I see is for you to agree to my request."

"You mean Bok's," he said sarcastically. "What's in it for you?"

"If Mr. Bok is happy, that is my reward."

He regarded her speculatively. "If what you say is true, why

78

didn't Elliot get the jade piece to Bok himself?"

"He intended to. He was to bring it to the shop the day he died."

"Why didn't he have it here in the shop in the first place?"

"It was something Elliot fancied for himself. You know how he was about beautiful things. When Mr. Bok made his offer, he was willing to reconsider."

"You know," Quentin said speculatively, "this whole story could be a fairy tale. I'm not sure I should get sucked into it."

She lifted her shoulders in a tiny shrug. "The choice is yours. I did not mention it until you came begging for money."

He flushed slightly. It always came down to that bottom line. He needed money and she was offering him a way to get it.

"Thirty thousand dollars, was it?" she asked quietly.

She was twisting the knife. "Bok's willing to pay that?"

"If you get him what he wants. Since the piece has not been inventoried through the store, there's no record of it here."

"Actually," he said with growing enthusiasm, "I need fifty thousand. I was hoping to make up the difference from another deal."

"Spare me your lies, Quentin. You've never been bashful about asking for exactly what you want. No matter how much you've gotten, it's never been enough!"

"It happens to be the truth," he said nastily. "I do need fifty thousand. If you can hold Bok up for another twenty—hell, he wants the piece bad enough to steal it, doesn't he? If he won't pay our price, tell him to find it himself."

She paled with anger. "You don't know what you're saying."

"Don't I? Suppose Elliot locked it up in a safe-deposit box? The bank would have sealed it the minute they heard he was dead, and nobody'd get into it until the state appraiser was there. And the only ones invited to the great unveiling are the immediate heirs. Arisa and *me*. One of us walks out with it in our pocket. It shouldn't be too hard to find another buyer. If it's worth thirty thousand to Bok, it's going to be worth at least that to some other collector. It won't be hard to find one."

Deline's breath was audible in the silence that followed. Her nostrils flared, then she smiled. "Do as you please, of course. But you should consider the fact that once Arisa knows about the piece, she can claim it is part of Elliot's collection, which was left to her. You may wind up with nothing."

He blew out a breath. He should have known he wouldn't get anywhere trying to con her. What she said was absolutely true. He had no guarantee, but his prospects were considerably better doing what she wanted.

"Okay," he said at last. "I'll see what I can do."

Along with her inheritance came the task of sorting through her father's things. She knew Quentin would want no part of it, so Arisa set about the distasteful chore the day after the funeral, determined to finish it as quickly as possible. She began in the master suite her parents had shared. The suite of bedroom, dressing room, and bath at the rear of the house was a study in Oriental simplicity. The simple lines of bamboo furniture were enriched by oyster-silk walls; the draperies and bedspreads were the same color, with blue flowering prunus drifting across the delicate background, as though nature had placed them with a careful hand. The lightest shade of blue was picked up by the carpeting and the fixtures in the bath so the rooms were coordinated and cool. Several pieces of Ming porcelain stood on racks and pedestals of carved sandalwood, whose rich, deep red color was the solitary accent to the theme of blue and white. The walls were unadorned except for a single picture, a pastel sketch done by an artist in Hong Kong. It was impressionistic, with feathery lines that blended the trees and house as though they were viewed through a fine mist, but there was no mistaking the house on Victoria Peak. The artist had captured its elegance as well as its ethereal beauty. He'd captured the *feeling* of the house.

She flung open the walk-in closet in the dressing room and snapped on the light. To her amazement, one side of the closet was completely empty. Her father's suits, shirts, sport coats, and slacks were still confined to the limits prescribed by Melisande. His shoes were on the long metal racks below, his folded sweaters in plastic drawers on the shelf above. It was as if he'd dared not go beyond the boundaries of his marital partnership, or had no desire to let his life expand into new areas. Fingering a cashmere jacket, Arisa was disturbed by the feeling that her father had lived these past years in a vacuum, that although he had to acknowledge his wife's death and his daughter's absence, he never quite accepted them. Seeing the deliberate emptiness of his life, she realized with a jolt how lonely he must have been. She'd misread his uneasiness and withdrawal on their occasional visits. He had not been ill at ease because he didn't love her, but because he did. He'd forced himself to give her space to recover from her grief . . . and she had never come back.

She walked the length of the closet slowly, pushing aside suits to examine them. Most were in good condition, but several were stained and rumpled. Without a wife to remind him, Elliot obviously put off little chores. A crumpled pair of slacks had slipped from a hanger and lay in a heap on the floor. She picked them up, then tossed them back. Closing the closet door firmly, she crossed to the phone and dialed information for the number of the Salvation Army, then called and arranged for a pick-up. Let them take everything.

She went through the drawers quickly but found nothing of significance except a small leather jewelry case which contained a Baume & Mercier watch, a pair of pearl cuff links, and a stickpin.

Carrying the case, she left the bedroom. Had her father faced the task of disposing of Melisande's things alone? Strange that so many things had never crossed her mind before. It was almost as though her mother's death had built a barrier between two segments of her life, and now at long last the wall had worn thin enough to be broken down. She felt a touch of pity for the suffering her father must have endured.

It took longer to go through her father's desk in the den downstairs. Like his study in Hong Kong, the room was masculine, secluded, and a catchall of mismatched furniture, dusty files, antiques, and shelves of books on Oriental art, ceramics and jade. The files were a hopeless jumble. She doubted they had value for anyone except the man who'd collected them over a lifetime: letters, newspaper clippings, articles clipped from magazines, brochures and catalogues from exhibitions and auctions—all in cryptically indexed folders. But the books lining the walls were a comprehensive and valuable reference collection. She studied the gold-leaf names on several leather-bound volumes. The bindings were fragile and the pages yellowed. A number were first editions, and two were printed in Chinese and hand-bound. The color plates and illustrations were magnificent, and Arisa had to force herself back to the task at hand rather than sit and lose herself in the world they represented.

The den reminded her of her father's study in the house on

Victoria Peak in Hong Kong. Glancing around, she identified several of the pieces of the collection he'd shown her when she was a child. The collection that had provided his start in Travish Imports. Some of the original pieces were gone, of course. He'd been forced to sell them to raise the capital he needed to begin an import business and their new life.

Arisa's first glimpse of California had been from the jetliner winging over the sandy shoreline crescenting the largest city she'd ever seen. She was dazzled by the sparkling sapphire swimming pools and the forests of industrial areas with belching smokestacks. The city was mostly flat, with only a few brown hills here and there until it began to climb up away from the ocean—became a full-fledged mountain range that lost itself in the hazy blue distance.

She'd turned to her mother, babbling excitedly. Melisande barely glanced out the window. Nothing would ever take the place of her beloved Hong Kong. She hated California, sight unseen. From his aisle seat, Arisa's father grinned and winked. Everything was going to be all right.

But it hadn't been, not then or for a long time afterward. California, the land of promise, was a mecca for youth. Surfers and hippies flocked to its beaches; the glamorous and ambitious pursued their never-ending quest for Hollywood fame. Youth, flighty or serious, congregated in Sunland. And American colleges were turning out a steady stream of architects and builders to meet the booming real estate surge.

Elliot found himself in competition with hundreds of bright young men who didn't have families to relocate. There were plenty of experienced men already in the field for whatever high positions companies had to offer, and a multitude of highly competent and competitive freelancers struggling to set up new businesses of their own. The market was glutted. Elliot was forced to take a job as a draftsman with a small Valley firm in order to supplement his rapidly dwindling savings. Arisa was enrolled in a public school, which she hated, and they moved into a furnished rental bungalow in Chatsworth, which Melisande hated more. Melisande discouraged Arisa from making friends in the neighborhood. It was only temporary, she said over and over; soon they would return to Hong Kong and all this would vanish. Arisa spent her after-school hours in the stifling, miniscule living room, listening to her mother's memories of the past and dreams of the future. For all Melisande's hatred of the Chinese, she longed to return to Hong Kong. To her, the colony was British, not Chinese at all.

Elliot, who loved Hong Kong and all things Chinese, refused to return. At first, Arisa thought her father was biding time because he was determined to succeed in his new job, but gradually she realized that his decision stemmed from some deeper determination. None of Melisande's arguments or tears moved him. The house on Victoria Peak and their old life were gone. He would not go back to something that could never be the same. They were in the United States now, and they would stay.

Even the menial drafting job did not change his mind. It wasn't any more to his liking than his wife's, but it was a job. He ignored Melisande's complaints, and when their discussions insidiously turned to bitter arguments, he fled the house to lick his wounds. He worked harder and longer hours to try to win some kind of promotion—any kind—that would solve their financial problems. It was a year before he realized it would never materialize. His boss gave him a pink slip one payday. He was sorry, he'd indicated, but business was bad and he had to cut back. In a way, Elliot was relieved that he no longer had to spend eight hours a day at work he hated. Melisande was triumphant—now he would listen to reason. There was nothing to hold them in California. Surely he wouldn't debase himself by groveling for another position which would lead nowhere. They had no ties in Los Angeles. They rarely saw Quentin, who was establishing his own career. There had been a few duty visits when they'd first arrived, but these had dwindled to an occasional phone call or a hastily scrawled note.

But just as Melisande never gave up her desire to return to Hong Kong, Elliot never wavered in his decision to remain in Los Angeles. After a particularly stormy scene, he left the bungalow and did not return for three days. Melisande was angry, then worried, then frightened. When Arisa returned from school on the third day, Melisande was sitting on the lumpy sofa staring vacantly. Her gaze flicked up as Arisa came in. There was stark terror in it. Arisa dropped her books and knelt before her mother.

"Are you all right?"

Arisa pressed the icy hands to her cheek. It was like holding a corpse. Tears stung Arisa's eyes. She wanted to reassure her mother but her own thoughts tumbled in confusion, and she couldn't find words. She realized suddenly that her mother lived a fantasy. Her life was a sad game of make-believe: they would return to Hong Kong . . . they would get back everything they'd lost . . . nothing had changed. With dreadful clarity and a wisdom beyond her thirteen years, Arisa realized that she had played the game too, either to please her mother, who found so few pleasures in life, or to escape the reality of her own lackluster life. Like her mother, she had not even tried to adjust to the changes forced on her.

She sniffled and brushed away warm tears as she took her mother in her arms. She held her close, like a child, and said gently, "There's nothing to worry about, Mother. Everything is going to be all right." When Melisande shook her head, Arisa stilled it with a firm hand. "It will be all right, Mother, you'll see . . . you'll see." She smiled at her mother's puzzled look and repeated, "You'll see."

And it was all right, but in a completely unexpected way. Elliot returned that evening as Arisa and Melisande were cleaning up the kitchen after dinner. Melisande tensed and poised like a statue, a dish towel and pan held before her like a drummer waiting for his cue. Arisa turned from the sink as the front door latch snapped and her father's footsteps crossed the bare floor. When he appeared in the doorway, she let out her breath slowly. The terrible weariness in his face was gone, and there was a light in his eyes she had not seen for a long time. She gave him a wavering smile.

"Hello, Daddy. Have you had your supper? I made *moo shu* pork—there's some left."

He smiled and put his arm around her. "I've had dinner, but I wouldn't mind a taste of my favorite dish." He kissed her cheek, then looked at Melisande. She had not stirred, except to turn her head to follow his movements. "How about making a pot of tea and sitting with me while I sample Arisa's culinary art?" He glanced at Arisa, who was already busy at the stove. "You too, baby. I've got something to tell you."

Melisande's sharp breath was audible. For a moment, her husband held her gaze hypnotically. Hope sparked, burned brightly, then faded. She looked away. As if seeing for the first time the pan she was holding, she began to dry it slowly. Victory was in his eyes . . . and peace. She'd lost, finally and completely.

Arisa dished up the *moo shu* pork and set out teacups. She settled into a chair and could hardly sit still as she waited for him to disclose his news. He looked happy—had an inner happiness, not just a smile on his face. And relieved, as though a heavy burden had been lifted and he could stand tall again. The silence became uncomfortable. Arisa wriggled.

"Did you find a new job, Daddy?"

He pursed his lips. "You might say that—but not an ordinary job like the one at Paget's. Not actually a job in the usual sense of the word." He glanced at Melisande as though willing her to speak, but she did not.

Arisa caught the excitement in his voice. "Tell us, Daddy, tell us!"

Elliot considered his words as carefully as a chess player advancing a key piece. "I'm going into the import business—art objects from the Orient."

Arisa clapped her hands with delight, thinking about his collection and the wonderful excursions to Hong Kong shops. He loved Chinese works of art more than architecture—she'd always known that. And now to make a living at it!

"What will you use for money?" Melisande asked in a tight voice. "It costs thousands to get started."

"I sold the Ch'ien Lung cup." For a moment, the only sound in the room was the hissing steam from the kettle.

"Oh, Daddy, your Ch'ien Lung?"

"*Your* Ch'ien Lung," he said gently. He took her hand and beseeched her with his eyes. "I haven't forgotten my promise that some day my collection would be yours, Arisa." A shadow darkened his eyes as though a cloud had overtaken him. "I'll make it up to you. Once the business is on its feet, I'll start a new collection even finer than this one. It takes capital to get going. I'll have to sell some of the other pieces, too. I already have a buyer lined up." He drew a deep breath and forced a smile. "I found a place on Melrose. I think I can get a one-year lease. It's a good location."

Arisa felt a tremor of excitement in his fingers. She jumped up and flung her arms around him, hugging him and kissing his ear. "I'm so happy, Daddy. I know it's going to work!" She danced around the chair, still bubbling. "Mama? Aren't you glad?"

Melisande seemed to shrink. "You don't know anything about running a business, Elliot," she said flatly.

"I know enough to get started. I can learn the rest. I know

Chinese art, that's what counts. Now that the political scene has quieted, I can bring things in from Hong Kong. With the contacts I have . . ." He stopped and his face sobered. "I admit it won't be easy, but I'll make a go of it. There was never any place for me in architecture. I don't want to spend another ten years working my way to a dead-end."

The kettle whistled shrilly, and Arisa ran to the stove. Pouring water into the pot, she glanced at her mother. Why wasn't she happy? Daddy's idea sounded exciting—and it had to be better than the job he had at Paget's—which he hated anyhow. Maybe they'd be able to move to a nicer house and Mama would be happy again. She just needed time to adjust to the news. Arisa carried the teapot back to the table and set it down to steep.

"When will the shop open, Daddy? Will it be like Fook Shing's?" She'd browsed many Hong Kong shops with her father. Fook Shing's, with its dark carpeting and tapestries and a gleaming brass gong beside the door, was her favorite.

He laughed. "Probably more like Mr. Chang's on Ladder Street to start," he said with a wink. They used to laugh over the unbelievable clutter of the tiny stall where Mr. Chang conducted business amid piles of old coins, carved jade, jewelry, and ivory netsukes. The stall looked like a helter-skelter accumulation of flotsam but represented three generations of collecting by the Chang family. Chang's father and grandfather had traded along the Pearl River, often taking trinkets in payment when a family had no money. Most of the pieces had little intrinsic value. Chang sold them to the parade of tourists who passed down the well-known street, or to local Chinese and foreigners who needed a bit of bric-a-brac to brighten a shelf. A few items were unusual and rare; these he kept in a wooden tray beneath his makeshift counter. Whenever Elliot Travish approached, Chang drew them out to spread on a square of black silk. Elliot had rarely gone away empty-handed and never disappointed.

Remembering, Arisa laughed. "And will you queue your hair and wear a black cap?"

He affected a pose with his hands tucked into imaginary sleeves, grinning and bowing as Chang had done. "You honor my humble house, Missy Travish. . . ."

Arisa giggled. How good it was to have her father back—and with such good news. She looked at her mother and beamed a silent message: everything is going to be all right. Didn't I promise? Everything is going to be all right. Finally, her mother rewarded her with a tiny smile. Her terror had vanished with Elliot's reappearance; now the confusion and doubt that had replaced it seemed to be ebbing. A touch of pink colored her cheeks.

Everything was going to be all right.

True to Elliot's prediction, the business took time to build. The first couple of years were filled with struggle and scrimping so that life was not much different than when he'd been employed at Paget's, except for the difference in Elliot himself. He was no longer a beaten man but an ambitious, driven one. He sold several other pieces from his collection and reinvested his profit in choice works of jade, porcelain and ivory. He dealt by letter with men he knew in Hong Kong; it was a year before he was able to make his first buying trip. By then the shop on Melrose had become popular with decorators and collectors. The trip was a dual celebration: the beginning of Travish Imports, and the turning point in their financial situation.

Elliot made a down payment on a small house on the outskirts of Beverly Hills, much closer to the shop than the rental unit in Chatsworth. It marked a turning point, too, in Melisande. Throughout the months Elliot struggled with the new business, she was unenthusiastic. She listened to his problems and triumphs passively, as though reserving commitment to his success or failure. She was relaxed and seemed happy, but when she was alone with Arisa, she still spoke wistfully of the life they'd known in the colony. It was as if in accepting Elliot's new venture, she might resign herself to the territory. She took an interest in the house, selecting furniture and decorating with taste and care. She never went to the shop; when Elliot described some piece that caught her fancy, she asked him to bring it home so she could try it on the mantle, table, or wall. If she saw something she liked in another shop, she relayed the description to her husband so he could secure or duplicate the piece from his own stock.

The first buying trip to Hong Kong was also the occasion of Deline Armitage's coming to work at Travish Imports. Faced with the choice of closing the shop while he was gone or hiring help, Elliot decided the time was right for expansion. With an assistant to run things while he was gone, he could spend more time searching for buys that would bring not only profit but prestige. Since Deline Armitage had been born and raised in Hong Kong, she was as familiar with fine Oriental art as Elliot himself. She would be a definite asset.

Travish Imports grew steadily. A year later, Elliot moved the shop to Beverly Hills. Arisa settled into high school. Freed of mourning the past, she accepted the present with the enthusiasm of youth. Memories of Hong Kong blurred as she became part of the corp of popular, pretty, sun-golden California girls. Outwardly, life was smooth; any ripples on the placid surface settled quickly. Beneath the surface, guilt nibbled at Arisa's conscience because she no longer encouraged her mother's confidences. She knew that Melisande had only submerged her hope of returning to Hong Kong, not abandoned it. She threw herself into civic and social activities, and though Elliot occasionally talked about having her accompany him on his buying trips to the East, nothing ever came of it.

For Arisa's sixteenth birthday, her father surprised her with a car. He'd accepted a ten-year-old convertible as payment for an eighteenth-century mirror-black bottle without character or period marks. Delighted, Arisa dubbed the car "Chang" after the crafty old merchant who'd inspired her father to barter. The car gave her freedom and self-confidence. There was an army of gangling youths and girls waiting to share any trip Arisa made—to or from school, to the beach, along the shady lanes off Coldwater Canyon or the bright moonlit strip of Mullholland Drive. Arisa was a competent driver. She'd never had an accident until the fateful day her mother insisted on going to Laguna for the opening of a gallery. A rain-slicked freeway . . . a Cadillac driver who changed lanes abruptly . . . wheels spinning and the convertible crushing like rice paper as it smashed into the guard rail. The flames were the worst part of the nightmare—searing, licking fingers of fire engulfing her mother's terror-stricken face. The flames . . . and the screams. Afterward she'd wake shaking and feverish, with her throat as parched as though she were still breathing the heavy, oily smoke.

She returned to school but the sympathy of her classmates and teachers was worse than the solitude of guilt. She dropped out of activities, cut classes, ignored assignments. In desperation, her father finally sought advice from the school psychologist.

"She blames herself for her mother's death," the doctor said.

"It may stem from a deeper guilt, but she won't talk about it. Until she does, there's not much I can do. Perhaps a therapist..."

Elliot broached the subject to Arisa that night. He'd been keeping shorter hours since the accident because he didn't like leaving Arisa alone. Deline Armitage came in at two and stayed until closing so he could be home when Arisa arrived. Arisa had been listless since the accident, and Elliot was unprepared for her violent refusal.

"I won't see any doctor! I'm not crazy. I know what I've done and no shrink is going to bring Mother back. Isn't it bad enough I killed her and ruined your life and mine? Leave me alone!" She ran out sobbing and locked herself in her room. Terrified she'd hurt herself, he begged her to open the door, promising he'd agree to whatever she wanted.

The door opened abruptly. Tears had left glittering trails on her cheeks, and there was a smudge across her chin where she'd wiped them away. Red-rimmed, her eyes were violet in the muted light. "I want to go away—I can't stay here."

He hesitated, but the cold gaze demanded the fulfillment of his promise. "Will you finish school?"

"Not here." She shook her head sharply.

"Somewhere else then? Switzerland? Remember the producer's daughter who went there?" He was grasping at straws, dredging his memory for anything that might entice her. "You said her letters made the school sound exciting. You can decide about college when the time comes." He was in no position to bargain. She had the whip hand, and he prayed she wouldn't use it. Still dispirited, she agreed. He slipped his arm around her. The crisis was past.

The rest of the school year at the academy...a summer with friends in Kent, then the decision that she would not return to California but enroll at an English university. California was locked behind a door as surely and securely as Hong Kong had been.

And now the doors were unlocked. She had to face the past as well as the future. She sat at her father's camphor-wood desk and began to sort through the papers littering its surface. Letters, catalogues and brochures were haphazardly mixed with receipts, bills, and indecipherable notes in her father's scrawl. She pulled open the drawers and looked at the hopeless filing system. She'd always thought of her father as a methodical man, but now she saw he was a pack rat, tucking everything away safely but in a way meaningless to anyone but him. If he kept the store's records the same way, an accountant would throw up his hands. Arisa was sure Deline had long ago assumed responsibility for the files, just as the bookkeeper had for the financial records. With a sigh, she began to sort things into neat piles.

It took her all day to establish a semblance of order. Even then, she didn't take time to study any of the papers. She read each briefly enough to decide into which category it fell, then went on to the next. Among the receipts, she found one for a safe-deposit box at Security Bank; was it the one opened by the key he'd mailed to Paris? There didn't seem to be any logical reason for him to do that. She'd ask Forbes. A state appraiser would have to be present when any box was opened; knowing Quentin, he'd insist on being on hand to make sure she didn't spirit away any stash of currency or jewelry Elliot might have had. She laughed as she looked at the stack of bills she'd unearthed. Without a checkbook, there was no way of telling which had been paid, and she hadn't found her father's checkbook. Another thing to ask Forbes about. Or Deline or Carter. Her father might have elected to have the company bookkeeper take care of his personal bills for convenience.

She fingered a credit card bill she'd found unopened. The total was more than five thousand dollars. Judging by the item- ized charges, most were restaurant bills. She recognized several posh Beverly Hills spots. Business expenses—they had to be. Why hadn't her father had the bill sent directly to the office? At the bottom of the bill was a notation that a portion of it was overdue. Shaking her head, she realized that if the desk were any example of how he'd handled paperwork, he'd let many things slide. Also, the bill might have arrived while he was preoccupied with the Hankow collection Tanner had mentioned; perhaps he hadn't bothered to look at it. She found an envelope and addressed it to Carter Montaigne. As executor, it was his responsibility now.

She stretched wearily and went to the kitchen to fix herself a drink. She wished now that she'd made plans for the evening. She had been in Los Angeles only a few days, but she was already restless and bored. She carried the drink into the living room and curled onto the sofa, her feet comfortably tucked up on the red velvet cushions.

Unless she took Carter's offer, after all, she couldn't go

back to Paris. She barely had the price of an airline ticket, much less the cash it would take to close the deal on the *galerie*. Maybe she should swallow her pride and admit her hasty declaration to Carter had come from anger, not logic. And then she imagined the smug expression on his face. She'd be playing right into his hands. Maybe it would be better to talk to Forbes before she reconsidered the offer. She had no idea what a fair price for her stock would be.

Restlessly, she finished her drink and carried the empty glass to the kitchen. No sense sitting around brooding. She couldn't make any major decisions tonight. And she couldn't sit around with nothing to do. If she was going to be in California any length of time, she'd have to keep herself busy. For tonight, a couple of hours of shopping and a quiet dinner somewhere. Tomorrow she'd approach Carter with the idea that was growing in her mind. If she put her time to good use at Travish-Montaigne, she could learn a lot about running a business of her own. And at the same time, she could become well-informed on the true state of the business she had inherited.

YEAR OF THE RABBIT

Lei Tong felt the cold metal of the rifle barrel in his hand. He always held it thus unless he raised it for firing. In the winter months, the cold steel measured the iciness of his heart. In the summer heat, it was an extension of his burning hatred, the fire that was never quenched within him. There were times when the hot pain lessened briefly, when heaven smiled and presented an opportunity to spend his energy against the hated foreigners, but these were too few. The army of the Kuomintang was weakening. He spat upon their willingness to give in to the demands for peaceable settlements with the strikers, and with the foreigners who ran the schools and missions, and brayed like asses about their gentle God. He spat upon them all.

He shifted the weight of the rifle to ease the ache in his crooked elbow. The bones had knit and his arm was strong enough to hold the heaviest weapon, but he had to steel his mind against the dull ache inside his flesh. There was no pain in his hand, though two of his fingers no longer obeyed his will as they hung crooked from his palm. It had taken weeks of training to learn to shoot with his second finger. The others laughed at his struggles and called him "Devil's Hand," but he shut his ears to them. At night in the camp, he flexed his good fingers in a pretense of shooting, aiming first at one sleeping companion, then another, until his muscles grew strong and sure. When at last the bullets from his rifle struck the target perfectly, they no longer laughed. He indeed had a devil's hand.

But now that devil's hand was ordered not to fire unless word came from Sun Fo, General Shan's lieutenant. Lei Tong glanced toward the officer who waited with the men. From the bank of the river, a fusillade of rifle shots made Lei Tong's finger tighten. Were he assigned to the river patrol, he would now be firing instead of standing like a stone figure.

The Bund was unnaturally quiet, the shops closed and barred

with heavy iron gratings. In the distance, a busload of comrades rattled past the Sun Company; Lei Tong saw another band of soldiers at the gates of the Canton Hospital. Suddenly the men around him began to stir with anticipation. Sun Fo's emissary was running back through the narrow street leading from the English school. He conferred quickly with the lieutenant, who immediately raised a signal. The men broke into a loping run.

Lei Tong's blood sang. His stride kept him abreast of his comrades, despite the pain that seared his loins, reminding him of his robbed manhood. The foreign devils were no better than the bandits who had raided the train and left him in agony. Drive out *all* those who would divide China like a rice cake and gobble up the crumbs. *Kill,* his mind screamed. *Kill!*

They spilled out of the narrow passage and spread a human net around the school. The frightened gatekeeper tried to draw the heavy doors, but a wall of men flung him back as they stormed across the courtyard. The red banner waved as soldiers blocked the way of two peasants trying to lead out a small herd of cattle. The frightened youths drew up abruptly, staring at the soldiers; then they dropped the ropes and scurried through the milling animals. One of the soldiers plunged after them, but a sharp command from Sun Fo brought him back. They were not after Chinese peasants who tended the foreigners' animals. Their target was the traitor who had fled their ranks and warned the English and Americans that their freedom was imperiled.

The soldiers filled the courtyard; a small band had already climbed the steps to the door. Their rifle butts crashed against the wood.

"Open by command of General Shan!" Lieutenant Sun shouted. Behind him, the men began to chant.

"Min-chu! Min-ch'uan! Min-sheng!"

"Drive out the foreign devils!"

Beside Lei Tong, Comrade Kok hissed air between his teeth. "Let them die like pigs on a spit," he whispered. "The Crimson Hand will avenge our people if General Shan and the woman-hearted Sun Fo lack the courage."

Lei Tong looked at his companion. "We strike?" Hope choked the words in his throat.

Kok extended his left hand to grasp Lei Tong's in the sign of brotherhood. Lei Tong's breath rushed like a raging river. The promise of revenge was to be fulfilled. The foreign devils would die, not merely be driven off. The pain in his loin and arm vanished with the balm of that promise. Slowly he moved toward the steps as the heavy brass-bound doors opened.

"We have come for the traitor Pook Yat!" Lieutenant Sun bellowed.

The foreign scholar called Downs blinked like an ancient owl. "By what authority does General Shan rout his friends from their dinner?" he demanded.

"Those who hide a traitor to the Kuomintang forsake their friendship with the people!"

"He is not here." Downs blinked as he tried to disguise his lie.

Sun shoved the old man aside and strode in. Lei Tong and Kok pushed through with his small cadre of men. The hall of the school was built in the foreign fashion, without pillars. A dozen doors closed off rooms along a passage that cut through the length of the building. Soldiers began to fling them open to search. Lei Tong and Kok moved to the stairs. Pook Yat would choose the darkest corner to hide in if he could not escape. And he could not, for the school was surrounded with soldiers who had the image of his face burned in their memories. Behind them, he heard Sun give the order for the men to look upstairs. Quickly, he led the way, his gleaming bayonet and rifle pointing.

The landing was dimly lighted by a window that was built into the roof. Here, too, the doors were closed. The foreigners built large houses, then shut themselves into cubicles. He flung a door open and went around the room methodically, stabbing his bayonet into clothing hung on pegs, ripping away the bed-clothes from the soft, thick mattress that stood on high legs, slashing pillows so that feathers drifted like falling snow. Cursing, he pushed out into the hall again and mingled with the others. Men were entering the rooms by twos, leaving no door unopened. Would that he and Kok were left to search alone! He walked the length of the hall to peer in each doorway to see if the quarry had been flushed. Two by two, the soldiers returned empty-handed and began to straggle downstairs.

Lei Tong felt a sharp pain in the pit of his belly. Had the cursed foreigners spirited Pook Yat away? Had they worked their evil magic to cause the traitor to vanish? There had been no hue and cry from outside nor from the men downstairs. He stood trembling with rage as he looked over the banister to the scene below.

"I tell you, he's not here!" Downs had regained some of his false courage and was shaking a fist at Sun Fo.

"The eyes of my men watched him enter. Do not lie, old man. I will kill you!" Sun Fo touched his bayonet to the man's belly.

"He's not here," the American said again, but his voice trembled like a leaf in the wind.

Breathing harshly, Lei Tong started for the stairs but was halted by his comrade's hand. Kok pointed to a door cut cleverly into a panel at the end of the hall. In the dim light, the others had missed it. Silently, the two went to it and eased it open. A narrow, dark flight of steps led to an attic. They crept up stealthily. The air was thick with dust and the cold seeped in from outside. Above their heads, another window in the roof offered murky light. The tiny room was crammed with boxes and trunks. The voices below were a low rumble like distant thunder. Kok paused, sniffing the air like an animal on a scent. Then he pointed to the scuffed dust near a steamer trunk of cracked leather.

In unison, they moved silently, flinging open the lid of the traveling box. Cowering inside were two figures. They covered their faces as they tried to make themselves invisible.

With a grunt, Kok yanked the dark head by the hair. He grinned. "So, comrade Pook Yat, you scurry behind a woman's skirts like a frightened child." Still holding the cowering man by the hair, he forced him out of the trunk. In the gloom, Pook Yat trembled visibly. The other figure in the trunk moved and Lei Tong grabbed out instantly. A woman—a female foreign devil!

"The dog lies with the bitch," he muttered. The woman was too frightened to answer. She yelped with pain as he dragged her to her feet. She shuddered as her eyes fell upon the wicked point of the bayonet Lei Tong raised to her breast.

Summoning her courage, the woman's tongue flicked across her lips before she spoke. "Pook Yat has done nothing, let him go." The words had no authority as they trembled from her lips. She begged for the traitor, not her own life. Lei Tong laughed softly. Pook Yat was silent. He would have fallen to his knees to beg for mercy if Kok had not held him fast. He knew the sentence of a traitor's death was upon his head. Nor would he die quickly from the plunge of a bayonet. His comrades had a torturous death ready as his reward. Lei Tong's gaze met Kok's. They knew what had to be done.

Kok pushed the prisoner toward the steps. Stumbling, Pook Yat scrambled as if dancing on a rope, lest his hair be torn out by the roots. The woman with Lei Tong shivered as though her clothing no longer warded off the chill. Lei Tong regarded her scornfully. He had seen the American scholar's wife on the Bund and in the stalls of the narrow streets of Canton. Her hair was golden fire and her flesh hung heavy at her jowls. The proud carriage with which she walked the city had vanished; her eyes were round with fear.

"I shall tell my husband of your senseless cruelty," she said. "General Shan has assured our safety. It was right that Pook Yat warned us of this dreadful communist revolt. You will not be permitted to get away with this." She set her jaw, but she could not hide the trembling of her lip.

"Quickly . . ." Only Kok's head was visible above the top of the stairs. The prisoner was already out of sight below him.

Lei Tong nodded as his comrade vanished like a mole into the dark opening. He turned to the woman. When she tried to clamber out of the trunk, he twisted her arm savagely. She yelped. With a single blow, he flung her backward. Her look turned to astonishment, then terror, as he shoved her again so that she folded like a puppet in the dark box. As he lifted the bayonet, her mouth opened. Lei Tong plunged the blade into her with a vicious thrust. Her scream bubbled and escaped like a whimpering moan. She lifted one hand to ward him off as he plunged the steel in again and again. At last she grew still, drenched in her own blood.

Her round blue eyes stared lifelessly as he wiped the bayonet on her skirt. His lips curled. Straightening, he flicked the bayonet tip to dislodge the pale hand that had fallen across the edge of the trunk.

"Sleep forever in the pits of hell, female dog," he said bitterly. He closed the trunk lid and made his way downstairs.

Sun had ordered the prisoner bound, and he was being led out by three soldiers. Their bayonets prodded and probed, forcing the traitor to dance foolishly as he stumbled down the steps and across the courtyard. The American scholar shouted above the jeers and laughter.

"This is inhuman! I shall speak to General Shan personally and see that each of you is punished." He prattled to the wind. The soldiers were already departing, flushed with victory and in high humor now that the traitor was in their hands.

Downs looked about helplessly, still sputtering.

Lieutenant Sun spoke sharply to his men and they began to file out. Lei Tong accosted him.

"And the American? Will you allow him to lead the Nationalists to us?"

Sun glanced at the white-haired foreigner scornfully. "It would please me greatly to sentence him to the same fate as Pook Yat."

"It is in your power," Lei Tong whispered harshly.

"He has the protection of General Li who listens to the promises of the foreign devils," Sun said. "With my own eyes, I saw the French gunboat on the river this very day. It is said that the English and Americans stand ready to invade the Pearl if their people are endangered." He glared at Downs, who had drawn back his shoulders at hearing about the power of his compatriots. "We must wait until . . ." Sun let his words drift on the tide of the unspoken promise.

The pain had begun to seep back into Lei Tong's body. The American would soon discover the dead filth in the trunk upstairs. He would run screaming to General Li.

"We go," Lieutenant Sun ordered. He strode out to join his jubilant men.

"You've not heard the last of this," the American shouted, but his gaze was already wandering to the stairs.

Silently, Lei Tong moved behind him. From his belt, he drew out a thin sharp dagger he kept hidden. It was over in an instant, soundlessly. Blood trickled in a thin line across Downs' throat, then gushed as Lei Tong put pressure on the blade. The old man gurgled pitifully as he crumpled to the floor.

"Quickly," Kok said with a satisfied glance at the twitching body.

The two made their way outside, closing the heavy door behind them.

The small rebel force made its camp in the derelict buildings north of the Academy. Though they claimed to be part of General Shan's unit, they neither had nor wanted his blessing or the burden of his orders. Sun Fo was not convinced that he should throw the lot of his warlord band in with the weak-willed paper soldiers who talked instead of fighting. To a man, his force believed the time for words was past.

In the compound behind the makeshift barracks, laughter and jeers filled the air as Pook Yat wriggled on the wooden cross to which he'd been tied. His face was a bloody mask, more animal than human. His tongue had been cut out so he would endure his dying in silence, and blood dripped down his chin and onto his clothing. His arms and legs were chafed raw under the ropes that held him.

A staggering soldier heaved an empty wine flask. It struck the prisoner's head and shattered to the ground. A wave of cheers rose like smoke in the crisp dusk.

"Pen, the marksman!" someone shouted.

"With so large and bright a target, only a crippled infant could miss," another jeered.

New wine flasks were passed among the men who pranced aimlessly, except when one paused to poke a blade tip into Pook Yat gleefully. A soldier stepped in front of the cross. Deftly, he slit Pook Yat's trousers to expose his flesh to the raw wind. Another drew a dagger and sliced it across Pook Yat's genitals. Delighted, others vied for room as they heaped this new indignity upon their victim.

Leaning against the wall, Lei Tong winced, remembering his own pain when the bandit on the train had shot him. A lifetime would never erase the memory. He raised the rice wine Kok had brought, and drank deeply. There had been no alarm from the English school. Did the bodies still lie in their own stink? Had the gateman not ventured inside, or had he fled in fear of his own life when he saw the carnage?

Sporadic firing from the Bund splintered the dusk. The gunboat had evacuated the French from their hospital, and it was said that other foreigners were fleeing the city. A band of rebels had set fire to the Central Bank of China; even now the red glow was bright against the sky. Soldiers were everywhere on the streets, spurred by the rumor that General Lei Fuk-lam of the Fifth Army was sending troops from Honam Island to run out those who wore the Red banner.

Lei Tong smiled and drank deeply from the wine flask. The White banners would be slain like foreign dogs. Let them suck at the breast of the pacifistic tin soldiers who cautioned the army against violence. Soon the Red army would sweep across all of China and free the people from bondage. Soon the glorious Red flag would wave over the Kuomintang. No more would Chiang Kai-shek dishonor the Revolution by holding back the tide of true nationalism.

Excited whispering drew his attention. A man dressed in merchant's garb stood beside Kok, talking with rapid gestures. Lei Tong recognized Ying Pow of the brotherhood. He straightened to extend his hand, but the other was too agitated to notice.

"The general has issued an order for the perpetrators to be captured. He sends a hundred men to scour the city."

Lei Tong's crippled hand tingled. Kok looked at him.

"The Americans have been found. The gatekeeper's wagging tongue has named us as the last to leave the school. We are already accused."

"Our comrades will stand behind us," Lei Tong boasted. "Our opportunity to stand against the Whites is at hand."

Kok squinted and tightened his lips in disgust. "At this hour General Shan negotiates to turn us over to Chiang Kai-shek's troops in exchange for their evacuation of Shameen. A small price for our army to pay, comrade, but a heavy one upon our heads." He passed a hand across his throat like a dagger. "We must go quickly."

"I will not run!"

Kok spoke as though he had not heard. "The brotherhood will hide us. We will make our way to Shanghai and join our comrades there. Live soldiers fight better than dead ones."

Lei Tong swigged the last of the wine from the bottle. The fight was far from finished. His friend spoke wisdom. Wiping his mouth on his sleeve, he drew back his arm and flung the empty flask at the cross in the center of the compound. It struck the back of a soldier who was smearing mud into the bloody cavern of Pook Yat's gaping mouth. The soldier did not even feel the blow as he cavorted wildly.

"To Shanghai, my friend," Lei Tong said drunkenly. "And to glorious victory."

The men huddled around a brazier that glowed red with coals but from which heat spread through only a small circle in the drafty room. Lei Tong stamped his feet to regain sensation, then winced as sharp needles tortured his soles. He had not been warm for weeks. He seemed frozen in an ice block in the northernmost part of Mongolia. *Aiii* . . . He moved restlessly and tucked his hands into the thick padded sleeves of his jacket. The pain in his crooked fingers had long ago ceased. His entire arm was numb.

The door opened and a blast of frigid wind struck like an avalanche, driving away the meager comfort of the brazier. Lei Tong shivered as he watched two men enter, force the door shut, then slide the heavy bolt. They were so bundled against the cold that they waddled like fat pandas. Only their eyes showed above the thick layers of their head wrappings.

The men around the brazier fell silent as the two approached. Lei Tong watched with a sense of excitement. He'd listened to chatter about the leaders of the Crimson Hand. Now at last he was meeting them and would become part of the active Shanghai *tong* that did not sit on its hands when there was work to be done. The two came across the room to grip each hand in the sign of the brotherhood. Lei Tong felt a current of power surge in his arm.

Quickly, the men took places around the bare wooden table. Gradually the shuffling sounds ceased and all eyes turned to Tan Tin-sum, who unwrapped his voluminous scarves with the air of a man displaying a portrait. His round face glowed. His eyes gave evidence that he was a leader. Lei Tong had met many officers, but none had the strength that Tan Tin-sum's eyes showed. They glittered like dark coals.

The man who had entered with him began to report the news from the city. Groups of Communist soldiers were returning from the hills of Kiangsi where they had been driven by Chiang Kai-shek's purge in the spring. The Red forces were gaining in number and strength. Key men had already infiltrated government and military headquarters. They would be in positions of authority when the revolt came. Chiang's puppets would fold like reeds in a typhoon, and the People's Republic would rise from the ashes of their bones. Mao Tse-tung was on his way to Shanghai now to take command of his army of the faithful.

A murmur spread through the group. Mao...

Tan Tin-sum raised a hand for silence. Every eye fixed on him as he spoke.

"We have done our work well. We are in readiness. If the Communists continue to uphold the ideals we have pledged ourselves to, we will fight at their sides. But we are a brotherhood with a purpose that supercedes all others. We have

vowed to return the Stones of Heaven to the Imperial Palace!"
His voice rose like the keening wind and his words struck each
heart.

"*Hai-hai*," the men agreed readily.

Tan Tin-sum's hand disappeared into his voluminous jacket
and brought out something in a closed fist. Lei Tong's pulse
danced with excitement. When he joined the brotherhood in
Canton, he was told of the Stone of Heaven that had come into
the hands of the Crimson Hand. It was guarded zealously by
Tan himself, never leaving the leader's possession. Had he not
killed the dog of a peasant who had stolen it? When Shanghai
fell to the rebels, looters had left Kwan-Yin Miu a sacked
desecration. The Stones of Heaven no longer rested in their
place of honor. Three had been recovered quickly from the
body of a soldier who fell under gunfire as the foreign army
rushed to quell the uprising. These had been taken to a remote
village for safekeeping. Another, the one he carried, had been
traced by Tan to a stupid peasant who thought fortune had
smiled on him when he found the Stone in the dust. The fifth
had vanished. Like the captured looters who were tortured for
information, Tan believed the American major had made off
with it. But the major had died in battle before two suns had
crossed the heavens. Tan himself had dug up the body where
it had been put in the ground before sandalwood had been
burned or fortune tellers consulted to determine the right time
for burial. The Stone of Heaven was not on the corpse, nor
was it inside the cavern of the body which Tan had slit open.
The fifth Stone of Heaven had not been seen since. Twenty-
four moons.

The room fell silent except for the hiss of the coals. Tan's
hand poised, then uncurled slowly to place the Stone of Heaven
on the table. The men stared in reverent silence.

Beneath the flickering oil lamp, the piece of jade glowed
like the eye of a god. The carvings had not grown faint during
the centuries since a master craftsman had designed it. Lei
Tong felt ice form in his belly. His crooked arm shot fire into
his chest. Surely the heat of the brazier at his back and the
iciness of the room in front were addling his mind. It could
not be. . . .

He did not know that a sound had come from his throat until
Kok stared at him. He swallowed quickly, too confused to
speak. Tan was picking up the Stone; he returned it to a place

of safety close to his body. The meeting was over. The men pushed away from the table and stood respectfully until their leader had departed; then they began to wrap themselves to face the bitter winter outside. Left alone with Lei Tong, Kok peered at him.

"Your face has seen the spirit of death," he said.

Lei Tong tried to speak, but a fit of trembling gripped him.

"What is it, comrade, are you ill?" There was a touch of scorn in Kok's words. There was no place for weakness in the Crimson Hand.

Lei Tong's belly was poisoned with uncertainty, but he could no longer keep his suspicion to himself. Meeting his friend's gaze, he said, "I have seen the fifth Stone of Heaven. I do not know how it can be, but my sister wears it about her neck."

4

Carter tossed the note on the desk. *Merde.* Arisa didn't even suspect, or else she didn't give a damn. Hadn't she seen the change in Elliot the last time he was in Paris? Either she was blind or completely wrapped up in herself. He suspected the latter was closer to the truth. Women like Arisa, the spoiled and pampered, didn't worry about mundane things such as where their money came from, not as long as it was there.

He ticked the note with the tip of his finger and read it again.

These bills are obviously business expenses. Pay them, please.

Arisa Travish

Her name was underscored with a curving line with two short strokes through it. The word "please" was set slightly apart—as if she'd suddenly remembered her boarding school manners. The note was written on Elliot's familiar scratch paper, which meant she'd been through his things.

Carter exhaled impatiently. Well, as Elliot's heir, Arisa was the one to do it. Better her than Quentin. He'd rummage like a ragpicker and pick off any choice tidbits that struck his fancy. Arisa, however, had apparently plucked out the garbage and dumped it in his lap. Granted, it was his job to see the bills were paid, but her attitude nettled him. He riffled through the slips that had come with Arisa's note. Elliot had run up chits all over town: credit card receipts from various restaurants, bills from a couple of places where he had a private tab, haberdasheries, even a boutique. That was probably for some pseudo-*chic* outfit for Lily Taylor. No wonder she'd been an easy mark when he needed cash.

He shuffled the bills together and slipped them back into the envelope as the intercom buzzed. He pressed the switch.

"Yes?"

Deline's voice was slightly muffled by the connection. "Tanner called about the throne cover Elliot purchased at the Hankow auction. He says it may be earlier Manchu than we thought. He doesn't think the damage should be repaired."

"Do you agree?"

There was a fractional hesitation. "Yes. Clients who appreciate early Oriental work expect flaws. Silk is very fragile and rots unless stored under perfect conditions." She paused again. "We can always have him do the work later if it attracts a decorator or casual buyer."

"All right. Have Tanner clean and mount it so we can put it in the textile display. The less it's handled, the better. Let's see what happens."

"One other thing . . ."

He scowled. "Yes?"

"Arisa just came in."

Carter swiveled his chair so he could look down into the showroom through the one-way glass. Arisa was standing near the Ming collection. The indirect lighting gave her hair a soft glint that put him in mind of a medieval madonna. The idea made him laugh. Madonna with brass balls, he thought. She glanced up toward the offices as though aware she was being watched, then started for the stairs.

"I want to talk with her," Carter said. Better get it over with. Arisa vanished in the curve of the stairs and reappeared on the second level. "If she hasn't already got me on her schedule, ask her to stop in before she leaves."

"I'll tell her."

He sensed faint disapproval in Deline's tone. He snapped off the intercom and watched Arisa come across the balcony. She moved like a dancer, perfectly balanced and effortlessly, as though walking came as naturally as breathing. She was wearing white, without frills. Good taste. Expensive. The sundress had thin shoulder straps that showed off her magnificent tan. Paris this time of year? More likely the Riviera . . . or a good health club.

He was still staring through the glass when he realized she hadn't gone past. The door opened abruptly. He lifted an eyebrow. Her boarding school manners didn't go as far as knocking.

"Good morning," he said with exaggerated politeness.

She settled lightly in the leather chair. Glancing around, she appraised the office as though it were going on the auction block.

"You've made changes," she said with a hostile look. "Where did you work while my father was here?"

He regarded her with a touch of amusement. She made him sound like a grave robber, claiming Elliot's space before the body was cold.

"Here."

"This was his office." Her eyes flashed.

"He didn't like paperwork. He used his office at home or the workroom downstairs."

"So you took over." The defenses had become a barricade.

"I could have shared an office with the bookkeeper, I suppose," he said dryly. "Would you find me more acceptable then?"

For a moment, he thought she was going to blush, but she lifted her chin and looked at him defiantly. "I don't intend to share an office with the bookkeeper, Mr. Montaigne."

"It never crossed my mind." What the hell was she intimating? An office? Damn. He wasn't going to have her underfoot everytime he turned around. He watched her guardedly. The corners of her shiny, raspberry-tinted lips twitched in a ghost of a smile.

"Good, then I'll expect this office to be ready for me tomorrow. I'll need sales records, an inventory, a profit and loss sheet for the first six months..."

"What you need is a damned good spanking." A muscle jumped at his jawline.

Her mouth opened, then shut as if unable to express her disdain. Her violet eyes became deep dark pools. He almost expected her to say "I beg your pardon?" with grand hauteur. Instead she let an icy silence say it for her.

He captured her cold amethyst gaze as he said, "Number one: I am not going to move out of this office. I've been appointed to manage the company until probate is settled. That means I'm in charge." He thumbed his chest. "*I*, not you. Not both of us. *I* am in charge. It's convenient for me to run the business from *this* office, so I don't intend to move, and I won't have you in here underfoot. Which brings us to number two: Being a stockholder, even the major stockholder, does not entitle you to disrupt the management of the company. You're neither an officer nor an employee. I appreciate your desire to learn more about the business, but you will not do it at my expense or the company's. I'll be glad to give you an opportunity to learn, just as I would any new personnel we took on. Newcomers usually begin in the workroom—uncrating, cataloging, gaining a general familiarity with the kind of merchandise we handle. In view of your identity and the fact that you have some art background, perhaps you can skip some of the chores such as sweeping, carrying out the trash..." He let his sarcasm thicken and gel. "I do think it would be gracious of you not to lord it over the others. After all, they're poor working folk trying to make a living."

He had to give her credit: she didn't move a muscle. No sputtering, no trembling, no outraged histrionics. Her violet eyes were like icebergs reflecting the cold northern sea.

At last she said, "I deserved that. I was being childish. You don't tend to bring out the best in me. When I saw you sitting behind my father's desk..." She shrugged. "I thought you were being smug."

She didn't apologize but he liked the honest admission.

More gently, he said, "I'm not exactly renowned for my honeyed tongue either. Now that we've cleared the air, we should discuss your plans as far as the company is concerned. I warn you, I'm quite serious about not letting you interfere. If you doubt I have the authority to make it stick, check with Forbes. Once you accept that, we can move on."

"My goal is to see a continuing profit. I want the name and reputation of Travish-Montaigne to rank at the top of the list in the mind of every collector and decorator in southern California. When they think art objects, I want them to think Travish-Montaigne. Your father made some excellent buys just before his death. Added to the merchandise we have on hand, it should give us a good season. Our inventory is substantial. If you're interested in studying it, Deline will supply you with a detailed list. She'll explain the code that tells if each piece is on display or somewhere else. As you may have noticed, the showroom is divided into sectors. Each salesperson is totally responsible for his own area. A couple of times we had a problem with things disappearing and..."

"Do you mean stolen?" She was incredulous. Her father had always trusted his employees and there'd never been a bit of trouble.

Carter shrugged. "Unaccounted for. Nothing valuable enough to create a fuss or a full-scale police investigation, no breaking and entering. Deline suspected one of the girls who worked here at the time, but it was impossible to prove anything. The girl left on her own accord. We instituted the new system for efficiency and better security. We've ruled out internal theft by making one person, and only one, responsible for a given amount of merchandise. So far the system seems to have prevented further losses. At any rate, to return to my point, each clerk knows his or her complete stock as well as what's coming in future shipments. Also what's being restored."

He tilted his head. "You've met Tanner Holmes. He does our restorations and cleaning. He's good, damned good. Your father respected him very highly."

Arisa nodded. She had liked Tanner at once, and somehow felt her father had too. But she was still trying to absorb everything Carter was saying. He was explaining the business as though he was willing or even expected her to take an active interest.

"Once you've had a chance to acquaint yourself with how we operate and what we own, you'll have a pretty good picture of where we stand at present. Financial statements are garbage unless you can project where you're going to be next month or the month after. The real test is whether we stay in the black or slide back into the red because we've loaded ourselves with merchandise that's going to sit. Or because we've taken on additional expenses that sales don't warrant."

He smiled disarmingly. "Such as hiring the major stockholder as office or sales help when we have a complete staff."

His point was well made. "I wasn't asking to be hired," she told him without rancor.

He met her gaze head on, his smile still touching his lips faintly. "Fine, then we have that settled. At the present, Travish-Montaigne can't afford to pay you. If you want to work within the boundaries I've prescribed, I'll have Deline instruct the staff to cooperate fully. Their regular duties will come first, naturally."

"Naturally." Her own acquiescence amazed her. She'd come in ready to state demands, and here she was meekly eating out of his hand. She lowered her gaze to the envelope on his desk. "I see you got the bills. I'm finding out my father wasn't the most orderly man when it came to bookkeeping. I didn't even find a checkbook for his household account."

"He didn't have one."

She looked up sharply. "Everyone has an account. He banked at Security."

"He closed the account last year." A small bending of the truth. The bank had closed the account because it was continually overdrawn and the company would no longer guarantee the overdrafts.

A frown rippled her brow as though a pebble had been tossed into the pool of her serenity. "That's ridiculous." She looked at him questioningly, waiting for him to refute her claim.

He chose his words carefully. "It would seem so on the surface, but it was in his best interests."

"That statement's loaded with innuendo." She was watching him, searching his face for a clue that would reveal an answer.

He tested the water with a careful toe. He didn't want to set off the spark of her stubbornness now that she was finally acting human. Still, she would learn the truth sooner or later. Maybe it was better if it came from him.

"You didn't see much of your father these past years, but I'm sure that even in his brief visits you must have noted some changes." She continued to watch him speculatively. "He was lonely. He tried to compensate in many ways. Lavishness was one of them. It got out of hand. Closing off his ready access to cash was a deterrent."

"Paying bills is hardly lavishness," she said evenly.

"We set up a system for his regular expenses to be paid out of his draw each month. With the company struggling, it was expedient to limit how much we took out of the profits. It was temporary, but the sacrifice had to be made. Another six or eight months would have seen us over the crisis."

Her eyes narrowed. "How long has this been going on?"

"The financial pinch built over a period of four or five years. The decision to curb expenses came after I joined the partnership."

She thought about the generous allowance checks she'd received steadily. Her father hadn't mentioned financial stress or made any suggestion that her allowance be cut. Had he considered her a child to be pampered and shielded from the hard knocks of reality? He'd always insisted that the small monthly checks from her mother's trust fund were "mad money." The allowance from him was to cover her living expenses.

As though reading her thoughts, Carter continued. "He didn't want to stop your allowance. Since he was forced to pay it out of his personal funds, it ate deeply into his savings."

"But surely he didn't have to deny himself!" The anger was returning, and her voice climbed.

"He did, that's just the point. He was spending a lot more than he was making. The company was being eaten up by expenses. There had to be a cut across the board. It's one thing to draw unlimited personal funds when your business is sound, but it's sheer folly when you're in trouble."

She inhaled sharply as she tried to quiet her churning thoughts and banish the guilt that seeped around their edges. Carter's steady gaze challenged her blind ignorance of her father's problems. She wanted to convince herself Carter was lying for some devious purpose, but the truth was beginning to congeal like a bad-tasting pudding. Travish Imports was not the fountain of prosperity she had believed it to be. Her father had been virtually broke. Carter had delivered a stunning blow that forced her to fight for survival. Not only was her future in the balance, but also her present.

She framed a careful question. "Does my allowance cease now that my father is dead?"

"Yes. His personal bills will be submitted to the court and paid by the estate. When probate closes, you'll have what's left of his earnings, but for the moment they're tied up too." He regarded her speculatively. "It was my understanding that you have a trust fund from your mother's estate. Will you be able to survive on that?"

He was suggesting the impossible. The trust fund check wasn't enough to cover bare essentials, even if she lived rent-free in the Wetherly Drive house. The clothes she'd charged yesterday . . .

He was still watching her with a curious mixture of interest and reticence. "If it's a problem, I'd be glad to advance money against the sale of your stock—if you should decide to sell. Otherwise, we can consider it a personal loan until things are settled. I wish we could work it out through the company, but it can't be done at present. Your father made some large purchases recently and we have a temporary cash flow problem."

"Are you referring to the items he bought from the Hankow collection?"

"I wasn't aware you knew about them."

"Tanner Holmes told me. He was sure that my father hadn't planned any trip to Hong Kong as that woman—Lily—claimed. He'd spent that entire week at the Hankow exhibition. I hope you told Lily Taylor to whistle for her thousand."

"I'm still checking into it."

"She's lying!"

"We'll see. If she can back her claim, we'll have to pay it, or she'll file against the estate and hold up probate. It has to be resolved eventually."

Arisa's stomach churned. Carter was more concerned about Lily than about her. *She* was expected to get by on whatever handout he chose to bestow. An angry flush stained her cheeks. She was thinking just like the spoiled juvenile Carter took her for.

"If he wasn't planning a trip, why would he borrow the money?" she asked more quietly.

"Personal expenses, most likely. Like these." He tapped the envelope addressed in her hand.

"Those are business expenses."

He fixed her with a piercing gaze. "They are not."

"Are you saying my father ran up those kinds of bills for his personal pleasure?" It was too farfetched. Thousands of dollars a month for entertaining!

"I'm afraid he did. He'd curb his spending for a few weeks, then go off the deep end with a mighty splash. He couldn't resist reaching for the check or standing a round of drinks..."

"I don't believe you!" She was out of the chair, her rage uncontainable. Carter had sweet-talked her into a vulnerable position and now he was moving in for the kill. She wasn't sure what his game was, but he was out to discredit her father completely.

"We had a separate credit card account in the company name. It was the only account we used for business expenses." He didn't tell her he had confiscated Elliot's card several months ago.

She was too furious to get words out coherently. She glared at Carter, then stormed out of the office. She'd find out why he was lying and fling the truth in his face! She'd...

The door of Deline's office opened and she ran headlong into Quentin.

"Arisa, what in the world..." He grabbed her to steady her and stared at her quizzically. "You look as though World War III had started."

"Oh—hello, Quent. What are you doing here?" Without waiting for an answer, she glanced at Carter's office and drew her shoulders back. "It has, in a way. That man!" She clenched her teeth and shook her head as though chasing a pesky fly. She let out a heavy breath. "Take me to lunch. I need a drink, and I want to talk to you."

He glanced at his watch. "I have an appointment at three."

"We have plenty of time."

He followed her down the stairs, half-skipping to keep up with her flying pace. When they came out of the shop and headed toward Santa Monica, she walked as though she were trying out for the Olympic marathons. By the time they reached La Scala, he was panting and flushed.

He was still trying to catch his breath when the hostess at the luncheon room told them it would be a half-hour wait. Arisa dismissed the prospect with annoyance.

"We'll eat in the main dining room." Without waiting for agreement from Quentin, she crossed the dim hall and stepped into the cool interior of the large dining room.

The posh room was deserted except for a trio of men in lightweight, three-piece suits at a far table. An army of hovering waiters and busboys materialized as soon as Arisa and Quentin were seated.

Quentin began to relax with his first martini. The high color ebbed from his face and the thin sheen of sweat vanished. He signaled the waiter for a refill when Arisa had barely tasted her vodka-and-tonic.

"Do you always belt them down like that?" Arisa asked peevishly.

"No, but I don't usually trot over here as if I were on the track at Los Alamitos," he snapped.

Arisa laughed sheepishly. "Sorry, Quent. I had to work off some excess frustration."

He looked at her with a knowing smile. "Carter Montaigne?"

She nodded. "How well do you know him?"

Quentin settled the empty martini glass with precision on the small cocktail napkin. "I haven't spent much time at the shop. I have my own business to tend."

Same old Quentin, she thought. "But you've had a chance to observe. Did Dad talk about him at all? You must know something."

He looked at her curiously as the waiter deftly removed the

empty glass and replaced it with a fresh drink. He glanced at Arisa's full glass and disappeared.

"I'm asking bluntly, Quent," she said. "Do you trust Carter Montaigne?"

He looked up. "I never gave it much thought one way or the other."

"Oh, for God's sake, Quent, you know what I mean. Do you think he screwed Dad in that partnership deal? Can we take his word for the state the company is in? He makes it sound as if we're hanging by our toes over a chasm, and only he can pull us back."

Quentin treated himself to a healthy gulp of his martini before he answered. "There's a lot involved." When she started to scold his caution, he held up a hand. "Just listen," he said patronizingly. She wanted to laugh but she pressed her lips together in forced patience.

"The partnership is aboveboard. Forbes drew up the papers, and they're uncontestable. It could be that Montaigne forced Father somehow, exerted undue pressure. Do you have reason to suspect him?"

"I'm not sure. I saw a financial statement. The company was in trouble. Forbes convinced me it would have gone under without the infusion of Montaigne's cash."

"Did he say why, after all these years, the company wasn't doing well? Where was the money going?"

She made a wry face. "Carter intimates that Dad was throwing it away on wild parties and gala entertaining. I find it hard to believe."

"So he spent a few bucks. I'm not talking about pennies."

"Neither is Carter. For last month alone there were over five thousand dollars in bills. Carter claims they're personal expenses."

Quentin blanched. "Five thousand?"

She nodded. "That doesn't include Lily Taylor's bid. Just who is she, Quent?"

"A girl. A friend of Elliot's."

"And yours?"

His face twitched. "I see her occasionally. She called and asked me to drive her to the funeral. I could hardly say no. I had no idea she was going to pull that stunt." He looked down at his glass which had somehow become empty again. The waiter started toward them.

"Was she one of the people he entertained so lavishly?" Disgust filled her as she thought of her father picking up women half his age in bars, or letting himself be picked up so that he didn't have to face a solitary evening. Loneliness did strange things to people, not always nice things. She realized she was judging Lily, but after the scene at the house, it was a fair assessment.

"He took her out, if that's what you mean." Quentin was eager to dismiss the subject of Lily. "Why do you ask about trusting Carter? I've never liked him. I wouldn't mind proving he blackmailed Elliot."

"That's a strong choice of words. Was there something Dad could be blackmailed about?"

"How should I know?" he said testily. "I suppose everyone has something about his life he'd like kept quiet. The point isn't whether or not Elliot was guilty but if Carter resorted to skulduggery. I wouldn't put it past him. I'd never heard of him and suddenly he was a partner."

"But you admit you rarely saw Dad. They could have known each other for years." She wasn't defending Carter's position, only probing for ammunition against him.

"All I know is that since he's been there, Elliot let him run things. He rarely went into the store this past year. Carter handled the money and decisions except when Elliot bought something at auction or through one of his old friends."

Arisa frowned. "That doesn't sound like him. The business was his life. Mother was always arguing with him to spend less time at the store and more with her." That wasn't exactly true. Her mother had only become upset when Elliot missed social engagements or made excuses not to attend the endless routine of parties and functions she adored.

"He changed after you left."

Again the intimation that her father was not the man she'd known. Why did that disturb her so? People changed. She had. But it was as if everyone was talking about a completely different person from the father she'd thought she knew.

"Frankly," Quentin said, "I didn't realize how much until I heard the terms of his will. I expected he'd leave the store to both of us."

His mouth was petulant. So he didn't like the terms of the will, no matter how fair Forbes claimed they were! She regarded him overtly. "Are you going to contest it?"

His mouth twitched. "It wouldn't do any good. I checked."

Arisa signaled the waiter to bring menus. Quentin toyed with his glass. "I was counting on some money." He looked at her, his head cocked slightly and his eyes dark. "I have a deal going that's the chance of a lifetime. I need cash to close it." He leaned forward, still watching her intently. "It's big, Arisa. Really big. There'll never be another one like it. I've got an opportunity to get in on the ground floor of a Tahoe development. You don't know what's been happening in California real estate. It's turned to pure gold, and this is the mother lode. With thirty thousand, I can have something that will set me up for life."

"Can't you raise it out of your brokerage business?"

His head jerked impatiently. "No, damn it! Everything is tied up right now. If I'd known two weeks ago..."

Known that their father was going to die? Known he wasn't going to have an inheritance in the offing? Arisa felt a wave of disgust at her brother's cold-heartedness.

He flushed. "What I meant was, I had a couple of deals pending when Father died. I plunged ahead with them because I thought..."

"There was more where that came from," she finished for him.

"You make it sound mercenary."

"Isn't it? Did you spare a minute's grief for Dad? Did you think about anything but the money you might get?"

"Of course I did." He was irritated and unconvincing. "That's beside the point now. The thing is, I need money. Will you lend it to me? This deal is—"

She laughed. "I haven't got it," she broke in to say.

"A sure-fire deal," he finished, then stopped abruptly to stare at her as though he'd just understood what she said. "You can get it, though. Put the stock up as collateral. Better still, sell now to Montaigne. I know he's made you an offer. You're a fool if you don't take it. Christ, Arisa, what the hell do you want to hang on for? Montaigne is hungry for that stock. Hold him up for top dollar. I've got a guy who can go over the figures..."

"Just one damned minute, Quent." His head snapped back as though she'd slapped him. "I told you I haven't made up my mind to sell and I don't like being ordered around. I'll decide if and when I sell. Right now, I have no intention of groveling to Carter Montaigne to further your interests. If that Tahoe deal is so important, borrow the money. You've got collateral."

He took a deep breath and his lower lip jutted. "I told you, I'm into other things. I'm in to my limit. Look, I'll pay two percent above prime on your money." He looked pained. "Or I'll cut you in for a percentage, if that's the way you want it."

"Thanks, but no thanks."

"Why?" He was incredulous that she wasn't jumping at his offer.

"I haven't made up my mind about a lot of things. It may come as a surprise, but I do have a life of my own, you know. There's a deal in Paris . . ." She didn't want to tell him about the *galerie*, not yet.

But he'd caught the scent. "A business venture? What is it? Don't you see, I'm offering you a chance to make a bundle. Look, I haven't told anyone. This deal at Tahoe is a combination resort and shopping complex. It's bigger and better than anything the community has seen, and it will take off like a shot. They've got a prime location, close enough to the Nevada border so people can gamble if they want to, but secluded so it will have all the amenities of a first-class resort. Golf, tennis, water sports—a complete, self-sufficient resort where guests don't have to walk more than a block to find what they want. Half the shops in the commercial section are already rented to some of the biggest names in retailing, and they haven't even broken ground yet. I tell you, it's dynamite. It will outclass the Mauna Kea in Hawaii or La Réserve in Geneva. When the money starts rolling in, you can write your own ticket in Paris or anywhere else."

"It happens that my deal in Paris is something that won't wait." She didn't tell him she'd already scraped together every dollar she had to put up good faith money. Or that she had only thirty days to come up with the rest of the downpayment. She realized with a sick feeling that seven of the thirty were already gone. She wondered if she would have considered borrowing the money from Quentin if he hadn't sprung his little surprise. The idea made her smile inwardly.

She scanned the menu the waiter had left, silent while her brother also gave the bill of fare his attention. When another waiter appeared to take their orders, she decided on the *vongole al forno* and *trota alla fiorentina*. Quentin spent another minute studying the menu, then ordered *saltimbocca alla romana*.

"And I'd like a glass of white wine," he said as the man turned to go. The waiter glanced at Arisa, who shook her head.

Quentin flipped open a gold case and snapped a thin Dunhill lighter to a cigarette.

"What about your trust fund?" he asked.

She masked her surprise. "What about it?"

"You can borrow against it."

"Maybe, but I won't." She was annoyed at his persistence. After all these years, he was coming on very strong for a brother who'd never paid any attention to her before. What made him think she'd back his project? If she borrowed against the trust fund or her stock, it would be for her own venture, not his.

His lips compressed to a tight line. "You're being foolish. This Tahoe thing is a chance in a million."

"Let's not talk about it anymore, not now."

"You mean you'll consider it?" His eyes sparked with renewed hope.

"Don't count on it. Let's enjoy our lunch."

After the waiter brought the salads, Quentin changed the subject. "I guess you've been left with the job of going through Elliot's things. I don't envy you."

"It's not fun," she admitted. "He left his papers in an incredible mess."

"Maybe Forbes or the accountant at the shop can help."

She was surprised at his solicitude. "I've at least got them sorted. It's a start."

"What about the house? Will you keep it?"

"At least until I decide what I'm going to do."

"Didn't Dad have a collection of jade and stuff? I seem to remember him talking about it."

"Yes, but I won't sell those. They meant a lot to him."

"It's not a good idea to leave them sitting around if you decide to go back to Paris. They should be in a safe place."

"I'd take them with me."

"I hope they're not just sitting out."

"You seem very concerned all of a sudden," she said with a curious smile.

"You should be too," he answered. "Do you know what the crime rate is in this city? It's not as though you live in a security high-rise. Beverly Hills is open preserve for thieves."

"I'll be careful." The house had been left alone for a long

time even before her father's death, she thought.

"At least make a list of everything, with detailed descriptions. If anything does happen, the police like to have an inventory—or photographs if possible."

"Oh, Quent..."

"It's not that big a chore, and you may have occasion to thank me someday. Let's hope not, but an ounce of prevention..."

"One more cliché and I'll lose my lunch."

He laughed. "All right, but you should do it. I tell you what, I have a good Polaroid. I'll come over and take pictures for you. It'll make me feel better and it can't hurt. How about tomorrow? I've got some time in the afternoon."

"Really, Quent..."

"I insist."

"Oh, all right. Make it after lunch."

He relaxed then, and she diverted him with questions about his brokerage business. He'd expanded into a larger office in one of the new buildings on Wilshire. Business was fantastic. He'd made some shrewd deals and survived the stock market slump when many brokers and investors had taken a bath. Several of the biggest names in Hollywood were his clients, he told her smugly.

She let him ramble while her thoughts were on her own plans. She was going to have to make some decisions soon. She'd led Carter to believe she wanted to stay in Los Angeles, but she wasn't really sure, deep down. The *galerie* wouldn't wait, and she had no cash. She'd have to talk to Forbes about the monthly checks from the trust fund. They'd always been sent directly to her bank in Paris. Maybe she could intercept the upcoming one.

She refused a second cup of coffee and excused herself. Ten minutes later, she returned to find a brass tray with the check on it in front of her place. Quentin grinned.

"I didn't expect to be taking anyone to lunch. I came away without any cash," he said. "Take care of it and I'll pay you back tomorrow."

"I don't have any cash either, Quent." He was pure gall.

"They take credit cards. I left mine at the office."

She tried to decide if he was putting her on. Then she laughed. "You forget, I'm fresh in from the French countryside. I don't have any American credit cards."

"None?" He looked doubtful.

"Not a one, dear heart, not a one." He looked so comical she laughed again. "What now, dear brother?"

He scowled, then laughed with her. "Poor little rich kids, eh? Well, I guess we charge it to Travish-Montaigne. I'll explain to Deline." Arisa pushed the check toward him like a conspirator. With a flourish, Quentin added a generous tip, signed his name and wrote out Travish-Montaigne Imports in bold letters under it as though he did it every day of the week.

"Shall we go?"

At the door, the maitre d' flashed a smile. "Good afternoon, signor . . . signorina . . ."

YEAR OF THE SNAKE

Hong Kong, December 1941

Abigail leaned heavily on her cane as she struggled from the chaise lounge in her bedroom. Watching her, Mei Shau felt the woman's pain in her own joints and wished her compassion had the power to ease the other's suffering.

"Ahhh, there we are," Abigail said with a sigh as she finally straightened. But she had sat still for so long, that she dared not try to walk immediately. She accepted the arm Mei Shau offered, then drew a breath as she forced herself into motion. The steady patter of rain against the windows and roof seemed to tighten the knots that had come with age. She moved painfully and slowly, making a small circle within the confines of the bedroom before she ventured to meet her guest.

"Yes . . . ready now, child. You must not let me doze so long in the chair." She scolded from force of habit. Mei Shau had been with her so long, she'd forgotten what the house was like without her. And Mai Yun—no longer a child but a beautiful girl of sixteen—the age Mei Shau had been . . .

They crossed the hall to the parlor. There was a fire in the fireplace and two lamps glowed softly, dispelling the gray gloom of the weather. Grantland Whitaker came from the hearth, where he'd been warming his damp clothes.

"You're looking fit this afternoon, Abigail," he said heartily in his clipped British accent. He clasped her hand and nodded Mei Shau away.

She ignored him until Abigail said, "Thank you, Mei Shau. I could do with a cup of tea, and I'm sure Grantland would welcome a spot of brandy with his."

Settling into one of the big chairs flanking the hearth, Abigail stiffened her back. Her wobbling stride irritated her. It was degrading not to be able to trust one's own limbs. So much had changed over the years, she thought with a sigh. She'd grown old, and Hong Kong had bounded upward with the exuberance of youth. Its population was more than double what it had been when she came to the colony in 1918. From a remote outpost, it had become a bustling metropolis. And from a peaceful jewel set in the blue waters of the China Sea, it had fallen under the shadow of the war on the mainland. She knew that was what her British friend had come to talk about. It seemed she alone on the island had no desire to discuss the new specter of war that darkened the horizon. The reports of the war underway at home made her shudder. London blitzed and left in rubble... Would Hong Kong now be laid waste?

"Caroline sends her best, Abigail. Sorry she couldn't join me, but with the wedding and the packing... Half the damned servants have run off as if the Japs were crossing the Bay this minute." He snorted. "The other half are too frightened to do what they're told. And as if that isn't enough, Melisande is weeping and wailing because we're taking her away from her young fellow right after the wedding." He snorted again. "We're saving her life, and all she can worry about is her young man."

Abigail smiled. "Too old to remember what love does to logic, Grantland? I thought I was the doddering old fool."

He laughed heartily. "I suppose you're right. I'm in sympathy with them, of course, but that may not stop the Japanese from carrying out their threats. I don't like the roll of thunder we're hearing from the north. It hasn't done a damned bit of good to block trade. I'm afraid we've put their backs to the wall. They have little choice but to attack."

"Nonsense, Grantland. The Japanese cabinet recognizes the folly of that kind of hasty move. They're already into Indochina. It's Russia they're after. The rumors and threats are nothing more than a bit of squeeze on the Americans. What does Melisande's young man say about it?"

"Elliot?" He shrugged. "The Americans have frozen Japanese assets and hit Tokyo hard in the purse. President Roosevelt's still negotiating, but American businessmen don't hold out much hope. They're the ones with the most to lose. The United States is safely beyond the range of Japanese bombers. We're the ones who will bear the brunt of war when it comes."

His tone alarmed her. They talked about the war often, but their chats had always been of the armchair-strategist variety, despite the reality of the war at home in England. "Is Elliot going home?"

"He'll stay on until after Christmas. His company is still

trying to bring in rice from Indochina. There are a few avenues the Japs haven't sealed off yet. With the news worsening every day, it's vital they bring in as much as they can, just in case . . ." He left the prediction unsaid. He peered at Abigail through his steel-rimmed spectacles.

"Elliot agrees Melisande should accompany us to Canada. He wants her out of harm's way. And we all agree that you must accompany us as well." He held up a hand when she tried to protest. "Spare me the arguments, Abigail. The picture is more ominous every day. Half our countrymen have already fled. Since the fall of the Konoe Cabinet, Tojo's been pushing steadily along a collision course. He believes that nonsense about the spiritual value of war. He's a ruthless, dangerous man. War is coming, mark my words. And when it does, none of us should be here." He sat back as Mei Shau came in with the tea tray and a decanter of brandy. She set them on the table and left him to pour his own liquor while she tended to the tea. After a swallow of the excellent cognac, he went on. "Let me tell Caroline you've agreed, eh?"

"You're rushing me, Grantland." Abigail accepted the delicate porcelain cup and let Mei Shau tuck the napkin across her broad lap.

"Rushing?" Whitaker boomed. "Good God, the Japs may be right at our back door, don't you understand?" He was immediately contrite, and lowered his voice though his face was still flushed. "We've dawdled a bit too long, hoping for a miracle. But it's not going to happen, Abigail. We've got to face that truth."

Sobered, Abigail pondered the suggestion. It wasn't the first time the subject had come up. She knew the danger was real; Grantland wasn't one to speak hastily or cry wolf. It was one thing his leaving the colony—he had a wife and family to concern him. But for her to flee . . . She'd been in Hong Kong so long, it seemed unthinkable to uproot herself. She wasn't young anymore. Her nursing career was done because she was too crippled to move about or lift patients. What would she do in Canada? Her savings wouldn't last long if she had to start over.

"I'll think about it, Grantland, you can tell Caroline that."

"There isn't much time."

"I know. Now, drink your tea and divert me with better news than you've imparted so far. What of your office? Are the architectual plans for the housing estates progressing?"

· He drained the brandy and took a sip of tea before setting the cup aside and refilling the snifter. "Everything is at a standstill," he said. "Refugees are streaming in as though Hong Kong were the last hope of the yellow race, and there isn't any place to put them."

"I suppose they prefer it to the mainland." She'd never gotten accustomed to the ability of the Chinese to live in such cramped quarters. Whole families lived in spaces half the size of her kitchen. She smiled, thinking how Mei Shau refused to move out of the tiny service porch even after Mai Yun was no longer an infant. The two were perfectly comfortable in the small cubicle. And happy . . . If she were to run off to Canada, what would become of them? She smothered a sigh and listened distractedly as Grantland talked about dwindling manpower and supplies for construction. The government was trying to accommodate the refugees without success. If the British fled, the Chinese would quickly move into vacated houses. Abigail tried to imagine the lovely rooms of the Whitaker house on the Peak filled with Chinese and the smell of fish cooking in chatties. It was too ludicrous, and she smiled. Mei Shau and Mai Yun would be able to stay right here, she'd make sure of that. Ah, but for how long? If Grantland was correct about the Japanese. . . .

Contemplating gathering her things, trying to decide what must stay and what she could take—all this wearied her. She wouldn't be happy living in a strange land where cold and snow filled so many months of the year. Better to die in Hong Kong.

She glanced at Grantland's ruddy face. She'd miss his visits. Caroline's and Melisande's, too, though not as much. Her true friendship was with Grantland rather than his pretty, socially-minded wife and daughter. But the war, if it came, would not last forever. The Whitakers would be back. God willing, she'd still be here. The steady drum of the rain lulled her thoughts. Her head nodded, and the teacup clattered against the saucer.

"Ho, I've overstayed my visit. You're dozing, Abigail." Grantland rescued the cup before it slid away. He put it aside and took her hand between his. "We're leaving next week, Abigail. There really isn't much time." His eyes were peculiarly sad, as though they held a vision of the future. "Not much time . . ." He squeezed the arthritic fingers quite gently and patted the hand back onto her lap.

"Mei Shau!" he bellowed.

She appeared instantly as though awaiting the summons, carrying his coat and hat.

"I'll drop by on Thursday. I'll see if I can't persuade Caroline to come along. But with the wedding on Saturday . . ." he shook his head at women's foibles. "At any rate, we will see you at the wedding. Melisande would never forgive either of us if you missed it. I'll send a car round."

"Give the child my love, Grantland. She hardly seems old enough to be marrying. The years have flown. Tell Caroline she shouldn't even attempt to come down on Thursday. She has enough on her mind. After the wedding, we'll have plenty of time to chat."

Grantland's face clouded, but he didn't remind her that they would be gone shortly. At the door, Mei Shau handed him his umbrella. She brushed spatters of rain from her skirt as she came back to help her mistress into bed.

When Abigail was settled under the warm comforter and had a cozy waterbottle at her knees, Mei Shau turned off the lamps except for a small night-light at the bedside.

"Thank you, Mei Shau. I don't know how I'd manage without you. This weather . . ." Abigail sighed, knowing the weather was only part of it.

"Will you go?" Mei Shau asked softly. In the dim light, her face was a pale moon with dark eyes.

Abigail was silent a moment. Mei Shau and Mai Yun were her family; she had no other. And like Grantland, she had to put them first. She smiled wearily.

"No, Mei Shau. My home is here. I will not go."

Mei Shau touched the mound of Abigail's feet gently. "Sleep well, Miss Abigail."

She closed her eyes and drifted in the half-dozing of old age. She felt better with her decision made. Now that she had committed herself to Mei Shau, it would be easier to disappoint Grantland and Caroline. Thank heaven there wouldn't be time for them to wheedle and coax; that was a blessing. The peace in Mei Shau's eyes was full reward, just as the years had been, she thought. How clearly she remembered the day she'd brought Mei Shau home . . . could it be sixteen years already? And Mai Yun, slender and lovely, though perhaps a bit pampered by the two women who adored her, had Mei Shau's grace and poise—and enough of her father's blood to soften her Eastern features to a rare blend of beauty.

Mei Shau never spoke of the father. It was as though the child's birth had severed the cord that bound her to his memory. Once when Abigail suggested that a letter might reach him in care of the company that had sent him to Hong Kong, Mei Shau's eyes were expressionless as she answered that her daughter's father was dead. A lie, of course, except to Mei Shau, who had killed her thoughts of him. It had been different when she heard about her brother's death. She had smiled with relief when Lei Tong's name appeared on the spotty lists of those who had died in the Communists' Long March of 1934. The death toll had been enormous in the high steppe lands and mountains of Szechwan. And not long after, Abigail learned through some of the personnel at the hospital that Mei Shau's father was also dead. The laundryman's body had been found several yards from his own doorstep. The police surmised he had been set upon by thugs and thieves after an evening of wine and mah-jongg, perhaps with a pocketful of winnings. He was badly beaten, but no one had heard any disturbance. There were hundreds of such deaths in the Chinese sectors every year. Little could be done to solve them or prevent them. Mei Shau had been surprised at the news, then relieved, as she had been about her brother. The two men who would have exiled her forever were gone now, and she had nothing more to fear.

Abigail wondered sleepily if she should have told Mei Shau about her visit to the shop on Sun Street. She had decided it was something she owed the Chinese mother, but Mei Shau would not understand. Abigail simply told Mei Shau's mother that her daughter was safe and well so that she could sleep peacefully at night. The old woman had bowed a dozen times, grateful and tearful. She'd believed her daughter was dead. The gods were merciful.

Abigail's thoughts wandered. Senseless death and cruelty . . . The Orientals seemed determined to kill each other off . . . or starve for lack of rice and space to breathe . . . Would they never be at peace . . . ? Would the world see peace again . . . ?

"I do not wish to go to the English wedding," Mai Yun said. Her pretty face, oval and delicate, enhanced by large dark eyes that were only slightly Oriental in appearance, was twisted in a determined scowl.

Her mother sighed softly. "You will hurt Miss Abigail by refusing her this. It does not give me pleasure to sit in the English church and see the foreigner wed. But the Whitakers are Miss Abigail's friends. We will go with her."

Mai Yun pouted, then went to the window and watched the relentless rain that had been falling for three days. Would it never cease? She was weary of the dampness, of sitting about her classes at the university with wet shoes and damp wool against her thighs. She longed for summer. And she longed for a way to escape the ordeal of Melisande Whitaker's wedding. Whenever the girl came to the house with her mother and father, she looked at Mai Yun as though she were a bit of garbage that had somehow fallen to the floor and escaped notice until it was ripe and rank. Once Melisande had turned the conversation to the subject of a "friend" who had fallen in love with a Chinese girl, but who had been sent off to Oxford by his parents before he could entertain the foolish notion that anything might come of such an alliance. Embarrassed, Mrs. Whitaker had quickly diverted the conversation to safer ground. But Mai Yun never forgot it, nor did she doubt that the story had been intended to belittle her mixed blood. Often Mai Yun cursed the accident of birth that made her neither Chinese nor American. She knew nothing about her father, except that he had come from America and gone back before she was born. Long ago, she'd given up asking her mother for more information. It was past, forgotten, dead.

But Melisande Whitaker reminded her of it with every glance. And now Mai Yun had to watch the marriage of the person she hated most in the world. She almost wished the Japanese would attack so the wedding could not take place, except that all she loved would be destroyed as well as the one she hated.

She felt her mother's touch on her arm. "The ceremony will only take an hour," Mei Shau said comfortingly. "We can survive that. We will go to the house of Kwan while Miss Abigail attends the reception that is to follow the ceremony. I will ring through to Kim Fai and ask her if we may visit."

Mai Yun smiled, her pique forgotten. A visit to the wealthy Kwan household was worth the price she must pay. Kwan Chan-ho had an exquisite collection of jade and porcelains that made her heart ache with their beauty. Most had belonged to

his family for generations. Kwan had succeeded in getting them
and his wife and children out of Shanghai before the Nationalists and Communists had divided up the city like a cold rice
cake. He'd been in Hong Kong for many years now, and had
rebuilt his wealth. Someday Mai Yun was going to live in a
house like Kwan's. Someday. . . .

Saturday dawned crystal clear with a light breeze playing
through the ever-restless bamboo. The Peak was sharply outlined against the azure sky as though an unskilled artist had
not yet learned the delicacies of shading. In contrast, St. John's
Church was a study in shadows: dark, gray-white beneath the
turrets and spires, and dazzling gold on the east facade as the
morning sun climbed through the cloudless heaven.

A propitious day for a wedding, Mai Yun thought sourly.
She sat beside her mother and Miss Abigail in a front pew
listening to the robed minister pronounce the vows that bound
Melisande Whitaker to Elliot Travish for life. Despite her annoyance at being forced to watch the spectacle, Mai Yun had
to admit the bride was beautiful. Her cheeks were highlighted
with a rosy flush and her blue eyes had a jewellike sparkle that
seemed to find its source in the man at her side.

Mai Yun studied Elliot Travish. She'd seen him a few times
when he'd come to the house with Melisande, but she had not
recognized his beauty until now. Beauty like that of a tall pine
or of waving marsh grass above dark water. His hair was the
color of nutmeg, his eyes so dark they might have contained
stones in the sockets. But not hard eyes . . . no, gentle—and
adoring as he faced his bride. And weak, she decided. Melisande would lead him about like the old grandfathers who
walked their birds in Victoria Park. Her cheeks grew warm as
she realized she was jealous. Jealous because the hateful, spite-
ful Melisande was finding joy . . . even though she would be
separated from her bridegroom in a matter of days. They would
leave the reception early, she knew, and they would lie in each
other's arms, discover each other's bodies. Mai Yun shivered
at the sensual thought. She had not yet known a man, and her
girlish fantasies were stirred. What would it be like to feel a
man's flesh warm and hard against her body? Her cheeks
flamed and she tried to change the course of her thoughts, lest
her mother sense the wicked path they had taken. She stared

at the couple at the front of the church, kneeling now as they repeated their vows.

When she married, would she be on display in an Anglican church like this or would she be closed in a marriage sedan until she reached her betrothed and was revealed to his eyes alone? The mixture of her blood and the two cultures in which she lived often left her confused and displaced. She loved her Chinese heritage, but she hated the upheaval China was in. She loved the antiquities, such as those Mr. Kwan collected, but she despised crowded, dirty stalls and streets on which they could be bought. She hated sharp-tongued, scornful foreigners like Melisande, but she envied the pleasure and ease of Melisande's life. She would never have to work in the house of another, as Mei Shau did, or fight for a job in a crowded Central office where she would be only another pair of hands to type or file, another pair of eyes to inspect ledgers and accounts.

The bride and groom kissed, and Mai Yun felt an ache in her heart. Melisande and Elliot were married. So early, so quickly. How long would it take for there to be a marriage of the two parts of Mai Yun?

Sunday, December 8, 1941

Another crystal clear morning made the winter season a thing of delight. Mai Yun rose early and took a bus to the top of the Peak, where she walked the paths among the elegant homes of Hong Kong's wealthy. She browsed along the park-like hillside, pausing to enjoy the rich, damp aroma of leaves and earth, and to look out across the blue-white city below. The English wedding the day before had left her restless and strangely dissatisfied; even the trip to the house of Kwan afterward had not broken the hypnotic spell that the nuptials had cast. Miss Abigail had reported that the reception was festive despite the bride's departure plans. Champagne, a lavish buffet, and a seven-tiered wedding cake kept the guests entertained while the bride and groom slipped away for their first night together. What had Melisande felt, she wondered. An awakening, an unfolding like a flower under the sun's warmth? Or was the haughty English girl as cold to her husband as she was to the outside world?

She thought of her own future. Had she been born into a

Chinese family, her marriage would have been arranged long
ago. She might now be wife to a merchant or perhaps a businessman of repute. She would know the feel of a man's body
entering her and unlocking the secrets that lay inside her spirit.
But she would also know the drudgery of family life—unless
her parents arranged a most fortuitous match. Her mother never
spoke of her own family or early life. Mei Shau had sealed off
the past. Mai Yun suspected that even the name she was called
was not the one to which her mother had been born. She
doubted that her birth had been preceded by marriage vows,
but she never broached the subject with her mother. It was a
burden enough to know that her American father was so un-
caring that he had never seen her. The weight of "bastard"
added to her name would be too much to bear.

   She came to the high place on Mount Austin Road where
she could look down over the city and the sparkling harbor.
In the distance, the sun glinted on the military planes at Kai
Tak Airport. Foreign planes sitting like vultures on Chinese
soil. Would the war come? It seemed remote, but even at school
the talk was of nothing but war. The war that raged on the
mainland . . . the war that might spread if Japan did not bend
to the demands of the Allies.

   She sighed and glanced at the distant hills of the Nine Dragons. A flock of birds swarmed over the ridge. For a moment
she thought she heard the drone of their wings. Shading her
eyes from the brilliance of the morning sun, she watched as
they dipped low past the barrier of hills, their wings gleaming
in the sun.

   Not birds—airplanes! She heard their roar distinctly now
in the clear, crisp air. One plane peeled off, its wings banking—
then another—and another—hurling themselves at Kai Tak
Airport, not leveling across the city as the landing planes did
but plummeting directly toward a goal. Suddenly, loud explosions rocked the quiet. Mai Yun couldn't be sure if the noise
had startled her or if the ground had actually shaken beneath
her feet. Stunned, she watched a cloud of black smoke mush-
room upward. Then the air was filled with explosions as the
planes roared over their target and dropped destruction. The
smoke was so thick, she could barely make out the glittering
planes as they circled and vanished beyond the hills, their
destruction accomplished. Flames licked through the dense
blackness over the airport. Sirens began to shrill, the sound

carried across the bay like a keening wind.

Bombs. War . . . She wanted to scream and run but stood watching in disbelief.

Behind her in one of the elegant Peak homes, a door was flung open and someone shouted, "The Japs have attacked!"

Somewhere a woman screamed.

Thursday, December 19, 1941

The roar of the planes came at the same instant as the wail of the sirens. Heart pounding, Mai Yun tumbled from her sleeping mat and groped for the flashlight Miss Abigail insisted each of them keep at hand. The inside of the bungalow was pitch black behind the tightly tacked curtains. Blackout. Black-in . . . The high-pitched whine of a bomb froze her hand in its search. She held her breath, counting. *Yat . . . yee . . . saam . . .*

The explosion rocked her back onto the mat. The windows rattled behind the curtains, and somewhere glass shattered. Another plane thundered above the noise, whistling as the bomb bays unleashed their terror.

Mai Yun covered her face with her hands. "Mama! Mama!" But she knew her mother had already gone to Miss Abigail. "Mama! Mama!"

When the explosion erupted the noise seemed part of her, filling her, tearing her apart with its force. She screamed as wood cracked, glass splintered, and choking dust engulfed her. She tried to get up but the floor buckled. She pitched headlong into the splinters. "Mama! Mama!"

She clawed her way across the debris, coughing and sputtering for breath. Her hands were wet with blood and her shoulder ached painfully. She had no memory of hitting it. She was too frightened to call out anymore, knowing the house was in the circle of the bomb's destruction. Around her, the walls shuddered and groaned. Desperately she searched for the door as the floor became an undulating, collapsing mass. A timber crashed against her arm, and she fell backward trying to escape the searing pain.

When she finally found the door, it was sprung from its hinges. She shoved it open with a crash. She blinked at the brightness. The front wall had been blown away, exposing the rooms to the holocaust outside and the stench of destruction.

Flames gorged on a house across the way, sending the charred framework into a yawning crater.

Mai Yun stumbled over the jumbled furniture, no longer feeling pain as her feet were slashed by the rubble and glass. In the eerie glow, she raced into Miss Abigail's room.

"Mama!" She stopped still.

A dozen small fires licked at the blackout curtains and the bedding. Oil from an overturned lamp had formed a pool on the table, and plumes of dark smoke eddied from it. In the center of the bed, two figures formed a bloody tangle.

"Mama!" She threw herself at them and pulled at her mother. "Mama!"

Her mother's eyes opened as though it caused her great pain. Her face was unrecognizable under the mask of dust and blood. Her eyes rolled.

Mai Yun wiped at the streaming blood on her mother's face, but it would not be staunched. Crying, she ripped off her pajama top and pressed it to the gaping wound at Mei Shau's brow. Her mother whimpered and tried to sit up.

The blood gushed again. "Don't move, Mama!"

Mei Shau's lips worked painfully.

"Don't talk."

"Mi—— Mi—— A—— Ab——"

"Shhh, lie still!" Mai Yun slapped out a nest of flame and lay her mother's head back gently. Her stomach churned as she looked at Miss Abigail. Swallowing nausea, she forced herself to lift one flabby, limp hand and put her finger to the woman's wrist. No one could have survived such an injury. Miss Abigail's head had been ripped open by a jagged length of wood that quivered in her skull like a bloody arrow, pinning her to the mattress. Mai Yun let the lifeless hand fall. Turning back, she lifted her mother and carried her from the room.

The fires had spread, turning the entire street into a holocaust. Houses were outlined against the glow for one moment, then collapsed into the soaring flames. Figures ran like dark shadows against the orange backdrop. Mai Yun pressed her face into her mother's bloody gown as a shower of sparks stung her naked shoulders. Sobbing, she forced her feet to move, no longer feeling the slivers and cuts as she struggled to breathe in the overpowering heat. Behind her, the bedroom burst into flames as the burning oil suddenly touched off the blankets. For a moment, Miss Abigail's body was outlined in the glow

of her funeral pyre. Mei Shau screamed agonizingly. Mai Yun
clutched her tightly and ran toward the yawning glow where
the front door had been.

Outside, the street was rubble. Where the bomb had hit, the
pavement buckled around a huge crater that was still smouldering and foaming thick black smoke. The steady wail of sirens
and the cries of the wounded filled the night. Tears stung Mai
Yun's eyes as she tried to orient herself without the familiar
landmarks of the street on which she'd lived all her life. In her
arms, her mother had subsided to pitiful sobbing.

Suddenly a figure loomed very close, blocking her way.
She tried to dart past but a strong arm blocked her.

"Miss Abigail—where is she?"

Mai Yun squinted at the man's face but it was a grotesque,
grimy mask. He grabbed her arm, then let it go quickly when
Mei Shau groaned and a fresh flow of blood gushed from her
head.

Still shouting to be heard over the roar of the flames and
the din of panic, Elliot Travish leaned close to Mai Yun.
"Where is Abigail?"

"Dead." Mai Yun let her gaze fasten on the inferno behind
them.

"Oh, my God. . . . !" Elliot felt sick. If only she'd gone with
Melisande and the Whitakers. God!

The girl was looking at him with dead eyes. He started to
walk away, but couldn't dismiss that helpless look of despair.
He took Mai Yun's arm and led her away from the crackling
flames and showering sparks. When they got to the lower end
of the street, he stopped and breathed the damp, cold air rolling
in from the harbor. In the light from a small pocket torch, he
examined Mei Shau. The blood had stopped running from her
wound, and her face was waxen. Even before he felt her temple,
he knew she was dead. Her flesh was already growing clammy.
Mai Yun watched him with frightened eyes.

"She's dead, Mai Yun. I'm sorry."

She didn't move. No hysteria, no tears, nothing. She just
stood holding her mother's corpse, and stared at him. Gently,
he took the dead woman from her arms and laid the body on
the grass near a banyon tree. The girl went down on her
haunches beside it, but he pulled her away.

She shuddered as if the biting wind had suddenly reached
her soul. She jerked her arm free and knelt beside the corpse.

"She's dead," Elliot said. "There's nothing you can do."

Trembling, she reached under her mother's bloody dress and found the jade pendant she always wore. Clasping it, she rose and looked up at Elliot. She began to cry soft whimpering sounds at first, then agonized sobs. His heart wrenched. He put his arms around her and held her against his chest, murmuring soothingly. He'd come to get Abigail and keep his promise to the Whitakers that he'd look after her. The past ten days had been sheer hell, with nightly raids by Jap bombers and the aftermath of fires and rampant looting. It had taken a week to get his name and Abigail's on a list to be taken across the harbor to try for Free China. A week ago it had been possible to fly out, if one had enough money, but people were crushed in the panic to board the few planes that had taken off. Now the Japanese completely controlled the skies. And it was rumored that within days an attack force would occupy the already beaten city.

It was too late for Abigail. He sighed. If he didn't go tonight, it would be too late for him. He tried to release the girl, but she clung pathetically. He realized for the first time that she was naked from the waist up. Gently, he disentangled her arms and slipped off his jacket. Coaxing her into it, he pulled it across her narrow shoulders and small upturned breasts. The sleeves hung almost to her knees and flapped as she folded her arms across her body to huddle in the coat's warmth. She looked like a lost puppy. He couldn't be sure she even recognized him. She was dazed and confused, but after what she'd been through, it wasn't surprising. What was he going to do with her? He couldn't leave her here to squat by her mother's corpse until the next bombs fell. If she survived that, she'd be defenseless when the Japs came. He gritted his teeth thinking about what would happen to her then.

"Okay, come on," he said at last. At her blank stare, he took her hand and started toward the ferry pier where he was to meet the boat. He'd paid dearly for two passages. One of them might as well give Abigail's protégée a chance at life.

5

After Arisa's unceremonious departure, Carter's anger dissipated quickly. He'd made the mistake of misjudging her before. She was mercurial, smiling one minute sweet as honey, and pure acid the next. But she was still trying to cope with a new image of her father she'd never seen before. Maybe she was feeling guilty about not paying more attention to him these past years. Elliot had needed her. Elliot had always needed someone. Some people avoided close ties and others couldn't survive without them. For all his shortcomings, Elliot had been a hell of a guy. He hoped Arisa was beginning to understand that.

She hadn't answered his question about her finances. Another touchy subject, he surmised. She'd probably been counting on the allowance that was no longer forthcoming. She was going to find out he wasn't the easy mark her father had been. If she wanted money from Travish-Montaigne, she'd have to work for it or sell her stock. The company couldn't afford her extravagant living anymore than Elliot had.

Sighing, he put Elliot's bills out of sight and Arisa out of mind, and gave his attention to the morning mail Deline had placed on his desk. He was halfway through the stack when his private line buzzed.

"Carter Montaigne . . ."

"Good morning, darling. I hoped you'd call but you're being very naughty, aren't you. Haven't you punished me enough?"

He settled back in his chair. "Good morning, Claire. Something special on your mind, or did you call on impulse?" He ignored the game she wanted to play. She hadn't forgiven him for their split; that wasn't in Claire's book of rules. She'd seen the signs as clearly as he that their affair had gone sour, but she wasn't ready to give him up. He'd still been too important to her in the studio, the one they'd started together and built from a wallpaper and drapery sample depot to a flourishing decorating business. The difference between them was that Claire didn't need the money the studio brought, and Carter did. He had a living to earn. Claire merely filled time, staving off boredom, getting her kicks out of playing in the working world. She fancied her name becoming a trademark in decorating, like Gloria Vanderbilt on the seat of a smart pair of jeans. The funny thing was she might make it.

"Both, love. How about flying to Paris with me?"

"Business or pleasure?"

She laughed silkily. "I believe in combining them. It makes life more fun."

"I'm pretty well tied up right now, Claire. Elliot's death has far-reaching effects."

"You've been running that place ever since you became a partner. I happen to know that you have everything well under control."

He didn't resent her snooping. She'd kept tabs on him since they parted business company. With her father's millions, it was routine to have a complete dossier on everyone who knew her.

"That doesn't mean there aren't tangled threads. Thanks for the invitation, but I'll have to take a rain check."

"There's the Matique sale," she tempted.

"I'll have to pass this year."

"I had a call from Harry last night. He's been off scrounging as usual. He claims to have a marvelous Vezzi original, but I'm dubious. You know how enthusiastic Harry gets about everything."

Carter tensed and came upright. Another of Claire's games: leading him along a smooth path, then dropping a meteor in front of him. An original Vezzi—an attention-getter for sure.

Claire was savoring his surprise. "I haven't seen a Vezzi in years. I thought they'd all been uncovered long before this. Harry's probably got an imitation—you know how many have been forged."

"Did he say what it was?" Carter tried to sound casual but knew he wasn't succeeding.

"Mmm...no. I didn't think to ask. I don't have anyone lined up for something like that. Besides, darling, you should have first go at it—providing it is an original. Your collectors will pay much more than any of my clients."

"Did Harry leave a number? Is he at his apartment in Paris?" A description of the Vezzi would help.

She laughed. "He was calling from someone's villa in Nice.

He only had a minute, poor darling. The countess was wailing about getting packed for their flight to Paris." There was a comic seriousness to her tone that made Carter smile. It was exactly the story Harry would tell when he didn't want someone to call back and rock whatever boat he was currently maneuvering.

Carter reached out to flip the pages of his calendar. Damn it, he really couldn't take time off, even a few days. But a Vezzi—it would more than pay the cost of the trip over, and then some. He scanned the calendar again.

"I do wish you'd reconsider, darling," Claire said. The bait had been dropped and taken. She was testing the line.

"When are you leaving?"

"Today. The Fairchilds are flying over to cruise the Mediterranean. They've invited us to spend a couple of days with them. We're stopping over in London. You've been planning to run in to Christie's—this is the perfect opportunity."

She'd known all along that the Vezzi would get him to Paris. If it were anyone but Harry, he'd suspect Claire had staged the whole thing just to get him alone for a couple of days. He'd been avoiding her, trying as gently as possible to sever the thread that bound them. Well, if he was going, he might as well score in at least one inning.

"I hate to bring up the subject, Claire, but there's the problem of money. Elliot's death has tied up our assets. I have a temporary cash flow problem," he lied. He smiled as he heard her soft breathing. "What are my chances of picking up the check you owe me? It was due on the tenth."

It took her only a second to know she had no choice. "Of course, darling. I thought Adam had sent it. God, I can't bear the thought of looking for another accountant, but if he gets any slower, one of these days I'll have to do something."

"I'm sure if you just tell him the checks have to be out to me by the tenth each quarter, he'll understand. Even if he's carving your accounts in stone, there's enough in petty cash to pay me on time. You forget, I see the earnings statement."

When they'd parted, Claire had let go reluctantly. She was extremely capable when she put her mind to it. Her earnings for the year were up. And the installment payments to him for his share of the partnership were no more than his salary and expenses had been.

She laughed softly, acknowledging that he'd won. "I'll see

that it's sent over today. I'll pick you up at four. That should give us plenty of time to get to Santa Monica and . . ."

"Hold everything, Claire. I'll go, but I can't possibly get away today. I'll catch Air France's flight Thursday."

"The Fairchilds . . ."

"Give them my love. Maybe I can see them next time."

With a sigh, she said, "All right, I'll meet your plane at de Gaulle. See you on Friday."

He smiled in satisfaction. A Vezzi. If it was an original, the price he'd get for it would put him in a place he'd been aiming for ever since getting into the business—ever since, in fact, he first learned there wasn't anything he couldn't get if he wanted it badly enough. The first thing he'd really wanted was to get out of the dirty, three-room apartment in Brooklyn, where his mother came home drunk every night so she wouldn't have to see the cracked walls and scurrying roaches. When she drank herself into an early grave like his old man, he'd moved a step up, but not a very big one—single room with a hot plate on the West Side, where he could walk to night classes at Columbia after driving a laundry truck all day. It was a stopping place, no more a home than the Red Hook apartment. He'd been drafted right from Columbia, something that hadn't been in his scheme of things, but which he'd made the best of. His early years had toughened him enough so that the mudholes and rice paddies of Vietnam weren't unendurable. He didn't like them any better than anyone else, but they were temporary—like Brooklyn and the West Side walk-up.

From then on it had been easier. He'd decided it paid to get the crap shoveled away first so you could settle down to what really had to be done. He worked at various jobs, always around antiques or art, gleaning knowledge, storing information, becoming acquainted with everything and everyone in the business. It had taken five years before his chance came with Claire, and four years before he knew he'd outgrown her and had moved on. One year with Elliot . . .

He buzzed Deline, but she was out of her office. He found her in the workroom uncrating a bronze urn. She carefully lifted it from its wrappings and brushed away bits of clinging excelsior before she set it on the table.

"Nice piece," he said appreciatively. The vessel was about fifteen inches high and rectangular in shape. The bowl rested on stylized animal-mask feet incised with archaic patterns. The metal had attained a soft patina that enhanced the designs.

Deline studied it with a pleased expression. "Elliot said it was beautiful. He was right."

"Elliot bought it?"

She nodded. "For Elbert Faus. He saw it on his last trip to Hong Kong, but it wasn't for sale. A few months ago, Elliot called Leun Kee and finally convinced him to sell it." Her expression saddened. "He was awaiting its arrival so eagerly."

Carter busied himself with the invoice. He didn't like being witness to Deline's rare show of grief. It disturbed him, though he wasn't sure why. The bronze was expensive, but he was sure Elliot knew what he was doing.

"I'll call Faus. Let's get it over to Tanner right away."

"He's coming by this afternoon. I'll attend to it." The momentary exposure of emotion was over. Her face was impassive.

He asked her about some Ming tables he wanted delivered to a client before he left for Paris.

She assured him they were ready. "I didn't know you had planned a trip."

"Something just came up. I don't like leaving, but I'm sure you can handle everything. Mrs. Sherbock is coming in Friday for the Eden Limoges. Give her my apologies. I'll call her when I get back and make sure she likes the set." He started to leave. "Incidentally," he said, turning back to the bench. "I told Arisa she was welcome to hang around as long as she didn't get in the way. Invent work for her if necessary. I've told her not to expect special favors."

"Isn't that a bit harsh?"

"I don't think so. She has to learn this is a business, not a family hobby. I'm not her father and I don't intend to act like him. She follows the rules and doesn't disrupt things."

Mildly reproving, Deline said, "She owns sixty-five percent of the stock."

"And I'm managing the company. She can't change that, at least not until probate is settled. Afterward, well, we'll see what happens. Maybe she'll be tired of it all and run back to Paris."

"If not?"

He grimaced.

Deline's laughter tinkled and her eyes sparkled like black pools catching a shaft of moonlight. "I'm sure Arisa is bright

enough to recognize what you've done for the company. I
imagine she'll keep you on."

"With pure delight, I'm sure. She'll have me unloading
trucks and carting out trash."

They both laughed. Carter dropped the invoice onto the
table and gazed at the bronze again. "It's a good piece. Ask
Tanner what kind of price tag he'd suggest. If you need me
I'll be at home. I'm going to catch the Thursday flight. I won't
be gone more than a few days."

"Quentin was in today," she said unexpectedly. At his questioning look, she went on. "You were with Arisa. They left
together. But he asked if I'd talk to you."

"About . . . ?"

"His stock. He's willing to̅ sell."

Carter lifted an eyebrow wonderingly. "Before probate?"

"Right away, if it can be arranged. He doesn't see any
advantage to holding on to five percent, no matter what Arisa
does with hers."

"He doesn't share her fanatic loyalty to the name of Travish?" Carter said wryly.

Deline's eyes flashed a danger signal. Carter realized he
was treading on hallowed ground. Deline had always been
friendly with Quentin, despite the gulf between him and Elliot.
At times she played the role of peacemaker between them, at
others she became a stern parent figure, scolding and chiding
when the two men argued.

"He's a businessman. He prefers to invest his capital for
shorter-term gains."

"Did he mention price?"

She shook her head, but he knew she just didn't want to get
involved. Quentin had probably told her exactly how much he
wanted—and the figure was undoubtedly top dollar.

"Okay, I'll talk to him as soon as I get back. Reschedule
my calendar for next week."

Deline watched him go, then carried the bronze to the desk
so she could catalog it. After affixing a coded tag to the base,
she sat admiring the piece. Elliot had an eye for beauty as well
as value. Carter lacked Elliot's appreciation even though he
was knowledgable. There were dozens like him in the trade—
people who saw the financial side of antiques, but who had
only enough interest in the pieces themselves to be sure they
didn't make gross errors in judgment. At least Carter admitted

his inadequacies with respect to Oriental fine art.

She thought about his trip to Paris and wondered what had prompted it so suddenly. Not that she minded. It would be pleasant to have the shop to herself for a few days. It had been her life so long that she was restless away from it. She smiled. She was getting as bad as Elliot had been before. She sighed. Before . . . So long ago.

The phone at her elbow chimed softly. The bell had been muted so it would not startle anyone. She moved the bronze out of harm's way before she reached for the phone.

"Deline Armitage," she said softly.

"This is Bok Lo-san, Madame Armitage." Even in English, Bok's voice retained the harsh tonal quality of Chinese.

Deline's annoyance was betrayed by her tapping finger. "Yes, Mr. Bok. How may I help you?"

"Have you received the merchandise I am waiting for?"

She stared at the wall where memos and notes were tacked. "I expect it shortly."

"That is what you told me several days ago," he said curtly.

She wanted to slam down the phone, but there was no hint of anger in her voice. "I am doing everything possible to facilitate its delivery, I assure you."

"I have had your assurances before, Madame Armitage. I am not a patient man in some matters."

"You will have delivery as promised," she said coldly. The tapping of her finger had become a steady, rapid tattoo. "It is sometimes better to exhibit patience than foolhardiness."

The sound of his breath hissed. "Forgive me, Madame Armitage. I lose sight of how much you have at stake in this matter. I am sure you have no desire to disappoint me. Forgive me if I indulge myself by giving you small reminders from time to time. I shall expect to hear from you very soon. Very soon."

The line clicked. Deline sat, still staring at the assortment of papers on the dove-gray wall. She had been so sure Quentin would find the jade. What the devil had Elliot done with it? If it was in a safe-deposit box, Bok would chafe at further delay. Perhaps she could suggest to Arisa . . . No, it was out of the question. Quentin might hurry the opening of such a box, though. Once they knew if the jade were there, they'd be able to devise a plan to get it away from Arisa. If need be, Bok could step in and handle the matter himself.

She had not anticipated Carter's trip and wondered what prompted it. Not that she minded. The business ran smoothly, and without his watchful eye, she could be away from the shop if necessary. Carter had reorganized the business efficiently. Differently than Elliot's way, but she couldn't deny the success. Carter was a forceful businessman. Like Bok. No, Bok had a passion that went deep. Bok was a fanatic. Any fanatic was dangerous.

A faint smile touched her lips as she took off the blue smock she always wore in the workroom. She hung it up neatly, then picked up a few fragments of string and paper from the table and deposited them in the wastebasket. She straightened the phone pad. Satisfied, she picked up the bronze and started back for her office.

Quentin stared out the wall of plate glass in his office at the gray-blue haze of Beverly Hills. Smog lowered over the basin as the temperature climbed. The sprint with Arisa had sapped his energy. He was out of shape. It was time to get back to a health club. Or maybe move to the beach. He wasn't sure he liked the idea of dampness and mildew and gritty sand, but Malibu had become a prestigious address. He should look into it, it wouldn't hurt.

It wouldn't do any damned good either, he thought sullenly. Not if he didn't swing that Tahoe deal. Christ, he was up to his ass and sinking fast. It would take six months for the Tahoe thing to pay off, but he could hang in there that long. Maybe.

He still couldn't believe Arisa's assertion that she didn't have a dime. Elliot had been sending her a generous allowance, and she had that trust fund—how much did she get from it?

He reached for the phone and asked his secretary to get him Jay Rogers. A moment later, the lawyer's voice came over the line.

"What can I do for you, Quentin? If it's money, save your breath. I'm not buying."

"The Conoct deal is still open, Jay. If you don't believe you're missing the greatest deal of your life, it's no rainbow out of my future. When you kick yourself some day, I'll resist the temptation to say 'I told you so.'"

"Thanks," Jay said drily.

"That's not what I called about though. I need a favor."

"Uh-uh, I smell trouble."

"I'm wounded to the quick," Quentin said sarcastically. "My sister Arisa has a trust fund from her mother. Find out for me how much she gets each month, will you?"

"Why don't you ask her?"

"I'd prefer not to. Let's see, my mother died eight years ago November. Justin Forbes handled the trust."

"Didn't mama leave her baby boy any pennies to play with?"

"I don't need your smart remarks."

"And I don't need anymore freebies from you. Why don't we talk about the sizable fee you already owe me and how long it's overdue? Then we can talk about favors."

Quentin compressed his lips and stifled his irritation. "I'm good for the money. I always am, you know that. You'd have received payment ten times over if you weren't so stubborn about the stocks I recommend." He sighed heavily. "But it's your loss."

"Sure."

"Anything else you need to know about the trust fund?"

"No, guess I got it all. I suppose you want the answer right away."

"I'd appreciate it." It was only a matter of a phone call, and Jay wouldn't even make that himself. That's what secretaries were for.

"I'll get back to you."

"Thanks. And if you change your mind about the Conoct..."

Jay had hung up. Quentin dropped the phone onto the cradle. Suppose Arisa was getting more than she let on? Would he be able to convince her to lend it to him? Like most women, she probably didn't know a blue chip from a commodity, but real estate was something else. California real estate, the pot of gold at the end of the rainbow. But if he promised to bring her in on the deal, maybe she'd give him the loan.

He sat back thinking about Deline's proposition. Right now, it was the only sure route he could go. The trick was to get his hands on the jade without arousing Arisa's suspicions. According to Deline, the piece wasn't part of Elliot's regular collection. That should mean Arisa didn't know about it. Should. But she'd been in the house alone for a few days already. Maybe she'd checked the place out more carefully than she let on. She hadn't reacted with any alarm when he'd mentioned thefts. Maybe she didn't know what the jade was worth. Or maybe she hadn't come across it.

The intercom buzzed and his secretary told him Jay Rogers was on the line. He picked up the phone expectantly.

"Yes, Jay?"

"Got what you want. Arisa Elizabeth Travish gets two hundred dollars a month from the trust fund set up by Melisande Whitaker Travish from funds . . ."

"Two hundred!?" Quentin's hopes crumbled.

"That's it, good buddy. Two hundred. And the trust is airtight. Even Arisa can't change the terms or borrow against it. There's no big payoff at age twenty-five or whatever the hell they do in movies. The two hundred comes in as long as your sister is alive and kicking. When she flies this earthly coop, the trust goes to her children, if she has any, or else to some hospital in Hong Kong. That's it, no other legal heirs, especially you, pal. Your dear mumsie spelled it out as plain as she could: the money came from her father's estate, not from any Travish enterprises. And it goes to Arisa, no one else."

"I see." He was shaken. Cold anger eddied in his stomach. So Arisa hadn't been lying. She'd been mistaken about being able to borrow against it, but she'd probably never tried.

"That's it then, Quentin. Do me a favor, will you?"

"Certainly."

"Pay your bill."

Quentin hung up, still thinking about the terms of the trust fund. No mistake about his being cut off like a black sheep. And there wasn't a thing he could do about it. Maybe that's why his father had always come across with money when he needed it—guilt because his wife hated Quentin. The trust fund hadn't mattered as long as he had Dad to tap when he needed cash. Now there was no money coming from Dad either. It was beginning to look like Deline's Mr. Bok was the only answer.

The Saloon began to fill up shortly after five. Lily checked out the bar with a sweeping glance. Her favorite seat was taken. She frowned. There was no action at the front of the bar. It was for couples who preferred informal camaraderie rather than the privacy of a table, or for uninitiated singles not yet wise to the caste system of Beverly Hills oases. She smiled at the bartender and made her way around the "L" toward the only empty stool. She slid onto the seat as Tony put down a cocktail napkin and gave her a favored-customer smile.

"The usual," she said, smiling back as she glanced sidelong at the men at either side of her. She recognized a television writer who talked endlessly about the great scripts he came up with, which story editors hacked to death with a blunt fork. If he could line up enough bread to produce his own show . . . She turned her back toward him to discourage conversation. The man on the other side was vaguely familiar. If she'd ever heard his name, she didn't remember it, but he always sat alone at the end seat. From time to time, people wandered over to him for brief conversations. He could have been a bookie anyplace but the Saloon. They wouldn't stand for that here. Several times when she was meeting Elliot, she'd asked him about the dark, mustached man, but he'd shrugged and answered vaguely. "Just a guy," he'd said. Now she smiled, friendly but without open invitation. She knew the type: he'd ignore a come-on; if he wanted conversation, he'd initiate it.

Tony set down her drink, and laid her tab face down. She sipped the tall rum and tonic, wishing she'd been able to get away from Jana's on time. She'd been stuck waiting on a tanned Beverly Hills matron with time and money to spare, who'd tried on a dozen outfits before settling for one lousy tennis skirt and top. Jana was adamant about not rushing customers, even at closing time, and Lily had lost out on her regular seat at the bar for a lousy twenty-dollar commission. If she hadn't needed the money so bad, she'd have told the pert blonde and Jana what they could do with their crummy tennis outfit. For all her polite charm, Lily hated the women who frequented Jana's. They thought nothing of dropping a grand in one shopping spree if the spirit moved them, or if they were bored or miffed at their husbands. Women with closets full of clothes that they wore once or twice and then passed on to their maids or the Motion Picture Charity Bazaar. Yet they inspected each garment they tried on for a loose thread or tiny snag they could scream about. Rich bitches.

She sipped slowly and surveyed the room in the mirror behind the bar. She never bought herself more than one drink. If no interesting contact had been made by then, she moved on. Sitting alone at a bar too long got you a reputation that screamed: looking but no takers. That killed your chances. You would wind up with some barfly who'd been cold-shouldered by every other woman in the place. Like that TV writer. Creep.

She glimpsed a tall, red-headed woman coming from the direction of the noisy no-service bar. Lily smiled in the mirror as she turned.

"Hi, Lily. I saw you come in. I waved."

"Sorry, Polly, you know how hard it is to recognize faces when you walk in. How've you been?"

The redhead shrugged. "Could be better, could be worse. Yourself?" Polly squeezed in between Lily and the mustached man, giving him an "excuse-me" smile. The TV writer glanced her way but went back to his drink when her gaze passed over him. He watched them in the mirror, even though Lily's back was an effective barrier to conversation.

"Great," Lily said with forced enthusiasm and a grin that displayed her perfect teeth. It was more for the dark-haired man's benefit than Polly's. It never hurt to try.

"Hey, I was sorry to hear about Elliot Travish. You were seeing him, weren't you? Tough break, going like that. He was a hell of a nice guy."

"The best," Lily said as she let the smile fade. "He was fun. I'm going to miss him."

"Yeah...I guess a lot of people will. Funny thing, his daughter came in the other night. I didn't even know he had one. She bought enough clothes to fill a trunk. I was surprised she came to us instead of you, what with you and Elliot being buddies and all." She smiled again, not sorry at all. "But I couldn't turn up my nose at that kind of commission."

"Sure, I know. That's the breaks. I met her at Elliot's funeral. She didn't like the idea that her papa could have any fun. She hasn't seen him for years and figures he lived in a museum with the other relics. Mr. Moneybags was all he was to her." Remembering Arisa's icy dismissal, Lily's stomach knotted. Arisa had as much as told her she could whistle for her grand, then turned around and dropped more than that amount on a new wardrobe for herself. It wasn't fair—and she wasn't going to let them get away with it. Carter Montaigne had been just as bad, treating her like she was some bum off the street begging for pennies. She'd told him a thing or two. She didn't know how to go about filing a claim against Elliot's estate, but she was sure as hell going to find out. She raised her drink and swallowed half of it before she remembered to slow down. She set down the glass and wiped her fingers daintily on the damp napkin.

Polly shook her head. "Would you believe she charged everything to Elliot's store? Said she didn't have any credit cards because she'd just arrived from Paris." She laughed. "That's one I haven't heard before, and I thought I'd heard 'em all. Georgie wasn't keen on the idea of billing it that way, but what could he do? It was go along with her or put everything back on the rack. And you know Georgie. He'd charge his mother's funeral clothes to the devil's account if it meant a sale."

So Arisa was charging her bills just as if Elliot was still around to pay them. It figured. And debts like her thousand went begging. So much for justice. Maybe she should do some more work on Quentin. He was human compared to his sister and Montaigne.

The dark-haired man on the end stool signaled the bartender. Lily was sure he was taking in every word of her conversation with Polly. Well, Elliot's private life was hardly any secret, not at this bar or others where he knew everyone and chattered freely. Lily realized with a pang that she missed him. It had never been a case of love. Not that they hadn't enjoyed going to bed together. Elliot had been lonely for companionship and someone to talk to. He was like a kid waiting for Christmas when his dreams would come true. He was always waiting. Poor Elliot.

"Hey, I'm sorry," Polly said, touching her fingertips to Lily's arm momentarily.

Lily gave her a puzzled look. "About what?"

"My crack about funerals. I didn't mean..."

"It's okay." She was content to let Polly attribute her distraction to grief. If people thought you'd just lost someone close to you, it took some of the stigma away from sitting in a bar alone. She flicked a glance at the man sitting behind Polly, but he hadn't looked up.

"Well, I gotta run," Polly said cheerily. "It was great seeing you. Let's have lunch soon."

"Sure. Call me." Lily turned back to the mirror as Polly made her way through the standees to the group she'd left at the back bar. Lily tried to make out their faces, but she couldn't in the haze of smoke and dim light. Polly hadn't invited her to join them. That meant Polly hadn't staked out a claim for the evening anymore than she had, Lily thought smugly. There was no resentment at Polly's lack of invitation. It was one of the subtleties of the singles' game.

Tony put a fresh drink in front of her and she looked at him questioningly. He tilted his head toward the man on the last stool. Lily gave Tony an appreciative wink.

"Thanks," she said, smiling at her benefactor. He wasn't bad-looking if you liked the swarthy type. She did.

The man looked up with a faint smile. "My pleasure."

"Lily Taylor," she said warmly. "I've seen you here before."

"I stop in once in awhile," he said noncommittally. "I heard your girl friend mention Elliot Travish. You a good friend of his?"

She sighed with the proper degree of grief, yet let him know clearly that she wasn't out of circulation because Elliot was dead. "We had some good times. He was a hell of a nice guy. A lot of people are going to miss him." She eyed him speculatively. "Did you know him?"

"We have mutual friends."

"I see." She didn't at all, but it seemed the right thing to say. She sensed he wasn't the type who liked a lot of questions. "His funeral was nice. Small. The family wanted it that way. Seems a shame when Elliot loved crowds, you know?" He hadn't been at Forest Lawn, she was sure of it. She would have noticed.

"I don't dig funerals. When you're gone, you're gone. I don't want anyone wailing over my coffin."

"Me either," she said. "If you don't get your kicks while you're alive, what does it matter?" She watched him for a clue to the direction of his thoughts. He hadn't spared her a glance until after he heard Elliot's name, and now he wasn't pursuing the subject. Still, she had the feeling he hadn't struck up an idle conversation. She sipped her drink and waited.

Finally, he asked, "You work around here?"

"Over on Brighton Way. Jana's Boutique. Know it?"

"I've seen it. Nice place. You the manager?"

She laughed. "Don't I wish. No, I'm a poor working girl."

His gaze turned directly to her for the first time and swept down her expensively cut designer crepe de chine. "Funny, you don't look poor." He grinned.

She relaxed. "I didn't think you noticed," she said playfully. "But when you work in a place like Jana's you have to look good. The discount helps."

"Where'd you meet Elliot?"

The quick shift of subject took her off guard. "Right here. I sometimes stopped in for a drink after work, so did he. We just started to talk."

"That shop of his—not a bad place, huh?"

She made a pert face. "Class. Elliot loved it. He built it up from nothing. He talked about it all the time. Jeez, he was always talking about Chinese antiques like they were diamonds or something."

"Who runs it now?"

"His partner." A frown marred her forehead. "And his daughter. At least she gets his stock."

He grinned. "You don't like them?"

"I didn't say that."

"You don't have to."

"Yeah, well, I guess it's no secret. His partner treats me like dirt, and Miss Rich Bitch acted like I was some kind of worm that crawled out from under a rock when I mentioned the money Elliot owed me."

"How much did he take you for?"

"A thousand. It was just a friendly loan, don't get me wrong. If he hadn't kicked off so suddenly, he'd have paid me back. He wasn't a deadbeat, you know."

"Maybe, but you weren't the only one he left with an empty hand. He owed this friend of mine."

"Really? I mean, I'm not really surprised. El was always short of cash and needing a hundred here or there, but he always paid people back."

"Except when he croaked."

"I guess you're right." She gave him a wry smile. "Look, tell your friend to put in a claim against the estate. That's what I'm doing. I'm not going to let them screw me."

"You got an IOU?"

She shook her head, and her smile faded. Damn it, she needed that money. It was hers.

The dark-haired man finished his drink and pushed his glass away. "Let me know how you make out," he said, smiling. He wagged a finger at Tony as the bartender picked up the glass for a refill. "See you."

She wasn't sure if the words were meant for Tony or for her. Both, she decided as she watched him vanish in the crowd along the bar. Sighing, she reached for her tab, but Tony already had it in his hand.

"Gentleman took care of it, Lily."

Pleased, she glanced down the bar but he was gone.

"He's a nice guy. I didn't get his name, Tony."

"Danny? Hell of a guy. He doesn't buy many girls drinks. You should be flattered."

"Does he have a last name?"

"Ladera. Don't tell him I told you, okay?"

"Sure." She laughed. "If you see him before I do, tell him I said thanks for the drinks."

"Sure, Lily. See you."

"Going so soon?" the TV writer asked. He swiveled to watch Lily slide off the barstool.

El Cheapo, all friendly now that her drinks were paid for. "Sorry, I didn't know you were buying," she said maliciously. It flustered him. If he wasn't such a bore, she'd sit down and make him pop for one. "Thanks anyhow, but I have a date." She waved jauntily and left him staring after her as she went out.

YEAR OF THE HORSE

China, May 1942

Elliot woke sluggishly. The drone of mosquitoes buzzed persistently in the heat. One settled on his naked foot, and he kicked lethargically. He sighed and rolled onto his side. One day he'd wake up and the bad dream would be over. He opened his eyes slowly. Not today....

The sun was creeping over the flat rice fields. Its reflection in the paddies held only a trace of blood-red dawn. Soon it would pale and bleach against the blue bowl of the sky. Its scorching heat would make the rice grow and men wither. He hated to get up but he knew he had to do it. He wondered if it was worth it.

Rising from the hard mat, he stretched wearily and flexed his limbs. His ankles were swollen with bites crowned with pinpoints of blood where he'd scratched them during the night. He glanced at his filthy feet. Dirt had caked in the cracks where his flesh hadn't yet toughened to leather. He'd been barefoot two months, but he still felt the sharp incision of reeds and broken rice shafts as he waded in the paddies. He still felt the sting of blood-sucking leeches that fastened greedily to his flesh as he worked the furrows. He wondered if it was worth it.

Standing in the doorway of the mud and straw hut, he eased a knot from the small of his back. He wasn't used to the constant bending or the demands being made on his body, which had never been accustomed to physical labor. Buying, inventorying and selling rice was a hell of a lot different than growing it. He wondered how many people who ate it would be willing to endure this end of the process.

Willing... He could quit anytime, as long as he gave up the idea of eating. You worked or you didn't eat. There was barely enough to keep them all alive as it was. Every grain was eked out of the flooded paddies like gold from hardpan. The villagers would probably applaud if he lay down and died. His portion of food would prolong someone else's life for a few days or weeks.

He walked around the hut to the latrine. Maybe he'd talk to Mai Yun about moving on. But where? There wasn't anyplace to go. Another village? The hills? Back toward Canton? At least here there was a measure of safety. Occasionally news filtered in to the village from outside. There was no way to tell what was fact and what was rumor, but it was easy to believe the worst. Singapore and the Phillippines had fallen . . . thousands of Allied soldiers had died while being marched from Bataan north to prison camps. . . . In the spring, a plane had gone down in flames in the hills about fifty miles north. A small band of Chinese who'd come through the village reported seeing it and claimed it was American. For awhile, hope and fear that an American counterattack was underway kept the village tense, but nothing came of it. There hadn't been a Jap bomber or fighter overhead for weeks now. Maybe the war was over. Maybe the world had ended. Maybe there was nothing left except this narrow valley between the river and the mountain ridge. Maybe you'd better quit daydreaming and get to work, he told himself.

The pungent smoke of the woodfire drifted from the central hut where the cooking was done. Communal cooking had been set up before he and Mai Yun arrived. There wasn't enough wood and brush unless the women and children went into the mountains in search of it. It was a day's journey up and another back, and they couldn't often spare anyone for that long. Sometimes they didn't come back at all. There were resistance groups in the hills, and occasionally Jap planes came in low and strafed everything above the floor of the valley.

Mai Yun had rolled up the sleeping mats and joined the women at the stone hearth where water was already boiling for rice. When she saw him, she brought over a cup of steaming tea.

"Good morning, Elliot."

He smiled. "Thanks." He sipped the hot tea and felt a spark of energy ignite inside him. It was amazing how she'd blossomed, despite the grueling trek and their struggle to exist. The flight across the harbor just before the Japanese took Hong Kong seemed to have toughened her instead of sapping her energy. Kowloon had been jammed with hysterical refugees trying to make their way out. The roads were clogged with cars, bicycles, carts—anything that would move. Those who had started out with possessions and food piled on their backs had been forced to abandon them when the relentless strafing began. Those who had nothing but the clothes they wore moved faster but got hungrier sooner. The shops and stalls in the north end of the city had been stripped by the flood of refugees who'd already passed. By the time they crossed the new territories through Lok Ma Chau and the river into Kwangtung Province, corpses littered the roadways. He'd been ready to give up, but Mai Yun refused to let him quit. Just "another mile" or "one more hour's walk to safety," she'd coaxed. And somehow she managed to scrounge enough food to keep them alive. He never asked where she got it.

With the city safely behind them, refugees scattered in small groups or singly, losing themselves in the anonymity of the countryside, which wasn't worthwhile for the Japs to occupy. They headed northwest, away from the huge rice fields and fertile land and populated areas. Safety lay in the sparse, bleak out-districts. They'd stopped in several villages before this one and been forced to move on when the people refused to accept a foreigner, or when Japanese troops came dangerously close. Here they were as safe as anyone could be in a ravaged land.

Mai Yun returned to the women and Elliot finished his tea quickly. There'd be several hours of work in the fields before the women brought them rice and more tea. The men worked silently, conserving their energy for their labor. It gave him too much time to think. Where would he be now if he'd gone with Melisande and her parents? Canada? California? As an American citizen, he wouldn't have had any problem crossing the border and going back to California. He could be working in the home office of Sheffield Importing, at the desk job he'd left when the chance to go abroad came his way. The thought made him smile as he pulled on a conical straw hat and rolled up his trouser legs. The company had probably closed shop or gone into some kind of defense work, since there was no place to import rice from anymore. It was here but there was no way to get it out. He sighed and picked up a long weeding pole, then waded into the sea of sprouting grain.

The long, lingering dusk hovered over the valley after the villagers had retired to their huts. Refreshed but still bone weary after a bath in the icy river pool half a mile downstream, Elliot sat in the doorway of the hut, watching streaks of deep gray encroach the sky like a blanket being pulled up from the horizon. He was aware of Mai Yun settling beside him, but he didn't turn.

After a long time, she said softly, "Darkness soothes the spirit. It's peaceful. . . ."

He stared at the distant horizon that had become indistinguishable in the gloom. "War and death are so close, but we can't see them."

"You mustn't think of it."

"We can't forget it, Mai Yun, it's there. It's there just as surely as our next breath, or the sun coming up tomorrow."

"But we are here," she said gently. "We can do nothing except stay alive so we can go back someday."

He looked at her oval face, pale in the dusk. "Will there be anything to go back to? What's left? Is there still a Hong Kong? Is there still a world?"

She was silent a moment and he imagined he saw a reflection of pain in the fathomless darkness of her eyes. "The world is in us," she said firmly. "It exists because we exist. It lives because we are alive. We cannot bury ourselves with the dead but must live to honor their spirits."

They never talked about her mother and Abigail. At first Elliot had been fearful of setting off hysteria and despair but gradually he came to realize she'd shut off the ugly past. She had nothing left in Hong Kong—no kin, no home, no hope. He felt guilty now about his own self-pitying thoughts. Still, she was comfortable cut off from civilization. He wasn't, though not so uncomfortable that he was willing to risk anything else. He turned his gaze back to the dark land that had become both his salvation and his prison.

She touched his shoulder gently. Her fingers were warm through the black shirt she'd miraculously produced for him a few days after they arrived in the village. His own had long since disintegrated in tatters.

"If there is no world beyond the perimeters of this valley, then we must make this place happy. If there is no time beyond the night, then this time must be ours forever."

"Let us eat and drink, for tomorrow we die. . . ." He sighed and pressed his cheek to her hand on his shoulder. "Sorry, I get morbid when I think of how futile it all is. I'm grateful for everything you've done. We wouldn't have made it without your guts."

Her hand tightened on his flesh. "Without me you might have found a way to escape."

"No, we were cut off before we got to Kowloon. And there's no other way out unless we climb our way into Burma. Sometimes I feel—I don't know, useless . . . and cowardly? Like I'm hiding out while everyone else is fighting for my survival as well as theirs. I keep wondering what's happening out there. Is the whole world in rubble and flames? How long can we run from it?"

"We are not running. We are living in the only way possible. There are millions like us and when the war is over, we will be the ones to rebuild the world."

He turned to look at her again. "You believe that, don't you," he said in surprise.

"Yes, and you must too. What purpose would it serve for us to throw ourselves under the bombs? Are we corpses that must be consumed by flames because we are frightened? Life is a struggle, and death is the reward that comes to those who have fought well. We fight the Japanese by staying alive, by eating this rice,"—she spread a hand toward the dark fields where a sliver of moon was mirrored in the shimmering surface—"so there is less for their bellies. They gobble up China but they will not devour us. We live so they will die."

He let his breath out slowly as her intense look turned gentle and lingered on his face. He lifted his hand and touched her cheek. "You're good for me, Mai Yun. You chase away my black moods."

She put her hand over his and pressed it to her cheek. "You are good for me," she whispered. She met his dark gaze and breathed softly. "Do you think of her often?"

He knew she was talking about Melisande, and guilt filled him. He rarely thought of Melisande. They'd had three nights and days together before her family had evacuated Hong Kong, but she was part of a vanished dream—not real, somehow, not part of him.

"I'm too tired to think most of the time," he lied. He didn't want to herd his thoughts along dangerous byways.

"A man needs a woman."

The words caressed the night, and he could not pull his gaze away from her. For months he'd been denying the growing knowledge that she'd become a woman and that his body longed for her physical touch. She soothed him with words and small comforts she could provide, while he resolutely told himself that she was a grateful child. In truth she was only a few years younger than Melisande. . . .

"I am yours," she whispered. "I am good for you."

His own words spoken from her lips were an alluring balm, drawing him helplessly. Desire crept through his weariness.

"Come." She held his hand to her hard breast beneath her cotton *san*.

He remembered the small upturned naked breasts that had pressed against him when she cried over her mother's corpse. He remembered her frail body in his arms.

"Come," she said again. She rose and drew him up without taking his hand away from her breast. She led him inside where dusk and moonlight blended to a soft gray. The bed mats were unrolled near the door where they'd capture the errant breeze that swayed the green, slender rice shoots and whispered through the thatched roof. When she finally released him, her hands feathered over his body and drew off his garments. Then, bathed in the sultry night, her *san* and *koo* fell away and she stood naked.

She poised, feline, her arms stretching toward him. In the hazy darkness he was acutely aware of her nearness. He moved slowly toward her. When her hands touched him, desire stabbed his body. Her arms encircled him, drawing him against her warm flesh. He felt the brush of her hair against his cheek as she buried her face on his chest. He heard her soft sob of pleasure, but the sound was drowned by the sudden pulsating of blood that coursed through him. He closed his hand on the silkiness of her hair and raised her face as his mouth searched. Her lips were unbelievably warm and eager. The soft outline of her body became part of him as he explored the gentle curve of her back and the rising swell of her breasts. The night exploded into billions of fragmented chips of light as passion swept away everything but his need.

He stumbled back, lowering her to the mat without releasing her mouth or body. His hunger swelled ravenously as her delicate fingers breathed across his flesh. When her hand claimed the swollen center of his desire, he groaned and pinned her back to the mat. Knowing, she spread her pale thighs, then clasped her legs around him as he plunged heedlessly. Everything was swept away except the fiery knowledge of her body. Warm . . . demanding . . . giving . . . He moaned as release came swiftly and fully. Her body arched, then stilled slowly as his energy and lust were drained. She drew him down to lie on top of her, and he was too weak to move. When his breathing quieted, he rolled sideways on the mat, and she moved with him, unwilling to relinquish the prize she'd won. They lay a long time in the quiet darkness until sleep weighed his eyes and lightened his body.

"I am good for you," she murmured against his lips.

Then they slept.

6

Arisa answered the door on the first ring. Tanner Holmes pursed his lips in a silent whistle. "Fetching," he said with a warm smile.

She was wearing one of the new outfits she'd bought on Rodeo Drive. It was a soft violet jersey wrap-around, piped in twin rows of deep green and white, and belted with strands of matching cords. A brief bolero covered its spaghetti-thin straps and her bare back, and framed her antique-gold-and-jade necklace—her only jewelry. Her tan was perfect for the white sandals.

"You always say exactly the right thing. Is it a talent or does it come of long practice?"

He cocked his head, still grinning. "That would be telling trade secrets."

"Come on in." She stepped back. "Would you like a drink?"

He followed her into the living room. The temperature had climbed into the high nineties, but she'd drawn the shades and switched on the air conditioner. The house was pleasantly cool.

"I thought that since we're eating Mexican, we might start the evening with a pitcher of margaritas. You like them?"

"Love them."

"I've got the makings on ice at my apartment. It's not far from the restaurant. That okay?"

"Fine. I'll get my purse."

A few minutes later he was holding open the door of an eight-year-old, coral convertible. The top was down, and sheepskin seat covers protected the black vinyl from the sun. She slid in and wedged her feet beside a stack of books on the floor.

"Whoops, feet of clay, this paragon," he said. He scooped up the books and dumped them into the narrow back seat. After slamming her door, he climbed behind the wheel and pulled away from the curb.

"I guess I just gave away my secret," he said with a grin.

"You know now that I really don't have the knack of this chivalry thing. But if you take pity on me often enough, I may get the hang of it. I warned you about old Henrietta here." He patted the car dash affectionately. "She's not much, but she's all I've got. I wouldn't trade her for a Caddie. Is it going to be too windy with the top down?"

"No, I like it." The sun was falling behind the mountain of buildings on Wilshire, but it was still hot. A faint breeze was already pushing in from the ocean, stirring the palms with promised coolness. She settled comfortably as Tanner followed Wetherly north to Burton, then went east to La Cienega. Friday night traffic was thick along Restaurant Row. Driveways and parking lots were jammed with Mercedes, Ferraris, Jaguars, Porches and a sprinkling of Rolls Royces. Anyplace but Los Angeles, heads would turn and traffic would come to a standstill as people gaped at the array of foreign cars.

Tanner whistled tunelessly, glancing at her from time to time or commenting on something they passed. The breeze ruffled his hair and gave him a boyish look. He was wearing tan slacks and an open-necked sportshirt that made Arisa glad she hadn't chosen one of the fancier dresses she'd bought.

When they turned onto Beverly Boulevard, the noise of the traffic quieted. "Are you an Angelino?" she asked.

He shook his head. "Transplanted. Isn't everyone? Natives are few and far between in these parts."

"It seems that way." Even in high school, most of her friends had come from families that had roots elsewhere. She wondered if she should try to look up any of the old crowd...

They crossed the busy intersection of Fairfax where the city temporarily took on an old-world flavor. Orthodox Jews in black caps and coats vied with women bent over the bins of clothing, shoes, and hardware outside the Bargain Fair. Shoppers crowded the produce stands, butcher shops, and bakeries, while others opted for the kosher delights of Canter's. Past Fairfax, the street quieted as outlying shops closed for the night. Beyond CBS, Sotheby Parke Bernet stood behind a dignified expanse of green lawn. A couple of blocks further, Tanner pulled deftly into a parking spot in front of a shop a few doors from the corner.

"This is it." He swept a hand toward the shop. There was no sign except a neatly lettered: T. HOLMES on the window, which was screened by a dark curtain.

The door was thick, solid wood. Tanner produced a key ring. "Would you like to see the shop or are you dying for those margaritas?"

"Both. The shop first."

He selected two keys and undid the double locks. Reaching inside, he snapped off a burglar alarm and turned on a battery of overhead lights. She saw that behind the black curtain the window was barred.

Except for a small desk near the door, the entire room was fitted out as a workshop. There were four different work tables, as well as bins, cupboards, and shelves where articles were stored. Bottles, tubes, jars and cans of solvents, pigments, glues, cleaners, and lacquers were neatly arranged on narrow shelves that ran down the side walls. Brushes stood in niches in a rack below. Cotton pads and rags had a special place under the counter. Arisa had never seen such organization in her life. Behind a Lucite panel at the end of the shop, a more conventional workshop was set up with a variety of carpentry tools. On a small dais, a desk with peeling inlays was being treated.

Arisa glanced around at the pieces awaiting restoration, or in the process. "You have enough work to last ten years," she said, impressed. The air conditioner hummed softly, and she realized that the heavy curtain at the window not only maintained privacy, but helped control the exact temperature and humidity, creating the perfect climate for the valuable articles entrusted to Tanner's care.

He laughed. "I'm not quite that slow, but my clients might agree with you. When something's been around five hundred years, you don't sweep a dustrag over it or put it together with scotch tape. Look here..." He led her to a table where a Meissen handle-less cup lay on a Lucite board. "I've been working on this for weeks. Some idiot got sloppy in packing, and it had a piece broken off. See there—I still have a few chips to fit in."

She inspected the cup. Except for a tiny flake in the gold edging, which he pointed out, the piece looked perfect. She complimented him.

"Not bad," he admitted, "but unfortunately its value drops drastically because some oaf was careless." He flicked a fingernail to the porcelain and cocked his head. "The ring is gone." He sounded as if he'd lost a friend.

"It's as beautiful as it ever was," she said. "That's more important than value."

He looked at her with a grin. "You sound like your father. He saw beauty first. What a piece sold for was immaterial. If he'd had his way, he'd have kept everything he ever bought. Too bad he had to make a living."

"When I was little, he used to show me his collection. It was like entering a shrine when he took me into his study. He taught me to love and respect Oriental work."

"Why did you turn your back on it?"

"The collection? I didn't. He sold some of the pieces to get started in business. The rest are still at the house. I'll always cherish them."

"You're avoiding the issue. I'm not referring to a few special pieces. Why didn't you follow up on that love and respect for Oriental art? You have a fine arts background. Europe is a gourmet table of Oriental things, especially porcelain ware. I've read that more than three million pieces of Chinese porcelain were shipped to Europe on Dutch ships during the first half of the seventeenth century alone. Even if you didn't want to work with your father, you could have done *some*thing with all that latent knowledge wherever you lived."

Her cheeks flushed. "Children aren't always inclined to follow in their fathers' footsteps."

He leaned against a work table. "Okay. It's none of my business. But it's a damned shame to putter with something half-heartedly when you should be energizing a God-given talent. Your father knew you had it, and I think that down under all that surface crap maybe you know it too. That's why you haven't really settled into anything. You're marking time."

"The right thing hasn't come along!" She was angry, but not at him. At herself. Because he was right. She had drifted around the edges of the antique world without making a commitment to it. The *galerie* in Paris would be the first decisive step.

"It so happens I plan to buy a small *galerie* as soon as I return to Paris. I've been working for other people long enough. I want my own place."

He was silent but his eyes searched her face relentlessly until she had to lower her gaze. The faint hum of the air conditioner was the only sound, except for the beating of her heart which suddenly was too loud and fast. Tanner had no right to accuse. Hadn't he refused to develop his own talent and simply drifted? Why was she uncomfortable with her own beliefs? She wasn't prone to childish tantrums just because someone's opinion differed from hers. Her angry confrontation with Carter flashed across her mind, and she felt her cheeks sting with color. That had been a tantrum, pure and simple. Or perhaps unpure and not so simple. She had to stop being so defensive about everything.

Tanner broke the silence. "Sure, I understand. I'm glad for you if that's what you really want. You'll make a go of it."

She was glad to dismiss the subject and have his compromised blessing. "Let's finish the tour of the shop and then get on to those margaritas you promised. Where are we going to eat? I've been wracking my brain trying to think where the best enchilada place in town is. I really don't know. When I was in school, we stayed pretty close to home for snacks. I guess I don't know Hollywood as well as I thought."

His serious demeanor vanished as he gave her a quick grin. "Ah, the best-kept secret in town, known only to a couple of million people. You'll see, pet, you'll see." He came upright like a lazy cat from a nap. "Okay, the tour. Let's see how much is tucked inside that pretty little head of yours. You should be able to identify some of these things. How about that?" He pointed to a small painting.

"Definitely Chinese," she said. "Probably late eighteenth century but I can't do any better than that."

"That's not bad." He took her arm and walked her along a glass-fronted cabinet. He stopped and peered through the spotless glass. "Ah, that one."

"A Liverpool coffee pot. Enland, 1770," she said unhesitatingly.

"Good, good. And that?"

"Early Haviland."

"And that?"

"Art Nouveau," she said grimacing. "Not my thing."

"But outstanding. That one's a Ginori."

"Looks a bit like the Wizard of Oz."

He laughed and steered her toward the next cabinet.

"Now down to basics. There, on the top shelf."

"Oh, it's lovely!" She studied the blue-on-white dish of Chinese porcelain. It was Ming, she was sure, but that dynasty covered such a span of time that it had become a catchall label. She looked at the plate carefully. The central fish motif was surrounded by a ring of flowers, then a narrower edging of overlaid shell designs. The blues were brilliant, despite their age. Finally she shook her head. "I give up. I could say early Ming but that would be a cop-out, wouldn't it?"

"Good guess," he said, opening the cabinet and taking out the dish to turn it over so she could see the base. "You're not too far off. It's fourteenth-century Yüan. Early Ming potters copied the traditional blue underglaze until they developed the polychrome techniques. This base wasn't glazed, so it turned orange in the firing."

"It's not marked. How can you be sure it isn't a later copy?"

"There never was a uniform system of marking before the nineteenth century. A single factory might use a dozen marks over a relatively short time, or the same mark could be drawn in different ways by different artists. A mark helps, but it's not infallible. We can tell by the pigments and glazes, sometimes by the craftsmanship itself in the case of a distinctive artist. Style is something that's pretty individual." He returned the dish to the cabinet and closed the glass door.

Arisa was captivated by his earnest explanation. He knew his art history, and he obviously put it to good use in work he loved. Like her father's, his voice had a note of reverence when he talked about rare specimens. Perhaps she'd been too quick to sell the range of his talents short.

They moved to a workbench and Arisa fingered a rectangular bronze urn. It seemed warm to her touch, like a fine Oriental carpet.

"That's Travish-Montaigne's," he said. "I just picked it up. Needs cleaning." He put a finger to it like a fussy housewife.

"It's an interesting piece."

"Deline said your father bought it from a dealer in Hong Kong. He had his eye on it for a long time."

"What period is it?" The subtle differences in bronze were difficult to detect readily.

He hitched his shoulders. "Eastern Han. Very old and a beautiful specimen." He stood up. "You've done very well with your first quiz at Holmes' College of Boring Details. You get a gold star on your margarita glass. Now it's your turn to check me out on my talents as a bartender *extraordinaire*. Let's go."

They retraced their way through the shop. Tanner reset the burglar alarm, turned off the lights, then carefully tested the door. The entrance to the apartment upstairs was right next to the shop; that door was double-locked too. They climbed a

narrow flight to the second floor, to another door with another
set of double locks. Arisa shook her head as Tanner found the
right keys and got it open.

"This is like breaking into the treasury," she joked.

"An ounce of prevention—and all that stuff. Do you have
any idea what some enterprising burglar could make in one
haul if he got in downstairs?" He whistled softly. "I don't like
to think about it. It would keep me awake nights."

"And your apartment?" She indicated the complicated security system.

"Aha, that's where I'm smarter than the average crook. Are
you aware, young lady, that the most vulnerable and least
protected part of a shop is not its rear but its *ceiling?* Ergo,
security system downstairs, security system upstairs. You'd be
surprised at what alarms would go off if you tried to sneak in
here some night. Watch out."

She smiled. He bounced from serious devotee of the arts
one minute to boyish prankster the next. A charming chame-
leon. She let him escort her inside after he'd gone through the
routine of deactivating the alarm system and snapping on the
lights.

The apartment was a surprise. She'd expected bachelor clutter and early Salvation Army mismatches that fit the image of
carelessness Tanner gave, but the apartment was tastefully furnished in deep earthtones, chrome, and glass. Bookcases and
curiocabinets lined the walls. A soft spotlight highlighted a
lavender-blue vase with crackled glaze. When he saw her admiring gaze, he said, "Your father gave it to me as a house-
warming gift when I opened the shop."

"It's lovely." The simple lines of the slender-necked vase
were pleasing and graceful. The lack of adornment enhanced
the rich violet-blue color and gave it unblemished depth. The
spotlight bathed it in soft light with only a few pinpointed
reflections.

"Ch'ing, K'ang-hsi period," he said automatically.

"Margarita," she said pointedly.

He snapped his fingers and went into the kitchen whistling.
A moment later she heard the blender whir.

"Can I help?"

"Turn on the stereo and make yourself at home. I'll be ready
in a sec'." His off-key whistling resumed.

She switched on the stereo and found a station with pleasant music. Fascinated by his collection of books and art work, she browsed. One chrome-and-black Lucite case was entirely filled with reference books on glass, porcelain, antique furniture, and jade. Some were handsomely bound and looked like collectors' items in their own right. She lifted one and felt the glove-soft leather as she opened it to look for a print date. 1878 . . . England. She turned the yellowed pages and saw magnificent illuminations and plates. She returned the book carefully to its niche. The next case had art books and a healthy sampling of best sellers. Instead of bookends, sculptures and ceramics supported the partially filled shelves. There was a dark stone carved walrus that she recognized as an Alaskan Eskimo carving. On a lower shelf, an African mask was slashed with bold colors. Near the floor, an exquisite glass bird, as though in flight, spread its wings between two rows of paperback thrillers.

"My tastes are unconventional to say the least," Tanner said behind her.

"Varied," she corrected. "Is there anything you *don't* like?"

"Pretense." He grinned. "The margaritas are ready. Come on." Responding to her inquisitive look as he started toward the kitchen, he said, "One more surprise in store. Then I'll settle down to being just plain Tanner, Boy Wonder." He led her through the compact kitchen where deep brown cupboards contrasted with yellow appliances and a tiled floor.

"Did you do this place yourself?" she demanded.

"I got the refrigerator from GE."

"Idiot. You know what I mean."

He shrugged and his tan sportscoat hunched up around the collar. "All I do is surround myself with things I like and that are comfortable for me. I usually don't care if anyone else likes them, but I'm glad you do." His smile was honest and warm. "Now come on before the margaritas lose their frost."

"Where?"

He was leading her out a rear door. To her amazement, it opened onto a small porch overlooking neighboring rooftops and garages. What he had done to the porch was beyond belief. It was completely screened with sun-deflecting mesh that kept out the heat but let the evening breeze waft through. The eight-by-eight floor was covered with artificial turf that would be envied by the greenskeeper of any golf course. Plants stood in baskets, ceramic pots, or on bamboo holders, and they hung from the ceiling in such abundance that the porch was a jungle.

It even smelled damp and cool—like a rain forest. Four cushioned patio chairs surrounded a white wrought-iron table with a glass top. On it, a tray with a blender full of frothy, frosty margaritas stood beside two thin-stemmed glasses. Tanner pulled out a chair.

"*Mademoiselle, s'il vous plaît.*"

He poured their drinks and sat beside her. She looked out over the city as dusk wrapped it in mauve-touched gray. Lights twinkled through the palm fronds, and the hum of traffic along Beverly Boulevard was only a whisper.

"It's incredible, Tanner. You've created an oasis in the middle of the Los Angeles desert."

He peered at her over the salty rim of the margarita glass and licked his lips. "You're not one of those people who's convinced L.A. is a wasteland, are you? I don't think I could stand it, now that I've decided you're bright as well as pretty."

"No, I was using the term in the true sense of the word. Most gardens or patios here have a dry feeling that makes you look around for cactus. But this . . ." She spread a hand. "The air is moist. It's *lush.*"

"A miracle of modern ingenuity," he said solemnly. He leaned close and whispered. "I put in an automatic sprinkler system."

"On a porch?" She was incredulous.

He nodded and made a silent sign with his finger to his lips. She began to laugh. He pretended hurt.

"I thought I was very clever, frankly. Look, it's hidden up there behind the plants. The landlord hasn't spotted it yet. As long as the timer doesn't go haywire so that I flood the building, I'm all right."

She thought about the shop downstairs and knew that he'd made very sure that could never happen.

"Three times a day it sprays a fine mist that these green monsters lap up. The screen keeps it from becoming a hothouse." He paused and looked out at the lights. "I like to be out here this time of evening."

"I don't blame you. It's delightful." She thought of the expensive Beverly Hills gardens that were sterile by comparison.

The margarita was the right combination of salty and tart. She raised her glass in a toast as they sat listening to the evening hush around the screened aerie. Arisa thought of Paris and tried to fit an evening like this into her life there. But the lush, rich, earth smell would not blend with the Paris she knew. A bouquet of violets, a pot of geraniums, a spray of blossoms in spring— that was Paris. This riot of greenery was more reminiscent of Hong Kong. Humidity heavy with fragrant growth, a cool breeze blowing across the Peak . . .

"A penny for your thoughts." When she snapped out of her reverie, Tanner quipped, "Maybe with inflation it should be a dime?"

"I was thinking about Paris and wondering if anyone has a garden like this."

"And do they?"

She shook her head. "I doubt it. I was thinking about Hong Kong too. You might have some competition there. Strange, I don't think I've really given Hong Kong a thought for eight years. Not since I left Los Angeles."

He refilled their glasses from the sweaty blender. "Did you like it there? I mean, when you lived there?"

"I was only a kid. Yes, I liked it. It was home, it was excitement, it was my world." She looked at him. "Where were you brought up, Tanner?"

"Minnesota."

"On a farm?"

"No, just outside of Minneapolis. A suburb really."

"Did *you* like it?"

He gave the question consideration, as if his answer might be truly important. "No," he said, turning to capture her gaze. "I felt trapped, like a changeling stolen from one kingdom and transported to another. Even though I'd lived there all my life, I didn't feel any roots. It was as though I was waiting to be picked up and moved again."

"Odd, I would have bet your answer would be the same as mine. I thought all kids felt secure in the first place they knew. The moves that come later are the ones that cause trouble."

"Maybe that's true for most kids. I never did fit any pattern." He smiled, but his eyes mirrored a strange sadness.

"Did you have an unhappy childhood?" she asked.

"Not by ordinary standards. I wasn't starved or beaten or neglected. I had the usual two parents that come with an average family. I can't say we understood each other very well, but what family really does these days?"

"You said you were in the service."

He nodded. "It finally got me out of Minnesota or I might still be there." He noted her empty glass and the layer of froth at the bottom of the pitcher. "I hear the bugler sounding mess. I'll bet you're starved." He got up and began to collect the glasses and tray.

"I am," she said. "I am not one of these women who picks at salads and calls them meals. I have a hearty appetite. Lead on, *caballero*."

"Got on your walking shoes?" He glanced at her thin-strapped sandals. "Oh-oh, guess we'll have to take Henrietta."

Downstairs he handed her into the car, then made a U-turn in the middle of the street at the first break in traffic. He grinned when she clung to the door. A few blocks later, he made a left into the driveway along the back of CBS. He winked conspiratorially when she looked at him.

The parking lot of the Farmer's Market was crowded. Cars and tour buses stood in solid lines under the arc lights as people took advantage of the market's summer hours. Tanner drove through the back lot and around the buildings that had been added to the original market. A minute later he found a parking place, and they walked through a tunnel of shops to the bustling, colorful interior of the market.

Arisa gazed around nostalgically. She hadn't been here for years. Knickknacks, candy souvenirs, clothing, fresh meat, coffee, mountains of fruit and vegetables. Canvas awnings flapped gently as passersby ducked under. Tourists with cameras slung over their shoulders strolled and gawked or stopped to buy *ti* logs imported from Hawaii or cheese made in Wisconsin.

They walked slowly up and down the aisles without any attempt at conversation since there was so much to see. Arisa remembered the open restaurants near the center of the maze and knew where Tanner was leading her. He held her hand as if they were kids at the fair, eager and expectant. When they reached the big Mexican food stand near the patio, Tanner stopped and glanced up at the posted menu.

"To start, may I suggest guacamole and chips, señorita?" His clipped tone imitated a stuffy headwaiter. Beside them, a young Chicana giggled. Tanner bestowed her a haughty look, which made her giggle even harder. "For a main course, enchiladas are our specialty. I would be wounded if the señorita does not try them." He smiled beatifically. "And our tacos—

mmm." He kissed his fingertips and closed his eyes. The young Chicana broke into a rapid burst of Spanish to her companion, and they moved off a few yards with their trays, still giggling and watching Tanner. Arisa couldn't suppress a grin.

"Our rice is the chef's special recipe, with just a kiss of spices and rich red tomatoes. Our refried beans—what can I say? *Magnifique!*" He looked at her questioningly. "Señorita, may I take your order?"

Entering into the spirit, Arisa took his suggestions. She stood inhaling the spicy aromas as a young Mexican behind the counter constructed their orders on paper plates and cardboard boats. Tanner piled extra hot sauce in small paper cups beside the plates and picked plastic silverware from a bin. They found a table in the crowded sidewalk cafe. Tanner settled her there while he went to get cold drinks. He came back whistling a few minutes later and carrying iced lemonades for both of them. Arisa couldn't remember when she'd had so much fun.

While they ate, Tanner encouraged Arisa to talk about herself. She found it easy to describe her life in Paris with just the right mixture of frivolity and candor, despite his earlier accusation that she was marking time. Tanner was attentive and relaxed. He occasionally asked a question or drew out details when she skimmed the surface. Some of her stories sounded silly in retrospect, and she found herself laughing with him.

When they finished their meal, they strolled up and down the aisles like tourists until shopkeepers began to draw the shutters and lock up for the night. When they finally made their way to the near-empty parking lot, Arisa told Tanner how much she'd enjoyed the evening.

"I'm glad," he said. "Maybe it will help convince you not to run back to Paris."

Her conscience stirred but she was unwilling to break the pleasant mood with a serious discussion. "If I ate like that every night, I'd weigh two hundred pounds and have a hard time fitting in a plane seat."

"Maybe I can come up with other persuasions not as fattening."

She glanced at his profile as he started the car and headed for Fairfax Avenue. She wondered if his hope of keeping her in Los Angeles stemmed from loyalty to her father or from personal interest. He hadn't made a single gesture that could be interpreted as romantic, yet there was a wistfulness in his voice at times. Smiling, she turned to watch the busy panorama of Fairfax Avenue as they turned south. He was taking her home. No suggestion of stopping at his apartment for a nightcap.

When they reached the house, he pulled into the driveway and walked her to the door. "Thanks for a pleasant evening, Arisa. You're good company."

"It's really the other way around, Tanner. This is the first time I've relaxed since I left Paris—thanks to you."

He looked solemn in the yellow light of the pagoda lamp installed beside the front door. "That's nice to hear. Anyone as beautiful as you deserves a good time. Good night, Arisa, sweet dreams."

"Good night, Tanner . . ."

She watched him walk down to the car and then let herself in. Dropping her handbag on the hall table, she paused, frowning, in the doorway of the living room, and glanced around uneasily. The lamp she'd left on cast a soft glow that kept the corners of the room in shadow, but it was bright enough to see that everything was in place. Yet a faint trickle of apprehension stroked the back of her neck. She glanced down the hall toward the dining room and kitchen. The shadows changed from gray to black gloom. She wished she'd left more lights on. She cocked her head and listened. The ticking of the clock in the dining room seemed loud in the silence.

She tried to shake her uneasiness by telling herself her imagination was working overtime. She stepped toward the door to call Tanner back but heard the sound of the car's engine as he pulled away. She chided herself for being such a ninny. Boldly, she snapped on the hall light. There was a faint rustle of sound from the end of the hall. Panicked, she snapped off the light, her heart pounding. Her father's study! During a moment of indecision about which way she should flee, the door of the study opened and a figure emerged. It was too dark to see anything but a blur as it sprang toward her with the swiftness of a panther. She whirled for the door but he was upon her and dragging her back savagely. Her spine arched under the pressure of his powerful grip as his hand clamped over her mouth to choke off her startled cry. Fighting for breath, she kicked viciously and clawed at his iron fingers, but she was no match for the brute strength of her assailant. While gripping her mouth with one hand, his other found the indentation at the base of her skull and deftly applied pressure. Arisa had the sensation of floating as she lost consciousness and slumped to the floor.

She woke slowly, still drifting in the gray-velvet fog that engulfed her. For several moments, memory eluded her, then she opened her eyes with a start. Her pulse raced as she recalled her attacker, and she looked around quickly. The house was quiet except for the loud ticking of the clock. Slowly, she sat up, not trusting her first appraisal. There was nothing—no one lurking in the shadows, no sound—to betray anyone's presence. She tasted blood at her lip where the rough hand of her assailant had held her. Shaking, she crawled to the phone stand. Her hand was trembling as she dialed the police emergency number pasted under the receiver. With her gaze glued to the dark end of the hall, she shivered until the call was answered.

"Beverly Hills Police Station."

"There's someone in my house..." Her voice broke into a panicked sob. She didn't realize she was whispering until the policeman asked her to repeat what she'd said.

"I—I surprised an intruder in my house..."

"Is he there now?" The voice was briskly efficient.

"I—I'm not sure."

"What's the address?"

She gave it to him.

"We'll have a car there right away. Where are you now?"

"In the front hall."

"Stay there. Don't wander through the house and don't go outside. Do you understand?"

She nodded, then realized he couldn't see her. "Yes," she said weakly.

She put the phone back and leaned against the wall. If the intruder were still there, he'd have heard her, she was sure. She stared into the shadows, trying to assure herself she was alone. My God, she could have been killed. She shuddered and hugged her arms around her body. *Get a grip on yourself... if he'd intended to harm you, he'd have done it when he had the chance. He's gone. Whatever he was after, he found it or you frightened him off.* She leaned sideways and peered into the dimly lit living room. Nothing had been disturbed. Summoning her courage, she got up and inspected the room more closely. The jade... the *sancai*... the T'ang horse... all where they

belonged. Instead of reassuring her, the fact frightened her all
the more.

The sound of a car stopping made her hurry to the front
door. She stood with her hand on the lock until a knock
sounded.

"Who is it?"

"Police."

She undid the door quickly. A uniformed man stepped inside.

"You called about an intruder?"

She nodded. "I'd been out to dinner. I surprised him."

"Where was he?"

She pointed down the hall. "In my father's study."

The man motioned her toward the living room and moved
quietly down the passage, his gun drawn. He stopped outside
the study door, standing to one side. Reaching for the knob,
he flung the door open and pressed back. He snaked an arm
around the jamb and found the light switch. In a split second,
he was in a crouch, gun aimed through the open doorway.
Slowly, he stood up and went inside. A minute later he came
out, turned on the kitchen light and then the one in the dining
room.

"What's upstairs?" he asked Arisa when he returned to the
archway from which she'd been unable to move.

"Three bedrooms. Mine is in the back. The other two are
in the front. There's a bath off the hall and two closets."

He moved to the foot of the stairs and flipped another light
switch. The upstairs hall brightened. A second uniformed man
entered the front door.

"Nothing around back, Jim."

"Stay with her," the policeman said as he began to climb.
When he reached eye level with the upper hall, he paused to
look carefully through the balustrades before he continued the
rest of the way.

The second cop stayed where he could see both Arisa and
the upper hall. He was tensed for any sound that would indicate
his partner was in danger. He relaxed visibly when Jim came
down again.

"Nothing. It doesn't look as if it's been ransacked, neither
does the study." He looked at Arisa. "You're sure someone
was here?"

"Positive." She'd regained some of her composure. "He

came out of my father's study and jumped me before I could get to the door."

"Are you hurt?" the second cop asked.

"More frightened than anything. He grabbed me from behind and covered my mouth. I struggled, but he did something to the back of my neck and I don't remember anything else. She glanced at the slim gold watch on her wrist. "I wasn't out more than a few minutes."

"Enough time to make his escape." Jim indicated the living room. "Would you like to sit down?"

Beside him, the phone shrilled and Arisa took two frightened steps backward. She stumbled, but the policeman caught her arm.

"You'd better sit down."

"No, I'm all right. It startled me." She reached for the phone. "Yes?"

"Arisa?"

"Yes?" She was so nervous it was difficult to get words out.

"This is Carter. Are you all right? You sound...Are you all right?"

She let out her breath. "Carter...yes, I'm all right. I've had a bit of excitement, that's all."

"What happened?"

"We're not sure. I was out and surprised a burglar in the house when I came back."

"Good God, are you hurt? I'm coming right over."

"No! I'm all right, really."

"I'm coming over." The line went dead.

Arisa shook her head and said foolishly, "He's coming over."

"Maybe it's a good idea for you to have someone here for awhile. Make you feel more secure," the policeman called Jim said. "Now, do you feel up to going through the house with us to see if anything's missing? The place looks intact, but you'll have to check."

They walked through room by room, as she looked at shelves, checked drawers, opened cupboards. As far as she could tell, nothing was missing. Valuable small objects that could easily have been pocketed were not disturbed. The only thing she could point to was that her father's desk had been gone through. "I sorted everything just a few days ago. It was neat when I left it." Now papers, pencils, and other items were askew as if they'd been pawed through hurriedly.

"Looks like he just got started. Either that or he knew where he wanted to look. Anything missing from the desk?"

She made a hopeless gesture. "I don't have an inventory, but there wasn't anything of value, I'm sure. My father died two weeks ago and I was called home from France. I went through everything."

"I'm sorry. . . . We can write up a report if you want to file an assault charge. Not much else we can do." He gave her an apologetic smile. "Any idea how he might have gotten in? There's no sign of forced entry, not that it rules out the possibility."

Arisa shook her head. "I'm sure I locked up before I left."

"Who else has a key to the house?"

"I—I'm not sure. My father insisted I keep mine. There's a cleaning woman. I have no idea how many other keys there are."

He led her back to the living room and took notes while she told him everything she could. When she mentioned the shop, he looked interested and asked if she kept any valuable pieces around the house. She indicated the furniture and art objects surrounding them. "Any of these would be worth a great deal. My parents collected them over a long time."

He looked surprised and a little impressed. "Then my bet is your intruder was looking for something special. Do you have any idea what he might have expected to find in the desk?"

"None whatever. I doubt that my father was in the habit of keeping large amounts of cash on hand." She thought ruefully of the stack of unpaid bills she'd sent to Carter.

"Did he have a gun?"

"I didn't see one. He moved so quickly—but I'm sure his hands were empty."

"I mean your father."

Startled, she shook her head. "No—at least I don't think so, unless he kept it at the shop."

The policeman turned as the doorbell rang. Arisa said, "That will be Carter Montaigne, my father's partner. He can answer that better than I."

Carter came directly to Arisa to assure himself she was all right. His handsome face was darkly angry. "Just what happened?" he demanded, facing the two policemen.

Not questioning his authority, the one called Jim related the events that had brought him and his partner to the house. Carter looked at Arisa when he heard she'd been knocked out.

"Are you hurt? Come over here and sit down."

She tried to protest but he led her firmly to the sofa. Unaccountably, her knees began to tremble as she sat down. Carter went to the door with the two officers and talked in a low tone for several minutes before he closed the door and snapped the bolt.

"Now then," he said, returning, "do you keep the booze in the same cupboard Elliot did?"

She nodded, and he vanished down the hall. She heard him scoop ice cubes. Now that it was over, her body began to react. The weakness in her legs radiated, dancing with needlelike sharpness through her until she shuddered and had to hug her arms. She didn't hear Carter come back until he was sitting beside her.

"Here, this will help." He pressed a cold glass into her hand. She started to tell him not to coddle her, but she was gripped by another wave of shakiness. She drank some of the liquor and began to feel better. She smiled.

"Feel like talking?"

"There's nothing to say. I'm confused..."

"You can't add anything to what the officer told me?"

"Not a thing. I haven't any idea who he was or what he wanted." She shuddered and swallowed some of the drink. "All I know is, I didn't like it one bit. I'm going to have new locks put on all the doors tomorrow—and chains!"

"I'll take care of it for you."

"That's not necessary!" It came out sharply and she saw the flash of annoyance in his eyes. She sighed and bit her lip. "I'm sorry, I didn't mean to snap. I guess my nerves are more on edge than I thought. I've never had anything like this happen before."

"No need to apologize." He put his arm across the back of the sofa and began to rub the back of her neck gently. She winced. "Tender?"

"Not really." His first touch had been electric and completely unexpected. As his fingers continued to work soothingly at her taut muscles, she began to relax.

His fingertips kneaded gently until the knotted muscles succumbed. "Feel better?"

"Mmmmm."

"All right, finish your drink while I double-check the doors and windows. You'll feel a lot different after a good night's sleep."

She listened as his footsteps went through the upstairs rooms, then the rear of the house. His presence was reassuring, but a shadowy edge of doubt began to niggle at her. Carter had never called before. Why tonight? After the way she'd stormed out of his office earlier, she'd expected him to be very angry and distant. Was there any connection between what had happened and his phone call? There couldn't be. Coincidence, nothing more.

She busied herself with her drink as he returned to the living room.

"I'll go now so you can get to bed. Bolt the door when I leave. Everything else is secure. I suggest you keep the air conditioner on tonight instead of opening windows, just to be on the safe side. I'll send a locksmith over in the morning before I leave."

"You're leaving?"

He gave an embarrassed laugh. "I completely forgot. That's what I called about. I'm going to Paris. I had a call this afternoon about a piece I've been wanting for a long time. The only way to get it is to go over for a few days. I had the bookkeeper draw up a voucher for expenses and a letter of credit. This may be just what we need."

Despite his warm manner, she felt anger stir inside her. "What about those corners Travish-Montaigne has to cut? The cash flow problems?"

He gave her a disarming smile. "If this deal works out the way I expect, it may put a permanent end to them."

"And if it doesn't?" She was being churlish, but she still resented his cavalier treatment.

His dark eyes held her in a studied gaze, as though he was making up his mind whether or not to be angry. Finally, he shrugged. "The trip won't be wasted. There are several other things I want to pick up. I've asked Deline to take you under her wing. You're free to come and go in the shop as you please. If there's anything Deline can't answer. I'll be back in a few days. I left some books on my desk you might find interesting. Now, if you're sure you're all right, I'll go."

She was already sorry she'd baited him. She got to her feet and walked to the door. "Thank you for coming over. I appreciate it. I'm sorry if I sounded snappish. It really helped having you here."

He smiled. "I'm just macho enough to like that." He lifted her chin with his hand and kissed her with such gentleness that her legs trembled.

"Good night, Arisa. Be sure to bolt the door." Then he was gone.

She slipped the dead bolt and leaned against the door. It was a day for surprises. His kiss was the last thing in the world she'd expected.... but then, Carter Montaigne seemed full of surprises. Smiling, she turned off the lights and went upstairs. To her amazement, she fell asleep quickly, and her dreams were not of dark, sinister burglars but of Carter's gentle touch.

YEAR OF THE MONKEY

China, August 1944

They first saw the Japanese soldiers about midday. Two children who'd gone to the river for water came running back into the village with the water jars bouncing on the poles and splashing their bare legs. Before the women could scold them for being careless, they broke into an excited babble, pointing and gesturing toward the eastern valley.

In the clearing where she and two other women were slapping sun-dried rice sheaves against bamboo screens, Mai Yun paused to listen to the breathless high-pitched voices. A hard knot gathered under her heart.

Soldiers . . . trucks . . . tanks . . .

She dropped the half-threshed sheaf and raced for the fields. The men were almost hidden by the tall ripe grain. The swish of their sickles hummed like the drone of insects. Shading her eyes, she searched until she saw Elliot at the end of the line. Ignoring the angry cries of the harvesters, she trampled a path through the grain as she raced to his side.

He looked up with surprise. "Mai Yun!"

"Quickly, come!"

"We're not finished."

Angrily, she yanked the sickle from his hand and threw it into the sea of swaying gold. "Do as I say!" She jerked his arm and pulled him back toward the huts.

Docile but reluctant, he stumbled after her. His hat slipped back and caught around his neck by its straw fastenings. It banged at his shoulders with every step. He tried to question her, but she only shook her head and urged him to move faster. After his first surprise, he realized something drastic had happened to put her in such a fright. The child? He began to run.

At the hut, he went immediately to the rice basket that had been made into a cradle. The child was sleeping peacefully. He whirled. Mai Yun was gathering up the few clothes they'd accumulated. He grabbed her and forced her to look at him.

"Will you tell me what the devil is wrong?" he demanded.

176

She cocked her head like a bird's. Outside a chorus of women's voices were calling men from the harvest. Mai Yun whispered, "Hurry, there is no time. Soldiers!"

"Here?" Elliot looked at her dumbfounded. She freed herself so she could bundle together their things.

"Whose?" he demanded, grabbing her arm again.

"The children saw them. We cannot stay here. They will be at the village within an hour."

Stunned, he stared through the doorway and wiped his face. "Maybe they're Chinese. Chiang Kai-shek..."

"Don't be a fool! The Japanese hold the entire coast. They must be Japanese!"

It made sense, but he fought logic. "Chiang Kai-shek's army is on the move."

"The soldiers come from Canton," she said savagely. "They are Japanese. We will be killed if we stay." She thrust the bundle of clothing into his arms. "We have not endured these years to be taken now." She went to the basket and scooped up the sleeping child. He whimpered softly, then settled in her arms. Mai Yun faced Elliot. Her jaw was set determinedly, her gaze hard.

Outside the babble had taken on a tinge of panic as the villagers scurried about. Elliot had mastered only a smattering of the difficult dialect, but it was enough to tell him that Mai Yun's verdict about the soldiers was general. The village was being evacuated before the tanks and trucks came far enough up the river to see the smoke.

The baby stirred as Mai Yun tucked him into a back sling and turned so Elliot could help her adjust it. She knotted the sashes quickly.

The soldiers would follow the river. Instinctively, the villagers turned the opposite way, moving toward the distant hills like a scurrying rat pack. A child wailed but was quickly hushed. Two middle-aged men carried a grandmother between them. Within minutes, only a thin trail of smoke from the fire showed where they had been.

An hour later, Po Mu, the village elder, halted them. By now, the soldiers would be approaching the village. Any movement of the plains grass would point a trail directly to them. He ordered everyone to scatter and lie flat so they could listen for sounds of pursuit.

The sun was hot and dry. Their clothes were filmed with

dust and bits of pollen. Mai Yun raised her *san* to nurse the baby as she settled beside Elliot, resting her head comfortably on his shoulder. The baby gurgled as he nuzzled the nipple, then quieted to contented sucking. Elliot pressed his hand at Mai Yun's shoulder, then closed his eyes and listened. Except for the high shrill of the cicadas, they were wrapped in silence.

What did it mean, Japanese soldiers coming west? There was nothing for hundreds of miles but tiny villages in the midst of paltry acres of rice land. Even though the countryside was technically in Chiang's sphere, not even the Chinese had ever found it worth laying hand to. Their village was remote and isolated—no weapons, no industry, only a pittance of food. The Japs couldn't be that desperate. No, they had to be on the move westward. They'd follow the river inland to—where?

He turned to look at the harsh sun-bleached sky and the far-off peaks of the western mountains. What was over there? Something worth fighting for? The Japs must think so. The few fragments of news the villagers had gleaned during the past two years gave only a hazy picture of how the war was going. It was said the tide had changed. If rumors were to be believed, the Phillippines were back in Allied hands. A good sign. Maybe it foreshadowed an end to the war. Maybe a push was being concentrated on China to drive out the invaders. He wanted to believe it, but the Japanese had been in China so long that he wondered if it was possible.

He thought about what his life had become. He rarely felt guilt anymore that he wasn't part of the war. Each man was destined to go his own way, whatever fate decreed. He'd come to believe Mai Yun in that. His life—their life—was here. There was a measure of contentment in his day-to-day living. Mai Yun was good for him. She was happy to take each day as it came. The baby was a source of joy to her from conception. He'd worried about her pregnancy in the harsh environs of the village, but she'd blossomed and grown strong instead of evidencing difficulty. Even the boy's birth had been uncomplicated and quick, accomplished in the span of the few afternoon hours he'd worked in the fields. When the men came in at the end of the day, Mai Yun greeted him as she worked over the hearth. The baby, his son, lay in the shade of the hut, squinting with unfocused gaze. She called him Dai-yat Tsai, first son.

That night, lying with Mai Yun in the circle of his arms, he'd dreamed of Melisande. He woke sweating in the cold spring wind and crept from the sleeping mat to sit outside and stare into the darkness.

Now, a sudden burst of rifle fire brought him up abruptly. Scowling, Mai Yun dragged him back. He realized the sounds had come from a distance, probably back at the village. He listened for a command from Po Mu, but the elder was silent.

Mai Yun drew him close to her whispering lips. "They are trying to flush the quarry. Their bullets cannot reach us here as long as we do not give away our presence."

Reassured, he settled back. Would the soldiers spread out and try to find the trail of the villagers? The fire left burning had told them they couldn't be far. A second volley of shots sang through the hills. Then the valley fell quiet. The sun crept another hour's passage before Elliot lifted his head above the tall grass and scanned the distance. A plume of smoke. Nothing else.

They spent the night in the field. At dawn, one of the men crept out silently. When he returned, he reported that the soldiers were under way, following the river westward. The village had been sacked and burned. The thrashed grain had been taken, but the fields had been left untouched.

When the sun reached the tip of the mountains, they made their way back to the village. They would begin again.

7

Carter emerged from customs and glanced around the waiting area without slowing his stride. People were jostling to greet the arrivals, but there was no sign of Claire's flaxen head. Despite her promise, he didn't really expect her to meet the plane. She was probably on Fairchild's yacht or off at some country villa. She wasn't one to sit around waiting.

He was still fresh after the long flight and his step was brisk. He'd read most of the way, catnapped briefly, and was totally rested. His inner time clock adapted readily to his demands, and he never suffered jet lag.

He moved away from the crowd and stepped outside, thinking about the tantalizing possibility that Harry had uncovered a Vezzi. Harry had a knack for ferreting out valuable antiques. He'd be a ne'er-do-well except for his charming ability to put together people and the things they wanted. "One man's junk is another man's treasure," Harry claimed. Harry found "junk" and turned it into treasure. And even when the owner knew it wasn't junk, Harry had a way of convincing him it was worth parting with for a price, usually about half of what he resold it for.

"Carter!"

A silver Ferrari was double-parked beyond a row of taxis. Claire stood in the open jaws of the driver's door, waving.

"Carter! Here!"

He edged between two tightly parked cabs as she scowled at a honking driver who was impatient to pass the stalled line of traffic. Tossing his bag, he climbed in as she settled behind the wheel.

"Damned traffic," she said leaning toward him. "I was afraid I'd miss you. You look great." Ignoring the blaring horns, she offered her mouth for a kiss. When he obliged, she prolonged it intimately as if they were alone in a secluded place.

"I'm glad you're here."

He grinned. "You'd better get us out of here before the guy

in the Citroën decides to go right over us."

She made a pert face. *"Fous le camp."*

He wasn't sure if it was directed at him or the driver behind. Skillfully she checked the rearview mirror as she shifted gears, let the clutch out, and shot the car into the moving traffic. She was attentive, despite her careless attitude. He settled back and stretched his legs.

"Have you seen Harry?"

She glanced at him sidelong. "Damn it, you could pretend you came to be with me."

He shrugged and gave her a smile. Claire never stopped trying.

She pouted. "I've seen him, but not the great Vezzi. He's waiting for you."

"Considerate of him," Carter said wryly. It paid to know where the bodies were hidden—or at least to have Harry think he did. "Did you arrange a meeting?"

She nodded. "Lunch tomorrow at Café Marie. I knew you'd want to see him as soon as possible." She tossed him a provocative smile. "Maybe when you get that over with, you'll feel like popping down to Monaco to catch up with the Fairchilds."

She made it sound like a quick trip to the suburbs for cocktails. For her, it was. The idle rich thought nothing of indulging themselves, and the hell with time or money. It was one of the things that had come between them and eventually split them apart. The fact that they'd had a business to run never prevented Claire from dashing off whenever pleasure beckoned.

"I can't ignore my friends," she always said. "They have houses and apartments—that makes them potential clients, darling." It was a rationale that made cockeyed sense because it worked. Claire kept up the social life and he minded the store. The difference between the heiress and the kid from Brooklyn. Except that she would have liked it better if he'd played truant with her more often. She had no need for the money from business endeavors. She'd dabbled in a few before the salon, and each had been successful to a degree. Clair was motivated by challenge and a need to win. But the game won was no longer a challenge, and she tossed it aside to go on to something new. He had refused to let the salon become one of her cast-offs. When he'd finally walked out, he'd tossed the gauntlet by predicting she'd give it up within a year instead of developing it to its full potential. Furious, she'd sworn to make him eat his words—and she'd refused to buy him outright and arranged his payoff over a period of three years. With her father's battery of lawyers, she'd made it stick. Carter had been replaced by Pierre Michel whom Carter himself had trained, and who moved up from assistant manager. The business was flourishing. To Claire, delayed checks were just another way of winning, an excuse to keep Carter on a tight leash. Much as she wouldn't admit it, Claire still relied on his advice.

"I wangled a catalogue for the Matique sale. Germaine's hoping you'll stay long enough to come. She claims you give tone to her little 'gatherings.'" She flicked him a shrewd glance. "She'd snatch you up in a minute if you'd move to Paris."

"She already has a kennel of pet poodles."

Claire threw back her head and laughed. "She'd have kittens if she heard you say that. She thinks it's only a matter of time until you fall into her bed."

He rolled his eyes expressively, and Claire laughed again. Germaine Garnier was seventy with a face like a basset hound. The glittering diamonds that drew her a coterie of sycophants also slashed them to bleeding shark-bait when she tired of them. But her gallery on Avenue George V was a showcase for collectors. For dealers she liked, Germaine offered choice pieces on a resale commission basis: a respectable quick profit and a small percentage of the buyer's eventual resale net. No one else did business that way, but then no one else had Germaine's nerve or steel-trap mind. She kept track of every antique in the business through her plexus of fawning dilletantes.

"I'm sure she'll survive in the meantime," Carter said.

Claire smiled. "A woman needs more than survival, darling. Ask me."

He gave her a skeptical look that showed he was aware of her game and wanted no part of it.

For an instant, her lips tightened. She spun the car out to pass a slow-moving Damlier, then zipped back into the lane so sharply there was a screech of brakes behind them. He smiled, unruffled. She still considered him one of her failures. He'd left unconquered.

After a moment, Claire flashed a smile. "Do you remember Nicolai Penzov?"

"The funny little Russian?"

She nodded. "I'm doing his apartment, if I don't wind up

a basket case first. His taste hasn't improved. He insists on keeping those monstrosities he calls heirlooms. His family would have done him a favor if they'd let that trash get burned in the Revolution. But I'm doing the best I can with his limited imagination. I went for simple lines in the upholstered pieces and relied on textures instead of prints. Earthtones with blue for contrast. I need a piece for the front corner that won't clash with that horrible gilt pier glass he refuses to move from that wall. I'm sure he has a safe behind it. He screams if I touch it." She drove with one hand as she made sweeping gestures. "So it's up to me to find a 'truly exotic and priceless piece,'" she mimicked, "to fit under it. I tried a *certosina cassone*, but he said it looked like a coffin." She sighed and made a gesture of resignation.

"If I remember correctly, that pier glass is a Kent-Goodison. The only other one is at the Victoria Albert in London."

"Too bad Nicolai doesn't donate this one." She gave a mock shudder.

"A table would be better than something low."

"Mmm, I considered that."

"Maybe glass to emphasize the mirror's surface instead of the frame. Christie's has a blue and amber Imperial table. It's got bronze and ormolu mounts, but they're understated and would tie the two pieces together."

Her eyes widened. "You may be right."

"The Russian origins should please him."

"Utterly delight him!" She wrinkled her nose. "I have a Christie catalogue at the apartment. I'll send a bid."

Her good humor was completely restored and her face was animated. She would take credit for the idea and lap up compliments like a preening cat. He glanced at the city skyline outlined against the changing light. The richly clouded sky was a pewter-and-blue dome over spires and rooftops. Within an hour, lights would paint a fireworks shower across the horizon. Claire was like Paris—dark and sulky one moment and ablaze with sparkling lights the next. No wonder Arisa reminded him of her.

He felt a flicker of surprise that Arisa popped into his thoughts so readily. He'd surprised himself last night when he'd kissed her; he still wasn't sure what had prompted it except that she looked so vulnerable. Just when he'd begun to think of her as a tough opponent. Easy, he cautioned himself. One fluttering leaf doesn't make an autumn.

Claire maneuvered the Ferrari through the traffic circle at L'Etoile and turned into Avenue Foch. She slowed along a solid line of parked vehicles, then made a wide sweep into a drive mid-block at a row of undistinguished flats, and brought the car to a halt. A doorman and parking valet materialized instantly.

"*Bonsoir*, Mademoiselle Prigent."

"*Bonsoir*, Henri. Put the car away, we won't be needing it tonight."

"*Oui*, mademoiselle."

Claire gestured toward Carter's suitcase. "Have it brought up."

"*Oui*, mademoiselle."

She tucked her arm through Carter's. "We'll have a quiet dinner. There's so much to talk about."

Knowing her, he hadn't expected otherwise. He smiled, wondering why he still felt affection for her in spite of everything. She thought she was winning a round by his ready acquiescence, but that was all right. Claire's rounds were very tempting and very temporary.

An attempt had been made to soften the starkness of the lobby by adding an Ottoman rug to the marble floor and placing several Louis XV chairs across from the concierge's table. The white-haired porter looked up with a brisk nod, showing he was permitting a resident to pass. The elevator was at the ground level. It rattled noisily, then settled to a smooth ascent to the top floor.

The concierge had called from the lobby, and a woman in tailored dove-gray was waiting at the door of the flat. She smiled as she recognized Carter.

"Good evening, Mr. Montaigne."

"Good evening, Mrs. Vals." Carter smiled warmly. The housekeeper had been with Claire for six years, maintaining the Paris apartment, one in London, and a penthouse in Brentwood. Despite her soft mien, she ruled the staffs with an iron hand; no breath of discord ever disrupted their even flow or reached her mistress's hearing. She coached maids, cooks and valets and supervised the accounts, menus, and countless details that made Claire a perfect hostess.

As they entered the flat, Claire asked for drinks to be brought to the living room. Mrs. Vals vanished.

Despite the ordinary appearance of the building's exterior, the flat was unashamedly luxurious. It had been completely done over to Claire's taste. A wall of mirrors and a mirrored console reflected an uncluttered, hard-edge image of white walls and parquet floor. Beside the lamp, a silver vase displayed a tall arrangement of white lilies and blood-red roses. In a large silver pot near the archway to the living room, a lush palm added a natural touch.

Claire unbuttoned the jacket of her white suit as they walked through to the spacious living room. She tossed it aside and flung herself onto the gray suede sofa. She patted the cushion beside her.

He ignored the suggestion and walked to the uncurtained windows to look out at the tree-lined avenue below. After a moment, he turned and surveyed the room. Claire had blended New York comfort with the rich elegance of aristocratic Paris. As many times as he'd been here, the place never failed to impress him, with its blend of the modern and the antique. Seeing what she'd done with this apartment had strongly influenced his decision to go into business with her five years ago. Too bad he hadn't seen the clues to her inconsistent personality in the unorthodox decor. But like the flat, Claire was pleasing and unusual in many ways.

"You look as if you should be leaning on a stone column with a cigarette dangling from the corner of your mouth. What evil thoughts are running around inside your head, Bogie?"

He laughed, glancing at a flower-filled Chinese porcelain vase resting on a glass pedestal. "Humphrey Bogart wouldn't be caught dead in this room."

"Thank heaven! Now come and sit—or would you rather I tell Mrs. Vals to delay dinner, and we'll take our drinks to the bedroom?"

"That's a Bacall line if I ever heard one."

"It worked for her."

He chuckled and sat at the other end of the long sofa. Claire made a moue and tucked her slim legs under her hip.

"You're very remote. Aren't you glad to see me?"

"Certainly, but I'm not a puppet on a string anymore, Claire. I didn't fly halfway around the world to pop into bed with you, no matter how enticing the idea may be. You know I came to see Harry's Vezzi. You knew it would get me here, that's why you dangled it as bait."

"All's fair..." She glanced around as a maid in a black uniform and white apron came in with a tray.

He waited until the drinks had been served and they were alone again. "The end of that quote is, 'in love and war,' if I'm not mistaken. Which is this?"

"Don't be absurd, darling." She was angry. When she looked at him, her eyes were icy. "Is it your new partner, your little protégée? Is that what you're so tense about?"

"Arisa?" he asked astonished.

She nodded, and her eyes were feral. She sipped her drink and regarded him over the rim of the Baccarat crystal.

"Whatever gave you an idea like that?" He laughed, but she didn't smile.

"I saw the way you looked at her. I thought you had had your fill of female partners. You told me that when you left."

"I didn't exactly choose Arisa."

"Is she going to stay?"

"I'm not sure. Does it matter?"

"It should to you."

He was annoyed. "Of course it does, but I can't do anything about it. I made her an offer. She refused, but I think she'll come around eventually."

"What about the brother?"

He snorted. "He's eager to sell, but unfortunately he doesn't have enough stock to worry about."

"I've met him, you know."

"Before the funeral?"

"Uh-huh. Halsey Holderbein gave a wrap party when they finished filming "The Thorn." We did the master suite for him when he bought that four-level in Malibu."

He remembered the account but hadn't gone to the party.

"Quentin Travish was there. Came with Peti Martin. I remember wondering how she survived the drive out. He was something from central casting—the typical bore every party must have. I don't know where Peti found him, but she threw him back fast. Several mutual friends refused to invite her anywhere if she brought him."

Carter smiled at the harsh appraisal of Quentin. Claire was given to excesses.

"Tried to corner half the people there about investments. It wouldn't have been so bad if he'd at least patted an ass or two—maybe some of the women might have gone for his line."

"Maybe some of the men, too," Carter said drily.

"I'm sure of it, but I don't think Quentin Travish even knows about the peccadillos of the birds and bees. I couldn't believe he was Elliot's son—I mean, really. Just consider yourself very fortunate, darling, that Quentin didn't inherit his father's share of the business. Not that *I* wouldn't prefer him to Arisa," she said pointedly.

"I believe you're jealous," Carter said with a smile.

"Would you care?"

He smiled and touched the hand on the cushion between them. "Of course I would."

She gazed at him searchingly, knowing he was lying but willing to accept it as an apology for his lack of passion. "Then come over here and convince me you're glad to be with me. . . ."

Without taking his gaze from her, he set his drink aside and took her in his arms. She melted against him and found his lips. In spite of himself, he felt desire stir. She tantalized him with her tongue. When he finally disengaged himself, she snuggled against him.

"That's much better," she sighed. "But only an appetizer."

"You'll have to wait for dessert."

"Patience isn't my long suit," she said, lazily playing a hand along his thigh. She was silent awhile, then asked, "What happened to the claim that girl made for the thousand dollars Elliot owed her?"

"Nothing yet. We've only got her word for it. Forbes doesn't want to pay her."

"I think she's probably telling the truth," Claire said.

Astonished, he pulled back to look at her. "What makes you say that?" She couldn't possibly know Lily.

Claire gave him an enigmatic smile. "Elliot was always borrowing cash, you know that."

"I don't know any such thing. What the devil are you talking about? He was a spender but . . ."

She shook her head ruefully. "Really, Carter, don't be naive. In the last two or three years he tapped me a dozen times."

"What!"

"I thought you knew." She laughed softly and reached for her drink. "Friendly little loans. He always paid them back— and he usually took me out to lunch or dinner as 'interest.' I'm sure if he hadn't died so suddenly, he would have paid Lily exactly when he said he would."

It was his evening for surprises. He hadn't even known that

Claire dated Elliot—if that's what it could be called. She saw the incredulity in his expression and chucked him under the chin.

"Jealous, darling?"

"Astonished is more like it. It would seem I didn't know Elliot as well as I thought." He'd faulted Arisa for that same shortcoming. What else didn't he know about Elliot Travish? He studied Claire's face. "I guess I didn't know you all that well either."

"Darling," she chided. "It was good business to know Elliot, you told me that yourself. We always went to him when we needed something Oriental."

Still puzzled, Carter frowned. "Did he ever say what the cash was for?"

She shrugged. "I never asked, but I had the feeling it was some kind of a running debt or obligation. I remember he laughed once about it being that time of the month again."

The maid reappeared and announced dinner. Claire insisted on an end to serious conversation while they enjoyed an intimate candlelight meal in the neoclassically inspired dining room done in vibrant reds and golds. Soft lights illuminated an adjoining terrace lush with greenery. The effect was of dining by moonlight. A Brahms symphony from a hidden stereo completed the seductive setting. When the cheese was cleared, they retired to the bedroom by mutual consent.

A hundred years earlier, Harry Cherney would have been called a dandy. He was thin, dapper, and had a pencil mustache and dark sensual eyes that women found irresistible. He claimed to have been born in France, but his English had a faint twang of midwest America. Carter suspected his background was as carefully designed as his perfectly tailored appearance. Half a dozen women turned to watch him cross the patio of the Cafe Marie. Harry glanced at each of them with a smile of promise.

When he spied Carter, he veered between the sun-dappled tables.

"Carter, my friend! How good to see you in our favorite place!" Bending, he grasped Carter's fingers in his slender, almost feminine hands. For a moment, Carter thought he was going to go through the hypocrisy of presenting his cheek, but Harry released him and drew a chair around so that it was out of the sun. "You look fantastic, but then you always do."

"Same old Harry."

The small man grinned. "I would disappoint a cast of thousands if I were to change, *non*?"

"A thousand women, anyway. How have you been?"

"Couldn't be better. Have you ordered?"

Carter shook his head, and Harry waggled his fingers to catch the eye of a waiter, who ducked past red-fringed umbrellas and came toward them.

"The usual?" Harry queried.

Carter nodded and let Harry order a bottle of Chambertin and *agneau à la broche*. Harry settled back and lit a Galoise with a gold lighter. He inhaled appreciatively.

"Claire says you're onto a Vezzi," Carter said without preamble.

Harry blew smoke lazily. "Always business, Carter, always business. I hoped you were glad to see an old friend."

"I'm overwhelmed, Harry, mainly because you have a Vezzi. Or at least you say you do."

Harry looked pained. His face was guileless except for a glint in his eyes that put Carter in mind of diamonds under a harsh jeweler's light. "I do have one, Carter." He sat forward and puffed a short blast of smoke. "I came across it in a villa near Cannes. The Marquise de Mativare—do you know her?"

"I've never had the pleasure."

Harry grinned. "Pleasure is in the eye of the beholder. The marquise affords more pleasure if one keeps his eyes closed. She is a veritable dragon but like all women, susceptible to charm. When I saw the bric-a-brac that her dear departed husband, the marquis, stuffed into that villa, believe me, I was my most charming. She's sitting on a fortune down there, and she doesn't give a damn. She already has so much money she'll never be able to count it in her lifetime, and she has no direct heirs to pass it on to." He wagged his head at the sorry thought.

"The Vezzi," Carter prompted.

"Ah, yes. I paid dearly for it, my friend—not in cash, since the marquise is not impressed by such mundane payment." He winked and sighed heavily. "After a week at the villa, I was able to persuade her to let me have a little memento of our *intimité*."

"Exactly what is the piece?"

"A chinoiserie vase."

"Is it marked?"

Harry bobbed his head and his eyes glinted. *"Venezia,* but I recognized it before I turned it over. It's genuine, Carter, trust me."

"That would be a bit like sending the wolf to babysit for grandma," Carter commented drily. Harry laughed good-naturedly. "Has anyone else looked at it?"

"Word may have slipped out that I possess this incredible treasure, but I have reserved first refusal for you, my friend."

It was probably closer to the truth that Harry had leaked the news of the Vezzi himself in order to stimulate excitement if he decided to put the vase up for competitive bidding. Unlike the marquise, Harry's thoughts were constantly on money.

The waiter arrived with glasses and a bottle of wine which he uncorked expertly. Pouring, he waited until Harry sampled it and pronounced his approval, then filled the glasses and set the bottle where it was out of the sun.

"I'd like to see it."

Harry sipped his wine. "I have it at my flat."

"You left it in that rat trap? A four-year-old could pick the lock on that door, Harry." Carter was astounded at Harry's lack of precaution. If the vase was indeed a Vezzi, it was worth a fortune.

Harry shrugged off the implication of danger. "Ah, but even a four-year-old would not bother to break into such an obvious hovel, *non?* What could he expect to find? The flat is the perfect place to keep it."

There was a crude logic to what he said, but it still made Carter nervous to think of a priceless work of art in Harry's Left Bank rooms. There were collectors who would kill for a genuine Vezzi.

"We'll go immediately after lunch," Carter said.

"You're interested?"

"Sure, but I want to see it—and I want another opinion." Vezzi was the most forged name in porcelain. There were hundreds of fakes sitting in various collections, because eager buyers were too greedy to take precautions.

"No problem," Harry said. He sat back with a confident air and refilled the wine glasses. The main item of business settled, he entertained Carter with a lively account of his week with the marquise and his *bon vivant* existence. He was a born raconteur, and an hour passed pleasantly as they enjoyed succulent broiled lamb, seasoned to perfection with herbs and a touch of garlic, as well as tiny fresh peas and new potatoes from Marie's own garden. Carter was invigorated by the magnificent summer day and the chance to be back in Paris. Overhead, a vagrant breeze ruffled leaves against a cerulean sky dotted with puffy clouds. Along one edge of the sidewalk cafe, artists had set up easels, hoping to coax wandering tourists to have portraits sketched or silhouettes cut. Camera shutters clicked as the glory of the day and the Parisian spirit was caught on film. It was a pity tourists had discovered every corner of the city, Carter thought. Less than a decade ago, the Café Marie had been a hideaway for a privileged few, and English was a rarity. He wondered if there were any unspoiled places left. He tried to envision Arisa sitting among the crowded tables. Did she frequent out-of-the-way places like the Café Marie or stay within the confines of the select territories of the *bonne compagnie?* She'd probably long ago dismissed the past and accepted the brittle life-style so many Americans enjoyed abroad.

When they finished dining, they walked across the traffic-jammed square of Place St. Michel. Students gathered around the curving parapet of the Fontaine St. Michel looked no different than when he'd been there last, Carter thought with a smile. A guitar player strummed boldly despite the fact that his music couldn't be heard above the chattering voices and laughter. As they turned into the high street of the student quarter, a gangly youth in worn jeans and a T-shirt lettered "Disneyland" emerged from a tiny cafe, where the dissonant melody of flippers jangled as steel balls slammed into jungles of bumpers, score flags, and poppers. The bearded youth two-stepped to intercept them.

"T'as pas cent balles?" he said, with a try at an all-American grin.

Harry hissed impolitely and the youth backed off shrugging, already eyeing another target.

"Damned kids don't want to work anymore," Harry complained.

Carter shot him a wry smile. Harry had never worked a day in his life. Carter stepped to the curb and flagged a taxi, miraculously on the first try.

After giving the driver an address in the district south of the Jardin du Luxembourg, Harry fell silent as he watched the familiar scene of the busy Boule Miche beyond the cab window. Carter was content with his own thoughts. If Harry had a genuine Vezzi, it might solve all his problems. The resale value was staggering. He knew a dozen collectors who'd want it; two in particular would never give him a moment's peace if they knew he had it. Elbert Faus, a Pasadena multimillionaire who had a more impressive collection than some museums, would pay any price. He already owned four excellent Vezzis; a fifth would be a feather in his cap. He'd given carte blanche to several dealers to find him more. And Ganrali Maracudo would top any offer Faus made if Carter entertained bidding on the vase. No, if the Vezzi was genuine, there'd be no problem selling it at a handsome profit, no matter how much Harry held him up for. Unfortunately, long-term credit wasn't in Harry's mode of operation, so the price Carter could pay was limited. A letter of credit for thirty thousand, and an additional ten he'd forced Claire to pay up.

The cab nudged along the narrow streets near Porte d'Orleans until it became hopelessly wedged in a traffic snarl created by an overturned fruit cart that had lost a battle of supremacy with a tour bus. Harry tapped the driver.

"We'll get out here." He let Carter pay the fare.

Harry's flat was in a small courtyard that opened off Rue de la Tombe-Issoire. The court had once been a haven for sculptors and artists who enjoyed the bohemian life. Over the years, the ateliers had been converted to flats to accommodate Paris's burgeoning population. Grass and flowerbeds had been paved over, except for a lone tree surrounded by a circular wooden bench. A child's tricycle lay on its side nearby, giving the scene a touch of desolation.

Carter recalled the first time he'd been here. The courtyard and building seemed impossible to correlate with Harry's impeccable appearance and the circles in which he traveled, but the inside of the apartment was an even greater surprise. Instead of nondescript leftovers from some former tenant, Harry had furnished the rooms with excellent pieces he'd culled from villas all over the continent. Gifts—Harry labeled them—from admiring female friends. The effect was to make one immediately forget the grubby courtyard and the no longer elegant street.

Harry unlocked the door and flicked on the lights. He kept the draperies closed at all times, preferring the pleasant internal scenery to the reality outside. He motioned Carter to a chair as he disappeared upstairs to the loft.

Carter settled on a Queen Anne settee done in brocaded silk, and listened to the muted sound of Harry's footsteps on the carpeted floor. He wondered where Harry kept the Vezzi. It still made him uneasy to think of the valuable porcelain lying around the apartment, but then Harry's furniture and personal belongings had been safe here long enough. Most antiques that Harry picked up on his travels were quickly sold, with no need for storage.

A few minutes later, Harry returned with a black canvas sack. He sat across from Carter and undid the cord, then drew out a plastic-wrapped bundle swathed in lambswool. He worked slowly, his slender fingers caressing each fold as he unsheathed the vase with meticulous care. Carter held his breath as the last wrapping fell away.

The vase was about eleven inches high. It was an off-white porcelain painted with flying cranes over an early European artist's conception of a Chinese pastoral scene. Carter held out his hands and moved to the end of the settee where the light was better. The porcelain was unmarred and the colors were true and bright. Holding the lid securely, he upended the jar and studied the factory mark. "Venezia." The *z* was slightly off kilter and the shadings of the letters uneven. The mark was followed by the characteristic dot. The weight was right for hard-paste porcelain. His pulse quickened. He tipped the jar to the light and examined the design with closer scrutiny. It was typical of the work done in the brief ten-year-life of the Vezzi factory. Polychromatic. Vibrant blues and rich cinnabars. Vezzi quality was often uneven and the color of the paste uncertain; the vase was one of the best he'd ever seen. His palms were damp and he set the jar down carefully.

"I still want an outside opinion, Harry."

Harry's eyes glinted. "Gricci?"

The former restoration expert from the Louvre was a good choice. "Is he in the city? I'd heard he retired to Brest."

"He's here. I spoke with him yesterday. I thought you'd insist on formality. He's waiting at his sister's flat on Rue Mouffetard."

"You think of everything."

"I try," Harry said with a grin. He began rewrapping the Vezzi.

"We haven't talked price," Carter reminded him. Better to settle it now than wait until his enthusiasm was out of bounds.

Harry let out a dramatic breath. "We are old friends, Carter."

"I'm sure that doesn't mean you're giving it to me. What figure did you have in mind?"

"Thirty thousand, American."

"You're crazy."

Harry shrugged.

"You didn't pay a dime for it. You admitted that."

"My time, dear Carter, my time. One does not convince the marquise to part with a family heirloom in five minutes."

"I'll give you twenty-five, providing Gricci authenticates it."

"He doesn't have access to the Louvre's equipment any longer. You'll have to rely on his eye."

"I'll risk that much," Carter agreed. Gricci was one of the finest in the business. "Twenty-five?"

"I could get more."

Carter was silent. They both knew that was true, but if Harry had wanted to go elsewhere with his find, he'd have done it. Nevertheless, if word reached too many ears that Harry was marketing art objects he collected from his friends and acquaintances, his sources would dry up rapidly.

"All right," Harry said at last. "But I must have cash."

Carter suspected Harry might be embarrassed if the government looked into his tax situation. "It's a deal. Can we go to Gricci now?"

"But of course." Harry grinned as he slipped the padded vase back into the canvas bag.

Gricci refused to stake his reputation on the authenticity of the vase, but he handled the treasure like a first grandchild. It was an excellent example of early Italian work, no question about it. If it was a forgery, it had probably been done in the late eighteenth or early nineteenth century, most likely by someone at Cozzi or Doccia. Even such a copy was far from worthless.

In light of Gricci's tinge of doubt, Carter argued Harry down five thousand dollars and promised to have the cash the following day. Harry insisted Carter take the vase with him, a gesture of complete trust. Before they parted, Carter asked for the name of a discreet but capable private investigator.

"Are you checking up on me?" Harry asked in a wounded tone.

"It's another matter completely."

Harry scribbled a name and number on the back of a match folder. "He can find evidence for the stickiest divorce situation, if that's what you're after."

Carter pocketed the matchbook. Later when he was alone in Claire's flat, he phoned the detective and arranged to see him. Then he locked the Vezzi in his suitcase. It was as safe in Clajre's flat as it would be anywhere.

That night, he and Claire dined at Le Grand Vefour with a middle-aged couple whose city mansion in the Marais Claire had been commissioned to decorate.

Throughout the meal, Claire deftly juggled subjects of conversation to reveal everything about the couple that would help her plan the perfect decor for them. By the time the evening was over, she knew their preferences in art, colors, periods and habits—everything she needed. They were totally enchanted with her without knowing how thoroughly she had pumped them.

Later Carter and Claire made love in the perfect setting of the luxurious, deep-toned bedroom. Afterward she rose and padded naked to open the draperies. She slid back the glass door leading to the balcony and stretched luxuriously. Her full breasts and slim waist were outlined against the star-sprinkled night sky. Carter watched her with pleasure. No matter what differences they had, his sexual attraction to Claire had not diminished over the years. He was perfectly aware that she had used him at dinner. She wanted him to meet the Badins so he could help her pick perfect works of art and antiques for their mansion. Before he left Paris, she'd have sketches and swatches—and a complete list of pieces Carter thought would enhance the rooms. She had already impressed the Badins with his prestige and reputation, as though he were an associate on whom she called frequently. He wondered if he resented it, but decided he didn't.

Claire stretched again and walked slowly toward the bed, her shoulders back and breasts thrusting. She was proud of her taut figure. There were no sags or bulges to attest to her thirty-five years. She sat cross-legged on the bed, her hip touching his thigh intimately as she ran a hand along his leg. He could sense her energy level through her cool fingertips.

"I've decided on neoclassical. The house cries out for it," she said animatedly. He knew she was talking about the Badin mansion and let her ramble. "Mahogany—what do you think of Étienne Avril?"

"Perfect." He relaxed under the sensuous, cool nibble of her fingertips. She was fondling him absently, not aware she was distracting his thoughts.

"Maybe one or two pieces with Sèvres inserts. I can do the room in blue."

"Mmm-mmm."

"Thank God the walls aren't overdone with fluting and friezes. I'll do them cool blue with the sculptured areas white. It'll be smashing. Remember the Marie Antoinette cupboard at Fontainebleau?"

"Mmm-mmm."

"I need something like that for the focal point."

"Try Soisson. They're bound to have something," he said lazily. The reflection of the street lights and the pale moon glow above the trees splashed her ivory skin with enticing shadows. A warm breeze bathed his naked flesh.

"I'll call them tomorrow."

"Mmm-mmm." He drew her down gently, threading his fingers into her hair and holding her lips against his. She sighed as she relaxed along his firm lean lines. Gradually, her body took on a renewed sensual throbbing, and thoughts of business were driven from her mind as she came to him eagerly.

YEAR OF THE DOG

They heard about the end of the war after the second harvest. Refugees who'd hidden in the countryside began streaming back toward the coast. Almost daily, some passed through the small valley. The villagers rejoiced at the news, since it meant there would be no more interruptions to their lives. Rice wine was brewed in great earthenware pots and drunk long before it was ready. With each wayfarer they toasted the new life that was beginning.

Elliot accepted the news with mixed feelings. No longer did he have to wonder about the world outside the valley. The United States had never endured bombings or shellings; it was intact, except for the thousands of soldiers who had died on foreign soil. The British Colony in Hong Kong had fared worse. Allied forces reached the colony to find heavy material damage from military operations, looting, and neglect. The work of rehabilitation was already underway.

As the village made preparations to welcome the Year of the Dog, Mai Yun told Elliot they must go back. He'd worried the idea in his own mind for several months, unsure of whether he wanted to give up the serenity of their simple life. He'd grown accustomed to the hard labor and the isolation, and for the first time in his life felt at peace with his surroundings. He wasn't eager to face the uncertainties that awaited him in Hong Kong.

"Our son must have something better than the scrabbling life of a peasant," Mai Yun insisted.

Elliot watched Dai-yat Tsai fling himself at the flapping clothes the women had hung to dry. The child laughed gleefully as the leg of a *koo* slapped at his flailing arms.

"He's happy here," Elliot said.

"He is an infant, barely a year in age. He does not know what awaits him," she said grimly.

"But we've been happy too, all things considered. We won't have this in Hong Kong."

"We will build a better life. He will go to school. He is a scholar, not a peasant. The old ways of China are gone. We must prepare him—and ourselves—for the new world."

He was silent a long time. The winter sun soaked through his flesh. His hands were calloused and hard. His skin was deeply tanned. Toughened like old leather, his feet had long ago become immune to cuts and bruises. Even the mosquitoes no longer plagued him. He'd become a peasant, he thought.

"We will leave on the second day of the new year," she declared. "The Year of the Dog is propitious for new starts."

He held out his arms as Dai-yat Tsai ran to him with the wobbling gait of an infant. He hugged the child as he squirmed and kicked for freedom. At last he set him down so he could crawl across the doorstep in search of new adventures.

Without turning to face Mai Yun, Elliot said, "I have a wife in Hong Kong." He heard her sharply indrawn breath and felt her stiffen.

After what seemed like an endless interval, Mai Yun said, "She fled. You put her on the airplane yourself—you told me so."

"She'll come back now the war's over."

"No!" It was a contemptuous sound. "She abandoned her husband and thought only of her own comfort. She will want no part of Hong Kong now that it can no longer give her the same life she once enjoyed. Hong Kong is in ruins."

He wished her prediction were true, but he could not let Mai Yun delude herself. Quietly he said, "Her father is a government man, an architect who plans houses and office buildings. He'll be one of the first back to help rebuild the city. And Melisande will come with him."

The name, spoken for the first time in more than three years, was uncomfortable on his tongue, and in the presence of Mai Yun. How beautiful she was. She'd matured without losing the bloom of youth. Her skin was clear and fresh, her eyes dark as the river pool that swirled over black rocks. She had delicate bones and a graceful carriage that made her seem like a palace maiden, but her strength equalled the stockiest peasant's. He'd watched her lift and carry heavy baskets without strain. He'd seen her spend hours over the threshing screens when the other women had to rest in the shade from time to time. And at night when they shared the bed mats, she was eager to please him in every way. She massaged his body sensuously, driving away his fatigue and rousing his desire. Was it any wonder his memory of Melisande had grown so dim or that he was reluctant to return to her? He sighed.

She finally met his gaze and he was taken aback by the fierce determination in her eyes. "We will go back, Elliot, and the three of us will remain together. Melisande can never take away what we have, and we cannot give up what we must do." She reached to her throat and removed the jade pendant that she'd taken from her mother's corpse. She held it out so that the sun struck its gleaming richness. "My mother wore this before I was born. It was the most important thing in her life. She would not speak of it, but I know it was given to her by the man who fathered me—an American. It became her bond to him, a symbol of hope and promise." She pressed it into his hand and closed his fingers over the warm stone. "It is our promise now. It is our future so that the past cannot harm us. It is your Chinese blood, just as your American blood flows in the child of my womb. We three are one."

He was silent again, knowing they would leave the village as she said. Maybe he'd always known they had to go back. Maybe he'd been waiting for it all along.

It was spring when they reached the liberated colony. The winter winds had softened as the monsoon shifted gradually to the southwest. The Peak, always green, grew lush. Below, the devastated city was being reborn.

The colony was under a military administration and reconstruction was well under way. Rubble had been cleared, bomb craters filled, and damaged buildings were being repaired or torn down. Many expatriots had already returned and industry had begun a slow comeback. Construction was limited by the amount and cost of materials that could be brought in, and the biggest problem was housing. Entire neighborhoods had been left in ruins, and a population that had been dense before the war had now burgeoned further with the great influx.

The street where Mai Yun had lived with Miss Abigail was demolished. Every house had been blown apart or burned to the ground. Bulldozers had leveled the entire area to make way for new construction which had not yet begun. Elliot's year in Hong Kong before the war had been a temporary assignment, and he'd lived first in rooms he rented in a private residence.

After meeting Melisande he'd spent most of his time at the Whitaker house on the Peak. Neither Elliot nor Mai Yun knew any other part of the city.

They were forced to take a room in a crowded tenement without indoor water or sanitation facilities. They were squatters, like thousands of others who'd come back. Elliot was repelled by the filth and the vermin. They would have done better to stay in the village like peasants than live here like animals, he told her. She didn't like the squalor any more than he did, but she refused to think about going back. And there was nowhere else to go.

Elliot eventually found a post in the office of a newly organized fishery cooperative. His experience in importing and shipping was weighty enough to land him the job even though he had no identification. He was told he would have to reapply for his American passport.

He wasted no time in going to make his application, and was emerging from the consulate building when someone called his name. "Elliot!"

He turned automatically before he realized the voice was British. He found himself face to face with Grantland Whitaker.

"Elliot, my God, I can't tell you how glad I am to see you! Melisande has been worried sick. We've hunted all over the colony for a trace of you—I was just on my way to talk to the consul again to see if he'd been able to learn what happened to you after the invasion." He clapped his son-in-law on the back, almost hugging him in his exuberance.

Elliot was too stunned to respond. In a lightweight gabardine suit and impeccable shirt and tie, Whitaker made Elliot terribly aware both of the cheap suit he'd bought in West Point and his toughened, calloused hands.

"Have you been in Hong Kong all this time? We were afraid you'd been interned at Stanley, or worse—you have no idea what a jumble the records are in." He clapped Elliot's shoulder again. "Let's go across the Mandarin. My word, it's good to see you. Melisande will be overjoyed."

Numb, Elliot let himself be led down the hill and across to the hotel. Grantland insisted his questions could wait until they were comfortably settled with a drink. Grantland put an arm across his shoulders and told him he looked remarkably fit, though thin.

In the Captain's Bar off the lobby of the Mandarin, Grantland ordered drinks as they settled on the leather banquette.

Elliot felt like an intruder in the luxurious surroundings. How long had it been...Lord!

Grantland raised his glass. "To a bright future." He took a long swallow of his drink, then set his glass down. "Excuse me, my boy, I'll be back in a moment." He winked and clapped Elliot's shoulder as he left the table and sprinted up the steps to the lobby.

Elliot stared at the European faces surrounding him. Laughter and conversation reverberated. A world he knew. Seeing it after so long made him feel as if he were suddenly caught between two worlds, and both were spinning too fast for him to choose between them. One part of him wanted to get up and run before Grantland returned. Back to Mai Yun and Dai-yat Tsai. The other part of him was drawn to the world he'd always known and those he'd lived among. There was no escaping the Europeans if he stayed in Victoria. His work would throw him in contact continually. It was inevitable that he'd run into someone he knew before long. He laughed wryly. Hadn't he told Mai Yun this very thing would happen? That Grantland Whitaker would return to Hong Kong? And Melisande?

He realized he was sweating under his suit coat. Grantland had gone to ring Melisande, of course. Elliot wanted to run, to plunge back into the limbo of the past three years. But that was gone, and he could never find it again. He'd been a fool to come back. Now he had no choice but to face Melisande and tell her the truth.

Grantland was beaming when he returned. He signaled the bartender for another round of drinks as he settled beside Elliot. "I promised Melisande and Caroline we'd have just one more and then I'd bring you home. Now, I want to hear the whole story—you'll be repeating it for the women, but I dare say there're parts that can be left out in that telling. Lord knows it's been hard enough on them being exiled to Canada and not knowing what happened to all their lovely things here, or where you were. Melisande did a lot of weeping, my boy. We knew there was no way for you to get a letter, but she posted one every day those first months. Hoping. Yes, she's a brave girl. Very well then, tell me the story, lad."

Hesitantly, Elliot began with the bombings that had wreaked havoc in the colony after the Whitakers' departure, and of his struggle to get himself and Abigail out. It seemed so long ago...a lifetime. When he told of the fire and Abigail's death, Grantland's face sobered.

"I was afraid of that. Poor thing." He shook his head gravely. "Go on, my boy."

Grantland didn't ask about the others in Abigail's house, and Elliot did not mention Mai Yun. He described in detail the flight across Kowloon and the countryside, his acceptance in the tiny village where he'd lived for three years. If Grantland assumed he'd been alone, he did not correct the impression. It would be hard enough telling Melisande the truth. Grantland wasn't satisfied until he'd heard the tale of Elliot's eventual return and the job he'd managed to find with the fishery co-op.

Grantland gaped. "Why didn't you go back to your old post, lad? They'd have taken you on in a minute. Every company in the colony is crying for experienced men to rebuild commerce."

"I thought a change might be in order. This post sounded interesting." He didn't add that it would require his moving to Aberdeen, far enough removed from Prince Street to lessen his chances of running into anyone he knew before the war. "Several men connected with the fishing industry were interned together at Stanley. To while away the time, they put their heads together on reorganizing the industry. They came up with some very workable plans. I think—"

"Mmm, we'll see, we'll see, lad. Now, let's finish up. The girls are waiting."

Melisande, the skirt of her pale yellow dress fluttering in the breeze, was standing in the door of the house on Mount Austin Road when the car pulled into the drive. She was smiling even as tears poured down her cheeks. When Elliot climbed the steps, she flung herself into his arms.

"Oh, Elliot!" She sobbed, pressing her face to the shoulder of his inexpensive suit, clinging to him as though afraid he might vanish again.

Elliot put his arms around her and soothed her. When she looked up expectantly, he kissed her gently.

"Oh, Elliot, it's so good to see you—to have you—oh, do come in. Mother is in the parlor. We just can't believe . . . Oh, it's *so* good to have you back!" She wiped a stream of tears she could not control.

Caroline Whitaker clasped his hands and pressed her cheek to his. "My dear Elliot!"

Then both women were babbling at once, asking questions, wanting to know everything that had happened since they last saw him. Melisande clung to his arm and led him to the verandah at the rear of the house where a maid quickly brought a steaming teapot to the already laid table. Melisande pulled her chair close to Elliot's and did not let go of his arm. Her gaze never left his face.

In view of her happiness, Elliot could not change the story he had told Grantland. He was honest in every detail except his involvement with Mai Yun. Like Grantland, neither woman thought to ask about Abigail's Chinese companions. It was as if Mai Yun and her mother had never existed.

When tea was over, the elder Whitakers retired discreetly, leaving the two young people alone. Melisande took Elliot's hand and started up the stairs. When he hesitated, she smiled and lowered her gaze. Whispering, she said, "I have dreamed of this moment so long, I can hardly believe it's here. Oh, Elliot, I want to be with you . . ."

He followed her up to the suite of rooms they'd shared after the wedding. The decor was completely changed, and he realized with a start that the entire house had been renovated, probably after severe damage by the Japanese occupation army. Grantland must have pulled strings to get the work done so promptly.

The suite overlooked the green jungle of the mountain and the harbor below. From here, the city looked pristine and perfect in the sunlight. The scars of war didn't show, nor did the poverty and dirt and squalor. Melisande put her arms around him as he stared out the wide, bay windows.

"Darling . . ."

His chest tightened. Dropping the starched white curtain back into place, he turned. Her eyes were shining ponds of tears that crept slowly over her cheeks.

"Melisande, I—" He cursed himself for not having blurted the truth to Grantland. It would have been easier man to man.

She pressed a finger to his lips. "Don't talk, not now." Her arms went around him again, no longer gently but with desperate clinging. Her fingers played at his neck and face. Her body pressed against his. Her lips sought his eagerly, and he could not refuse her kiss. His mind whirled. He had to tell her about Mai Yun, but the years seemed to be swept into a haze he was reluctant to disturb.

"Elliot . . . I can't tell you how dreadful it's been without you, constantly wondering if you were safe." She gazed at him longingly, still unable to believe she was with him once again.

He heard himself tell her the horror was over . . . and then he was believing it himself. He led her to the bed where they undressed slowly, almost shyly, watching each other and smiling secret smiles. And when she came into his arms, all thoughts of Mai Yun were erased as he once more became Melisande's husband. During their brief honeymoon, she had been a passive lover, but now she was eager and responsive. His desire for her was rekindled. There was no pretense in the pleasure he found in their lovemaking. It was totally satisfying to them both.

Afterward, they lay in each other's arms, their bodies warm and damp. Melisande talked of the future—their future. Her father had promised to buy them a house, she told him. She would begin to look at property immediately. And her father's tailor would measure Elliot for a new wardrobe. The pitiful suit he was wearing could be consigned to the rag bag or given to the hospital charity. When he told her laughingly that he'd worn ragged Chinese garments for three years, she wrinkled her nose comically. She took his roughened hand and bent his fingers over hers.

"You don't ever have to pretend to be Chinese again," she told him. "You're home now, darling."

Guiltily he thought of Mai Yun waiting for him in the dismal tenement. Every minute he delayed telling Melisande the truth only made it harder. But what was the truth? He'd been so sure a life with Mai Yun was what he wanted—until now. Being back among the people and things he'd always known was so natural. Could he have made love to Melisande if he didn't still feel the bond that had once united them? Could he have held back the truth now if he didn't belong among his own people? But there was Dai-yat Tsai—his son. He loved the child and couldn't abandon him to the pitiful life that would be his without a father. He didn't realize he'd sighed until Melisande looked at him questioningly.

"What is it, Elliot?" she asked softly, a smile playing at her moist lips.

He said hesitantly, "So much has happened, Melisande . . ."

"I know, but it's over now, darling. We're together again, that's all that matters."

He could not meet her gaze. "Can it ever be over?"

"Of course. You must put it all from your mind. This is the beginning of our life together, that's all that matters."

"There's—there's something I must tell you."

She raised herself to look at him. "I don't want to hear it." She looked near tears, and her lip trembled. "It was a horrible war and it won't do any good to relive it. We must start fresh, start from now, not from 1941. From now, Elliot."

She looked at him with such determination that his stomach knotted. He brushed back a tendril of chestnut hair that had fallen across her cheek. "Please, Melisande, try to understand."

She shook her head. "Don't say it, please." Her gaze fell. "I know..."

"You can't possibly."

"Don't you think I've faced the possibility all these past years? I've tortured myself with all kinds of dreadful visions. We had so little time together, I vowed that when we found each other again, nothing else would matter. Nothing, Elliot, do you understand? If you have slept with other women, I know it was from despair and loneliness and the uncertainty of the war. Other wives had to face the same dread. The most difficult part was making up one's mind that it could well happen to any one of us. It frightened me, but I knew that as long as you were safe, I could forgive anything."

He was silent a moment, overcome with tenderness. When she buried her face in his shoulder, he stroked her hair gently. Almost in a whisper, he forced the words out. "Can you forgive a child, Melisande? I have a son...."

She was very still, so still that the thin whisper of the curtain at the window became a harsh, rasping sound. Her body tensed, then trembled. "A child..." So soft were the words that he thought they might be an echo of guilt in his own mind. Then he felt her hot tears on his skin as she began to tremble.

Painfully, he forced himself to tell the portion of the story he'd kept from her. Finding Mai Yun with her dying mother in her arms, their flight, the refuge they'd found in the village... and the measure of peace he'd eventually found with Mai Yun and Dai-yat Tsai among the humble peasants.

She was silent a long time, then without raising her head, she said, "But you left them at the village?" The question was pitiful and hopeful.

"No. Mai Yun wanted to come back to the city so the boy would have a decent life."

Her head jerked. "They are here?"

"Yes." He thought again of the crowded, dark room and the woman and child waiting for him. He wouldn't blame Melisande if she pushed him away and said she never wanted to see him again. But instead she tightened her arms around him.

"You are mine," she said, the strength in her voice startling him. "I've waited all this time, and I won't let you go. I deserve a chance to be your wife. You owe me that much. I deserve the chance." Her voice broke, and she clung to him as fresh tears fell on his naked flesh.

He felt strangely in limbo, devoid of pain or love, and was silent. That Melisande would forgive him so readily was something he had not expected, just as he had not expected Mai Yun's strength when they'd fled the city, the long exile among a people he scarcely knew, or the birth of a son. Was that what war did to people? Take away their expectations so that each day was lived as it came? Would he have stayed in the village if Mai Yun had not insisted on coming back? He thought about the job he'd gotten with the fishing co-op. It had been the first step back toward the life he'd always known, which was inevitable here in the colony. He couldn't live as a Chinese laborer. Both he and Mai Yun had known that all along. They both wanted more out of life for themselves and for Dai-yat Tsai.

He felt Melisande's tears drying on his skin, pulling like small stitches in his flesh. As though reading his thoughts, she said, "You are not Chinese, Elliot. Even though the child has your blood, he is. So is she." She could not bring herself to say the other woman's name. "Do you realize what kind of life you'd have here as a family? The Chinese won't accept you any more than the British colony will. You will never be able to live comfortably in either world. They're not like us." She stopped abruptly, unwilling to tread on ground that might give way underfoot too readily. Surely he had to recognize the folly of such an alliance.

He thought about his dark-haired son who did not look Chinese at all, and of Mai Yun who did, but whose beauty was enhanced by the mixture of an Oriental and Caucasian heritage. In which world did they fit? Mai Yun wanted his world, one that would provide for their son the kind of life she'd always enjoyed under the protection of Abigail. A pleasant home, good schools, escape from the poverty and drudgery of the average

Chinese family life. Mai Yun wanted it so much she was willing to risk coming back to Hong Kong rather than stay where they had been safe. He had let himself be led back, just as he had let Mai Yun lead him across the war-torn land to a place where there was hope.

"Elliot?" It was barely a whisper.

He'd have to tell her, and he'd have to provide for the child. The child was innocent.

"Elliot?"

"I'll stay," he said finally. "I'll stay, Melisande." He felt her tears again, and he held her close.

Mai Yun listened with ice forming around her heart. She'd known when he had not returned that she had lost him, that he had slipped away into the foreign world where she could not follow. He'd been reclaimed like a prize of war that had been abandoned temporarily to the enemy. She had forced him to take the risk, and she had lost.

Elliot could not read her expression. Her eyes were unfathomable pools. If only she would weep or scream or call him the names he deserved, but she stared at him wordlessly.

"I'll provide for you and Dai-yat Tsai," he told her. "Grantland Whitaker has already arranged a post for me in the office of his company. I'll make double the salary I would have at the fishery. He's promised to get you a flat in the first urban services housing that's available. You won't suffer...." He realized how inane the promise was. He looked away.

She spoke for the first time. "He is very powerful."

It was a condemnation. Of Whitaker or of him? Elliot tried to stem the rising guilt. "Dai Yat-tsai will go to school, just as we planned. I'm not abandoning him." He stopped again, aware that he *was* abandoning *her*. Grantland and Caroline Whitaker had been shocked, then hurt and angry when they heard his story. Melisande had stood by Elliot's side and staunchly defended him. The past was gone, she insisted. Elliot was back and their life was beginning. She would not let him go. If her parents could not accept them, she would leave with Elliot. Caroline wept and dabbed at her swollen eyes. Grantland's face was stony. And Melisande had won, though her father insisted on certain conditions. Elliot had to tell the "Chinese girl" he would not see her again. There would be enough money to provide her and the child a decent life, he'd see to that, but there must be no contact with Elliot and Melisande. A small flat in the buildings where Chinese refugees and displaced people were being housed would be appropriate.

Melisande had squeezed his hand reassuringly, desperately, and Elliot had agreed, except that he wanted to tell Mai Yun himself.

"Very well, but tell her that if she doesn't agree, she'll find life can be a lot less pleasant than what she was accustomed to, living off dear Abigail." Whitaker's lips twisted cruelly.

Caroline erupted in sobs again. "My poor friend—when I think that she took that ungrateful Mei Shau into her home and treated her like a daughter—and now this!"

"Be quiet, Caroline!"

Elliot flushed, remembering. He glanced around the dismal room. There was nothing he wanted to take with him, no clothes, no possessions except the memory of Mai Yun's strength and Dai-yat Tsai's laughter. The boy was asleep on a mat at one side of the cubicle, his thin body curled as though blocking out the world from his dreams. Elliot felt a sharp pain under his breastbone.

Mai Yun rose and went to light a tiny spirit burner from the flickering oil lamp that was the room's only illumination. She settled it on a small table and put a battered kettle on to boil. As she readied a teapot, Elliot spoke impatiently.

"I've got to go, Mai Yun." Melisande had insisted on accompanying him and was waiting downstairs in her father's car.

"Good-bye, Elliot," Mai Yun said without turning.

He went to her and forced her to turn around. "For God's sake, Mai Yun . . ." His eyes stung with tears. "I—we—It wasn't as if we didn't know. It was wrong of me to pretend . . ." God, what more could he say to her?

Her lips trembled slightly. "It is never wrong to love. I have loved you, Elliot, and I know you loved me. I do not regret that."

"Nor I!" he said desperately. How could he regret her strength, the joy she'd given him, the life they'd had?

"You will not change your mind about this?" she asked quietly.

He hesitated. "No." He'd already agonized over the decision. It would do no good to torture himself again.

"Then go," she said. "Go now."

He stood with his hands outstretched helplessly. The room was very quiet and sounds from the warren of neighboring rooms tried to fill it. The strident tones of two men arguing, the soft cry of an infant, the click of mah-jongg tiles...

Elliot glanced at the sleeping child. He reached into his pocket and drew out the jade amulet Mai Yun had given him in the village. For a moment, his hand clasped over it, then he opened his fingers and held it out to her.

"It is yours... and his."

She glanced at the pale stone. For a moment, it held her gaze hypnotically. She seemed to shudder and draw away, but she had not moved.

"It is your blood," she said tonelessly. "The China you will never leave. My blood and your son's." Abruptly, she turned back to the teapot.

He stood a moment staring at her rigid back. He wanted to force the jade on her, but it seemed fused to his flesh. His blood... Sighing, he bowed his head and walked out.

Like so many distasteful things, news of the cholera epidemic that summer did not reach the Peak until it had scoured the lower reaches of the Chinese sectors and begun to claim its toll. Melisande heard the gossip from three young Peak wives with whom she played bridge twice a week. She discussed it with Elliot after dinner as they sat on the screened verandah of the house her father had built for them immediately after Elliot's return. There was only a faint breeze stirring the muggy heat. Even the Peak, often cool when the city sweltered, seemed to be wrapped in the depressing humidity.

"Jane's uncle says it's because of the terrible crowding and filth. It's confined mainly to the squalid sectors of Wanchai and Causeway Bay, thank heaven. The boat people seem to be hit the hardest, but there have been cases reported as close in as West Point. I worry that some of the infected may be wandering about Central, exposing everyone." She looked at him with such concern that he smiled.

"No sense panicking. You're perfectly safe here. It might be best not to venture down into the city until the danger is past, though. When cool weather comes..."

"But I worry about you," she said. She reached over and clasped his hand. "You will be careful? I mean, no lunches in Chinese restaurants—no matter how clean you think they are?

And don't walk about the streets anymore than is absolutely necessary."

He smiled again. "I promise. Besides, your father keeps me so busy, I rarely have time to grab more than a quick bite at the hotel."

"He says you are learning very fast," she said proudly, the epidemic dismissed, her duty done. "He thinks that with a bit of training, you could join the architectural staff instead of staying in the office. I agree with him."

"I'm not sure that I want to compete with all the bright men he already has there. I'm content."

"That's just the point, darling, you are content too easily." Her tone was chiding, despite her smile. "The university is getting back to normal scheduling. There's an architectural program beginning in the fall. The company wants to send you."

He frowned. "I'm too old to be a schoolboy again, Melisande."

"Nonsense. It would be a challenge, and it would lead to something very prestigious. Ian Quimby will be retiring in a few years and you . . ."

"There are four men in the department capable of filling his shoes," Elliot said. Admittedly, he had some flair for architectural planning, but he didn't want to devote his energies to it. His sketching was doodling more than anything else, usually prompted by the desire to soften some of the stark lines turned out by the company staff. They were well into reconstruction projects, and Elliot was dismayed by the unimaginative, strictly utilitarian buildings Grantland's staff continued to design. Each would house thousands of Chinese in boxlike warrens that were cleaner but no less depressing than the tenements they replaced.

"You would outshine any of them," she declared.

"You have a very prejudiced view," he said wryly.

"But a very practical one. We've our future to consider. You don't want to be a clerk all your life." Her tone was quiet but there was reproach in it.

He felt a faint stir of resentment, but said only, "We'll see." It seemed a man ought to be able to find pleasure in his work, not simply do it because he had a living to make. The war had been over only a year, and Hong Kong was pushing reconstruction so rapidly that the entire colony seemed to have a single goal in mind. Sometimes he longed for the unhurried pace of the village. He firmly steered his thoughts from that dangerous path. The past was gone. He rarely thought of Mai Yun these days, but it was a different matter with Dai-yat Tsai. The boy's face haunted his dreams. He'd be growing fast, perhaps talking by now. Did he remember his father, or had Mai Yun blotted the memory from his young mind? Elliot knew they were still in the city. Grantland had arranged a flat for them, though he didn't tell Elliot where. The news was given only to prove Grantland had kept his promise. And to remind Elliot he must keep his.

The following day, a reason to break that promise came. A note addressed in an unfamiliar hand was delivered to Elliot mid-morning as he was drafting a letter. He opened the note and glanced at the signature, not recognizing the name. He read it quickly.

> Mr. Elliot Travish, Esq.
> Sir:
> I am writing at the request of a patient who was admitted yesterday. Though it is not my general policy to do so, the woman, an Eurasian by the name of Long Mai Yun, has persuaded me to communicate with you. She is in an advanced stage of cholera, and it is questionable whether her life can be saved. She speaks constantly of a child, who is also ill, though no child was admitted with her. She begs you to look after him. It is the feeling of the resident surgeon assigned to the wards that having this matter resolved in Mrs. Long's mind might encourage the healing of her body.
> Yrs. truly,
> H. R. Meadows
> Matron, Tung Wah Hsptl.

He stared at the blurring words and realized his hand was trembling. The skin around his neck shrank to a tight band that threatened to cut off his breath. His son . . . His uneasiness about the cholera epidemic became a focused fear. The crowded Chinese sectors . . . he'd thought only in terms of the tenements, but the urban services buildings were as crowded and as susceptible. Mai Yun probably shopped in stalls along the narrow streets, buying food that had been handled by those who eked out an existence there. Cholera—transmitted by contaminated hands.

Shaking, he rose from his desk, pulled on his coat, and ran from the office.

* * *

The stiffly starched uniform of a nurse rustled as she led him along the corridor. Cholera patients were confined to a long ward at one end of the wing. Approaching it, Elliot's knees weakened at the stench of death and dying that was not quite covered by the heavy medicinal odors and anticeptics. He glanced sidelong at the rows of beds as he was led to the end of the room. The nurse halted and indicated a slight figure under a gray spread.

Elliot's breath caught. The figure lay so still, he could not detect any breathing. The nurse said softly, "She had a sedative not long ago. She may not wake fully, but she will hear you." The woman's shoes whispered away on the linoleum.

Elliot moved close. He'd been warned not to touch anything, and he had to draw back his hand as it went out automatically to Mai Yun's pinched face. Her skin was waxy and damp, her ebony hair plastered around her face like the fingers of death.

"Mai Yun..." His lips moved but no sound emerged. He cleared his throat and tried again. "Mai Yun?"

She did not move. He studied the fine tracery of veins in her translucent eyelids.

"Mai Yun, can you hear me? It's Elliot. I've come." Pain tore at his chest. He was trembling again and, without thinking, he reached out to steady himself on the edge of the bed, then drew back his hands as though they'd touched glowing coals. He locked his fingers behind his back.

Behind him, he heard an agonized moan of pain as a patient was gripped with a terrible spasm. He did not take his gaze from Mai Yun's drawn face. Had she moved? Was there a flutter of sooty lashes against her cheek? He leaned close and spoke her name again.

Her eyes opened slowly, unfocused for a moment, then settling on the face staring at her. Her breath fluttered.

"It's Elliot," he said softly. "The matron wrote..."

Half delirious, she spoke in Chinese. Her voice was so low that he caught only the child's name.

"Mai Yun, where is he?" Elliot said.

She seemed to consider his words a long time, then whispered in English. "In the care of An Po."

"Where?" When she did not answer, he realized the effort it cost her to speak. He asked questions she could answer simply.

"A nurse?" (With her head she indicated "no.") "A neighbor?" ("Yes," she nodded.)

"In the estates?" (Yes.)

"Does he have—is he ill?" A tear squeezed from her eye.

"I'll find him," Elliot promised. "I'll find him and I'll see he's taken care of."

"Forever?" The words barely fluttered her lips.

"Don't think such things. You will get well. You'll see him soon. Please, don't worry—I'll see to him, I swear."

Her eyes closed and her breathing became shallow again. He hunched over the bed watching her until he was sure sleep had claimed her, not death. Then he slowly made his way out.

He found the matron and secured the address from which Mai Yun had been brought. Promising to return, he set out immediately for the housing by taxi. He was numb with guilt and fear. If he had not abandoned Mai Yun and the child, this would not be happening. If he had insisted on seeing for himself that they were well cared for . . . He tormented himself with restless thoughts of what he should have done as he recalled the pathetic figure in the hospital bed. But even in his grief and pain, he realized he'd felt no love for Mai Yun beyond that of compassion. The thought seemed callous, and he tried to examine his feelings. Had he ever really loved her, or had he only sought refuge in her strength at a time when his own failed? He'd been ready to give up many times during the flight from Hong Kong, but Mai Yun had urged him on, pushed him on, by refusing to let him quit. And it was she who had set the balance of their relationship, demanded and gotten what she determined was good for them. He'd responded as willingly to her gentleness as to her strength.

Just as he'd succumbed to Melisande's gentleness and strength. He was a damned puppet, letting his actions be dictated by others. *Why?*

The taxi crept through a littered narrow street in Kennedy Town as the driver shook his head and intoned curses upon the foreigner who brought him so far from people who could afford his services. Elliot spoke sharply in Cantonese.

"You will have a passenger back and your money as well. Now find the address!"

Startled, the man nodded and cursed instead the street vendors and straggling pedestrians who clogged the roadway. He blared the horn and screamed at those who did not move fast enough. Finally he stopped at a corner where rows of three-story buildings were lined up like fatigued soldiers. When Elliot was about to disembark without settling the fare, the driver grabbed his arm and demanded payment.

"I want you to wait. I'll be going back." But the man shook his arm violently and insisted on getting his money. Exasperated, Elliot paid him double the fare and ordered him to stay right where he was if he wanted to match the amount. Smiling, the driver settled behind the wheel with his newspaper as Elliot made his way along the row of buildings that were a far cry from the plans that he'd seen in Grantland's office. The houses were habitable, but not much more than that. Signs of their hasty construction showed even in the most cursory inspection. Granted that materials were still in short supply and difficult to come by, but when he thought of the quality and quantity of European housing that had blossomed on the Peak in the past year, he felt sick.

A cluster of wide-eyed, half-naked children stared at him as he crossed a littered yard and entered the second building. The hall was dark and narrow, heavy with the smell of stale cooking, refuse, and nightsoil. He had to knock at five doors before he found someone who recognized Mai Yun's name and directed him to a flat on the third floor. His knock there brought a gaunt-faced woman. He spoke to her in Cantonese.

"I'm looking for the child of Long Mai Yun. I have come from the hospital."

Her eyes mirrored fear.

"Is he here?" Elliot demanded. "The child—Dai-yat Tsai."

She stepped back and let him into the flat. It was barely the size of his dressing room at the Peak house. Two windows, screened now by flapping clothes strung out to dry on poles set in a maze of hooks, took up the entire outside wall of the room. Along another were piled half a dozen rolled sleeping mats. A small brick stove took up one corner, and a table, two chairs, and a single small chest were piled high with folded clothing. An elderly woman sat cross-legged on a mat as two small children clung to her, gazing wonderingly at Elliot. Another child slept beside the woman on the mat, his body curled so that only his round buttocks and a thatch of dark hair showed. The woman who had opened the door pointed to the sleeping child.

"Dai-yat Tsai," she said quickly. "I have taken the very best care of him."

Elliot crossed and bent over the boy. The other children edged around the old woman, who stared silently. Elliot knelt and turned the sleeping child, who opened his eyes and wriggled uncomfortably. With relief, Elliot saw no sign of the horrible pinching effects of cholera. He was pale but neither feverish nor clammy. He realized the woman was jabbering animatedly. She paid Mai Yun five Hong Kong dollars a month to sublet a portion of the room, and she cared for the boy while the mother worked. She cooked well, and she washed the clothes every day.

He waved her off impatiently. "Dress him," he told her, pointing to Dai-yat Tsai. "I m taking him away."

She looked frightened but went quickly to the chest and pulled out garments, then knelt beside the mat. When she had put him into a pair of short trousers and a faded clean shirt, she pushed the boy toward Elliot. Dai-yat Tsai whimpered and stuffed a hand into his mouth, looking at Elliot without recognition, only fear.

Sick at heart, Elliot picked him up. To the woman, he said, "Mai Yun is very ill, and to worry over the child is not good for her. I am taking him to a place where he will be cared for and she will know he is safe. She thanks you for your kindness. She will return as soon as she is well."

Fear was ebbing from the woman's dark eyes, replaced by relief at no longer having to be responsible for the child. Elliot wondered if she had moved the old woman and children into the flat after depositing Mai Yun at the hospital. It was inconceivable that Mai Yun would have accommodated so many people in the small space for any price. He thought wryly of the government suggestion that thirty-five square feet per adult be allotted in relocation projects, half that amount per child. He reached into his pocket and gave the woman a note equal to about ten dollars.

"See that the rent is paid on time," he warned her. "If it is not, you will all be thrown out, is that clear?"

She bobbed her head, smiling.

During the taxi ride to the Peak, Elliot tried to make friends with Dai-yat Tsai, but the boy retreated behind a silent, frightened stare. When they arrived at the white-painted stone house on Mount Austin Road, Elliot paid the driver and carried his son inside.

Melisande was waiting, her face white with rage, her lips

a tight line. Her father stood behind her.

"How dare you bring that child here?" Melisande said in a stony voice.

Grantland squeezed her shoulder and stepped between them. "You gave your word. It was not conditional on the woman's health or anything else."

Elliot realized he'd dropped the note from the matron on his office desk, and Grantland had probably found it. Well, that saved the need for an explanation.

His anger boiled. "You gave your word that they'd be well cared for, that they'd lack for nothing. Have you been inside the miserable place that is called decent habitation?"

"Those buildings have the government's approval. They meet specifications right down the line." Grantland said angrily. "We are not responsible for what these people do to them after they'd been given a decent place to live." He flicked a disdainful glance at the boy in Elliot's arms. "No matter how they live, it does not give you license to break the vow you made to my daughter, and to me and her mother. We will not tolerate this. Get him out of here at once."

Elliot shifted his gaze to Melisande. "Does your father speak for you?"

She was silent, her lips a tight line, her eyes as cold as sleet.

Elliot said evenly, "If he goes, I go with him. I was a fool to believe I could walk away from that child and never see him again. He is my flesh and blood."

"You dare—" Whitaker sputtered and his fists clenched. "Get out of here at once!"

"I'll go pack my clothes." Elliot defied him with a glance. Behind her father, Melisande's already pale face blanched. Elliot strode past and started up the stairs. He heard Whitaker's spurt of rage and Melisande's quick, "Father!" He felt their eyes on him until he closed the bedroom door. The child in his arms was like a statue, still too frightened to cry. Elliot sat him down on the bed and spoke to him gently in Cantonese.

"I am going to take care of you until your mother is well. Now sit a moment and we'll be out of here in no time." He forced a smile for the solemn eyes. Inside, he was sick. He began piling clothes from the dresser and closet on the bed. He didn't own a suitcase. No matter, a pillowslip would do.

He heard the door and turned. Melisande came in and leaned

against the door, watching him. She still had not looked at the child.

"Do you love her?" she asked in a quiet, controlled voice.

Elliot went on stuffing his clothes into the pillowslip.

"Do you love her, Elliot?" she asked again.

"Does it matter?"

"Yes. Please answer my question."

He looked up. "No. I am grateful to her for what she did for me during the war. I have compassion for her because she's desperately ill, but in spite of it, her concern was for the boy. So much so, she risked everything, gave everything—do you understand? I'm sure, even in delirium, she knows the scope of your father's vengeance, and that he will not give her a penny from now on. Her concern was for the child!" His rage was gone, and he was filled with shame at his own shortcomings. "I'm grateful to her for showing me my own selfishness."

"Are you going back to her?"

"No, but I intend to take care of my son and see that he has the chance your father did not give Mai Yun."

"He means that much to you?" She sounded bewildered.

"He is an innocent child. My child." He had not answered her question because he did not know how.

"You are willing to give up everything we have for him?"

"If I must."

"No!" she declared sharply. "I won't let you!"

"You can't stop me. Not this time."

She came toward him, her eyes blazing. He quickly stepped between her and the bed. She stopped as though he had struck her. High spots of color flamed at her cheeks. Suddenly her eyes brimmed with tears.

"I love you, Elliot. I don't want you to go."

He stared at her. "Your father has ordered me out. I'm in no position to argue since it is his house."

"It was a gift to us," she said evenly. "It is my house, and yours, not his. I want you to stay."

"And the boy?" He studied her face. Was she playing a game, expecting him to back down? He realized with a start that he had never crossed her before, never demanded anything since he'd known her.

For the first time, she let her glance touch the child sitting on the bed. She seemed to study his features individually, assuring herself they did not bear an obvious stigma of the

Oriental. Dai-yat Tsai stared back solemnly. When she looked back at Elliot, he could not read her expression.

"Do you love me, Elliot?"

He hesitated as he searched his heart. Finally he said, "Yes."

She drew a long breath and let it out slowly. "That is all I ask. Stay. The child too."

"And your father? What will he say to this?" Elliot looked at her warily, still trying to understand her motives.

"I will take care of him. He has my happiness at heart. He thinks he is protecting me. I'll talk to him, it will be all right."

Still cautious, Elliot said, "I must see Mai Yun again and tell her the boy is all right."

Melisande retreated momentarily behind a veiled expression, then said, "I understand."

A smile touched Elliot's lips as relief flooded him. "Thank God." He felt the tight grip of tension across his shoulders ease.

"Does that mean you'll stay?"

"Yes."

She flung herself into his arms and pressed her face against his shoulder. Her body and voice trembled. "Oh, Elliot, I was so frightened. I could not bear the thought of living without you. I wanted to die..."

Drained physically and emotionally by his victory, he could only stand and caress her hair. They embraced for a long time before she smiled up at him.

"I'll go tell my father."

"I'll go with you." He picked up the child and followed her downstairs.

Grantland Whitaker was pacing the verandah. His face tightened as he saw the three enter the parlor. He came in immediately and waited for his daughter to speak.

When she told him their decision in a quiet voice, his eyes narrowed.

"Are you sure this is what you want, Melisande?"

"It's what we both want." She sounded very sure.

"If the mother dies?"

"We'll adopt the child."

Whitaker blanched. "And if she survives?"

"We'll do whatever's right," Melisande said. "It will be some time before she's well enough to go back to work. If she demands the child back, the decision must be Elliot's." She gave her husband a reassuring glance.

Whitaker accepted his defeat. "Very well, if your mind is made up, I will not try to dissuade you. Your happiness is my primary concern."

"Then be a dear and ask mother to send one of the servants over to help us take care of the boy until I can find an *amah*."

That night as they lay nestled against each other after gentle lovemaking, Melisande whispered how much she'd hoped to be able to tell Elliot that they would soon have a child of their own. But a visit to the doctor had proved her hopes groundless, at least for now. Did he want a child—another child? He kissed her ear and said honestly that he did, more than anything in the world. Would he mind if they called Dai-yat Tsai by a more Christian name while he was with them? No, whatever pleased her. Quentin, she decided. A lovely Christian name. They fell asleep still entwined in each other's arms.

8

Arisa woke in the faint chill of the air-conditioned house. With the shades drawn, the room was dim, and her first thought was to wonder why she had sealed herself in instead of opening the bedroom to the evening breeze and the morning sun. She remembered with a start and glanced about apprehensively. Then she laughed. The break-in the night before was only a bad memory, dispelled by a decent night's sleep, thanks to Carter's reassurances and precautions. She stretched lazily and flung back the covers.

Before she finished breakfast, the locksmith called and promised to come within an hour. Carter got results, she thought gratefully. What had taken him to Paris so suddenly? Neither he nor Deline had mentioned the trip at the shop. Carter said he'd called to tell her about it. In retrospect, she found that strange. After she'd stormed out of his office at noon, it would be more like him to be angry and to exclude her from any of his personal affairs. Maybe he was softening a bit, or maybe he realized he was stuck with her whether he liked it or not. He had, after all, kept his promise to help her familiarize herself with the workings of the shop.

When the doorbell rang, she was surprised to find a curly-haired delivery boy with a florist's box.

"Miss Travish?"

"Yes."

He presented the box to her and went down the steps whistling.

In the kitchen she opened it quickly. Two dozen long-stemmed yellow roses were nestled in green tissue. Amazed, she opened the small enclosure card.

To chase away any lingering shadows.

Carter

Smiling, she found a vase and arranged the flowers. She considered calling him, but his plane had undoubtedly left already. She'd have to thank him when he got back.

The locksmith arrived soon after, and when he had completed his work, Arisa drove to Travish-Montaigne, determined to fill her day with work that would occupy her hands and mind. To her surprise, Deline already knew about the break-in.

"So many crimes," Deline said, shaking her head. "The city is no longer safe. How terrible for you to have such an ugly experience so soon after your return." She peered at Arisa, frowning. "Are you sure you should be working? Carter was concerned about you. He insists that you see a doctor."

"It isn't necessary," Arisa assured her. "The intruder knew exactly how to black me out without putting me in real danger. I imagine the police are right, he only wanted time to get away."

"Still, both Carter and I would feel better if you were checked. I'll make an appointment."

"No," Arisa said firmly. She felt foolish enough about the whole thing as it was. "Let's let it go. Tell me, Deline, how many people have keys to the house? I know there's the cleaning woman..."

"She has the highest recommendations, I checked them personally."

"I'm not accusing her. Heaven knows I can't find fault with her work. And it doesn't matter, since I've already had the locks changed. My father may have given out a dozen keys. I'm sure Quentin has one, and maybe Forbes."

"And I," Deline said softly.

Arisa laughed. "I know *you* weren't the one who jumped me last night. Besides, the police admit the lock could have been picked. The puzzling thing is that nothing was taken."

"Be thankful," Deline said.

"Well, enough of that morbid subject. The police will be by with a statement for me to sign. That'll be the end of it, unless they catch the man. Now I'm ready to get to work. Suppose you tell me where to begin." She smiled at Deline. "You know, I'm really looking forward to this. I'm excited about getting acquainted with my father's business at last."

"That would please him."

"Yes, I think it would. I've just begun to realize how selfish I've been these past years. Everyone knows—knew—my father better than I did."

They walked toward the workroom, where a young Oriental man Deline introduced as David Chan was unpacking a shipment that had just arrived. Deline asked him to explain the cataloging system to Arisa and then left. She returned a moment later.

"I forgot to ask if you would do me the honor of attending a party with me tomorrow evening."

Arisa hesitated.

Deline smiled. "Carter's instructions. It is a fund raising event for the Tucker Museum. We buy two tickets every year. With Carter off to Paris, you and I have inherited them. Will you come?"

"I'd love to."

When Deline left, David Chan whistled softly. "Neat."

She gave him an amused but puzzled glance.

"Maracudo—that's who's giving the bash. You know him?" When Arisa shook her head, David said, "One of the richest guys in town. He got tired of collecting money so he collects art. He's already filled up his mansion in Bel-Air so he endowed a museum. He raises a million or so every year with this party. You will be among the elite, the talk of the town."

"I'm impressed," she said, half joking. But David was serious.

"You should be, it's a big night. Movie stars, TV—the works."

"I'll try to behave myself so I don't embarrass Travish-Montaigne," she said laughingly.

David suddenly remembered whom he was talking to, and his face flushed. "I didn't mean . . ."

"Don't spoil everything by apologizing, David. I promise I'll tell you all about it on Monday."

He grinned. "Okay, Miss Travish, now where should we start?" He glanced around the cluttered workroom.

"At the beginning," she said honestly. "And call me Arisa. I'm afraid I'll drop something if I have to live up to 'Miss Travish.'"

The Bel-Air mansion sprawled on a mountaintop like a languid sunbather. It was ablaze with lights and the long, sweeping drive was parked with cars. Deline had insisted on picking Arisa up, and now Arisa sat back enjoying the grand entrance they were making. Two red-jacketed valets opened the doors, gave Deline a numbered tag, then spirited the car away into the darkness. At the house, a butler accepted their invitation, and a maid directed them to a powder room.

There was no formal receiving line. Guests were on their own in the huge ballroom. Arisa was dazzled by the expensive gowns and jewelry in evidence. She'd never seen so much wealth flaunted in one room, even at posh Paris parties. It seemed every woman was trying to outdo the others. By contrast, her own dress was deceptively simple. She was glad she'd spent the morning shopping, and that she'd stayed with her own taste rather than the more dramatic gowns the saleswoman had shown her.

Her white dress was cut on soft lines that highlighted her slim figure. The bloused bodice bared her shoulders and the bands wrapped loosely about her throat fell free. Gathered at the waist by a slender rope of gold, the skirt swirled to mid-calf, a length she preferred for evening. She'd chosen white multi-strapped high-heeled sandals and plain gold earrings. Her hair, drawn back and twisted to a loose rope threaded with gold, completed her look of simple elegance.

Deline was wearing a striking *cheongsam* of black silk with pale green flowers embroidered randomly. Around her throat, an exquisite jade necklace with a pendant of deep green splashed the black silk dramatically. She'd done her hair in a soft chignon that gave her a petite doll-like look. Arisa marveled at her perennial look of youth.

They drifted among the crowd, pausing as Deline introduced Arisa to people she knew. She gave a capsule biography of each.

"Roger Meyer is a San Francisco antique dealer. His shop near the St. Francis attracts collectors the world over."

"Daphne Coates is one of our most prominent civic and social leaders. She's on the board of the Tucker Museum."

"Randolph Grimes is the editor of Heritage Antiques Library books."

She knew many of the guests, and Arisa struggled to file their faces in her memory. When her head was ringing with names, she begged Deline to stop.

"I know there are a hundred people you want to talk to, so just go ahead. I'll get acquainted on my own, and I'll catch up with you later."

"You're sure?" Deline poised like a protective bird.

"I'm positive. Go on now." She watched as Deline made her way to a group of people near an archway.

The room was enormous, what would have been called a ballroom years ago, she supposed. The high ceiling was decorated with frescoes and giltwork, the walls covered with tapestries, paintings, and a few excellent pieces of statuary in recessed niches. Arisa longed to see the room when it was not crowded with people blocking the view. She thought of David Chan's assessment of Ganrali Maracudo's wealth. It was certainly flaunted by using a ballroom as a gallery!

A buffet table had been set up near a wall of open French windows that led out to a terrace. Waiters in crisp white jackets circulated with silver trays of champagne and hors d'ouevres. Diamonds of lights danced from the huge crystal chandeliers. Arisa accepted a thin-stemmed Baccarat champagne glass as she moved toward the windows. She discovered a rangy blond man watching her.

"Aren't you Arisa Travish?" he asked, inclining his head to study her inquisitively.

"Why yes . . ." She tried to recall his face, not sure that she knew him. His sun-streaked hair and deep tan gave him the California look she was not yet accustomed to seeing at every turn.

He looked delighted. "Paul Russell. We were at Beverly Hills High together."

She searched her memory and came up with a blurred picture of a lanky football player who'd been in several of her classes. She smiled. "English 902, Art 16 . . ."

"The same. I'd heard you were back, but I didn't think I'd have the luck to run into you so soon. Believe it or not, I planned to phone you."

She laughed softly. "Sounds like the same line you gave to all those girls who flocked around the football field."

He grinned. "That's the trouble with old friends, they drag up the past. But it's not a line, I was going to call. I heard about your father's death, and I wanted to extend my condolences. I don't imagine you've kept in touch with many people here. I know I probably wouldn't if I lived in Paris."

"You know an incredible lot about me," she chided.

"Art dealers are an incestuous little group."

"You're a dealer?"

"I'm with Sotheby Parke Bernet. I used to run into your father frequently. He didn't miss many exhibitions and sales. He was always on the lookout for something special. I was sorry to hear about his death." His serious mien relaxed to a smile. "But at least it has given me a chance to see you again. You look marvelous."

"Thank you."

"Will you be living in Los Angeles now?"

"I'm not sure. Things are unsettled. I'll be here for awhile, though . . ." She glanced at the mingling crowd. "This is quite a party."

"Maracudo's invitations are command performances," he said lightly.

"I came quite by chance."

He gave a short laugh. "You represent Travish-Montaigne, that's no accident."

"Are you saying there's a connection?"

He shrugged and his blue eyes flashed. "Maracudo likes to be at the head of the line when something exciting comes along. He wants dealers to call him first."

"And do they?"

"Most. A few holdouts like Carter Montaigne irk the hell out of him, so he watches them like a hawk."

Annoyance ticked at her. "He seems a very demanding man. I don't think I'm going to like him."

"You'll have lots of company. But be careful, he can be very charming, and he'll try to win you over. He needs an ally against Montaigne."

"I don't understand."

He gave her another engaging smile. "Maybe I've said too much already. I don't mean to ripple still waters."

"But now that you have, please explain. I own most of Travish-Montaigne now, and I want to know anything that pertains to it. Why are he and Carter at odds?"

"Two strong, stubborn men meeting head-on. Maracudo has the money to buy whatever he fancies. He's an egoist. His ambition is to acquire the most extensive and unusual collection in the world. He doesn't channel his interests to any period or kind—he snaps things up like an undernourished dragon. Bidding against him at auction is futile if his mind is made up. I call him the 'Hungry Tiger.'" His gaze swept the room. "Small, struggling dealers stand in line to be gobbled up. You can always tell who's been invited to a Maracudo party for the first time." She followed his gaze toward a knot of people across the room. An imposing, portly man with steel gray hair and a cold smile was the center of attention. "He has a regular modus operandi," Paul said. "He gets them to tell him what they've got, then he tells them what he wants. By Monday those six will be combing their sources to find something they can bring Maracudo to try for a shot on his preferred list. Maybe one or two a year make it."

"And the rest turn green with envy?"

"That's about the size of it."

"In which position is Carter Montaigne?"

"Neither. Ganrali wants him on the list. Carter's willing to deal, but he won't give Maracudo anything exclusive. Maracudo isn't happy, but he can't kiss off Carter and risk missing out on something good."

Arisa caught the implication that Travish-Montaigne's reputation was noteworthy. She was fascinated by this outside view of the company. "I presume some of his collection has come by way of our company. Did my father deal with him?"

"Your father got Maracudo interested in Oriental art. Maracudo relied on him more than any other single dealer."

"Carter isn't an expert on the Orient. He's the first to admit it."

"But Deline Armitage is, and Maracudo's banking on her upholding that end of the business. Carter wouldn't close off such a lucrative portion of his trade." Paul gave Arisa an earnest, blue stare. "Just between you and me, I suspect Maracudo is delighted that Carter isn't in town tonight. It gives him a chance to work on you."

"He doesn't even know I'm here!"

"Don't be too sure. And don't look now, but our gentleman host doth approach. Smile pretty but watch out for the fangs."

Arisa felt the gray-haired man's presence before he moved into her line of vision. He radiated an aura of strength that commanded attention; she resisted the compulsion to turn around before he spoke. Paul eased the tension by making introductions.

"Good evening, Mr. Maracudo. I don't believe you've met Arisa Travish. Arisa, our genial host." There wasn't any trace of resentment or hostility in his tone.

Maracudo smiled, clasping Arisa's hand as though he had

been waiting a lifetime for the moment. "I can't tell you how happy I was when I heard you'd be coming tonight."

Arisa noted the accuracy of Paul's prediction and wondered how the millionaire got his information. "I'm glad I had the opportunity."

His gray gaze flicked a hint of approval when she did not gush or fawn. Maracudo lifted a hand to shoulder level. Instantly a waiter appeared with a champagne tray. Maracudo took two glasses and handed one to Arisa, motioning the waiter to claim her empty. Paul was left to fend for himself.

"I admired your father. He knew his business—I like that in a man. I'm not sure how I'm going to like it in such a beautiful woman," he said smoothly. "I'm afraid I won't be able to keep my mind on business when I work with you."

He smiled so warmly that she felt herself being drawn into the circle of charm Paul had warned about. She accepted the compliment with a smile. Again, she detected a glimmer behind the slate-colored gaze. Surprise or approval?

He changed tactics adroitly. "One of the pieces I'm exhibiting tonight came from Travish-Montaigne. Your father got it for me in Hong Kong. I think you'll find it interesting. You lived in Hong Kong, didn't you?"

"Yes, until I was twelve."

"Damned Commies," he said absently. "Your father knew a lot of people there. No wonder he came up with some of the best items in the business." He cocked his head like a listening dog. "I'm sure you'll do the same. Will you be making trips to Hong Kong? I've been thinking about going over before the end of the year. I'd consider it a pleasure and privilege to have you show me the city."

She laughed softly. "My memories as a twelve-year-old would hardly be fascinating, I'm afraid. The city has changed. I may not know it myself."

"But you *are* going?" he pressed.

Again she felt a peculiar uncertainty about his motives. "I really hadn't thought about it. I've been in L.A. less than a week. That's not enough time to assimilate everything I need to know about the shop and decide what kind of an active part I'll play in running it."

"When you decide, my dear, be assured I'll meet you at the airport personally each time you come back from a buying trip. I have the feeling that you have your father's talent." He winked broadly. "It won't be difficult for you to pick up his contacts. Why, you probably knew them when you were a tyke—maybe even sat on the old Chinamen's knees. Didn't your father tell me you were acquainted with Kai Tang?"

She frowned as she pondered the name. "I believe he had a small shop near the Peninsula Hotel. He sold jade and ivory."

"Yes, yes..."

"I visited the shop a few times but my father and Tang chattered in Cantonese while I browsed."

"Do you speak Cantonese?" Paul interjected.

She'd almost forgotten his presence, so compelling was Ganrali Maracudo. She smiled. "I'd hate to have to get very far on it. I haven't brushed up in years, but I was fairly fluent as a child. I had an old Chinese *amah* who was convinced the foreign devils cast spells with their words. She refused to learn a word of English. My mother communicated in sign language or through an interpreter, though I suspect the old woman understood a lot more than she let on. I learned Cantonese from her."

Maracudo demanded her attention again. "Sounds like a lot of clattering and wailing to me, but I'm told that's part of it."

"A tonal language," Arisa agreed. "Children pick it up readily but it presents a problem for many adults. My mother never mastered it even though she lived in Hong Kong most of her life."

"I'd be the same," he declared adamantly. "English is challenge enough for me." He turned to look at a group near the buffet table. He singled out someone and drew his attention by the power of concentration. A minute later, a white-haired Oriental in a dark business suit came toward them. He was slender as a reed with a slight stoop to his walk, as though age had sapped his strength. His face was lined but his eyes were bright.

"Kai Tang," Maracudo said jovially. "This is an old friend, Arisa Travish."

The old man smiled and waited for Arisa to speak. She took his translucent, blue-veined hand. "How good to see you after so many years, Kai Tang."

"Daughter of the mountain," he said in a rustling papery voice.

Tang had always called her that! With nostalgic delight, Arisa saw herself as an eager, wide-eyed child standing before the sparkling glass counters of Tang's shop. The childish fear she'd had of him as a toddler had given way to respect as she grew up. Tang was almost wraithlike in his fragility; in his hands, works of jade or ivory seemed an extension of his rare, ancient quality. Her child's eye had viewed him as inscrutable. Even the name he called her had an air of mystery until her father laughingly told her it was because they lived at the summit of Victoria Peak that Tang had chosen it.

"I feel eight years old when you address me so," she said with a smile. "Does your family prosper?" Automatically, she slipped into a formal Chinese mode of greeting.

"Fortune smiles on them."

Arisa glanced sidelong at Maracudo. He was relaxed but attentive. She suspected he'd summoned the Hong Kong dealer for a purpose other than to reacquaint her with an old friend.

"I didn't expect to see so many old friends this evening." She smiled at Maracudo, then at Paul and Tang.

For several minutes, she and Tang engaged in small talk about Hong Kong. Like Maracudo, Tang hoped she would step in to fill her father's shoes and make frequent trips to the Orient. Strangely, she found the idea attractive. If she stayed with Travish-Montaigne, it would offer interesting possibilities rather than the limited visits she first envisioned.

"Your father had plans to journey to the Fragrant Harbor before the winter monsoon," Tang said sadly. He smiled. "If you come in his stead, you must promise to call upon me."

"I promise." It would be fun to see Hong Kong again. She wondered what Carter would think of the idea.

"Now, I beg your pardon most humbly. I have left men who have further need to speak with me." He bowed, then made his way back to the group he'd left.

Maracudo excused himself too and wandered toward the door where a mass of newcomers had accumulated. Paul watched him for an interval, then turned his attention back to Arisa.

"He's up to something," he said thoughtfully.

"What do you mean?"

"He's circulating. Usually he stays in place and lets people come to him. He made a special point of talking to you, you know that."

She refused to entertain sinister notions. "You said he wanted to cement relations with Travish-Montaigne. What better way than to be nice to me?"

"I have a hunch there's more to it than that." He snapped

back from his wandering thoughts as an attractive woman in a shocking pink satin jumpsuit came up to them.

"Here you are, darling. I've been looking for you." The dark-haired woman flicked a glance at Arisa and her eyes narrowed slightly. It gave her the look of a bisque doll.

"Hi, Helen. I ran into an old friend. This is Arisa Travish. You remember her father."

"I'm Paul's wife," Helen said pointedly, giving Arisa a look that clearly warned "hands off." "I saw Ganrali talking to you." Her gaze flicked at her husband. "Anything interesting?"

"He's trying to line Arisa up for his team," Paul said. "You know how he operates."

"Don't I! I could kill him. He's kept me dangling for three months now and I can't budge him."

Paul said to Arisa, "Helen's a decorator. Maracudo is always doing a room or suite somewhere."

"If you'd get him that Chou jade he wants, he'd let me do the whole goddamned house."

Paul gave a sharp laugh. "If I could locate the Chou, you could do our house too, pet."

Arisa looked at him with puzzled interest. He explained.

"There's been a rumor for a couple of weeks now that some pieces of Chou Dynasty jade have come out of Shanghai. Everybody wants them but so far no one's traced them. The exportation of cultural objects from Shanghai is frowned upon, shall we say, by the People's Republic, so it's impossible to separate hearsay from fact. Every dealer in town is hoping to get an inside track." He looked at her speculatively. "Your father would have been able to get at the truth. That's probably why Maracudo was trying to find out what your plans are."

"Flattering, if I don't take it personally."

Paul grinned but gave her a serious look. "Don't make the mistake of thinking Maracudo won't mix pleasure with business if it helps him get what he wants. He'd prefer dealing with a beautiful woman any day. It makes the game more fun." He didn't look at his wife, but Arisa felt her tense. Had it been an oblique hint of something between Helen and Maracudo?

"So far your predictions and suppositions have been one hundred percent accurate," Arisa told him. "I'll keep it in mind."

"Good girl."

"And now *you'd* better be a good boy and get into that

discussion Marti Wallace has going over there." Helen flitted a glance toward a corner where a willowy blonde in black crepe de chine was holding court. "She's planning a segment for *Your Town Is My Town* about the Tucker Museum, and about some private dealers and collections. Sotheby doesn't fit the mold, but she'll need something to compare them with." Looking at Arisa, she said, "You'll excuse us?" She linked her arm through her husband's and led him away.

Arisa watched as they joined the group around the blonde woman. Judging from Helen's remark, Marti Wallace was a television personality. She made a mental note to check. Television exposure would fit Carter's plan to make Travish-Montaigne a household name.

She was intrigued by Helen and Paul's chatter about the Chou jade. If there was truth to the rumor, it would be a major find. Chou work was rare, and it commanded top prices. For a long time it was assumed that the last pieces had been confiscated by the Chinese Communist government, which was allegedly dedicated to protecting China's cultural heritage. Antiquities such as Chou craftsmanship, which was more than two thousand years old, were strictly regulated. Whoever owned these pieces obviously had been successful in hiding them from the authorities. She wondered about the ethics of buying such pieces. And who among her father's contacts might lead her to the jade? Suddenly she realized she was entertaining the idea of trying to locate the rare pieces. Could she do it? More important, would Carter let her try? He'd have to finance the venture; she couldn't get as far as San Francisco on her own. And what about the cost of the jade itself? They'd have to have financial backing, unless Carter had a private source of money he hadn't revealed.

She found the idea intriguing. She was more excited than she'd been about anything for a long time.

"You look as if you've just made a great discovery," a voice said at her elbow.

She turned to a wispy stoop-shouldered man who was smiling at her. "One of those rare moments of insight we all get."

"In the middle of the greatest party of the season?" he said seriously, but his eyes gleamed with humor.

She laughed. "I was daydreaming, I'm afraid."

"Ah, that's better. It is our dreams and hopes that give purpose to our lives."

"I don't think we've met," Arisa said. "I'm Arisa Travish."

"I know. I'm Elbert Faus. Your father and I were friends and he introduced me to the wonders of Oriental art."

She'd gotten over being surprised that everyone recognized her. "I'm beginning to realize how many people my father knew."

"He was very well-liked. And an expert in his field."

"I'm beginning to realize that too."

"I'm told Carter is in Paris."

"Yes, rather unexpectedly. He'll only be gone a few days."

"I'm sure I'll see him soon after he returns."

"If you like, I'll ask him to call you."

The old man smiled. His sparse white hair looked silver under the light refracted through the crystals of the fixture overhead. "It's not necessary, my dear. If he's gone to Paris, he's probably found some delightful piece I cannot do without. He'll be in touch."

She laughed. "Another faithful client? Travish-Montaigne seems quite popular tonight."

The old man's eyes were piercing, but the smile never left his lips. "Others have been asking about Carter?"

"In a way. And about me, and about our plans for the future."

"I saw you chatting with our host. I'm sure he's vitally interested in your plans. He is not a connoisseur but he is an avid collector. I imagine he sees you as a link to the Chou jade."

This time she couldn't hide her amazement. She stared at him open-mouthed.

Faus's eyes twinkled and a smile creased his wrinkled face. "I see you've heard the rumors of the fabled jade. It's quite the topic of conversation tonight, and everyone believes it's an absolute secret. I'm sure if you are fortunate enough to locate and acquire it, you'll honor me with first refusal?"

She couldn't suppress a laugh. "You are delightful," she told him. "Unlike Mr. Maracudo, you let a person know exactly where you stand. But I can't speak for the company on my own. I'll have to talk to Carter."

"Of course. Now, I've taken enough of your time, my dear. Thank you for brightening an old man's evening." He made the suggestion of a bow and moved off.

At the buffet table, Deline was ending a conversation with

a stout woman wearing a glittering tiara of diamonds. Arisa started toward her, but at the same moment an Oriental man came from the opposite direction and claimed Deline's attention. Arisa felt a tug of recognition. Lord, she was going to have to work on names and faces. Coming back to Los Angeles was taxing her memory. Someone her father had known? No, more recent . . . Of course, he'd been with Deline at her father's funeral. They were already in earnest conversation as the man led Deline out onto the lantern-lit terrace.

YEAR OF THE BOAR

He studied her across the desk. The illness had left her frail without destroying her beauty. Her thin hands were clasped demurely in her lap and he could detect no sign of nervousness. One would think she was called into the offices of the Chartered Bank every day of the week. He'd arranged to meet her here so there'd be no chance of Elliot seeing her.

Without rising, he said, "Grantland Whitaker, Miss Long. I think you may remember me?"

Her eyes flickered. "I can hardly forget the man who has seen to my welfare so admirably this past year," she said.

Her lack of humility irritated him, and he wondered if he imagined the irony in her tone. "I am glad to see you have recovered so well from your bout with cholera. I dare say you are more fortunate than many. How have you been getting along?"

He knew the answer but wanted her relaxed and off guard. He'd had her watched closely ever since the day Elliot had visited her in the hospital and told her the boy was with him. She'd still been very ill, and the surgeons had given her less than an even chance at recovery. Undernourished like most Chinese people, she should have succumbed. But she hadn't, and now he was faced with the problem of what to do with her.

"Well enough, thank you," she answered calmly.

He changed tack abruptly. "I received your message about the boy."

She said nothing. Her dark gaze studied his face. Damned Orientals, he thought. Devoid of civilized emotion. He frowned. "My daughter has grown quite fond of the lad. He is well cared for, as you know." Her silent stare was neither reproachful nor grateful. "His father dotes on him." That brought a tiny flicker to her lips. A smile?

"Now, while I understand your desire to have the boy returned to your care, I do not believe it is in his best interests."

234

Ah, a touch of fear now. He plunged ahead. "I believe you are employed four hours a day at the Gloucester Factory." He consulted a sheaf of papers in a folder on the desk—a complete dossier on her since her release from the hospital. "Your wages total nine dollars a week, less than one-third the amount I contribute to your support. Is that correct?"

"Yes."

"And you now express an interest in going back to the university as well as having the child returned to you." He fixed a hard gaze on her. "With a child to care for, how do you propose to manage your time and expenses?"

Mai Yun's chest tightened as her fears were realized. He did not intend to return her son without a fight. She counted ten heartbeats before she answered. "I have talked with the university offices about a scholarship. I can continue working, and a neighbor will care for Dai-yat Tsai."

The Chinese name unsettled him momentarily. He'd thought of the child as Quentin for so long, he'd almost forgotten he'd had another name before. "I see. And if the scholarship is not forthcoming?"

She sat taller as she shriveled inside. She had not considered the possibility that his influence was that far-reaching. Did he control people at the university as he controlled her life? Fear was bitter on her tongue and she tried to hide it. "I will be forced to manage in other ways."

He pursed his lips and moved his head in a deprecating gesture. He scanned the papers again, turning pages slowly, as though searching for something in the text. Finally he regarded her once more. "Are you aware that thousands of refugees still pour into the colony? The pressure is being felt at every level, especially industry and the schools. Your employer consented to allow you part-time work as a special favor to me. He has a hundred applicants who are eager to work nine hours a day, seven days a week. Naturally his production schedules are better served by workers who produce steadily. The university has seventy-four applicants for every scholarship available. I dare say your ambitious plans are unrealistic, though most commendable."

Her anger blazed in spite of her resolve to face him calmly. "I had your word that I would be helped."

"I do not deny that, nor am I now denying that help. As your benefactor, however, I am entitled to certain considera-

tions and a hand in the planning of your future, since I am
paying for it."

"I want only to better myself in order to provide for my
son!"

"Precisely. For that reason, I have a proposal to make that
will help you reach that end."

Her heart fluttered like wind through rustling trees, and she
laced her fingers to hide their trembling. Lies, all lies. She had
been forced to accept his hollow promises because she was too
weak to fight him or to plead with Elliot for justice. Her eyes
burned with hate as she stared at the man across the desk.

Grantland settled back in the cushioned chair, increasing
the distance between them. She knew she was beaten; he saw
it in her eyes. "I believe you are interested in Oriental Studies.
An excellent choice. I'm told you show a flair for the arts. I've
given consideration to what you might do with such an education once you completed it. A shop girl for one of the local
dealers, I suppose. With the economy being restored, I'm sure
trade in art objects will flourish. One can always aspire to a
teaching post, I suppose, but they are severely limited. No
matter, there's time for that. At the moment our consideration
is the present." Abruptly he brought the springed chair upright
and leaned toward her. "What would you say to a guarantee
of the education you desire and the promise of an excellent job
when you finish?"

She was so taken by surprise, it took her a minute to answer,
"I would ask what price I must pay."

Grantland gave a snorting laugh. "Quite so, quite so. Everything has its price, eh? Very well. The price, as you put it, is
that you let the boy stay with his father and my daughter. They
want to keep him. Formal adoption is not necessary since Elliot
is the biological father. The child will naturally be brought up
as a Caucasian. His Chinese blood is unnoticeable for the most
part. He will be educated in British schools, and he will have
every advantage that can be provided for him. I have had papers
drawn up to establish a trust that guarantees his education at
the university of his choice. Naturally, he must not be torn
between loyalties. We must remove any chance of contact with
you, accidental or otherwise. To this end, you must leave Hong
Kong."

Her blood flowed like an icy mountain stream. She had
imagined many things, but never this. Was he proposing to

send her to Canton? Shanghai? His assurance of her education ruled out some remote village in the interior, though she was sure that would be his preference.

"As I said before," Grantland went on, "Hong Kong is overrun with refugees. Many like yourself hope to improve their lot. At best, you will face overwhelming competition in everything you undertake. The arts program at the university is in a fledgling stage. In a few years, I have no doubt it will be one of the finest in the world, but right now it is hampered by the more pressing need to emphasize technical and scientific courses. There are other well-established schools that do not face this problem as keenly. You would do well at one of them, and it would solve the dilemma of your presence in Hong Kong. My first choice would be, of course, an English university, but unfortunately England was hard hit by the war, more so than Hong Kong. Her recovery period will be lengthy. There are excellent American schools, however."

Her composure had returned and she said carefully, "It is difficult for Chinese," she gave the word a slight mocking emphasis, "to get visas to America."

"Granted, but that can be taken care of. If you are successful in your studies and later employment, your application for citizenship can also be arranged."

Until now, her fears had been channeled only toward surviving the power he wielded in Hong Kong. She had underestimated him. Had Elliot played a part in suggesting America, his land? For a moment, the thought of him conquered her anger.

"Because of prejudices and regulations, it would facilitate matters if you adopted a more anglicized name. I will have the legal papers drawn up, if you agree."

She was being stripped of all identity. So Elliot could never trace her? So her son would also be stripped of his past?

As he let the silence build, Mai Yun realized she had no choice. The matter was being put before her as a proposal, but it was an ultimatum. She thought about Dai-yat Tsai, about never seeing him again. But he was being given the life she wanted for him. To take him from it would be foolhardy. And impossible. She knew enough about the law to know his father could claim him legally, especially with Grantland Whitaker's money and power behind him. She found it difficult to believe that Elliot's wife accepted the child so readily and loved him.

She thought about Dai-yat Tsai's solemn face and his trembling body as she nursed him through the illness that had befallen him just before her own. She'd been terrified he had cholera and tended him so unceasingly that her own strength was sapped and she'd neglected precautions for her own health. Dai-yat Tsai's illness had been nothing more than childhood dysentery; her own had cost her her son.

"Do you agree?" Grantland asked briskly.

"Have you already chosen a name for me?" she asked bitterly.

He shrugged. "It's of little consequence. My secretary suggested Deline Armitage. Seems she read a novel where the heroine had the name. If you have another in mind, it will do as well."

Deline Armitage. It felt new and foreign in her mind. English? Perhaps. Or even American. "It will do," she said.

"Then you agree to all the conditions?"

Ice solidified around her heart. "I agree."

"Good. My solicitor is waiting outside. He has papers for you to sign." He pressed a buzzer on the desk, and the door opened to admit a stern-faced man with a briefcase under his arm.

9

The plane was filled to capacity. Carter made no effort to engage in conversation with the imposing, bearded man who shared the first-class row. Before the jet cleared the runway at de Gaulle, he opened his attaché case and took out the report the detective had given him. Adjusting the overhead light, he settled back to study it.

Subject: Arisa Elizabeth Travish
Address: 14 rue Charmagne
Place of Employment: Galerie Saint-Gerons, 777 Place de la Concorde.
Proprietor: Eduoard Saint-Gerons (subject left position w/ St.-Gerons immediately prior to her departure for U.S.A.)

Carter quickly scanned the credit and financial data. Arisa was not the thriftiest woman alive. The small trust from her mother's estate and the allowance Elliot sent were deposited directly into an account. Amounts were drawn over four-week periods to correspond with her living expenses. The apartment was moderately priced, which surprised him. Her accounts at several haute couture shops were high, which didn't surprise him at all. He'd noted her clothes.

His gaze swept the column of expenses the detective had unearthed. Arisa had not lived as extravagantly as he imagined. Well, but not lavishly.

A withdrawal from her account caught his eye. He flipped the page to read the detective's report, scanning until he found what he wanted.

On June 12, subject withdrew 10,000 francs in the form of a cashier's *chèque* to use as earnest money on Larousse, a *galerie antique*, located at 81 rue de la Tremóille. Subject has 30 days to pay balance of 30,000 francs as down payment to be applied against total purchase price of 150,000 francs. Terms of agreement attached.

He flipped the pages to read the purchase agreement. So Arisa was buying a gallery. He made a mental note to call Paris as soon as he landed to get more details. Had all her talk about wanting to stay in Los Angeles and take over her father's work been bullshit? Had she intended all the time to return to Paris as soon as possible?

He'd been a fool to believe her for a minute. He smiled to himself. With the profit on the Vezzi, he'd be able to make her an offer she couldn't resist.

He turned to the report on Arisa's social life. She certainly hadn't been a nun, he thought wryly. Several familiar names cropped up among her associates. Her name was linked romantically with half a dozen men, the most recent being her former employer, Eduoard Saint-Gerons. He wondered how Saint-Gerons had taken the news of her leaving? Did he know about the *galerie?* Former lovers often got sticky about competitors rising from their beds. He grinned, thinking of Claire.

When he'd digested the report, he slipped it back into the attaché case and stared out the window. He'd misjudged Arisa. She wasn't the flighty socialite he'd envisioned. Elliot had known his daughter after all. But why the devil was she so stubborn now if she had her future mapped out? She couldn't run both Larousse and Travish-Montaigne. He wondered if she had had enough experience to run even a small shop. She'd worked at half a dozen different jobs the past few years: at art galleries, antique dealers, even a stint as a guide at the Louvre. Maybe she'd been gathering knowledge and courage to branch out on her own. She might not be a specialist in Oriental art, but she sure as hell was following in her father's footsteps.

It puzzled him that she had such a naive opinion of Elliot. To her, he seemed to be the father who'd granted wishes like a fairy godmother, not a flesh-and-blood man with passions and weaknesses. Yet at times, Carter sensed a bond under Arisa's ignorance and guilt. Did she suspect there were things about her father she'd never known? He wondered what her reaction would be to finding out about Elliot's reputation in local Beverly Hills bars. What the devil made a man change like that? He'd known Elliot for six years; he'd been on top, had the antique world at his feet; then suddenly he'd flung himself into a race as though to see how fast he could destroy himself. The drinking, heavy spending, bets. Lily Taylor was right about one thing, Elliot never welshed on a loan or bet. Mr. Good Guy, right to the end. Carter wondered what the thousand from Lily had been for? Or the countless other thousands he borrowed after his expense account had been cut off. Funny, Carter had never been able to shake the feeling that there was something haunted about Elliot this past year. Maybe it was better not knowing. . . .

He pigeonholed the past and concentrated on the Vezzi. He was disappointed that Gricci hadn't been more convinced about its authenticity. He'd get another opinion. Tanner would be able to put him on to the top experts. If the Vezzi was authenticated, it would triple or quadruple his investment. If it wasn't . . . He wouldn't think about that now.

He'd call Faus first. He imagined the old man's excitement. Vezzis didn't turn up every day of the week. All in all, the trip had been successful. He leaned back and closed his eyes. Even being with Claire had had its moments. He wondered how long it would take her to give up hope of having him at her beck and call? At least he'd gotten the matter of his quarterly payments straightened out.

"Would you like a drink, sir?"

He looked at the pretty French flight attendant and smiled. "Scotch and water." A drink to celebrate victory.

Arisa relaxed as she sat across the desk from him. She was wearing a shirtwaist dress that was somehow blue and violet at the same time.

"When did you get back?" she asked.

"Last night. How have you been?"

"Fine. Thank you for the roses." A warm smile lit her eyes. Deep violet today, they blended with her dress. She had a flair for colors.

"You're very welcome. You didn't suffer any ill effects from that night, I hope."

She shook her head and her hair sprayed on her shoulders like a waterfall. "None. And the locksmith came. I'm all secure again. I had only two sets of keys made, and I have both of them."

He nodded approval. "Did the police come up with anything?"

"No, but they never did sound very encouraging."

"Deline tells me you've been hard at work and learning fast."

"There's a tremendous amount to absorb. I had no idea there

was so much work involved in running a shop."

He thought about the Larousse, but she was so guileless he couldn't read anything sinister into her remark. "I suppose there is, but a division of labor makes it easier. I hear, too, that you attended the Tucker Museum event. Did you enjoy it?"

"How could anyone not! I've never been exposed to that side of Los Angeles. I had no idea there were so many serious collectors and dealers in one place. At Paris parties they're always outnumbered by the dilletantes and fringe groups."

He laughed. "Paris will never outgrow its Bohemian air. It's too fashionable to set up a street easel and announce you're part of the art world. Paris patrons are always willing to sponsor anyone with a modicum of talent. They see another Rembrandt or Gaugin on every corner."

"Maybe that accounts for why Paris has the greatest number of masterpieces and promising neophytes," she said.

"Yes, but that's part of the starve-in-a-garret school you don't find in many other places. It certainly isn't an old American custom. That's one reason there are so few hangers-on at parties like Maracudo's. His money helps too," he added wryly.

She smiled. "I didn't see a single pair of blue jeans," she admitted. "The closest was a satin jumpsuit by Halston and boots by Gucci."

He knew she'd worn something equally costly. The bill, along with several others she'd charged, was in his desk. The accountant had presented them hesitantly that morning, unwilling to confront Arisa himself with the news that her personal expenses could not be charged to the store.

"I'm sorry I missed it, but I'm glad you had a good time. There'll be others coming up we can both enjoy."

She wondered if that was an invitation. She'd enjoy going to parties with him if he continued being as pleasant as he'd suddenly become. "I ran into several people I knew," she said. When he arched an eyebrow, she elaborated. "Paul Russell of Sotheby's. He and I went to high school together. And Kai Tang, a dealer from Hong Kong was there. My father used to take me to his shop. He remembered me after twenty years. Seeing Kai Tang brought back a lot of old memories. "I haven't really thought about Hong Kong for a long time, now I'm thinking about going."

"Oh?"

She leaned forward, and her golden hair fell across her

cheek. She brushed it back absently. "Carter, there's a rumor that some Chou jade is being brought out of Shanghai. If we can get it before anyone else— Do you realize the price it would bring in this country?" Her cheeks took on a pink glow as she tried unsuccessfully to control her excitement.

He frowned a moment, then said carefully, "I recall your father mentioning it casually." He hadn't paid much attention at the time. Elliot had been excited but secretive, saying only that it would be the find of the century if the rumor had substance. It had come up right after his last trip to Hong Kong. Carter had partially discounted the story because Elliot was always enthused about something, often items they couldn't afford.

She shook her head emphatically, and her shining hair sprayed again. "My father could never be casual about Chou jade. He probably wanted to verify the story before he got you all fired up. That would be his way."

Her appraisal of Elliot was on target. Carter silently admitted again that he'd underestimated the bond between father and daughter.

"I talked with Tanner about it," she said. "He agrees that if there's some Chou work coming into circulation, we'd be crazy not to go after it."

That carried more weight than anything she'd said so far. Interesting that she'd gone to Tanner instead of Deline. He'd check with both of them. He tried to recall the dates of the Chou Dynasty but only knew that it was one of the early periods. Most work that old was probably in museums. And very high-priced.

"And you want to go to Hong Kong to look for it."

"Yes. My father had so many contacts, I'm sure I can locate it."

She was talking about the jade as if it were free for the asking. He frowned. "How many pieces are there? How much will they cost?"

She looked startled for a moment and said almost defensively, "I don't know. The thing is that if we don't act fast, someone else will get to them and we'll be out in the cold."

"The thing is," he said as gently as he could, "that we have to be able to pay for anything we buy. We're still at a stage where our credit is a bit shaky."

"What better way to improve our position than to turn a

substantial profit on something like this? If we can locate the jade and get it on consignment . . ."

"That's not very likely. If what you say is true, there'll be enough dealers after it that it will go as an outright sale. We'll need cash, which we don't have."

Her eyes blazed. "That didn't bother you when you took off for Paris to buy something that caught your fancy! You seem to forget that even though you are running the company, I have a say in it."

Her words stung like a lash. He'd forgotten. He'd let himself be lulled into considering Arisa a manageable nuisance. He'd let his head be overruled by . . . He took a deep breath.

"Do you have a say then about where we can get the backing we need for the kind of expenditure you're suggesting?"

"What about the profit on the Vezzi?"

How did she know?

"I talked to Tanner this morning," she said, answering his question before it was asked. "A conservative estimate would be about fifty thousand dollars. That's a start. I've been going through my father's papers. Chou work has sold for phenomenal prices in this country. I admit, we may have to gamble everything we've got, but it'll pay off, I know it will."

"*If* you can locate it."

"Damn it, it's worth a try." She lifted her chin and glared at him.

"Is that an order?" he said, irritated.

Her gaze didn't flinch. "If you want to consider it one."

Carefully, he said, "I'll give it some thought."

She started to say something, then changed her mind. "All right."

He'd talk to Tanner and see what kind of an investment it would take. And he'd put a rush on the Vezzi authentication. The vase had already been delivered to Tanner's shop.

She rose and stood looking at him. "I don't want to belabor the point, but there isn't any time to lose. Rumors about the jade were circulating at the Maracudo party. We won't be the only ones looking for it. Ganrali Maracudo wants it. He practically offered to sponsor the purchase if I'd work exclusively for him."

Carter felt the muscles at the back of his neck pull. "I don't do business that way. Maracudo may be able to pressure other dealers into working directly for him that way, but not Travish-Montaigne."

Abruptly, she sat down and leaned on the desk. "Good. I don't want to work that way either. So let's go after the jade on our own and laugh in his face!" She smiled, and the violet lights came back into her eyes.

He looked surprised, then laughed. "Okay, you set me up for that one. Let me work on it. I should be able to have an answer soon. In the meantime, will you have dinner with me tonight?"

It was her turn to be astonished. There wasn't a reason in the world to refuse. "All right."

"Good. I'll pick you up at eight."

She got to her feet again, smiled, and went out. He watched her swing along the hall and down the stairs at a bouncy gait. He wasn't sure what had prompted his invitation to dinner, but he was already looking forward to it. Smiling, he picked up the phone and dialed Tanner Holmes.

After a few minutes, he was convinced Arisa had a right to be enthusiastic about the Chou jade.

"A single piece would probably bring something in the neighborhood of a quarter of a million dollars on the American market if it's in good condition," Tanner told him. When Carter whistled softly, Tanner explained. "There haven't been any for sale since the Communists closed up China."

"Has much of it come to light over the centuries?"

"A bit here and there. It's conceivable there's a lot tucked away somewhere, though it wasn't a dynasty known for art work. Most scholars figure what there was has probably been destroyed in one war or another. If some is actually coming on the market, it'll be a find."

"What kind of money are we talking about if we can buy it?" Carter doodled on a pad, biting his lip until Tanner answered.

"It would only be a guess."

"Guess then."

"Could be as much as a hundred or a hundred and fifty thousand. Unless of course the guy who's got it decides to auction it from the start. Then the sky's the limit. I hear Maracudo already has feelers out."

"Is that from Arisa or have you heard it elsewhere?"

"Arisa says there was plenty of talk about it at that bash last weekend. And you can bet if Maracudo heard it he's got feelers out. Maybe a dragnet."

"Luckily he doesn't know a Chou jade from an artichoke.

He'll need someone to front for him."

"He won't have any trouble there."

Carter didn't argue. Maracudo could sponsor the purchase through half a dozen dealers.

"Okay, thanks, Tanner. Any word on the Vezzi?"

"Have a heart, it's only been a few hours. It looks great to me but to be on the safe side, I took it over to the university and pressured a buddy there to do a carbon dating on it. That's the only way to tell for sure."

"How long will it take to get an answer?"

"I promised him a case of Anchor Steam beer if he gets it by tomorrow. It means overtime, but he'll probably do it. You pay for the beer."

"I'll spring for a case for each of you," Carter said with a laugh.

When he hung up, Carter stared at the framed Chinnery painting on the wall. He'd considered taking it down when he moved into the office, but now, with the rumor of the Chou jade, the Chinese scene seemed like a good omen. Smiling, he opened the desk drawer and took out the bills Arisa had charged to the store. He went through them, tallying them mentally. Two thousand dollars. Seven hundred for a single gown. Judging by the date, she'd worn it to Maracudo's party. He wondered if he'd ever get to see it. He let his imagination create a sketch of Arisa dancing in his arms in a "white silk de la Renta . . . $700.00." Sighing, he took out his personal checkbook and began to write.

"You had a call from Mr. Paxton," his secretary said. "He'd like you to call back as soon as possible." The girl was young and beautiful, one of the Hollywood hopefuls who clung to a belief that she'd get a break soon; the secretarial job was a fill-in until a movie part—or even a walk-on TV spot—came along. Occasionally she asked for time off to make a cattle call. With the salary Quentin was paying, she felt she was entitled to it.

"Is he at his office?" Quentin glanced at the clock. It was almost eleven. He'd stepped out for a quick cup of coffee. Lousy timing.

She stretched across the glass and chrome desk to hand him the message slip. Her silky blue dress gapped to show a tantalizing amount of cleavage. "He left a number."

"Get him for me and hold any other calls."

At his desk, Quentin had only a few seconds' wait before the intercom buzzed.

"I have Mr. Paxton on the line, Mr. Travish."

He picked up the phone. "Mr. Paxton—good to hear from you," he said heartily. He'd delivered the twenty thousand as promised. He hoped to hell Paxton wasn't moving up the due date on the rest of the money.

"Good morning, Quentin."

Quentin smiled at the use of his first name. A good sign.

"I wonder if you might be able to have lunch with me today? I realize it's short notice . . ."

"It happens I just had a cancellation. I'm free."

"Would one o'clock be convenient?"

"Perfect."

"Would you mind meeting me at my club? I have several matters to take care of there."

"Of course." Quentin jotted down the name and address. One of the best in Beverly Hills. When Paxton rang off, Quentin was elated, but a thin edge of apprehension crept around his thoughts. Why did Paxton want to talk to him? Was it purely social now that he was part of the California Planners group? The check had cleared, no problem there. Maybe Paxton had another deal in the offing. Quentin's neck tingled at the prospect. Something bigger than Tahoe? Jesus! Meeting Paxton was the greatest break of his life. For a few moments, his imagination soared. No telling where this could lead. He came back to reality with a thud. Hell, he still didn't have the thirty grand he needed to close this deal. Where would he scrape up cash for another? Where was he going to come up with the thirty grand? He'd taken polaroids of everything Arisa had at the house, ostensibly for insurance, but the jade piece that Deline's Mr. Bok wanted wasn't among them. He'd made Deline go through the photographs twice, but she was adamant. The only place left was a safe-deposit box, so he'd checked with Forbes. Elliot had one all right; Forbes had already requested an appraiser to set a date for the box to be opened. If the jade was there, Quentin knew he'd have to think up something mighty convincing to get it away from Arisa. So far he hadn't come up with any bright ideas, and time was running out. Would he be able to play on Arisa's sympathies? Maybe

convince her he wanted one memento? She wasn't likely to
believe that. Maybe Deline would have a suggestion. Hell, she
was the one who'd promised Bok the jade. Let her do some
of the work. Even as the idea formed, he knew it wasn't the
answer. If Deline could convince Arisa to part with the jade,
she'd just sell it to Bok herself and cut him out. Damn!

Paxton's club exuded subdued, masculine elegance. Pan-
elled walls, excellent paintings, thick carpeting, and discreet,
flawless service made it the perfect setting for business discussions. Quentin recognized five top executives among the
diners.

Paxton suggested the *boeuf bourguignon,* which they ordered along with their second martinis. Quentin had just about
convinced himself the lunch was nothing more than a friendly
overture. He was relaxed and confident as they talked about
the stock market, real estate, and half a dozen other general
topics. Paxton didn't get down to business until the salad was
cleared.

"I met last night with one of our investors," he said by way
of introduction. His smile was easy. "The man who recommended letting you into our group."

"I'm looking forward to meeting him. I have a lot to thank
him for," Quentin said. "I hope you've conveyed my appreciation."

Paxton nodded. "He knows you're grateful. Did I mention
that he knew your father?"

Surprised, Quentin said no.

"I never had the pleasure of meeting your father, but I'm
told he was one of the top men in his field. Hate to admit it,
but I'm not into Oriental art. Not that it isn't beautiful, just not
my thing."

"That's understandable. Tastes vary. I tend to agree with
you, though I do have a few pieces my father gave me as gifts."
He was improvising. His apartment was strictly modern and
Elliot had never given him anything, but he wanted a nice, safe
middle ground between Paxton and his investor.

"I imagine you've been exposed to it all your life. You
probably know a lot more about it than I do."

Quentin shrugged. What the hell was he getting at? He had
a definite feeling that this wasn't just chit chat.

"At any rate," Paxton said genially, "this investor wondered if you might do him a favor."

"Name it. I owe him one." He wondered if Paxton was going to keep the man's name a secret forever.

"He has his heart set on a certain Oriental objet d'art and he thought you might arrange for him to get it."

"I don't see how— That is, I'd be glad to, if I can. I'm not directly connected with Travish-Montaigne's operation, if that's what he had in mind. Of course I'd be happy to use my influence to persuade my sister and Montaigne to sell him any piece he fancies."

"I knew you would," Paxton commented pleasantly. "The problem is Travish-Montaigne doesn't have the piece, but we have good reason to believe they may soon. We'd like to be assured then that we'll know about it first. And be able to buy it."

"I'll have to know more about the piece and about the gentleman who wants it." He couldn't bargain blindly. He'd put it to Deline, she'd know how to handle it. It would be like Montaigne and Arisa to get their backs up if the proposition came from him.

"Naturally," Paxton said. He went on eating as though the deal were already settled in his mind. "He'd like very much to meet you and discuss this personally."

Quentin almost laughed. Here he'd been worried he was being kept in the dark, and the guy wanted to meet him all along. Paxton's little game. Well, it didn't matter. "I'd like to meet him too."

"Fine. He's joining us for brandy in the library as soon as we finish."

"He's here?" The question popped out before Quentin could mask his surprise.

"Yes. He should be free soon." He glanced at his watch. "Twenty minutes or so. Unless you'd like dessert?"

"No, no. The beef is delicious. I see why you recommended it."

They filled the rest of the meal with small talk. Quentin didn't glance at his watch, but he would have staked his life that it was twenty minutes to the second when Paxton put down his napkin and pushed back his chair.

"Shall we move to the library?"

Quentin noted that Paxton wasn't even asked to sign the check. Class.

The library was a huge room with walls of books and small

groupings of chairs set well apart from each other. Several magnificent Oriental rugs covered the floor and deadened any sound. Some chairs were occupied, but not a whisper carried beyond the tight circles. Quentin couldn't resist a glance at the ceiling to see if it was soundproofed with acoustical tile. It wasn't.

Paxton led the way to a corner where three high-backed leather chairs formed a triangle around a marble-topped table. One chair was occupied by a heavy-set man in a gray suit. He looked up as they came in and watched them come toward him.

"I trust we haven't kept you waiting," Paxton said with a smile. The man's expression didn't change. His steel gray gaze touched each of them. "Mr. Maracudo, this is Quentin Travish." Paxton didn't repeat the introduction the other way around. There was no need to. Quentin put out his hand.

"It's a pleasure to meet you, Mr. Maracudo." Maracudo! Wow! He sure as hell hadn't expected this. No wonder Paxton hadn't balked at taking on a penny ante investor. When Maracudo talked, everyone listened.

Maracudo shook his hand with an iron grip, then waited for them to sit. A decanter of brandy and three snifters stood on the table. A waiter appeared from nowhere to pour. Maracudo waited until he left.

"You look like your father," he said. "Strong resemblance." Without shifting his gaze, he said to Paxton, "You've told Mr. Travish what I have in mind?"

"The essentials," Paxton said quickly. His voice no longer had the bored superiority Quentin had been aware of earlier.

"Good, then we can get down to details."

"Anything I can do——" Quentin started.

Maracudo went on as if he hadn't heard. "Your father and I did business. As you may know, I'm something of a collector. I like only the best."

Quentin wished to hell he'd been inside the Tucker Museum. It would help to know something about the art works Maracudo was interested in. All he knew was that both his private collection and the museum's were said to be the best in the country.

"A few months back, Elliot mentioned some jade he was hoping to get. They were pieces I'd be interested in. With Elliot gone, I'd like a guarantee that I'll have first crack at it."

Quentin was reluctant to say again that he wasn't in control of Travish-Montaigne. He didn't want to get off on the wrong foot by sounding hesitant. Besides, Maracudo probably knew more about him than he did himself. "I'll do anything I can, Mr. Maracudo."

Maracudo inhaled the aroma of the brandy then rolled a mouthful over his tongue appreciatively. "Good."

Uncomfortable under his scrutiny, Quentin said, "If you'll tell me more about it, I'll be able to give it some thought."

"I don't want thought, Mr. Travish. I want some very special pieces of jade that are coming out of China."

China. Christ, how the hell was he supposed to . . .

"I have every reason to believe your sister and Montaigne may come into possession of that jade," Maracudo said. "I've done some asking around. They'll have competition, but your father knew a lot of people, and he made contacts on the jade the last time he was in Hong Kong."

"I see." Quentin stalled for time. "I'm afraid I don't know many of the people my father knew in Hong Kong," he said carefully. "I came to California when I went to college and I haven't been back since." No way around it.

Maracudo savored the brandy again. "Your father has a woman working for him who does. Deline Armitage knows everyone he did business with. Maybe your sister does too."

It was possible, but Quentin didn't see how that brought him into the picture. He waited.

"I want to know if your sister and Montaigne plan to go after the jade. If they do, I want it. Montaigne isn't willing to give me an exclusive." He swirled the snifter and watched the amber liquor film the glass. "I'm going to be perfectly frank with you, Travish. Montaigne and I have not established the same kind of relationship I had with your father. A pity. I think your sister may be more agreeable. I'd like you to influence her in my favor. I want that jade. I'm willing to pay a commission to whoever gets it for me, and I'm willing to repay favors."

The brandy had warmed him and the temperature of the room seemed to climb. Quentin was already figuring ways to pressure Arisa. Maybe that deal she wanted in Paris. If she'd work with him, they could ace Carter out.

Finally, he said, "I'm eager to repay the favor you've done me by recommending me to California Planners."

Maracudo nodded. "Your father owed me some money," he said abruptly.

Quentin's hand jerked and he had to steady the brandy snifter.

"Naturally I don't want to make a claim against the estate. That sort of thing holds up probate. It wasn't so large an amount that I'm not willing to write it off if you see to it I get the jade. It won't come out of the commission I have in mind for you. You'll have that, plus his note."

Maracudo was watching him like a gray shark. Quentin felt the first sting of sharp teeth.

"What I propose," Maracudo went on, "is putting up the money for the purchase of the jade. You will act as my agent in buying it. If your sister is willing to work with you, fine. If not, I'm sure you can find a way around that. You'll need an expert once you locate the jade. I have a man in Hong Kong. I don't want anything but the originals."

"You want me to go to Hong Kong?" It was ludicrous. He'd be bumbling around without the slightest idea what he was doing.

"I want you to go to Hong Kong. If I'm correct about your sister having the right people to contact, she's going to get wind of that jade first. When she does..." He shrugged, the implication clear.

He was to buy it out from under her. Easier said than done. He saw Paxton watching him, and frowned. "There's one problem, Mr. Maracudo. I have a business to run." He flicked a glance at Paxton. "There are some things I have to take care of in order to meet my commitment to California Planners. The agreement was thirty days on the balance of my investment. Naturally, I want to meet that commitment. It might take a week or two to do what you're asking." No way was he going to lose out on the Tahoe deal.

Maracudo smiled for the first time. Quentin thought again of a great gray shark ready to make its kill.

"I understand. What would you say to my underwriting the balance? Thirty thousand, isn't it? I'll give California Planners a note for the full amount. That way you won't have that on your mind while you're getting the jade for me. We'll call it half of your commission, if you like. You don't lose out on the Tahoe project, and I get what I want. How does that sound?"

It sounded bloody unbelievable. *Half* of his commission! Another thirty grand—and no more sweat?! Maracudo's reputation was well-deserved. He was a man who knew how to get what he wanted. Quentin arranged his face in a comfortable smile. "It sounds perfect, Mr. Maracudo. Perfect."

10

Arisa was ready a half hour before Carter was due. She smiled at her reflection in the mirror, not wanting to admit that she was excited about the prospect of dinner with him. She studied the pale violet eyeshadow she'd applied and touched a fingertip to a tiny smudge. Satisfied, she gave herself a final inspection in the full-length mirror. Her green silk dress fell in soft lines that were striking. The dress was by a California designer who was new to her, but the choice had been a good one. It struck a perfect note between elegance and California casual. She was beginning to appreciate many things about California, she decided.

Downstairs, she settled on one of the sofas to read. After a few minutes she realized she hadn't turned a page. She closed the book and let her thoughts wander to the prospect of going to Hong Kong. The colony was bound to have changed. Maybe she'd been hasty in assuring Carter she'd be able to find the Chou jade. The antique dealers she remembered might be gone. Her father's friends might not remember her. Just because Kai Tang had was no assurance that others would. And even if they did, would they be willing to help?

The soft chime of the phone startled her, and the book fell from her lap as she hurried to answer it.

"Hello."

"Arisa? Darling, how are you?"

It took a moment to recognize the voice. "Eduoard!" It was the middle of the night in Paris!

"You promised to let me know how everything is. Are you all right? Is the horrible part over?"

She smiled. "Yes, thanks. It's sweet of you to call. I planned to," she fibbed, "but I've been busy."

"I understand. The main thing is you're all right. Funerals are depressing. When are you coming home?"

Home. She realized she hadn't thought of Paris for several days, except in terms of Carter's trip. "I'm not sure. There's still a lot to be settled."

"I miss you, darling," he said gently. "It seems you've been gone much longer than two weeks. I've done a lot of thinking about us. You were right, I've gotten too caught up in the shop. I didn't recognize it until you said you were leaving."

She bit her lip. There wasn't any point in going over this again. "Please, Eduoard . . ."

"No, listen. I've never been more sincere. I didn't realize how much you meant to me. I've been a fool. I want to make it up to you—if that's possible. I want to start over. I'll take a month off as soon as you come back. We can go to Switzerland, or the Greek Islands, wherever you'd like. Just the two of us. And when we get back, if you still want to buy that other place, fine. I'll lend you the money if you need it. I know I can't tie you here forever. You have to try your wings."

When she didn't answer immediately, he asked, "Will you think about it? Can you give me that much?"

Through the front window, she saw Carter's Mercedes pull up at the curb. Where did she belong? Paris or Los Angeles? Carter's head and shoulders appeared over the car.

"I'll think about it, Eduoard, but no promises," she said at last.

"That's good enough." His voice was relieved. "It's wonderful talking to you. Keep in touch. If there's anything you need, call. Promise?"

"Yes. Good-bye, Eduoard." Carter was coming up the walk.

"Good-bye, darling."

The doorbell rang as she hung up.

"I like the dress," Carter said with an appreciative survey when she opened the door. "The color is spectacular on you."

"Why, thank you. Come in. I just have to pick up my purse—unless you'd like a drink?"

He shook his head. "I made reservations for eight forty-five. I took a chance on your being the prompt type," he said with a grin. "I like that, too."

"You're easy to please."

"Not really." He was still smiling, but she had the feeling his answer was serious. For some reason, her cheeks warmed. She went to pick up her purse so he wouldn't notice.

"You may need a wrap. We're going to the beach."

She opened the closet and took out a white shawl. "It's hard to get used to the cool nights here. I'd forgotten how delightful they are. All set."

His touch at her arm as they went down the path made her shiver, as though the cool night breeze had already sprung up. Seated beside him as he drove, she resisted the impulse to study his profile.

They drove out the winding vista of Sunset Drive, past magnificent estates that stood behind high walls and iron fences, their grandeur masked by the shadows of evening and thick, lush foliage. Passing UCLA, he asked her about her schooling in England, and she found herself talking about her past without pain. Past Pacific Palisades, they began the winding descent to the ocean as they felt the cool relief of the sea breeze.

The restaurant he'd chosen was beyond Malibu, nestled against the shoreline like a sandpiper at rest. He had reserved a window table, and they were seated in a small alcove that reached to the edge of the frothy aftermath of the pounding waves. The throbbing sound provided a gentle undertone to their conversation.

Arisa was entranced by the diamonds of light dancing on the water. The sun was close to the horizon, a ball of glowing fire about to be quenched. Streaks of mauve and deep red hovered between sky and water like a blanket ready to be folded over the day.

She smiled at Carter. "I'll bet you chose this place for the sunset."

"It is magnificent. I hoped you'd like it."

"There are so many things I'd forgotten about southern California." She glanced at the sun beginning to disappear into the night ocean. "Like this. No matter what else Paris has, it can't boast an ocean view."

"You must have seen many beautiful sunsets in Hong Kong."

"Mmm, that was so long ago."

"You sound ancient," he chided, but his eyes twinkled.

"It's strange how one can shut off segments of one's life. I always felt my mother closed doors on the past and never looked back. Maybe I've done the same."

"It's all right to close doors, but an occasional glance over your shoulder can be useful to remind you where you've come from as well. Tell me about Hong Kong."

She stirred the frosty daiquiri with the miniature straws. "It's a busy city. Exciting. People seeing it for the first time find it an overload on the senses. Colors, sights, sounds . . . There are quiet places too. The Peak is beautiful, or at least it was." Her brow puckered in a small frown.

"You left during the riots in '67?"

"Yes. I don't like to think about it."

"Maybe it's one of those glances over the shoulder."

She lifted her gaze to his gently probing one. "You mean because I may be going back?"

"Partly, but mostly because you're here. Whatever happened then is part of now."

She glanced out at the darkening water. The diamonds had been engulfed by black velvet. Only a thin disc of the sun clung to the horizon. As she watched, it plunged out of sight.

"The Year of the Ram," she said softly. For a moment, she groped to unlock the closed door of her memory. "No one had any idea the situation would become so violent. I remember the New Year festivities." She looked back at him, her eyes shining. "I loved the Chinese New Year. It was as though all the color and noise and drama of the city were pulled together in one huge festival. Banners and pendants everywhere. Paper lanterns, fluttering ribbons. *Gung hay fat choy!*" She smiled nostalgically. "You couldn't walk down any street without being caught up in the fever. Shopkeepers hung lettuce and dollar bills on their doors so that they could feed the dragon and ward off evil spirits that might be lurking about. Everybody wanted only good luck for the year. My father took me to watch the parades. I never tired of them even though my mother insisted I was getting too old for such childish things. But Daddy and I adored them." She blushed. "I haven't called him 'Daddy' for a long time . . ."

Carter encouraged her with a smile.

"There was no hint of trouble then. It hardly seems possible that in a few months . . ." She shuddered. "I suppose the pot was boiling, but as a child I was unaware of it. My mother helped in that respect. She wasn't one to become involved in anything outside her own little circle."

"She was brought up in Hong Kong, wasn't she?"

"Her parents moved there when she was four. My father met her shortly before the war. They didn't have much of a honeymoon. They were married on December 7, 1941, then separated for the rest of the war. I remember my grandfather as stern and very British, but both he and my grandmother died when I was quite young. My mother used to show me the big house they lived in. My grandfather had it completely renovated after the war." A small sigh escaped her lips. "I've often wondered what became of our house, whether anyone rebuilt it."

"It was destroyed? I had the impression the rioting wasn't that serious."

"It wasn't. Most of it took place in the city streets, more in Kowloon than Victoria—rock throwing, sticks, homemade bombs that were more firecracker powder than explosives. It began with strikes and demonstrations. Of course people were hurt and killed, but not as many as some of the newspapers claimed. The Communists overturned buses, took over the ferry system, that sort of thing." She gave a wry smile. "In their typical, very British way, most people considered it all a bloody nuisance rather than any serious threat. My father got caught in it unwittingly."

"How so?"

"His office was in Central, only a block from Queen's Road, where a lot of the violence was centered. One day some rioters overturned buses and set fire to a taxi carrying three government people. It was frightening enough to make other drivers abandon their vehicles and simply run. It created a monumental traffic jam. When offices let out, no one could get through in either direction. My father made the mistake of trying to plow through the mass. He was set upon by young hoodlums who'd been drinking and were in an ugly mood. He fought them off and managed to get away, but they followed him. By the time he reached the tram, they'd gathered a crowd and were shrieking and screaming about foreign imperialism. He evaded them by running across the street and boarding a bus that was just leaving for the Peak, but after dark, there they were—right at our doorstep."

"The same group?"

"It seemed impossible and my father couldn't be sure, of course, but who else could have singled out our house for attack? It was just one of those senseless things. My father admitted he'd hit one of the lads hard enough to draw blood— he suspected he might have broken the fellow's nose. But to extract such revenge..." She shuddered, remembering the crash of rocks through the windows, the fire bombs, her mother's screams. "They besieged the house. It was horrible. Every window, my mother's beautiful things going up in flames..."

He reached across to take her hand, sorry he'd stirred such

ugly memories. "Don't dwell on it. It was a long time ago. So you came to California?"

She nodded. "The Chinese servants ran off. My father gathered together our passports and what money he had and a few things he didn't want to abandon. My arms were stuffed." She gave a rueful smile. "Mother wasn't much help. She was hysterical. My father had to half-carry her out as we escaped the back way and climbed the wall to a neighbor's house. It's all pretty blurred in my memory. Someone called the police and the fire department. But we watched that beautiful house burn to the ground. There was nothing left but rubble and ashes."

She was silent as she toyed with her drink. "The next day my father said we were coming to the United States. My mother was in no condition to argue. She always believed it was temporary. For a long time, she talked about going back, but then my father got into the importing business and we stayed. You know the rest."

"It turned out for the best."

She looked at him, aware that her hand was still in his. "I've often wondered..."

"That way lies madness," he said with a smile. "Your father looked back and got new direction from the past. He kept the good things and set aside the bad. He loved his work."

"I know. You're right. I'm being maudlin. I guess that's part of the reason I reacted the way I did about finding out you were part of the business. I wanted it to be all his, to pay for all the struggle and suffering, to make it all worthwhile."

"I think he'd be the first to agree it was worth it, even though he had problems toward the end."

They were getting dangerously close to another door she didn't want to open. He sensed it and changed the subject.

"Enough somber thoughts. First I suggest the sand dabs or the red snapper if you like fish. Then let's talk about how to find that Chou jade in Hong Kong."

"Oh, Carter—you've decided I can go?" She didn't realize he was still holding her hand until he squeezed it.

"Not you—us. If my idea works out, I'm going along to handle the financial end. You're the detective. I talked with Tanner, and at the prices he's guessing, it's going to take some doing to borrow the money. We're in no position to swing it alone, even with the Vezzi."

"Do you have contacts in Hong Kong?" she asked, amazed.

"I wish I did. No, I have someone in mind who may advance the money. We'll have to repay it as soon as we sell the jade, but even with interest, we'll come out well."

She sat back, and he let go of her hand reluctantly. Her eyes danced like prisms in the sun's last rays.

"Suppose we start by your telling me what you know about Chou jade. Tanner gave me a brief sketch, but I confess ignorance about everything but its age and value. Do you think there are many pieces? What are they apt to be? Did you hear any rumors about specific work? What——"

"One question at a time!" she protested.

She started hesitantly, giving him the historical highlights of the Chou Dynasty and the legends and facts she'd unearthed about art work of the period. Since the night of Maracudo's party, she'd devoured everything she could find on the subject in her father's collection of books. Information was scanty, but she had found one very interesting item in her father's file of clippings.

"I'm not sure it's significant, but my father saved an article from an obscure periodical called *Oriental Art World*. If he'd heard about the jade, as you say, he might have thought there was a connection. It was written by a professor of art history at Hong Kong University. He tells how some of the later work of the period was directly related to religious beliefs. That was about the time Confucius's teachings were being expanded and widely accepted. One of these was that the government had to bring humanity into harmony with the Will of Heaven. The Emperor was the Son of Heaven, not by divine descent but because of his position of moral responsibility. As long as he met this responsibility, he had the Mandate of Heaven— sort of his divine right to rule. Actually it was the other way around. When things went well, the people believed he had the Mandate of Heaven. If things went sour and there were natural disasters or wars or invasions, they thought the Mandate was being withdrawn or had expired. They believed it gave them the right to rebel and overthrow the government. It usually ushered in a new dynasty. New dynasty, new mandate—so it went through the centuries."

"What about the Chou jade?"

"According to the professor, there were reputed to be five pieces of jade that were called the "Stones of Heaven." They were carved by the leading craftsman of the period under Imperial edict. Each stone represented one of the five branches of the family that had carried on the dynasty. The jade was exquisite, the best that could be found. This, plus workmanship, made them priceless, but they derived special value from the fact that the Imperial family claimed they were the manifestation of the Mandate of Heaven. Whoever had them had the divine right to rule. They were guarded like the Crown Jewels. They were kept in a special shrine at the palace and watched over by eunuchs day and night." She paused to nibble some of the delicate fish and crisp broccoli.

"Naturally, the dynasty eventually came to an end. China was never without wars for very long. The Chous were overthrown and a new government came to power. But before they were driven out, the Imperial family managed to pack up most of the palace treasures—including the Stones of Heaven. They reasoned that if they hung on to the Stones, the Mandate would revert to them before long. Or at least so the professor theorizes. That part is all legend. But five pieces of jade did show up during the Ching dynasty—about 1800. They were from the Chou period and the old legend was revived. The pieces eventually wound up in a museum in Shanghai." She paused to eat again as Carter encouraged her not to let the food get cold.

"From here on, the story becomes fact, again according to the professor. In the early 1920s, revolutionary plots were being hatched all over China. The Nationalists set out on a campaign to drive out the Manchu warlords. There was hardly a province that wasn't fighting at some time. Shanghai was an international city with its own militia, which was made up of all nationalities, but invariably had a British colonel and an American major." She looked sheepish. "Am I telling you history you already know? I don't mean to sound pedagogic."

"I'm fascinated. Go on."

"Well, one day one of the powerful warlords swooped into Shanghai, bent on driving out the foreign invaders. He didn't consider himself or any of the Manchus invaders, of course. During the fracas, his men stormed some of the government buildings. One was the museum where the Stones of Heaven and other artifacts were kept. It became a general free-for-all when the militia came. The Manchu warlord went wild when he saw the foreigners. There was more shooting and hand-to-hand fighting than the situation warranted. The militia put down the uprising but, in the process, many of the cases in which art work was displayed were smashed and looted."

"And the Stones of Heaven disappeared?" He looked at her quizzically.

She laughed. "So the story goes. I warned you there was a fanciful blend of superstition and fact. Let's say five pieces of Chou jade vanished. Lots of other pieces too. Some were recovered. Now that I've made such a long story of it, I'll get to the point," she teased.

"There's more? It's beginning to sound like a thriller."

She wagged a finger at him. "Remember, my father saved the clipping. Why?"

"Maybe he liked legends."

She shook her head. "I'll bet he thought there was a connection between the Chou jade he'd heard about and the Stones of Heaven."

"I don't follow the logic."

"The professor described the Stones in the article and there was a very fuzzy picture taken back in the twenties when the jade was in the Shanghai museum. Also, the professor had seen one of the Stones. It was brought to him by someone who wanted an opinion on it, a peasant who'd escaped from Red China—I should say the Republic of China. He was one of the countless refugees who'd gotten out by boat and a final desperate swim. You've read the stories. Anyhow, this man claimed the jade had been in his family for years, but the professor suspected he'd stolen it from God knows where or come across it by accident. It wasn't the kind of thing the average peasant has lying about. He tried to convince him to leave it with him, but the man refused. The professor settled it by giving him the names of two reputable dealers who might handle the sale for him. He never saw the man again and he doesn't know what happened to the Stone."

"The dealers?"

She shrugged. "The professor didn't say. He did mention one other thing though. More legend. Since the Stones of Heaven disappeared from the museum in Shanghai, violence seems to have sprung up around them. Bits of stories here and there. People who own the stones seem to die rather abruptly. The professor didn't endorse the curse theory. He said it's more likely that because of the value of the jade, men are willing to kill for it. So you have your choice on that one. Anyhow, the main point is that the professor examined the jade, and in his judgment it may be one of the so-called Stones of Heaven. He says the peasant hinted that he had three more to sell."

"Three? I thought there were five stones."

"Four out of five isn't bad. What do you want from a legend?" She was delighted when he laughed with her.

"Okay," he said, "tie it all up for me. We have the professor's article, which your father saved. Where's the connection to the current Chou jade story?"

She laid her knife and fork across her plate and leaned forward. "First, there's the timing. My father was in Hong Kong approximately three months ago. You said he mentioned the Chou jade when he came back. The article was dated almost four months ago, and my father penciled it in red and kept it. There was a paper clip at one corner and a scrap of yellow sheet, as though there'd been correspondence attached to it. But I couldn't find it. My father's files were—still are—a mess, so I have no guarantee there were letters, but it seems likely that my father wrote to the professor and probably visited him on that last trip. When we get to Hong Kong, I suggest we see the professor first. He may be able to tell us something."

Carter was pensive. "Ninety percent of Oriental art dealers probably read the professor's article."

"Maybe, but it's not one of the big journals in the field. It's more a scholarly thing put out by the university. Besides," she said with a grin, "I never said it was going to be easy."

"True. What with legendary curses and Mandates of Heaven... It's a great yarn though. And if the Chou jade turns out to be these fabulous Stones of Heaven, it'll triple the price. Legends and curses are worth their weight in gold in this business."

She hadn't realized how the time had passed. It was totally dark outside now, the ocean and sky blending together in a black mass. A few boat lights twinkled and bobbed. A spotlight at the end of the pier jutting out beyond the restaurant cast wavering ribbons of white across the waves. The night itself was like a legend.

Over coffee and liqueurs, they talked about Hong Kong again. Arisa had begun a list of people her father knew, working from memory and the files in his desk. Carter promised to open the office files for her to see if there were any names she'd missed.

When they left the restaurant, Carter drove slowly along the Coast Highway as they enjoyed the refreshing ocean breeze.

Arisa's excitement had calmed to pleasant anticipation, though her mind was busy exploring all the side trails the trip to Hong Kong might bring. If they got the jade, Travish-Montaigne would be out of the woods financially. There'd be no excuse for her not making a decision, and she had the feeling Carter would insist on it. She thought about Eduoard's call, and about returning to Paris. Strangely, it seemed as remote now as the idea of returning to Los Angeles had once been. She wondered if Carter's new attitude had anything to do with her own. Was his eagerness to go to Hong Kong strictly financial? She realized they had not crossed swords once during the entire evening, and the thought made her smile. Maybe he was beginning to realize she was not quite the albatross he'd imagined.

When they reached the house, he walked inside with her. "I want to make sure there's no one lurking in the shadows to knock you out," he said with a grin.

Amused, she watched him go through the house. She stood in the hall as he snapped on lights and prowled the lower floor, then she followed him upstairs as he completed the tour. In the doorway of her bedroom, she waited until he had checked the closet and gone down on his knees to look under the bed. She laughed softly. Grinning, he rose with a satisfied nod.

"Really, Carter, you handpicked the locksmith, remember?" she chided good-naturedly.

"Can't be too careful," he said with mock seriousness. His grin softened to a tender smile. "I'm not taking any chances where you're concerned."

Surprised at his gentle tone, she tried to make light of the comment. "Ah, you realize at last what an asset I am to Travish-Montaigne."

He came toward her, his gaze caressing. "To Montaigne at least. Do you know how many times I've thought about you these past few days?"

Her breath caught.

"It's been a wonderful evening, Arisa. Does it have to end so soon?" His gaze did not relinquish hers as he closed the distance between them and took her in his arms. "You're incredibly beautiful," he said softly, "and unbelievably desirable." He drew her into the circle of his embrace and captured her lips.

Arisa's mind whirled as she discarded all the reasons she once might have used to put him off. She couldn't deny the desire that stirred at his touch. Nor could she erase the memory of her own restlessness after their first evening together had ended with only a kiss. Her legs trembled as his tongue caressed her lips and spoke its silent invitation. Desire and need filled her, and she responded eagerly. His fingers were cool at the nape of her neck, then warm and lingering as they traced a path to the pulse below her ear. His hand stroked the smooth curve of her back as though urging her to become part of him.

When at last he released her lips, he stared into the violet pools of her eyes. "Your eyes tell me what I want to know," he whispered.

She didn't—couldn't—deny it. Slowly he began to undo the fastenings of her dress and slip it off. When she shivered, they both knew it was not with chill but yielding desire. His gaze lingered on her high, firm breasts as he quickly removed his own garments and then drew her to the bed.

She lay quietly as he sat beside her and explored the sleek, wondrous contours of her body. He was a gentle, provocative lover, bringing her to passion tenderly and lingeringly, arousing her need to unbearable heights so that she lost all inhibition and made her own demands on his flesh. Her hands and lips were as eager as his until at last their bodies joined in exquisite union. A slow, steady throb filled Arisa as his power became part of her. She abandoned herself to the sublime torment of wanting him and knowing her desire would be completely fulfilled. Her senses reeled as she felt the hard, rippling muscles of his shoulders quiver. Her body arched as she reached the precipice of fulfillment and was rewarded by his answering promise of release. Breathlessly, they soared to the pinnacle of orgasm and were swept into its heady, ebbing tide.

She lay comfortable under the pressure of his arm flung across her breasts. It was a long time before he roused himself and got up to dress, watching her with a smile. Then he came to sit beside her again. He brushed her damp hair from her cheeks.

"Sleep well, Arisa. I'll see you in the morning." He bent and kissed her lingeringly and then, with a tender smile, he left.

She listened to his footsteps fade and the front door close quietly. A moment later the soft purr of the Mercedes engine disturbed the night briefly, then was gone. She let out her breath in a tremulous sigh, her lips still savoring the touch of his kiss.

11

When Carter returned to his apartment, he poured himself a Courvoisier and dialed the operator to put through a call to Claire. With any luck, she'd still be trying to put together the basics for the Badin job. If she'd taken off for the Mediterranean, it might be days before he could catch her. He was sorry now he hadn't gone along with his inclination to follow through on Arisa's idea from the start.

The phone rang and he picked it up quickly. The operator had his party; he listened to the muffled series of connections. Finally Claire's voice came on the line.

"Darling, what a delightful surprise."

"I'm glad I caught you, Claire. I hate doing business by long distance phone, but something's come up. I have a proposition for you."

She laughed softly, eagerly. "Anytime, darling."

He ignored her coquettishness. "Strictly business. What would you say to backing a purchase I want to make? I need two hundred thousand. I'm willing to give you a note for the entire amount plus interest, payable within sixty days. Or you can write off the balance due me on the salon at a six-percent discount and take the remainder in cash, sixty days net."

She was silent. Carter imagined her eyes narrowing as she juggled figures. She knew he was asking a personal favor, money from her own funds, not the business. He'd always been disdainful of her fortune, refusing to let her finance anything he couldn't match.

"You're serious?" she asked finally.

"Absolutely."

"Two hundred thousand? My God, what are you going to buy?"

He hedged. "Something special from the Orient."

She paused again. She wasn't interested in money, but he knew she was calculating what else she might get out of it. If she wrote off his debt on the salon, she'd lose her tenuous hold on him.

"I'd have to know more about it, darling."

"It's some very old jade. I've just learned that Elliot was working on a purchase before he died." He wasn't sure why he didn't tell her the whole story. Probably because he didn't trust her completely. She was capable of finding a way to work things to her advantage.

"It must be very old and *very* special. I'll have to think about it, Carter. It's a lot of money."

"I need an answer right away. There's another dealer interested."

"Surely you can put it off a few days. I can finish up here and fly back. We'll discuss it then. Maybe I should have a look at this fabulous jade and not buy a pig in a poke."

How much should he tell her? Damn. "Actually the jade isn't here. It involves a trip to Hong Kong. I don't want to wait."

"Hong Kong? I haven't been there for ages. All right, I'll meet you there. The Mandarin or the Peninsula?"

His temper knife-edged and he held it back painfully. Making her mad wouldn't help. In as patient a tone as he could muster, he said, "I'm not going over without assurance that I can buy what I want." He was already gambling on Arisa, but he didn't mention her name.

"I see."

"Yes or no, Claire? I'll have to go elsewhere if you don't want to do it." He was bluffing, but she couldn't be sure.

She let him hang a few moments. "Well, it sounds very important, darling. I guess I can trust your judgment."

"Is that a yes?"

"I'll phone my lawyer. Will a letter of credit do?"

"Fine."

"I'll have him draw up the agreement and call you tomorrow. When are you leaving?"

"As soon as I can arrange a flight."

"Mmm, well, good luck, darling, whatever it is."

"Thanks, Claire—for the money and the luck. I'll see you when you get back. Have fun with the Fairchilds."

He hung up, elated. He wanted to call Arisa but a glance at the clock changed his mind. She'd be asleep by now. He'd tell her tomorrow after he had the letter of credit from Claire's attorney.

One of the first things on Carter's agenda in the morning

was a talk with Tanner. He wanted to deliver the Vezzi to Faus right away. Faus's check in the bank would make him feel a lot better about the expenses of the trip to Hong Kong.

He knew as soon as he heard Tanner's voice.

"Oh, hi, Carter. I was going to call."

"The Vezzi?"

"I'm afraid you're in for a disappointment. The carbon dating shows it's at least a hundred years after Vezzi. Chances are it's a Doccia reproduction. A damned good one, though. Whoever put on the Venezia mark knew what he was doing."

A copy. Carter swore silently, disappointment and anger churning at his guts. He'd gambled and placed—not won.

"You're sure?"

"Afraid so. Listen, this piece would fool ninety percent of the people around. You said even Gricci pegged it for an original. I would have agreed if it hadn't been for the carbon dating. That's the trouble with scientific methods, they don't leave room for argument."

Carter let out a long, tired breath. "Okay, thanks, Tanner."

"Sorry to spoil your day."

"It happens. I appreciate your friend getting it done so fast. Send him that beer and charge it to the shop."

"Anyone who appreciates Vezzi will appreciate this piece. It's superb work."

"I know I won't have any trouble selling it," Carter said. "But I'd been reserving it for Elbert Faus. That's down the tube now."

"Sure, well, it happens, like you said."

Carter hung up. He stabbed the pencil he'd been doodling with so hard that the lead snapped. Angrily, he swept it off the desk. He'd been a fool to call Faus before he was sure, but he couldn't undo that now. He'd promised to bring the Vezzi to Faus's house today, and he knew the old man was looking forward to it. Maybe he should drive out anyhow. He wasn't eager to face Arisa with bad news just yet. He'd been counting on the Vezzi, both financially and to prove himself with Arisa. Or to himself? When he'd gone into partnership with Elliot, he'd vowed to reach a turning point within twelve months. The year was about up, and Travish-Montaigne was still rolling right down the middle of the road. His only hope now was the Chou jade. He hoped to hell Arisa would be able to find it before the other vultures swooped in.

*   *   *

A Santa Ana wind had washed the basin clean, and the mountains were etched in sharp relief against the blue bowl of the sky. Like everything else, freedom from smog had its price. The heat was enervating. He'd put the top up on the convertible and turned on the air-conditioning full blast. Turning from Arroyo Parkway onto Colorado, Carter tried to clear his mind for the meeting with Faus. He was sorry as hell to disappoint the old man. Faus was a good client.

Crossing the bridge, he drove along Arroyo until he came to the steep drive leading to the millionaire's mansion. It was visible for miles, perched like an eagle's aerie on a hilltop overlooking the canyon. Carter rolled the Mercedes to a stop in front of the twelve-foot-high iron gate. As he lowered the window to press the bell, heat poured over him. A disembodied voice said, "Yes?" He turned his face toward the hidden camera fitted into the stanchion. "Carter Montaigne. Mr. Faus is expecting me."

A moment later the heavy gates swung open. He started the Mercedes up the steep climb. The drive was graveled instead of paved. Faus once had explained that it forced vehicles to maintain a discreet speed and also prevented heavy runoffs during the winter rains. The drive bed was six feet deep, layered sand and gravel. In the fifty-five years since the mansion had been built, there had never been any erosion of the hillside. Faus had been an architect in his younger years, on a par with Stanford White for his time. In the thirties and forties, half the important buildings in Los Angeles were Faus-designed. Most of them had given way now to slabs of steel and glass, but there were still a few around.

The house was invisible from the drive, screened by the lush overhang of cypresses and jacaranda in a mosaic of green. The car purred upward until the drive leveled into a sweeping turn-around. Under the bleached azure sky, the mansion was a dramatic statement of simplicity and elegance. Grillwork balconies commanded a spectacular view of the city beyond the vista of garden bordered by the drive. The sight never failed to impress Carter, and he sat a moment looking at it before he climbed out of the car.

A black-jacketed butler answered his ring and ushered him into the huge hall.

"Mr. Faus is in the study, sir."

Carter always felt he should have a top hat and gloves to hand over to the impeccable servant. Suppressing a smile, he followed the man across the marble foyer with its glittering Czechoslovakian crystal chandelier. Beyond a pilastered arch, a grand staircase swept to the second story. The iron grillwork of the balustrade created a frame for part of Faus's collection of masterpieces on the wall. A hall led off the second foyer. Under subdued lighting, it was another gallery of paintings: Seurat, Renoir, Picasso.

Faus received him in a study tucked into a rear corner of the house. It was Faus's private domain, a man's room, comfortable, yet timeless in design and decor. Its rich paneling and pegged flooring gave it warmth and incorporated a feeling of openness with the yard outside which was a serene backdrop of gardens, fountains, and shrubbery. Faus extended a hand from the depths of a gilded beechwood *bergère*.

"Hello, Carter. You're empty-handed. I was hoping to see the Vezzi." A disappointed smile made his wrinkled face quiver like slow-rippling water when a pebble disturbs its surface.

Carter released the man's blue-veined hand and seated himself where Faus would not have to crane his neck. "That's what I've come about, Elbert. I'm afraid I have disappointing news."

The old man frowned and was silent.

Carter didn't hedge. "I was carried away by enthusiasm. I've just learned that the vase isn't a genuine Vezzi. It had a lot of people convinced, including me, but I've just had a carbon dating. It's an early reproduction, probably a Doccia."

The light in Faus's eyes dimmed a hundred candlepower. "A shame," he said.

"I know you don't collect Doccia, but you might want to take a look at it. It's a remarkably good piece."

Faus shook his head. "I think not, but thank you. I'm getting too old to take on new adventures in collecting. I prefer to spend my energy and money in quest of the few pieces I want."

"I'm sorry, Elbert."

Faus cleared his throat. "I appreciate your driving all the way out here to tell me, Carter. I always considered you an honest man to deal with." There was a change in inflection that lent a shadow of question to the statement.

"Past tense?" Carter asked, cocking his head inquisitively.

The old man sighed. "I'll come right to the point. As you

know, I have very few Oriental *objets d'art*. Elliot interested me in them because of their unquestionable beauty and their connection to European work, especially in the eighteenth and nineteenth centuries. He convinced me that a few pieces would fit well here." He raised a finger to indicate the room. Carter didn't have to look away from the old man's face. He knew exactly where the Chieng-Sen Buddha and the blue and white Qianlong moon flask were. With an uneasy feeling, he waited for Faus to continue.

"Shortly before his death, Elliot told me about a bronze urn he had coming from Hong Kong. He wanted me to have it."

"The Han," Carter said.

"Correct."

"I thought it was to be delivered to you last week as soon as it had been cleaned."

"It was." He turned his head toward the cases that held leather-bound books interspersed with art objects.

Carter saw the urn highlighted be a small recessed light. He looked back to Faus.

"It's a fake, Carter."

"It can't be!" Carter was on his feet, striding across the room. He lifted the urn and felt the unevenness of its weight. Frowning, he tipped it to the light and examined the mark on the base.

Faus said, "The mold is definitely machined—you can see the tooling marks if you examine the surface. Original signatures were pressed into the hot metal with a hand-carved die, not gouged with a stenciling tool afterward."

Carter carried the urn back. "I'm at a loss for words, Elbert. The piece was in the hands of several of our top people before it was delivered to you." Surely Deline or Tanner would have spotted the obvious flaws. How could...? "Have you talked to anyone at the shop?"

Faus shook his head. "I thought it better to wait for you."

"Thank you, Elbert. I'll refund your money immediately, of course. And I'll find out how this happened. I'm sorry you were embarrassed by someone's carelessness." His mind was tabulating possibilities. A mistake in packing? A distracted clerk mixing up two urns? No, it couldn't be that simple. The shop didn't carry junk like this.

"I would say someone's having a joke at your expense, Carter," Faus said.

"Needless to say, I'll get to the bottom of it. We've never had anything like this happen before. I don't understand. How was it delivered?"

"The courier service. Mason signed for it and brought it to me unopened."

Carter shook his head, still staring at the horrible cheap fake. As a joke, it wasn't very funny.

"I'll see nothing like this ever happens again, I assure you, Elbert. And when I find out who's responsible, he'll wish he'd never tried."

"I hope so, Carter. An incident like this can ruin a reputation that's taken years to build."

Carter grunted savagely. Once a dealer had the taint of forgery on his record, he might as well change his sign from "antiques" to "junk" and get himself a pushcart.

He met Faus's delft-blue gaze. "Thank you, Elbert, I mean that. I appreciate your reserving judgment and action until we talked."

The old man gave him a rippling smile. "I'm seldom wrong in my assessment of a man's character. Or a woman's. I met Elliot's daughter at the Tucker Museum benefit. Quite a young lady. She has her father's keenness."

Carter smiled. "I'm just beginning to realize that. We got off on the wrong foot when we first met. We were laboring under preconceived notions."

"A luxury of youth when there's plenty of time to correct your mistakes. The girl's a good listener. Unusual in a woman. She's interested in the shop. Will she be filling Elliot's place?"

"I'm—she's not sure. I believe she has some interests in Paris that may claim prior importance."

"A pity. She's personable. She'd do well. I suspect Maracudo was pumping her about her intentions. He spent a considerable time talking to her. If she's going to become part of the business, he wants to make sure she knows who he is." Faus lowered his chin and peered at Carter. "Are you going after that Chou jade everyone's buzzing about?"

Surprised, Carter grinned. "Arisa's convinced me it may be worth the effort."

"I'm not an expert, but judging from the talk and the interest Ganrali Maracudo is showing, I'd say she's right. From what I hear, he has prospectors out digging. He wants that jade."

Carter shrugged. "So far it seems to be mostly speculation.

Does the jade really exist? Can it be brought out of the People's Republic? Has it? Who'll be the lucky person to get to it first?"

Faus cackled softly. "Don't discount rumors, my boy. Would it surprise you to know Elliot talked to me about it some months back? He heard the story in Hong Kong and was trying to track it down."

"It surprises the hell out of me." Carter admitted. "He did mention it to me but mostly as a passing thing."

"He'd want to be sure before he asked for your commitment. He was a very proud man, but he was obsessed with the idea he'd disappoint a lot of people. He wanted to prove himself for a lot of reasons."

Again Carter was surprised. He'd never seen that side of Elliot, never suspected it. But Elliot and Faus had been friends a long time, and he didn't doubt what the old man was saying. Shifting the brass urn to the crook of his arm, he got to his feet.

"Thanks again, Elbert. I'll be in touch as soon as I find out about this. I think Travish-Montaigne owes you an explanation as well as a refund."

Faus pushed himself up from the chair and walked with Carter to the hall. "Thank you for coming out. It's always a pleasure to see you. Good luck in placing the Doccia, I'm sure you won't have any trouble. It was a good factory, some very fine work. And Carter . . ."

"Yes?"

"If you get that Chou jade, I'd appreciate a look at it. I asked Arisa for first refusal but she wouldn't commit herself without talking to you." His eyes twinkled. "Girl's got a head on her shoulders."

"I'll see what we can do."

They shook hands again and Faus turned back to the study as the butler appeared to show Carter out. He tossed the spurious Han urn in the back seat. Now that his shock had eased, cold fury filled him. He'd find out who was responsible for this if it was the last thing he did.

He assembled them in his office within minutes of his return to the shop. Arisa and Deline came up together from the workshop where they'd been cataloging a shipment of Ming porcelains. Tanner drove over from his shop, combining an answer to Carter's summons with delivery of the Doccia vase.

Tanner glanced at the women and smiled. "I didn't know it was going to be a convention. Hi, Arisa, how's it going? Deline?" Then he saw Carter's face. "Uh-oh, storm clouds. What's up?" He set the canvas bag containing the Doccia on Carter's file cabinet.

Carter waited for him to settle. Deline had already offered to make tea but he'd refused. He'd come to the conclusion there was no right way to approach this subject, so he plunged in headlong.

"I just came back from Elbert Faus's. He's returned the Han bronze we sold him last week. With good reason." His gaze impaled each of them in turn. "It's a fake."

"What?" It was a chorus from Arisa and Tanner. Deline's mouth opened but no sound came out.

"Not only a fake but the cheapest kind of substitution possible. I want to know how it happened and who's responsible."

"Surely you're not suggesting any of us had something to do with it!"

"I know better than that," Carter said. "But it happened. It had to be a deliberate attempt to discredit us. Whoever did it knew the fake would be detected as soon as the package was opened." He reached into the cabinet and brought out the urn, setting it on the desk. Tanner reached for it immediately.

He grimaced. "These things are turned out by the thousands all over the Orient. Junk. Tourist bait." He handed the urn to Arisa when she held out her hands. "It sure as hell isn't the same piece I cleaned. I picked up and delivered back a second-century bronze. If you'd sent this piece of junk over, I'd have tossed it in the garbage. Come on now, Carter."

Arisa passed the urn to Deline, whose face was pale as she examined it. She shook her head in disbelief. "This is not the same urn, of course." She glanced at Carter. "You were in the workshop when I uncrated it. Just before you went to Paris."

He'd forgotten. "So we agree that a genuine piece arrived here," he said. "The question remains, how did this one get to Faus?"

Tanner scowled. "I picked it up. It didn't need much more than a dusting. Leun Kee takes good care of his stuff. As I remember, I brought it back the next afternoon." He glanced at Deline for verification.

She nodded. "That's correct. It was quite late. I did not

have an opportunity to pack it until the following day. The transfer people picked it up the next morning—no, it was the weekend. They do not deliver on Saturday. They picked it up on Monday. I can check my records."

"Where was it during that time?"

Her brow puckered. "In the cabinet reserved for merchandise awaiting shipment."

"And the courier service?"

"The same one we always use. They have been completely reliable until now."

Arisa spoke for the first time. Carter's bombshell had stunned her, and a sick feeling was growing. "If the shop had been broken into, we would have known. That indicates the substitution was made after the urn left the shop."

"Unless someone had an opportunity over the weekend."

Deline pressed a finger to the furrow between her brows. "We do not receive deliveries on Saturday, so no one is assigned to the workroom. Had anyone been away from his or her post long enough to copy, make up, and substitute a package for the one I'd prepared, I'm sure the others would have noticed."

Arisa recalled Carter telling her of the steps he'd taken to tighten security after several small items had disappeared. They'd been effective until now. But this was more than petty theft. Someone had known the urn well enough to substitute one similar in size and shape. It seemed to rule out the courier. Carter seemed to be following the same line of thought.

"Deline, call the service and get a copy of the driver's log. I want to know how much time elapsed between the pick-up and the delivery. A copy of Faus's signed receipt too."

Deline nodded.

Tanner shook his head. "It sure leaves a lousy taste in my mouth. It comes down to a thief within Travish-Montaigne or to one of us lying."

"I don't want a word of this to go beyond this room," Carter said slowly. "You all know what it can do to our reputation. Deline, make copies of everything the police will need. I'll take them over personally. I'm sure I can persuade the detectives to handle this discreetly. We can't afford to look like fools."

"What about Mr. Faus?" Arisa asked. She recalled the pleasant elderly man at the Tucker Museum party.

"He's not going to make trouble. He agrees someone may

be deliberately trying to discredit us."

"Why?" Tanner demanded in astonishment.

"If I could answer that, we'd be a lot closer to how and who. Faus waited to talk to me. I appreciate that, but at the same time, it's given the thief several days. Do you have a sketch or a picture, Tanner? We'll circulate a description with the FBI's Art Squad, but there's a damned good possibility it's gone underground already."

Tanner shook his head. "I feel like I've fallen into the middle of a grade B movie. Maybe we should get Charlie Chan."

Carter's tension eased for the first time since he'd left Elbert Faus. Tanner had the rare talent of giving a light touch to any situation. "Okay, Number-One Son," he said, "get on this case. Let's assemble everything as quickly as possible. I'd like to take it over to police headquarters today."

Tanner unfolded himself from the chair and went out muttering. Deline glanced at Arisa, then followed Tanner, closing the door behind her.

"I'm still in a state of shock," Arisa said. "Is this going to hurt us financially?"

"The insurance will cover it," Carter said wearily. "I'm a lot more concerned about why it was done. What does someone have to gain by it? It isn't as if our reputation endangers anyone. Who are we a threat to?" He was talking to himself as much as to her. On top of the non-Vezzi, it was too much. He sighed. "We're all set on Hong Kong. I got the backing."

"Oh, Carter, that's wonderful!"

"I asked Deline to have the travel agent make reservations. We'll stay at the Mandarin if that's all right." When she nodded, he said, "Can you be ready to take the first available flight?"

"I can be ready any time." She studied the drawn lines of his face. He really was worried. There was no sign of the passion or tenderness she'd seen last night. She tried to put her own feelings in perspective. He seemed able to turn tenderness off and on like a tap. No, that wasn't fair, she told herself. He was worried about the bronze. And with cause.

She rose. "Carter, if there's anything I can do to help with this Han thing, you only need to ask. I know it's a blow coming on the heels of the Vezzi, but we'll make up for it all with the Chou jade, you'll see."

"Tanner told you, then." He'd forgotten how much the two discussed.

She nodded. "I respect your integrity. Not many dealers would go to the lengths you did to validate something they'd already bought as an original."

He rubbed his temple. "Invalidate," he said ruefully. "Well, if there's one great lesson I've learned in life, it's not to gnash my teeth over what's done." He smiled as he realized she was still looking at him as though he'd sprouted a gold-plated halo. "The Hong Kong trip takes on a whole new importance now."

She knew he was talking about the company's finances, but her cheeks warmed as she remembered his lovemaking the night before. "I have the list just about complete," she told him. "Tanner mentioned a few names I didn't have."

"All right. I'll let you know as soon as we have flight times. Now I'd better get organized if I'm going to get everything done." He watched her until the door closed, wondering if she understood just how crucial the Chou jade was to them now. And somewhere in a dark corner of his mind, he wondered if he was falling in love with her.

Deline closed the door of her office, still shaking inwardly. With a quick phone conversation to the owner of the courier service, she arranged for the information they needed to be delivered to Carter's office within the hour. Her second call she did not trust to any office line. She left the shop and drove to her house in a cul-de-sac off Coldwater Canyon. She dialed Bok's number.

"What can I do for you, Madame Armitage?"

"I have just learned of the Han bronze. What is the meaning of this? Don't deny it is your work!" Her hand trembled and she pressed the phone against the side of her head until her skull ached.

"I do not deny it. On the contrary, I wanted you to know I had arranged the deception." His voice was deadly cold.

Deline felt suddenly weak and sat down in the satin-cushioned tea chair that graced the hall. He wanted her to know...A warning...A suggestion of the reach of his power and the extent of his intention. Fear replaced the anger in her voice. "I am powerless to hasten the thing we both want most," she said. "I can only urge Quentin to pressure his sister subtly. It has not been effective. And now there will be a further delay. Arisa is going to Hong Kong."

"The reason?" he rasped.

"To purchase the Chou jade."

Bok's explosion was so violent that Deline held the phone away from her ear. She smiled, even though she knew his fury would not be abated by the invectives and curses he spewed forth. At last he said very coldly, "I remind you, Madame Armitage, time is running out, along with my patience. You will find that my next 'reminders' are not as subtle. Perhaps you can persuade Miss Travish to turn over the jade before she suffers another 'burglary' or another confusion in shipment."

He hung up abruptly, and Deline cradled the phone. Bok was dangerous, and he was angry. An evil combination. What did he expect her to do? The jade was not in the house. Quentin had verified this, then Bok himself—with almost disastrous results. The jade was not in the shop. It could only be at Elliot's bank—unless he had sold it. No, he would not have done that, she could not entertain such a thought. Years ago when the business was just starting out, he'd spoken of it often. There would be no reason for him to part with it after so many years. No reason at all. It was the tie that bound him to her—in California just as it had in China. His blood.

12

Arisa gazed at the incredible skyline. Since the plane had come in over Kowloon, she'd felt as if she were dancing backward and forward in time. She was instantly enveloped by the sensory perceptions she'd described earlier to Carter. At the same time she was astonished at the urban jungle the city had become. It had spread outward and upward and inward like a river that had burst its levee. Towering resettlement estates overshadowed the crowded lanes and streets from Kennedy Town to North Point, colorful splashes on monuments of white. Clusters of high-rises dominated the mid-levels and reached cautious tentacles toward the Peak. Even on that green-capped skyline, white concrete sentinels intruded majestically.

"Has it changed so much?" Carter asked.

With a guilty start, Arisa drew her attention back to the comfortable Harlequin Bar at the top of the Mandarin. Carter had insisted she relax after the long flight, but she was too excited now that they were here. During the trip, they'd gone over their plans. They'd talk with the professor first, then start on the list of dealers Arisa had compiled.

"It's unbelievable," she told him with a smile. "When we lived here, we thought the city was already bursting at the seams. My father used to lament the changes. He thought it was a shame that there was so little effort to recapture any of the Chinese or even colonial charms as the city was rebuilt." She glanced through the expanse of glass windows at the sprawling city that was confined now only by the contours of the island. "All that concrete and glass. I wonder what he thought of it."

"Maybe he was able to concentrate on the things that were the same," he said.

Yes, her father had probably done exactly that: shut out the influences he didn't endorse and focus on the Chinese things he loved. There were plenty of those. During the cab ride from Kai Tak Airport, she'd glimpsed narrow streets with tiny stalls and crowded shops that were the Chinese way of life. And she knew that within a block of the hotel, she could lose herself in the Hong Kong she remembered.

"Sometimes I get the feeling you knew my father very well," she told him.

"He was full of surprises. Sometimes I get the feeling I didn't know him at all."

That brought a smile to her lips. "I've felt the same way so many times these past weeks. I'm beginning to realize he was a very complex man. I had tunnel vision, I'm afraid."

"It's a common failing. We're all guilty of it to a degree."

His searching look personalized the remark, and she glanced away again. "The university isn't far. The secretary said Professor Sun is usually in his office from three to four. Maybe we should go."

Carter caught the waiter's eye. When the man brought the check, Carter signed it and they left the cool bar to descend to the street level. The commotion of Connaught Road had not diminished. The sidewalks were thronged, and the honking, roaring traffic was a steady stream. Two doormen snaked in and out of the inching vehicles as they tried to flag cabs for guests who had queued up. When they finally settled into a taxi, Carter grinned.

"Is it always like this?"

"It gets worse during rush hour or if it rains," she said, laughing. "Drivers don't usually stop if you flag them on the street. Even people from the offices wait in front of the hotels."

"I'll rent a car," he said emphatically. Then, with a rueful glance at the darting, swerving lines of traffic, he added, "Maybe."

At the university, a pleasant-faced young girl told them that Professor Sun was engaged at the moment. If they cared to wait, she was sure it wouldn't be long. They sat in a reception room that was well-stocked with periodicals dealing with Oriental customs, art work, history, and the like. Carter browsed through one while Arisa let her mind wander over the possible approaches to Professor Sun. She had tried to learn more about him, but he seemed a minor academician with only a budding reputation outside the university circle. He was considered an expert in the history of early Chinese dynasties. It accounted for his emphasis in the article on the historical significance of the Chou Stones of Heaven rather than their value in the art world. Would he be willing to aid a commercial venture?

"Miss Travish, Mr. Montaigne—Professor Sun will see you now." The girl ushered them through a sparse, uncluttered waiting room to the professor's office. The difference was as shocking as the transition from the quiet Harlequin Bar to the noisy street.

Sun sat behind a desk that was covered with towers of papers, magazines, and files. Behind the desk, a large library table was buried under less organized piles, as though the professor had given up any attempt to sort them. Books were stacked on the floor; even a windowsill had been pressed into use as a shelf, and the pages of a magazine fluttered restlessly in the breeze from the open window. Miraculously, two wooden chairs were vacant. The professor asked them to sit.

"I am delighted to meet you, Miss Travish, and you, Mr. Montaigne. I've been looking forward to seeing Mr. Travish again." Sun was sparse and frail with an ageless Oriental face. His black hair was combed severely back and cut short.

Arisa said, "Elliot Travish was my father. He passed away recently."

"I'm sorry . . ."

Sun settled his wire-rimmed glasses more firmly on the bridge of his nose.

"I take it my father came to see you," Arisa went on. "That's partly why we're here."

Arisa glanced at Carter, and he gave her a sign that he was leaving the dialogue in her hands. She seemed to have a knack for understanding the Chinese readily, and he was content to listen.

"Mr. Montaigne and I are following up on some matters my father left incomplete. I came across your article on Chou jade among my father's papers. I assume that is what he came to see you about."

"Yes. He was so interested, I thought I'd hear from him again."

"Could you tell us the gist of his inquiry?" Arisa asked. When Sun blinked and peered, she smiled disarmingly. "Like yourself, my father was too busy to keep up with the task of filing. I am handicapped by not understanding his methods and because I haven't had time to go through everything."

Sun glanced around at the clutter and nodded. "There are more important things to do."

He rocked back in his swivel chair. "He wanted to know about the Stones of Heaven. He'd never heard the legend before, but he thought he might have seen one of the Stones at one time. He wanted a more detailed description. I, in turn, requested more information on where he had seen the stone. If it is the fifth stone and not one of those already accounted for, you can imagine the value of the find." He looked at her hopefully. "Do you know where he saw it?"

"I'm afraid not, or at least that would be my answer until I, too, have a better description of the Stone. It's possible either Mr. Montaigne or myself may also have seen it at some time."

Sun's dark eyes shifted to Carter. "What is your interest in the jade?"

"As Mr. Travish's partner, my interest is commercial. We deal with many collectors who would prize these excellent examples of Chou work highly," Carter said.

Professor Sun sighed. "Naturally, I'd like to see the pieces in a museum instead of in the hands of a private collector, but I suppose that's unrealistic. I've already had other inquiries."

Arisa glanced at Carter. "Other dealers?" he asked quickly.

The professor nodded.

"What did you tell them?"

"Only what I can tell you. I don't know where the man went from here. I gave him the names of two reputable men who might be interested in buying the jade. Neither admits acquiring the piece I examined, but that may be a safeguard to protect their investment. I'll be happy to give you the names."

"Thank you," Arisa said. "Can you describe the pieces more fully? I'm still interested in the idea that my father may have seen one."

"I can do better than that. I have a photograph of the one that was brought to me." He began rummaging in a drawer and finally found two polaroid prints, which he passed over to her. Carter leaned over her shoulder to study them.

The photos were not professional. The flash had reflected on the surface of the stone and erased most of the detail. The piece of jade was laid against a ruler that showed it was an inch and a half wide and slightly longer. It resembled a beetle or cicada in shape though the lines of the carving were barely discernable. The second shot was of the underside of the stone. The rich color of the jade was more prominent and the details finer, as though Sun had profited by his first effort and corrected his lighting. A delicate scroll design was worked so perfectly around the edges of the stone that it gave an appearance of a rolled edging. In the center, several ideographs were enclosed in a circle. At first glance they seemed to be a chop mark, but closer scrutiny showed it was a lengthier text.

"What does it say?" Arisa queried.

"As near as I've been able to determine, they are names. Chinese ideographs have changed considerably over the centuries. This is an archaic scholarly form of writing."

"Do all the stones have it?"

"I suspect so, since each was to represent a branch of the dynasty family. Each Stone undoubtedly lists the family members. They'd be different, of course, but the inscription would probably be similar in appearance." He gave Arisa and Carter a hopeful gaze. "Have you seen the stone Mr. Travish mentioned?"

"I haven't," Carter said. "Arisa?"

"I'm afraid not. At first it seemed vaguely familiar, but I'm sure it's just the general shape. The cicada is a popular theme."

Sun couldn't hide his disappointment. "A pity. One always hopes. May I ask a favor?"

"Of course."

"If you are fortunate enough to acquire any of the jade you seek, will you give me the privilege of viewing it before you take it back?"

"Certainly," Carter promised. "And now we've taken a lot of your time. If you'll give us the names of the dealers, we'll let you get back to your work."

"David Fung on Queen's Road, Central, and Yue Hin on Hollywood Road."

Carter noted both names on a pocket secretary, then rose. "Thank you, Professor Sun. We hope to be in touch before long."

As they descended the hill toward the street, Arisa said, "We may be in luck. I remember David Fung. He's been in business a long time. He lived on the Peak not far from us. I'll bet my father stayed in touch with him. The other name is on our list too."

"Let's hope so, and let's hope one of them is the lucky man who got the Chou jade."

She sighed. "And let's hope he's still got it. If Professor

Sun has had inquiries, we may not be the first in line."

"We'll cross that bridge when we come to it. What do you say we head for Mr. Fung's shop right now?"

She smiled. "It's right on our way."

David Fung was not in. A middle-aged Chinese clerk said he was not expected back. Arisa suggested they walk to Yue Hin's shop, which was only a few blocks away. Carter let himself be led through a narrow street that was like nothing he'd ever seen. It wasn't wide enough for vehicles. Shops and stalls overflowed the sidewalks, barely leaving room for the crush of pedestrian traffic that filled it. Umbrellas and shoes crowded against colorful toys. Dark cubbyholes burgeoned with complex electronic equipment or fishing gear. Bright, lush piles of fruit formed colorful mountains atop handwoven baskets where women paused to select the choicest pomegranates or oranges. Rows of mass-produced cotton housedresses, silk blouses and *cheongsams* fluttered like banners from awnings and racks that were jammed into any available space. Hardware, housewares, baskets, plastics—an unending array of shoppers' choices.

When at last they came out onto Hollywood Road, Carter breathed an exaggerated sigh of relief. "That has to be worse than a bargain basement sale!"

She laughed with delight. "There are hundreds of streets just like it."

"The Chinese must spend all their time shopping."

"It looks that way, doesn't it." She was enjoying being able to introduce him to the colorful sights of the city and to see his reaction. She'd been gone so long, she'd forgotten the heady sense of excitement she'd always found here. Glancing at the occasional numbered buildings, she headed in the direction of the shop they were looking for. When she finally stopped in front of a curio shop, he gave her a surprised look.

"This is it?" He stared at the cluttered window piled with brass, ivory, and wood carvings.

"In Hong Kong, you learn never to judge a book by its cover," she told him. "My father loved these old shops. He always said he found the best bargains here." She thought nostalgically of Fook Shing's stall on Ladder Street and the treasures it produced.

They went up the two steps. A brass bell tinkled as they opened the door and stepped inside. A huge stone Buddha smiled a permanent welcome. They edged past and made their way to the narrow counter at the rear of the shop. In a dusty display case, carved jade caught her eye immediately. With a smile at the old man sitting behind it, Arisa bent for a closer look. Most of the jade was mediocre quality and work, but at one side several exquisite pieces lay in a black velvet tray.

"Are you Yue Hin?" she asked the man.

"Yes, how may I help you?"

"We're looking for some very special jade."

"I have some fine pieces," he said, reaching to slide open the back of the cabinet.

"The brushrest..." His hand moved to lift an opaque gray stone with olive-brown markings. Arisa took it and studied it carefully. "It's Ch'ing, isn't it?"

"Late eighteenth century," he said. "You are familiar with jade." There was no surprise in his voice.

"A bit. My father taught me well. He made many purchases in Hong Kong. Perhaps even here."

"Many people come to my shop."

"Elliot Travish, perhaps you know him?"

The old man pursed his lips. "The name is not unfamiliar."

Arisa smiled and held up the brushrest to Carter. "Look at the magnificent workmanship. The magic vapor issuing from the ram's mouth holds up a yin-yang disc."

Carter pretended to examine the carving, playing along with whatever it was Arisa was up to. Winning the old man's confidence?

When she set it back on the counter, Arisa said, "We are looking for something older."

"I have some excellent carved ivory from the Han period," Yue Hin said.

"Perhaps some jade from the Chou period?" she countered with a smile.

"Very rare," he said noncommitally.

"Do you know of some?"

He considered his answer a long time. "It is very difficult to find these days. Perhaps in one of the larger shops..."

"We prefer to deal with men of reputation, like yourself," she said.

Again, he considered his answer. "I would be happy to

search for what you want. If I am fortunate enought to find it, where may I contact you?"

"At the Mandarin Hotel. Thank you, Mr. Yue. Good day." He bowed without rising.

"What was that all about?" Carter asked when the proprietor could no longer see them through the window.

"Doing business the Chinese way. We've introduced ourselves and told him what we want. Now he'll consider it."

"Do you think he's got the jade?"

"I doubt it. The game would have gone on longer if he was in a position to bargain. But I think he knows something. The peasant who showed the jade to Professor Sun probably came by for an appraisal."

"You got all that out of those few words? Incredible. Okay, detective, what now?"

"Now we go back to the hotel and begin phoning. I'll start with David Fung at home. Since we used to be neighbors, maybe we can pay him a call."

When they reached the hotel, Arisa made half a dozen phone calls before she gave in to the luxury of a delightful soak in a hot tub to wash away her weariness. Even though she hadn't gotten any spectacular results, she was encouraged by her conversations with some of the dealers. David Fung was not at home, but Mrs. Fung remembered the Travish family and insisted that her husband would be delighted to talk with Arisa. As a matter of fact, they were entertaining the following night. Would Arisa and her father's partner join them? Three other dealers were most cordial though not very hopeful about the Chou jade. Cautious was more the word for it. None denied knowing about the jade but neither did they admit to having it or knowing who did. Arisa got the distinct impression that something of a conspiracy of silence had grown up around the archaic jade because no dealer had yet given up hope he might be the fortunate one to secure it.

She lay back in the soothing water and soaked in delight as she considered the past twenty-four hours. During the flight, Carter had been pleasant and attentive; since their arrival, she couldn't ask for anyone more charming. She knew he was bitterly disappointed about the Vezzi, but he had not moaned over the loss. It seemed he had the ability to do what he had encouraged her to do—learn from the past without letting its mistakes haunt you. She wished she had mastered the lesson before her father had died so that they could have recaptured some of the closeness they'd known when she was a child. Being back in Hong Kong had unlocked memories that had been hidden a long time. When she thought about it now, it seemed her happiest memories were of times spent with her father. Maybe it was because he was so interested in the Oriental side of the colony. She couldn't deny its fascination to her even now.

At last she roused herself and turned on the shower for a minute to shampoo her hair. Then she wrapped herself in the heavy terry cloth robe the hotel furnished and wound a towel around her head. The face that looked back at her from the mirror was the young Arisa who had loved Hong Kong.

Carter had insisted she choose a place for dinner, and she thumbed through the *Tourist Association Guidebook* she found in the desk. She was amazed at the number of new fancy restaurants—The Beefeater, Au Trou Normand, La Taverna, Lindy's—an international polyglot that could be found as easily in Los Angeles or London. She tossed the book aside and picked up the more flamboyant weekly tourist newspaper. Carter's first evening in Hong Kong had to be Chinese. If he'd been dazzled by Shin Hing Street, he had to experience the wonder of a Chinese restaurant. She found what she was looking for—a garish floating barge restaurant in Aberdeen Harbor. Excited, she phoned down to the desk and made arrangements for a reservation and a car to transport them. When Carter phoned at eight, she kept their destination a surprise.

"I arranged for a hotel car," she told him. "It will be easier than battling for a taxi. The driver will bring us back when we're finished."

The Mercedes and driver were waiting, and they settled back to enjoy the ride over the mountain and through the dusk-laden hills of the south end of the island. She told him about the fishing village to which they were going, where the more than 3,000 sampans crowded into the harbor were home for twenty thousand people. "There are three Typhoon Shelters on the island where boat people live their lives as a floating population. Some never set foot on land, though I imagine that picture is changing like everything else. Living in major cities of the western world, we really aren't terribly aware of the amount or degree of poverty there is in the world."

He smiled, thinking momentarily of his childhood and wondering what her reaction would be to his background. As they started the long descent into Aberdeen, the lights of the village were coming on like fireflies.

"High-rises," Arisa said with a resigned air. "They seem sacriligious here. It was a sleepy little village..."

The car entered the city and made its way along the traffic on the waterfront. Seeing the harbor, Arisa forgot her disappointment in the village itself. The harbor was more exciting than she recalled. It was a floating city with low, rounded sampans taking the place of squatters' shacks or resettlement estates. Despite the poverty, the crowded sampans offered an air of the exotic. They hugged the shoreline and spread out into the harbor in long lines with only narrow channels between them. Bright scraps of color waved as clothing dried on poles or walla-wallas displayed their banners. The entire harbor was overlaid with wispy smoke from braziers and the aroma of cooking.

"Here we are," Arisa told him. The car stopped at a narrow wooden walkway that led down to a small jetty. A launch was boarding passengers for the ride out to the floating palace. Strings of lights outlined the vessel and twinkled the name JUMBO in red from the upper deck.

The launch puttered slowly through the channels created by anchored sampans. The boats were so close together, Carter was sure it would be possible to step from one to another from shore all the way to the end of the line in the distance. Incredible. He was fascinated by the sight of families preparing dinner over small charcoal braziers and sitting down to eat on upended crates that served as tables. He caught glimpses of deeper recesses of the sampans where children slept on mats. Each boat was piled high with boxes and baskets, the worldly goods of several generations. The launch came almost close enough to brush the bare feet of the children who sat on boat sterns, their legs dangling over the sides. He wondered how many of then would ever escape this poverty. On one boat, a young woman in a stylish *cheongsam* put the finishing touches to her makeup while a barefoot old woman in traditional black peasant's garb squatted at the gunwale, washing clothes.

The restaurant offered a bright contrast. They entered through a magnificent foyer hung with tapestries and murals. Lights blazed from paper and bamboo chandeliers covered with Oriental designs and calligraphy. They went up a curved stair-

way to the dining room, which was huge and noisy. Hundreds
of diners sat at large round tables set with sparkling linen and
a large revolving server in the center. Ceiling lights twinkled
like giant stars, and a chandelier similar to the one downstairs
was suspended in the center of the room. A row of windows
around the upper portion of the room gave a skylight effect to
the darkening night sky.

They were seated with eight others who'd come on the
launch. At Carter's questioning look, Arisa assured him it was
more fun to dine family-style so they could sample a larger
variety of the cuisine. Portions of a dozen different dishes made
it possible for everyone to tempt his palate with a taste, yet
leave him ready for the next surprise. Carter put himself in her
hands.

Introductions were made round the table and within minutes,
the multi-national group was chatting comfortably. The meal
progressed through shark fin soup, amazingly delicious despite
its name, drunken shrimp, beggar's chicken, fried rice in lotus
leaves, steamed bean curd stuffed with shrimp in a light wine
sauce, and three varieties of fish done in as many sauces, each
more tantalizing than the one before. Glasses were kept filled
with a light wine that cleared the palate yet imparted a delicate
flavor all its own. Carter protested when Arisa insisted they
must sample dessert as well but was pleased to find it was tiny
dumplings with only a hint of sweetness. When at last Arisa
laid her chopsticks across her plate, with the tips toward the
center of the table, an indication that she had finished eating,
Carter followed suit gratefully. He was delighted with the evening and Arisa's spontaneous laughter at so many little things.
As the dinner party broke up, people moved congenially back
to the lower lobby to wait for the launch, then said their good-
byes when they finally reached the dock. The hotel car was
waiting for Arisa and Carter, and they settled back comfortably.

During the ride back to Victoria, Arisa basked in the magic
of Hong Kong. The city had recaptured her heart with its blend
of East and West that never quite homogenized but were never
totally separated. She wondered if she would feel this way if
she'd never left Hong Kong or if her pleasure came partly from
being able to share Carter's first impression of the colony.

As they came around Mt. Gough and started down the harbor
side of the island, the view was breathtaking. The city lay like
a tray of sparkling gems splashed on black velvet. Ruby and

sapphire bracelets were entwined among the diamonds. The harbor was a dark crescent of onyx that imprisoned chips of emerald and garnet as ferries plowed their way to and from Kowloon. A glittering world unto itself.

"What are you thinking about?" Carter asked softly.

She smiled. "How good it is to be back. You were right about the value of looking into the past. I have a lot of happy memories here. I'm enjoying them."

He reached for her hand. "I'm glad. You're beautiful when you smile."

Her cheeks warmed. "Be careful, you're succumbing to the romance of the Orient. It's been known to fell sane and hardy men."

"Never let it be said I'm not sane and hardy." He threaded his fingers with hers, pressed her hand to his lips, then held it against his chest intimately.

She could feel his heartbeat offset her own pulse, and she shivered delectably. She warned herself not to fall victim to the malady against which she was cautioning him, but she couldn't control the riot of pleasant emotions that overcame her. His nearness was as heady and arousing as it had been when he shared her bed. She had never felt so attracted to a man. Her romance with Eduoard and others before him had lacked the emotional bond she felt with Carter. She tried to examine it logically but it would not be defined. Was it because he'd known her father, or because they were in Hong Kong, a city of romance and memories? Or was it because they were on a quest that meant so much to both of them? Or was she falling in love, real love, for the first time?

She was glad for his silent contentment during the rest of the ride down the hill. Her thoughts were too turbulent to be trusted to words.

At the hotel, they crossed the busy lobby to the elevators and rode to the twenty-second floor in companionable silence. When Carter took the room key from her hand, unlocked the door, and followed her inside, she knew neither of them had to say aloud that they didn't want the evening to end. For several moments, they stood looking at each other, gazes filled with tenderness and desire. His mouth curved in an assured smile as he took her in his arms. Her lips parted as she raised her face to his kiss. Then the world spun, vanished, settled within their closely embracing bodies. Arisa was aware of a soft moaning sound long before she realized she was making it. She was mesmerized by his strong hands moving gently over her flesh, cupping a breast, stroking the curve of a hip. Breathless, she found herself on the bed without realizing she had moved. When she would have unzipped her dress, he withdrew her hands gently and claimed the pleasure for himself. The amber silk rustled like a whispering breeze among spring blossoms as it fell from her flesh and freed her naked breasts for his devouring gaze.

When at last he looked at her face, she traced her quivering lips with a moist tongue. Another small moan escaped her lips. She stood and let the dress fall as he removed his clothing. And when their naked flesh came together, they did not try to curb the hunger that raged in both of them. They lay entwined, touching, enjoying, exciting, murmuring without words.

Arisa was alive with sensations that were exquisitely new yet torturously familiar. She no longer wondered about her feelings but gave herself completely to the pleasure Carter offered. And when he finally stilled her torment with rapturous delight, she was aware of the ebbing tide of passion fulfilled. She nestled dreamily in his arms until sleep claimed her. And that night he stayed with her till morning.

13

They spent the day browsing the streets and shops of Victoria and Kowloon in hope of turning up some lead to the Chou jade. Many of the places Arisa remembered had been swallowed up by the city's growth; at the ones that still existed, they encountered diverse reactions. Some were under new management or taken over by descendants of the men who had once owned them. Elliot Travish's name brought only an apologetic shake of the head. At others, Elliot was known, but when Arisa brought up the subject of the Chou jade, they couldn't offer any help. One, wrinkled old man who ran a small shop on the laddered, narrow passage of Po Hing Fong Street folded his hands into the sleeves of his jacket. He had heard of the Chou jade and knew men who claimed to have seen it. Seven pieces in all, he told them. A chape for attachment to a scabbard, a dragon plaque, a carved fish, and four insect-shaped stones. "The Stones of Heaven?" Arisa asked him.

So it was said, he replied, and the story was believed by many.

By him?

He nodded sagely. Two men had already died because the Stones had passed through their hands. Was that not proof enough?

Arisa pursued the story to learn that the peasant who'd brought the jade into Hong Kong had been found murdered on the street. His brother, into whose care the stones were entrusted part of the time, had been found floating in the bay. The stones were believed to have been taken by yet a third man who was now trying to sell them, but many dealers in Hong Kong refused to let the Stones come into their shops.

Where was this man, Arisa asked.

Ngaw m-jee, ngaw m-jee. (I do not know, I do not know.)

She could get no more from him. He was frightened, as though the curse of the Stones might fall on him if he talked too much about them.

Over tea in the Peninsula Hotel lobby, Arisa and Carter reviewed their lack of success. "At least we're certain the Chou jade isn't rumor," she said. "It exists and it did come to Hong Kong."

"But where is it now? We're no closer than we were when we started."

"David Fung may have the answer," she said. "If we can believe Professor Sun, the stones were probably taken to him for appraisal. And we have an invitation to his house this evening. If memory serves me right, the Fungs always did a lot of entertaining and their parties include many others in the antique business. It could be a small-scale Maracudo affair."

"All right, we'll dress to the nines and see what we can unearth. I hope you're right."

Arisa was stunning in a white gown he presumed was the De la Renta he'd paid for. It was worth every dollar. After an appraising glance, he took her in his arms and kissed her. A flush of color rose to her cheeks when he told her how beautiful she looked. She picked up a soft white cape which he draped over her bare shoulders, letting his fingers brush the loosely coiled hair that was drawn to one side of her head.

Having lived in California as long as he had, Carter wasn't accustomed to taking cabs or depending on limousine service. He rented a Mercedes through the hotel manager and got directions to the Fung house. With Arisa to navigate, he felt at ease with the right-hand drive even in the hopeless congestion of the city. Once they were above the city, traffic thinned as the road switched back and twisted toward the summit. Houses became fewer, too; walled yards and lush shrubbery replaced the jungle of multi-level concrete. Houses set back from the road attested to the wealth of those who lived there—private domains above the crowded warrens below. Peak Road circled around the south side of the mountain until it finally brought them to the station where the tram finalized its climb. Arisa directed him to a narrow road that continued upward.

Mount Austin Road led to a loftly knoll that crowned the island. Arisa pointed to an entrance between white stone pillars. The yard was ablaze with lights, and a white-jacketed attendant bowed and spoke in Cantonese.

"I presume he wants to park the car," Carter said with a grin.

"Right." To the boy, she said, *"M-goy."* He bowed again.

"You're very impressive when you speak Chinese," Carter told her. He took her arm as they went up the broad steps toward the door.

The house was a tasteful blend of Oriental and Western. The roof sloped in graceful pagoda lines of blue tile. The front door was set in a crimson circle—a moongate door, Arisa told him. It was surrounded by bas-relief carvings of dragons, lions and serpents. Several windows, octagonal in shape and made of opaque mullioned glass, overlooked the courtyard. The second story of the house had large clear windows to take advantage of the view.

Carter pulled the ancient brass door-pull shaped like a dragon's head. A maid opened the door and bowed as they came in. Arisa slid out of her cape, then tucked her arm through Carter's and winked. They followed the maid through the paneled entry hall, which was bare except for two carved camphorwood benches between stone pillars at either side, and a magnificent Oriental rug. An arched doorway led to a large reception room, which in turn opened onto a wide glass-enclosed veranda. Both rooms had been opened to contain the party, which seemed to be well underway. Arisa judged there were thirty to forty people standing about with cocktail glasses, yet the rooms were far from crowded. She glanced at an exquisite tapestry covering one wall. It had been there when she was a child. Her father had told her it had been hand-stitched by twenty young maids for an Imperial Princess of the Ming Dynasty. One of Mrs. Fung's ancestors had brought it from Peking shortly after the colony was settled. The intricate work was done in vermilion, blue, green, black and gold threads to depict the family quarters at the Summer Palace.

Beneath the tapestry, Mr. and Mrs. Fung greeted their guests. Arisa led Carter to them.

David Fung smiled broadly. "Arisa Travish. What a delightful honor to welcome you once more to our home." He rose and took her hand warmly. "It has been—fourteen years?" He shook his head as though he couldn't believe the swift passage of time. He was a slight man with a proud bearing and an easy smile. His hair was untouched by gray, and his dark eyes sparkled with youthful vigor, though Arisa knew he was close to seventy. She smiled and introduced Carter, who thanked them for inviting unexpected visitors.

"We are delighted. So you are Elliot's partner. He talked

a great deal about you. He put great store in your talents."

"I'm happy to hear that. I hope I can live up to his expectations," Carter said warmly.

Mrs. Fung said, "We were grieved to hear of your father's death, Arisa. Please accept our expression of joy that his spirit is at rest. He was a good man. There are many who will miss his presence."

"Thank you."

"And now you and your brother are continuing the work he loved so well. A fitting tribute," David Fung commented.

The reference to Quentin surprised Arisa. She was not aware that the Fungs had known her brother, but then he *had* lived eighteen years on the Peak.

"Quentin is only peripherally concerned with the business," Carter said. Arisa detected a note of hardness in his tone, but he was smiling genially at the Fungs. "It's Arisa who is carrying on the work."

David Fung looked mildly surprised. "I am mistaken in my impression then, forgive me."

"The fault is mine," Mrs. Fung said with an apologetic glance at Arisa. "I sometimes find the vagaries of the English language difficult to my Chinese mind. When your brother introduced himself, I interpreted his mention of Travish-Montaigne incorrectly."

It was Arisa's turn to be surprised. "You spoke with my brother?"

Mrs. Fung's soft laughter tinkled like a windchime. "Like yourself, he is an unexpected but most welcome guest." She glanced beyond the arched doorways to the sun porch.

Arisa's head turned to follow her gaze. Quentin stood just past the French doors talking to a young Chinese man. Beside her, Carter tensed as Arisa tried to recover her aplomb. Quentin was the last person she'd expected to see. What in the world was he doing here? He half-turned in their direction, and she gave him a murderous glance. Then, arranging her features in a pleasant smile, she apologized to the Fungs.

"I'm sorry, I didn't know he was making the trip. He had other pressing business."

"How fortunate he concluded it successfully," Carter said with a touch of venom. His hand was still on Arisa's arm, and she felt his fingers dig into her flesh.

"Did you see Elliot the last time he was in Hong Kong?" he asked the Fungs.

"I had the pleasure," David Fung said. "My son was in the shop working in my stead, so Elliot visited me here. I claim the privilege of a few days off each week now that Robert is as knowledgable as I in matters of business. An old man doesn't like to admit the young can replace him, but I must if I am to enjoy my last years."

His wife chided him gently. "You are not old, David. You have earned your leisure and some time with me." Their eyes spoke silently as he clasped her hand. She smiled at Arisa and Carter. "We enjoyed your father's visits so much. David was delighted when his old friend chose to go into the importing business. He always said Elliot was a lotus among the thorns as an architect."

"Now, dear." It was David Fung's turn to chide. "Elliot did well and was happy in his architectural work."

Mrs. Fung's face remained impassive. The discussion was not new to them, and each read the other perfectly. Arisa was puzzled and a bit confused that such an early portion of her father's life had been subject to such scrutiny. She had only vague memories of her father's work in those early years. She had never questioned his contentment in it; she knew only that all the highlights of that part of her past seemed to center on Oriental art—his collection, trips to shops and stalls, and the Oriental motifs in his architectural drawings.

She used the opportunity to change the subject and introduce the purpose of their visit. "My father derived a great deal of pleasure from the shop and his work. And I know it gave him special pleasure to return to Hong Kong where he had so many friends. Did he speak with you of the Chou jade he hoped to buy?"

Carter masked his surprise. With other dealers Arisa had bandied subtleties; now she was plunging headlong into the subject. David Fung was special because of past friendship or present contact. Or maybe Arisa felt time was running out.

David Fung nodded as though he had been expecting the question. "We discussed it at length."

Arisa's breath caught. She was right—David Fung was the key. Her pulse quickened and she felt Carter's gaze on her. She plunged in without further hesitation. "Carter and I are here to buy the jade if we can. Or at least part of it. I hear there are seven pieces in all."

"Yes. Superb workmanship, the finest detail. The jade is the finest quality from Turkestan."

"You've seen them?"

"Yes. They were brought to me for appraisal."

Arisa sensed a faint hesitation in his words. "And you did not buy them?"

David Fung sighed. "The man who brought them into Hong Kong was determined to get the highest price, so he refused to take my opinion alone. He planned to secure others. Which he did. But unfortunately . . ."

"David," his wife said softly.

He seemed to rechoose his words. "One cannot blame him for wanting the best price. The value of such work cannot be reckoned by firm rules."

Puzzled, Arisa knew she had been sidetracked expertly. What had Fung been about to say before his wife cautioned him? Her bewilderment was surpassed by elation at the news that she and Carter were not too late. "We're very eager to see the jade. Can you put us in touch with the man who has it?"

"Of course. He will be arriving soon."

"Here?" Surprise again.

Mrs. Fung glanced sidelong at her husband and answered for him. "We are pleased to present to so many people the opportunity to make offers on the jade. Now, we must greet our other guests." She inclined her head in a polite bow, dismissing them. As Arisa turned to go, Mrs. Fung's hand touched her arm in a friendly gesture. "So good to see you. We must talk soon."

"What in the world was that all about?" Carter asked quietly, smiling as they passed people and received courteous glances.

"I'm not sure. It seems too easy after all the mystery we've encountered up until now. A party and open bidding? Mrs. Fung makes it sound as if David is going to auction the jade personally. How can he if he doesn't own it?"

"Commission broker?"

She sighed. "Anything is possible, but why would he work that way when he wants that jade so badly? Why not just buy it for himself or offer to top any bid someone else makes?"

"I don't like the idea of its going up on offer. We may be cut out of the running early in the game." He was thinking of the letter of credit for two hundred thousand dollars.

"I suspect they'll break the lot up. He'll get more by selling the pieces individually. We'll have a good chance." She squeezed his arm reassuringly.

They went through the open doorway to the veranda, and Arisa deliberately steered for Quentin. He looked flustered for an instant, then forced a smile.

"I had no idea you planned a trip to Hong Kong, Quentin," she said bluntly.

"Ahhh, the prospect came up unexpectedly. I flew over with a friend."

"What a delightful coincidence," she said with a tinge of sarcasm. "Do you find it exhilarating after so many years?"

He shrugged. "It was never my favorite place." With a quick glance at the young man he'd been talking to, Quentin added, "Except for good friends from school."

The man smiled at Arisa. "You don't remember me."

She shook her head.

"I am Robert Fung. I used to visit your house occasionally."

"Robert and I were chums in school," Quentin said jovially, clapping a hand on the other man's shoulder. Robert Fung's face tightened. Obviously he didn't share Quentin's sense of camaraderie.

"I once walked you for your baby *amah*," Robert said with a teasing grin. "I recall you wore a pink dress and a bow in your hair."

"Good heavens!" Arisa laughed. "That is a long time ago!" She drew Carter into the circle. "Robert, this is Carter Montaigne, my father's partner, and now mine. Your parents mentioned that you have become part of your father's business too."

"For some years." He put out a hand to Carter, who shook it warmly.

"Tell me," Arisa said. "What's the inside information on the fabulous Chou jade? Your father talked about it without telling me very much."

Robert Fung smiled. "For all his years and wisdom, my father belongs to a generation that finds it impossible to throw off the old ways. One never loses face among one's colleagues."

"I don't understand," Arisa said.

"My father made a promise he cannot now keep," Robert said. "It disturbs his tranquillity."

"What promise?"

Robert Fung smiled and his gaze lingered on Arisa's face. To Carter, it was obvious the man found her charming and was probably regretting all the years she'd been out of touch. He felt a small shockwave of pleasure that she was so attractive to others. His surprise at her direct approach with the Fungs had also subsided, and he was eager to hear her questions answered. Robert glanced at Quentin, who was fidgeting as though impatient to get away. Carter wondered what was holding him.

"A promise to your father that he would work with him to get the famed Stones of Heaven, part of the collection of the Chou jade recently brought from Shanghai."

Arisa frowned. "Are you saying my father wanted only the Stones of Heaven, not the rest of the pieces?"

Robert smiled. "He would have loved to have them all, as would any collector, but like all of us, he was not without financial considerations. The entire collection would be far beyond any one man's means."

That accounted for the sale of individual pieces—the highest price for each, and each buyer willing to stretch to the limit.

"Your father mentioned that the man who brought the jade into Hong Kong will be here tonight. Has he arrived?"

Robert's face sobered. "Not the man who brought it in, the man who holds it now." He glanced toward his parents who were talking with a distinguished-looking woman in a sequined gown the color of ice. "The original owner died under rather unusual circumstances."

"The curse?" Arisa said with a touch of amusement. Surely Robert didn't believe such things.

"My father thinks it is within the realm of possibility," Robert said guardedly. "Your father's sad passing has offered my parent an escape from his promise, for which he was very much relieved until you and Quentin came along to inquire about the jade. Now my mother fears he will consider his obligation renewed to his friend's offspring."

"He's already promised to introduce me to the man who has the jade," Arisa said. She hadn't missed his comment that Quentin had asked about the jade, nor the tense reaction it elicited from Carter. What the devil was Quentin up to? And where had he suddenly come up with the money even to consider buying the jade? Last time they'd talked, he was trying to tap her for a loan.

Robert smiled suddenly. "And so he will. I think you'll have no trouble buying what you want. The ranks of competitors have thinned considerably these past weeks."

"Why is that?" Carter asked.

Robert shrugged. "Many dealers belong to the same generation as my father."

"And so believe the legends?"

"Yes."

"How about you?"

"I represent my father in business. I cannot go against his wishes." He glanced toward the door where some people were just arriving. "Excuse me. We'll talk again." He bowed.

When he was out of earshot, Arisa glared at Quentin and demanded, "What's this about your wanting to buy the jade? Since when have you become a collector or importer? You know you have no authority to speak for Travish-Montaigne. What the hell are you up to?!"

Quentin's face mottled with anger and embarrassment. "I never claimed any. If people misunderstood . . ." He shrugged.

"Why are you here?" Arisa demanded again.

He was recovering from the surprise attack, and his arrogance returned. "I don't have to account to you for what I do. I'm a free agent."

Furious, Arisa gaped, then clamped her mouth into a tight line and stalked away. Carter eyed Quentin evenly.

"You'll have to account to me if there's any more of this crap about your speaking for the partnership. And I don't give a damn what you're up to, just stay out of my way, understand?"

Quentin's face darkened and his eyes flashed, but Carter whirled and followed Arisa before he could answer. She was standing in the glass enclosure of the veranda, staring at the view. Carter stood so close his arm touched her shoulder. He listened to her tight, harsh breathing as she tried to control her anger. After a few moments, he said gently, "This view takes my breath away."

Arisa took a deep breath and focused on the magnificent sight of the jewellike city below them. After dark, the Peak was a superb viewpoint for the panorama of the city. The windows of the veranda had been planned to take complete advantage of it. Arisa's breathing began to quiet and she looked at Carter.

"Thanks."

"He's a pompous ass." Carter grinned.

"What do you suppose he's doing here?"

"I haven't the slightest idea, but I doubt his actions will be in our best interests. I'll keep an eye on him. It would almost be worth letting him have the Stones of Heaven so he'd fall under the curse." He dropped his voice to a register worthy of an old-time radio horror-show announcer, and Arisa had to laugh.

Soft music came over a hidden speaker system. It was an Oriental version of Western music, with additional flutes and bells that added a charming dimension. Arisa glanced around the room speculatively, wondering about the friend Quentin claimed to have flown over with. She recognized several dealers whose shops she and Carter had visited: Yue Hin, James Wu, Han Shan-tak—even Kai Tang, the old man she'd known as a child and had last seen at Ganrali Maracudo's party. The story of the cursed jade hadn't kept dealers away. Did they all plan to bid, or were they curious to see who and what would happen. Arisa suspected the legend of the curse wouldn't deter everyone. Greed was powerful enough to offset fear.

She smiled. "Well, I guess we'd better start circulating and listening. I'd like to talk to Robert again without Quentin around."

"I'll see to it, go ahead."

She squeezed his hand and moved across the room then paused by a small knot of people near the elegantly columned archway to the dining room. An attractive red-headed woman in flowered green crepe de chine was staring at her open-mouthed. With a laugh, Arisa rushed toward her.

"Jane Bentley!"

"Arisa? Arisa! My word, what are you doing here? Such a shock! I never—how long has it been?"

Arisa grimaced. "Fourteen years."

"I don't believe it! You vanish overnight, then pop up again fourteen years later! If you aren't something!" She grabbed the arm of a tall, awkward-looking man beside her. "Teddy, you remember Arisa Travish. She used to live in the house where Talmadge's is now."

Teddy blinked, frowning. "Of course. Hello there." He didn't remember her at all but came up with the polite answer that was expected of him. Arisa noticed the wide gold band on his finger that matched the one Jane wore. She wondered if she'd ever known Teddy. Or what his last name—and Jane's—was.

Jane was already splashing ahead with enthusiasm. "How long have you been here? Are you staying? You must come to the house. There's so much to talk about!"

Smiling, Arisa let herself be drawn aside as Teddy turned back to the others. She didn't recognize any of the faces, all definitely English. The Peak's young marrieds, she suspected. Jane slipped her arm through Arisa's with girlish enthusiasm.

"Now, tell me everything! We heard about the fire and the rioters, of course. Bless heaven none of you was hurt. Naturally, we all expected you'd come back, not simply vanish into never-never land!"

Arisa laughed. "Several million Californians would take umbrage at that remark, Jane."

"Oh, darling, you know what I mean."

They'd been best friends so long as children that neither took offense. Arisa gave her a quick sketch of what had followed her family's flight from Hong Kong, compressing the years into a few pertinent highlights, and omitting the trauma and emotion that had accompanied them. When she finished, Jane shook her head.

"I wish I'd known your father was in the habit of regular visits to the colony. How we would have loved to see him. Why didn't you keep in touch?" she scolded. "Not a word!"

"Everything was so unsettled." She didn't want to admit she'd believed they'd come back. It all seemed so long ago. "And now you're married. Any children?"

"One little monster. Theodore Harper Judson the Third." Jane grimaced. "Actually, he's cherubic at age two, but thank heaven the baby *amah* has him most of the day!"

Judson. She recognized the name. Theodore Judson Senior owned the largest shipping company in the colony. Jane had done well for herself. "Do you still live on the Peak?"

"In Repulse Bay. It's become quite metropolitan, hardly the remote country it used to be. You must come out. Of course there are dreadful squatters' shacks everywhere, but thank heaven we face the bay and don't have to look at them every minute. The government is making an effort to clear them out, but refugees pour in faster than estates can be built to house them. So your father went into the antique business," she said, changing the subject abruptly. "A drastic change from architecture, but if he was happy—and it has brought you back at last, so I must say I'm delighted. I imagine like half the people here, you're interested in that old jade everyone is talking about."

Arisa nodded. "Know anything that will give me an edge?"

Jane grinned. "Darling, I know everything that goes on in the colony!" They laughed conspiratorially. "Now, what do you want to know? The man who has it is named Lo Bat. He claims to be a cousin of the men who brought the jade out of Shanghai, but more likely he made off with the jade before or after the two brothers died. You've heard that story?" When Arisa nodded, Jane went on. "He's a weasley little man, not at all the type you'd want to deal with, but there's no choice. David Fung wants to see the stones go to someone reputable— for the sake of preserving the art work rather than for the profit they'll bring Lo Bat, especially if he stole them, as most suspect. He can't be sure that the dreadful curse, whatever it is, won't catch up with him before he gets the money and can run off somewhere. I'm sure you remember Din Solun—she was in our class. Remember how she just vanished from school in third form because her father thought he'd fallen under the spell of some evil god or other who was punishing him for sending his children to study with the foreigners? Well, Lo Bat figures he can counteract any evil spells by getting rid of the jade as quickly as possible, and then making himself hard to find. I suppose if he believes it, it works, just like the curse works on those who believe it. I say it would be a good thing for the jade to get into American or English hands so all the nonsense can end."

"How do you know about Lo Bat? Have you ever seen him?" If she could talk with him before the others converged . . .

"Teddy was having lunch with Robert Fung. They've been friends all these years. It accounts for our invitation tonight. Robert likes a little variety in party guests. He says he gets enough business seven days a week at the shop. Robert told him the story. He's furious with his father for refusing to handle the jade himself. Of course it's Su-san's doing."

"Su-san?"

"Mrs. Fung. She clings to the old ways, despite all of this." Jane waggled her fingers to indicate the lovely house that departed from traditional Chinese. "Do you know her mother has lily feet? She lives in an apartment upstairs. You can smell the joss from the hall."

It was difficult to keep up with Jane's hopscotch conversation, but Arisa deduced that Mrs. Fung had persuaded her husband not to defy ancient superstitions concerning the Chou jade.

"I'm surprised David Fung would consent to be middle-man," Arisa commented.

"He's determined to see the jade preserved, I suppose. This is one way to do it."

"Will you introduce me to Lo Bat?"

"I'll see that Teddy does. He's met the man. I've hogged you long enough, though. Come on, I'll introduce you to the others." She led Arisa back toward the cluster of young people where they traded names and greetings. Jane babbled happily about including Arisa in social activities that were planned for the weekend. A petite, dark-haired girl who'd been introduced as Sheila Stone, and her husband Charles who was an executive with the Hong Kong and Shanghai Banking Corporation, extended a dinner invitation for the following night. Arisa did not commit herself but said she would discuss it with Carter.

"That handsome man you came in with? We'd love to have him too," Sheila said eagerly.

"Handsome man—you didn't tell me," Jane scolded. "Who is he?" She glanced around eagerly.

Arisa identified Carter where he stood talking to a man she had never seen before. Obviously an American, he was short and dark-haired and somehow looked out of place. He wore a black sport coat over an open-necked shirt. His gray gabardine trousers had a knife-edge crease, and his black boots were shined to a mirror finish. Hollywood. He'd be perfect at any Hollywood party, Arisa decided; that's why he didn't seem to fit here. His eyes were black glass that missed nothing and revealed nothing. While he listened to Carter, he seemed to be watching everyone and everything in the room.

"This is a night for strangers in our midst," a ruddy-faced man with a sprinkling of freckles across his nose commented. "I wonder who *she* is."

The obvious interest in his tone caused them all to look toward the entry. A tall, extremely attractive woman in a striking crimson gown stood surveying the room haughtily. A sun-tanned man with her was poised and equally haughty in a navy blazer and white pants. He looked as if he'd just removed a yachting cap.

A cold knot formed in Arisa's chest. "Her name is Claire

Prigent. She's a decorator from Los Angeles."

"*The* Claire Prigent?" Charles Stone was watching Claire glide across the room toward the Fungs to be introduced.

"I assume there's only one," Arisa said tightly.

"There certainly is," Charles said appreciatively, his gaze still on Claire. Sheila gave him a petulant look. "I'll have to meet her," he said with a smile. "Her father does eight million dollars worth of business with us a year."

"You mean Nesbitt Prigent, the steel magnate?" Teddy Judson sounded incredulous.

"The same. I didn't know she was in the colony." Charles smiled at Arisa. "Will you introduce me?"

She was suddenly cold as she saw Carter detach himself from the American and make his way toward Claire. "My partner is much better acquainted with her than I am. I'm sure he'll do the honors."

Claire smiled at Carter and slipped her arm through his, lifting her lips to kiss his cheek before turning to say something to the Fungs as she led Carter away.

Claire and Carter disappeared onto the veranda. The men brought their attention back to the group reluctantly, though their gazes strayed frequently to the splash of red that could be seen through the open French doors. The conversation resumed and centered around Claire's father. Arisa absorbed bits and pieces through her anger. Steel supplied for eighty percent of the government housing estates...yachts... Prigent a friend of the governor...power. To Hong Kong's young elite, it gave Claire an intriguing allure. Sheila Stone said nervously they would have to invite her to the dinner party. Did Charles think she would come? Jane said maliciously that if she did, they'd better tie short leashes to their husbands. Nervous laughter followed her remark.

"I just read a bit about the madcap heiress in this morning's *Post*, now that I think of it," one of the men said. "A Paris tidbit about her and her latest conquest. Dining at Maxim's or some such thing. The usual chit-chat."

"She seems to have made another," the freckle-faced man then blushed as he caught Arisa's angry stare. Carter and Claire had disappeared from sight on the veranda but they hadn't reentered the room.

Arisa forced a smile. "I'm sure Carter can take care of himself. If not, he'd better learn fast."

They all laughed and the tension eased. Charles repeated his request for an introduction, and Arisa was grateful when Jane took her arm and spirited her away with a comment that there were other people she wanted to introduce her to.

"You looked decidedly uncomfortable," Jane said sotto voce. "I take it Carter is something special in your life."

"Not at all." But the flush of her cheeks told more than her denial. She was grateful Jane didn't pursue the subject.

"I think the mysterious Lo Bat just came in. Everyone's suddenly very interested in that little man over there." She tilted her head toward the door. "Just a sec, I'll ask Teddy." She hurried back to her husband for a whispered consultation.

Robert Fung detached himself from the men he was conversing with. Several others started toward the door, then hesitated as Robert claimed the newcomer and took him toward his parents. The newcomer was thin and nervous-looking, with a coarse complexion. The black suit he wore was ill-fitting and slightly rumpled. Jane returned with Teddy in tow.

"That's him," she said. "Come on, we'll claim him before anyone else gets to him." She took Arisa's arm and walked between her and Teddy to the K'eng chair where David and Su-san Fung were holding court. Robert assumed the duties of host and introduced the two women to Lo Bat, whose eyes glinted when he heard the name Travish.

"Miss Travish has taken on her father's work," Robert said carefully. "The house of Fung is honored to do business with her, as we did him."

Lo Bat's stare still dismissed her as a mere woman. He said nothing.

David Fung said sternly, "We know you will show her the courtesy of dealing with her as you would her honorable father. The name of Travish is highly respected."

Arisa dipped her head in polite acknowledgment and spoke softly in Cantonese. "I am honored to meet the man who has Chou jade to sell. It was my father's wish to acquire some of the exquisite work you possess. It is my wish to honor his spirit by fulfilling that desire."

There was only a momentary glint of surprise in Lo Bat's eyes as he heard the flawless Cantonese flow from American lips. Then his impenetrable mask fell once more.

"Lo Bat wishes to make an appointment with prospective buyers," Robert said. "I am sure he will honor you with an invitation." He spoke to Arisa, but his steady gaze was on Lo Bat. "Tonight he wishes only to acquaint himself with the faces of those who will come so that he is sure to recognize them."

A precaution, Arisa decided. The wily peasant didn't want to be taken by surprise and set himself up for a possible robbery.

"Where will the meeting take place?" she asked.

Lo Bat spoke for the first time. His Cantonese was the dialect of a southern province, and his voice was low and sibilant. "Each dealer will be called and told where."

She reached into the white velvet evening purse that hung from a golden cord at her shoulder. Quickly, she wrote out her hotel number and her room extension and presented it to him. *"M-goy, m-goy."*

Arisa was aware that some of the other dealers had surmised Lo Bat's identity and were gathering quickly. She was glad to edge away. Jane gave a shudder.

"Creepy little man. Don't go meeting him in any of the Chinese districts!"

Teddy said, "Robert told me a house here on the Peak is being made available. I suspect Lo Bat feels safer away from those jammed streets and dark apartments if he's carrying the jade. Still, Arisa, you'd do well to take Montaigne with you. You never know."

"Thanks, I'll be careful. The jade's no good to me if I don't survive to take it back to California."

"Don't say such a thing!" Jane shuddered again. "Now let's get back in a party mood. I came for an enjoyable evening away from dear little Teddy the third. Is there dancing on the terrace, darling?"

"If not, we'll start some." Teddy put his arm around his wife affectionately and they walked toward a wide door beyond which Arisa glimpsed gently swaying lanterns over a paved terrace. Several couples were dancing to sedate music that came over the speaker system.

She glanced casually toward the veranda. Was Carter still out there with Claire? Jealousy pinched at her. She didn't like Claire, it was that simple. Because she'd worked with Carter and knew him well enough to claim him possessively each time they were together? Nonsense, she told herself. What right did she have to resent it? None, her mind told her. Every right, her emotions cried. For a moment, the memory of Carter holding her, making love to her was overwhelming. She pushed it aside savagely.

A maid in a black uniform and white apron and cap offered her a glass of champagne from an antique lacquerware tray. Arisa sipped as she wandered toward the French doors. The American Carter had been talking to earlier gave her a curious smile as she neared.

"If you're looking for your boyfriend, he's out there with the blonde chick," he said in an amused tone.

"I wasn't looking for anyone, and he's not my boyfriend," she countered, annoyed.

"Whatever." His gaze seemed to undress her, and she stared at him icily. "I came with your brother," he said, still smiling as if he knew a lot more than he was saying.

"Oh?" She was right about Hollywood, she decided. Curious, she asked, "Have you known him long?"

"We have mutual friends."

"Are you in the art business, Mr.——?"

"Danny Ladera. In a way."

"In what way?"

He laughed. "This mutual friend."

"You work for him?"

"Yeah, you could say that. I watch out for his interests."

"And what might those be in Hong Kong?" She wasn't going to let his game go unchallenged.

"What's everybody interested in?" His gaze swept her figure and personalized the remark obscenely.

She ignored it. "The Chou jade."

His mouth twisted in a grin. "You got it, baby. I saw you talking to the Chinaman. Is he the guy?"

"If you're so devoted to your friend's interests, why don't you find out for yourself?"

His expression didn't change as he shrugged. "That's your brother's job. I'm just along for the ride."

"And to protect your friend's interests."

"Yeah."

She was decidely uncomfortable talking to him. What was Quentin's connection with him, and who was the "mutual friend" Ladera alluded to? Whoever he was, he was powerful enough to develop Quentin's sudden interest in Oriental art where none had ever existed. She saw that Quentin had joined the dealers clustered around Lo Bat. A bull in a China shop, she thought. How in the world did he expect to compete with so many experts? She doubted Ladera was any more an expert than her brother on the subject of jade. A strange combination to be sent on so important an errand.

She saw Carter and Claire come in from the veranda and turned away quickly so it wouldn't seem she'd been watching. But Carter headed straight for her, despite Claire's annoyed look. Carter smiled, but not before she saw the tight anger in his face.

"Arisa, you remember Claire," he said.

"Of course." She returned the bored look Claire gave her. "Are you decorating houses in Hong Kong?" she asked sweetly.

"Purely a social visit," Claire said with a meaningful look at Carter.

Arisa clenched her jaw. "How nice." From the corner of her eye, she saw Charles Stone head for them. She smiled in relief. "Charles," she called, as though the idea for him to join them was hers. "You haven't met Claire Prigent. *The* Claire Prigent. Charles Stone of the Hong Kong and Shanghai Bank, Claire. He's been eager to meet you."

Charles held out a hand and Claire gave him hers with a flirtatious smile. "How delightful to meet you, Charles. Peter talks about you all the time. Have you seen him?" She glanced around the room carefully in search of her escort. "Let's go find him. He was just saying how nice it would be if you could join us on the boat. We're anchored in Repulse Bay."

They drifted away, Claire clinging and Charles fawning. When they were out of earshot, Carter said, "What were you talking to your brother's buddy about?"

"Who? Oh, you mean . . . Nothing much. He informed me that he and my brother came to Hong Kong to buy the Chou jade."

"Do you find that surprising?"

"Astonishing would be more like it. But I've ceased being surprised by anything my dear brother does. Just who is Danny Ladera?"

Carter frowned. "Is that his name? I've heard it before." His frown deepened to a scowl as he tried to recall where.

Arisa forgot her pique over Claire. "He seems to be Quentin's watchdog on this trip. He's protecting their mysterious employer's interests, he claims, but he was very careful not to name any names."

Carter's gaze swung to the group Quentin was part of. "Is that the man who has the Chou jade?"

"Yes, the infamous Lo Bat. I talked with him and he's

promised to call us. He's being cautious in sizing up the prospects ahead of time."

"What are our chances?"

"David Fung and Robert are on our side. They still feel an obligation to my father."

"Will it help?"

"I don't know, but if anything will, maybe their recommendation will carry weight." She was amazed at how quickly her thoughts had been sidetracked from Claire. She wondered if Carter had done it deliberately. When she looked searchingly at him, he smiled.

"We'll have to hope it does then. Are you enjoying getting reacquainted with your old friends?"

"Jane and I went to school together. She introduced me to the others. We have a dinner invitation tomorrow night if you're free. The Stones—that was Charles who just fell into Claire's clutches. His wife Sheila is the pretty dark-haired one in lavender."

He didn't react to the barb about Claire. "Maybe if the meeting with Lo Bat goes well, we'll have something to celebrate." His gaze went back to the group of dealers. Quentin had moved away and was walking toward the veranda. Danny Ladera set down his drink and followed. Carter would have given anything to listen in on their conversation. Who the hell had chosen Quentin as an emissary? And Ladera was obviously a high-class punk, a strong man, an errand boy. It didn't make sense.

14

The pace of the party picked up slightly, but it was quite subdued even with the young people Robert had invited to enliven it. The older Chinese and a sprinkling of British guests sat exchanging gossip and making small talk. Most of the dealers eyed each other and tried to ingratiate themselves with David Fung, with an eye toward special consideration on the Chou jade which had brought them all together. Young couples, mostly foreigners but mixed with a few Chinese, danced on the terrace or sat on the veranda, enjoying the view while they drank the mild cocktails the Fungs permitted to be served in their otherwise abstemious household.

No one could deny that Claire Prigent and her playboy escort, Peter Karo, grandson of the Greek shipping magnate, Dimitrius Karopolis, were a party bonus that made the evening click. The men swarmed around the laughing, flirtatious Claire, who granted dance favors like a fairy godmother bestowing wishes. Peter danced or lounged at the parapet above the gardens, never lacking eager competition for his company. When he asked Arisa to dance, she acquiesced out of curiosity. After a few desultory comments about the music, he asked her how long she'd known Claire. When she told him she had only met her once before, he seemed surprised.

"The way she talks, I thought you were old friends, or is that a poor choice of word?"

"I don't know what you mean."

"Rivals? I can't blame her for being worried, poor darling. You'd give any woman a run for her money with Carter or any other man. You've cast a bit of a shadow on Claire's limelight tonight, and don't think she hasn't noticed." He glanced past Arisa to where Claire was dancing with one of the young Englishmen.

"I wasn't aware there was a race," Arisa said coolly.

"Life is a constant race with Claire. And she always wins." He arched an eyebrow as if in warning.

"Not many people set out deliberately to lose at anything, if you look at it practically." She really didn't give a damn about Claire, and she resented the inference that she should be on her guard. "I certainly don't, do you?"

He laughed. "I only go in for spectator sports, except where women are concerned." His hand pressed hers suggestively.

"I think that would make life a little boring," she said with a smile. He was so typical of the vapid assemblage of dilettantes who collected around Eduoard and his friends.

"Not when the women are as beautiful as you."

"And Claire?" She hadn't missed the covetous glance he'd cast on her.

"She's gorgeous."

"Are you in love with her?"

It startled him, and he laughed. "I've asked her to marry me a dozen times but she holds me at bay like a lion tamer."

"So you purr and obey."

He gave her a discerning look. "I watch and wait. Someday she'll get tired and I won't look so terrible after all."

The idea of any woman considering the young multimillionaire "terrible" made Arisa smile. He was looking past at the other dancing couples again, then his gaze slid toward the table where Carter was chatting with the Judsons.

"If she doesn't break down his resistance first," Peter said. "She's been at him so long, I can't help but wonder if she really means it."

Arisa felt a cold fingertip of panic at her heart. "They were business partners," she said foolishly.

"Not at first, and not now," he said enigmatically.

Lovers . . .? Did she believe Carter was a monk just because she'd been playing nun these past weeks? Until three nights ago, she thought, and her cheeks warmed.

"I was surprised when she said she was coming to Hong Kong on a business deal with him. Even when they were partners, she left the buying of antiques to him for the most part. Now suddenly she has to see where her money is going."

"Are you saying she's here to buy something?" Arisa didn't know what her thoughts about Claire's presence at the party had been. She'd been too annoyed at seeing her and having her claim Carter to wonder beyond that. The Chou jade?

"Claire doesn't shop, she has it done for her."

Her touch of fear became an avalanche of anger. The music

ended, and Claire and her partner wandered off the floor, directly to the table where Carter was sitting. Claire's blonde head dipped close to Carter's as she whispered something. Smiling, Carter excused himself and walked inside with her. Claire's crystal laughter floated back to the terrace before the music resumed.

"Another dance?" Peter tried to take her in his arms.

"No, thank you. I . . ." He was watching her stare after the two vanishing figures. Suddenly she realized how foolish she was acting. She gave him a bold smile. "On second thought I'd love to dance again."

"Atta girl," he said, grinning.

They moved to the music again. For a few moments, Arisa was tense and stiff, still thinking about Peter's remarks. She'd been so elated about the Chou jade, she hadn't asked where the money was coming from. Claire! And Peter was saying Carter was buying for *her*, not Travish-Montaigne. He'd made a fool of her, romancing her and using her to lead him to the jade—for him and Claire! He'd been using her all along. He wanted the jade, and he wanted Travish-Montaigne.

She realized Peter was talking to her and forced her attention back. He was suggesting she might like to spend some time on his yacht. Eyes flashing, she asked if the invitation was designed to provide a thorn in Claire's side, and he laughed good-naturedly.

"I won't say the idea didn't cross my mind, but it's only a fringe benefit. I really would like you to come."

She promised she'd consider it.

When the number ended, she released him to the other women who had been casting envious glances, and excused herself. Inside, she found David Fung and thanked him for a lovely evening.

"You're not leaving so soon?"

"Yes, but I'm looking forward to seeing you again. I won't leave Hong Kong without saying good-bye."

"The next time you visit, we'd be honored to have you as our guest."

She clasped his hand warmly. "Thank you. And thank you for introducing me to Lo Bat."

The old man's eyes hooded. "Be careful, Arisa. He is not a man to be trusted completely. He is hunted."

"Hunted? Because of the jade?"

"Forgive an old man's foolishness, but one cannot ignore

everything one was brought up to believe."

"Do you mean the superstition about evil that follows the Imperial Stones of Heaven?" There had been hints and innuendos all evening, but she'd discounted them for the most part. David Fung was too enlightened to take them seriously.

"The power of the mind is awesome," he said carefully. "What man believes destines the pattern of his actions. There are those who believe strongly enough to create the danger their minds conceive. The Stones of Heaven are already bathed in blood. Whether it is the work of the gods or of evil men, the blood flows the same."

She studied his somber face. "How did my father feel about this?"

His eyes were black glass that reflected the shimmering glow from the candelabra. "Your father was a wise man. He understood the Eastern mind and respected tradition."

She didn't understand fully, but he would say no more. He walked with her to the door. As they stepped out into the cool Peak breeze, he paused under the entrance lights. "I will try to convince Lo Bat to give you special consideration, but he is a difficult man to deal with."

She thanked him warmly, then insisted that he return to his guests. The valet brought the car around, but Arisa told him the gentleman would be taking it. She was tempted to leave Carter stranded, but it would be like him to take off with Claire instead. Let him worry about the car he'd rented. She didn't need it—or him.

The soft summer wind was pleasant as she walked down the hill toward the Peak Tram. The sky was midnight blue, pinpricked by galaxies of stars that were a special feature of ocean nights. The road was bathed in moonlight and she had no trouble finding her way. She was looking forward to the tram ride. It had always given her a sense of solitude and peace to descend the mountain surrounded first by the trees and shrubbery of the upper Peak, then through the more populated areas of the mid-levels until the city itself engulfed her. She felt as if she were gathering up the city and becoming part of it.

Car lights flashed behind her and she stepped to the side of the roadway. The car slowed to a stop beside her.

"Pretty ladies shouldn't be walking alone. Get in." Danny Ladera's head poked from the open window.

"I'm enjoying the air."

"Get in," he said. "You'll break your bird in those heels."

He grinned and leaned across to open the car door.

She hesitated, then went around the car to climb in beside him. "I was enjoying the walk," she said.

"So now you can enjoy the ride. I saw you leave." He released the brake and the car began to roll. "It ain't the best place for a stroll."

"I don't mind."

"Why'd you take off like that?" He glanced at her before he returned his attention to the winding road.

"Why did you?"

He laughed. "Foxy lady. I like you. Okay, so I followed you. As far as I'm concerned, the party's over when you go."

"What about my brother?"

"Let him walk down."

She laughed and studied his angled profile in the dim light from the dash. "I thought you were his watchdog."

"I know where to find him."

They negotiated the steep hill that brought them out to the plateau where the Peak Tower glittered like a lighthouse. The windows of the circular dining aerie were bright as late-night diners feasted on the view as well as the food. Arisa settled back as Ladera started down Peak Road.

"This Chinaman with the jade—what do you know about him?" he said unexpectedly.

"Nothing more than you do. He's got it and wants to sell it."

"You believe all that crap about the curse?"

He'd done a lot of listening, she thought. "Do you?" she countered.

"Foxy lady." He grinned as he gave her a quick glance. "You always answer questions with a question."

"Only when I'm not sure why I'm being questioned in the first place. You've already admitted that you and my brother are after the Chou jade, just as I am. That makes us competitors, so I hardly feel obliged to share any information with you."

"Fair enough," he said grudgingly. "I had you pegged as a sensible broad. Sensible enough to go along with a good proposition. You play cards with me and you'll come out of this with a nice profit for your work."

In the shadowy light, his face was expressionless except for the hard set of his jaw. For a moment, an uncomfortable sensation prickled the back of her neck. Was he threatening her?

She turned to stare at the swaying slash pines and mahogany trees along the roadside.

The car swept around the long switchback that brought them around the east side of the Peak. Ladera drove effortlessly, as though a road once traveled was instantly recalled. Did he recognize Quentin's limitations in acting as emissary for the jade? There were a dozen questions she wanted to ask, but she knew he wouldn't answer. He'd already made it clear that he expected answers from her, not the other way around. Still, he'd have to tell her more if he wanted any kind of reply.

"Just what do you have in mind, Mr. Ladera?"

He turned, grinning. "Call me Danny. I like you." He looked back to the road. "I think you got an inside track on the jade. I saw you talking to Fung, and he's the guy who's pulling the strings. He puts in the word, maybe you get the jade, you know? Now that would be nice for you but not so good for me. My friend wants me to deliver, and I don't like to disappoint him. Your brother..." He shrugged. "I ain't so sure he can do what he's supposed to. Now we're this far, he's excess baggage. You and me can work without him."

"How did you and Quentin manage an invitation to Fung's party?"

He was thoughtful a moment. "It was arranged. Your brother found out where you were staying. I asked around and found out Montaigne rented a car. He was dumb enough to ask for instructions how to get to Fung's. A couple of phone calls... The rest was easy."

She was certain Quentin didn't have any connections in Hong Kong, which meant that Ladera or his employer did.

"He did his bit with the Chinaman. I don't like the idea of waiting until the gook calls us, you know? At first, Fung was all buddy-buddy but he cooled off after you showed up. It's easy to figure Quent ain't got what it takes. You have."

"You forget I already have a partner," she said guardedly.

"Montaigne?" he laughed. "Hell, I saw the way you were looking at him after that Prigent dame arrived. When you run out on him, I know you're not sitting around cooling your heels while he tumbles blondie." He glanced at her again. "We both know she ain't gonna put up the dough for the jade and let you waltz off with it and her guy."

Arisa's stomach churned and her throat was sour with nausea. Peter had intimated the same thing, now it was being flung at her again. Carter and Claire— lovers and still partners. Her stomach settled to a dull ache that crept upward under her breastbone. They came to the intersection at Wan Chai Gap; when Ladera hesitated, she directed him onto Stubbs Road.

"I'm giving you a way to get back at both of them and still handle the jade. My boss will pay you the commission, so you come out ahead all the way around. We all get what we want."

Except Carter and Quentin, she thought. If Ladera's employer paid her the commission, Quentin would be cut out. And if she worked without Carter, whatever arrangement he had with Claire would be quashed—they'd both be out. The vengeful idea was tempting, but she knew it would be foolhardy to agree. Ladera's proposition might well be fraught with more hidden dangers than those she already faced.

"Who are you working for?" she asked boldly.

He grinned. "What's it they say in all them TV shows? 'I'm not at liberty to say.' Yeah, I'm not at liberty to say."

"Then I can't give you an answer, Mr Ladera."

He frowned and pursed his lips. "Tell you what—I'll ask him. If he says okay, you get his name. If not, you'll just have to know. And trust me."

Her mouth twitched in a smile. She had him in a corner, and he knew it. She had no intention of working with him if there was any other way around the problem, but he didn't have to know that. And she was consumed by curiosity about his strange offer and the man he worked for.

They came into the crowded streets of Wan Chai. Danny Ladera cursed a slow-moving bus that kept them at a snail's pace as they passed the glittering lights of the theaters, shops, and restaurants.

"One big goddamned Chinatown," he commented. "This is a swinging place." The bus moved on, and he shoved the gas pedal, screeching ahead only to halt again when cross traffic blocked an intersection.

"Take a right here," Arisa said. "It'll take us to the flyaway and we can go across on Connaught. It's faster."

He followed her instructions and breathed a sigh of relief when they were in the moving traffic along the bay. "You know your way around."

A few minutes later, they were in the drive-through of the hotel. Ladera tossed the keys to the valet and followed Arisa into the hotel.

"You hungry? We skipped out before the food was served."

"No. I just want to go to my room."

"Alone?"

"Alone."

He nodded. "Okay. Think about what I said. I'll talk to you tomorrow." He winked and doubled back toward the Captain's Bar, where lively music of a dance band mingled with voices and laughter.

In her room, Arisa flung her cape across a chair and stared out the window, still fighting the fury that had been festering all evening. She felt betrayed. Duped. To think that she had been taken in by Carter's scheme was infuriating. She'd had plenty of warning, yet she'd succumbed to his sweet talk and romance like a schoolgirl. He didn't give a damn about anything but getting Travish-Montaigne for himself. Well, she wouldn't let him succeed! He couldn't get the jade without her. She was the one Lo Bat would call—and she wouldn't tell Carter anything. Let him and Claire cool their heels waiting.

Finally, she picked up the phone, dialed room service, and ordered a sandwich and tea. While she was waiting, she took off her white gown and put on a robe and slippers. If she didn't confide in Carter, where would she get the money for the purchase? Ladera? That idea wasn't appealing. She wondered again how Quentin fit into the picture. No matter which way she turned, she came up against a stone wall. She recalled Eduoard's phone call. He'd offered to lend her money for the *galerie*. Would he be able or willing to lend the sum it would take to finance the Chou jade? But asking him would obligate her return to Paris and a new try at that hopeless romance. That would put her in the same class as Carter and Claire.

When a knock sounded at the door, she went to let in the room service boy. She recoiled physically when she saw Carter.

"Why did you run off like that?" he demanded, pushing his way inside before she could slam the door. He shut it firmly behind him. He studied her, assuring himself she was all right. He'd imagined all sorts of things and hurried after her as soon as he'd discovered she'd left the party on foot.

"I'm tired and want to go to bed. If you'll just leave . . ."

"I won't leave without an explanation. What the devil has gotten into you? Did something happen? I was worried out of my mind."

She snorted. "You didn't look too concerned the last time I noticed you slipping off with Claire."

"She has nothing to do with this!"

"Really?" She inhaled sharply and drew her shoulders back. "Why didn't you tell me she was the financial backer for this trip?"

"Would it have made a difference?" he asked coldly. "We needed two hundred thousand dollars. Do you have any better ideas where we could get it?"

She couldn't control her frustration and anger. She wanted to fling Peter Karo's innuendos and Danny Ladera's comments at him, but she held her tongue. Let him believe she'd acted out of petty jealousy. She needed time to think. She turned away and sat in one of the blue satin chairs near the writing desk. He strode over and looked down at her.

"All right," he said. "I'm sorry if it upset you. I went to Claire because she's the only one I know who would consider the proposition I offered. She owes me money and I gave her a way to wipe out the debt and make some money at the same time."

Incredulous, Arisa snapped. "*She* owes you money? The stories I hear make that hard to believe!"

"If you'd listen a minute instead of exploding every time I open my mouth I'll be happy to explain."

"Please do." She sat back and folded her arms across her breasts to hide her shaking.

"Claire and I were in business together. When I decided I wanted to get out, she didn't like the idea, so she insisted on time payments that would keep me dangling on a string. Now I've offered her a cut on the balance due and interest on the rest in exchange for a sixty-day note. I picked up a letter of credit from her bank. That's the whole story. Whatever else you're thinking is garbage."

"She's here," Arisa said. She still wasn't mollified.

"God, she knows people all over the world. I was as surprised as you to see her walk in, but it doesn't change anything." Exasperated, he raked his fingers through his hair. "I was more surprised to see Quentin. Did you know he was coming?"

"Of course not!"

"Do you know who his friend is—the one he came with?"

She stared at him, not ready to divulge her conversation with Danny Ladera until she was sure of her ground.

"I finally remembered where I've heard the name," Carter said. "He works for Ganrali Maracudo."

"What!" Her astonishment was genuine.

"That's right, Maracudo. That means Maracudo wants the Chou jade and he doesn't care how he gets it. He isn't going to wait around and hope we sell it to him."

Weakly, she said, "Quentin doesn't know anything about jade. Why him?"

"That's something I mean to find out. Ladera isn't any expert either. He's nothing but a punk. I suspect they're working with someone here, maybe Kai Tang. He was there tonight and you said he was at Maracudo's party."

She shook her head as if to dispel the fog that had closed around her brain. What had started out as a brilliant idea to put Travish-Montaigne on its feet had become a nightmare of intrigue with a cast of characters too complicated to follow. If she believed Carter, then what? If she didn't, her options were even more limited.

There was another rap at the door and Arisa jumped. Carter was across the room before she could get out of the chair. The room service boy smiled politely and entered with the tray. When he sat it down, Arisa signed the chit and he left.

Carter said, "Think about what I've said, Arisa. Don't make the mistake of thinking Maracudo won't go to any lengths to get what he wants. He's greedy and ruthless. I don't know what part your brother is playing in this but he may be in over his head. For that matter, we may be too. There's still time to pull out, if you want to."

"No!" She hadn't come this far to back away now and leave the jade to Maracudo—or Claire. Carter had presented a logical argument for Claire's presence, but he'd skillfully avoided any implication that there might be more to their business arrangement than he admitted. Or their romantic one. Peter Karo and Danny Ladera both read a great deal more into their "accidental" meeting.

"All right then. Have your dinner and get some sleep. Call me as soon as you hear from Lo Bat. Let's hope I'm wrong about a lot of things." With that, he let himself out and she sat staring at the door.

Angry and confused, she poured a cup of tea and attacked the roast beef sandwich. She felt as though she were on a merry-go-round, circling inanely, plunging up and down on a grinning painted horse. Somehow she knew that her father was holding the brass ring, but it was just beyond her reach, no matter how hard she tried.

When she'd finished eating, she brushed her teeth and removed her makeup, then climbed into bed. But sleep wouldn't come, for her thoughts kaleidescoped wildly. Could she believe Carter? If he was honest about the jade purchase, did she care whether or not he was involved with Claire? There hadn't been any sign of tenderness in his visit tonight. Had she imagined he cared for her, or had she foolishly closed her eyes to his true purpose?

Sighing, she finally switched on the lamp and got up. That morning's edition of the *South China Morning Post* was on the luggage rack where she had tossed it earlier. She picked it up and settled in bed with it. She didn't realize she was looking for the article someone at the party had mentioned until she found herself scrutinizing the women's pages. She found it in a brief gossipy item wedged in with fashion news:

PARIS, June 29—Socialite Claire Prigent, daughter of millionaire steel magnate Nesbitt Prigent of Philadelphia, dined last night at *Le Grand Lefour* with Henri and Eloise Badin and her frequent escort and business partner, Carter Montaigne. Mlle. Prigent has just been commissioned to decorate the newly acquired mansion the prominent Badins have purchased in the *Marais*. Mlle. Prigent has gained a worldwide reputation in her work, which can be found in Paris, New York, Los Angeles, San Francisco, London, Hong Kong, Manila, and other major cities throughout the world.

Arisa crumpled the newspaper and flung it into the waste basket. Business partner! Frequent escort! Damn! She wasn't sure which infuriated her more as she flung herself back onto the bed. She snapped off the light and lay staring into the darkness until her anger subsided and at last she fell asleep.

She waited tensely for the call from Lo Bat. The hours ticked away slowly. When the phone rang, she leaped to snatch it up, then snapped irritably when Carter asked if she'd heard anything yet. She told him a curt "no" and he hung up without offering to join her and help pass the time. Her pique had been replaced by cold determination that she would succeed in buying the Chou jade. It had become more than a financial salvation for Travish-Montaigne. It was the symbol of everything her father had worked for, what he had sacrificed. It was her legacy.

The second call was from Quentin, who wanted to talk with her about combining their efforts now that they were so close to the finish line. She put him off with a curt reply and hung up. Late that afternoon, the call from Lo Bat finally came. His sibilant Cantonese told her to meet him at the Fung house on the Peak. Arisa hesitated, then called Carter.

"I'm to meet him in an hour," she told him.

"I'll pick you up in ten minutes."

It was less than ten minutes when Arisa opened the door to him. She looked fresh but there were tiny lines under her eyes, and she lacked the bubbly spirit that had filled her since their arrival in Hong Kong. She was silent during the ride up to the Peak.

By daylight, the house was sedate and isolated behind its high wall. Several cars were parked in the turn-around like predatory blackbirds. Arisa was out and ringing the dragon bell before Carter climbed the stairs.

They were admitted by David Fung, who smiled, though his face was drawn.

"Please, come in. The others are in the reception room. If you'll join them, we'll be ready shortly."

He ushered them into the room which had been cleared of all traces of the party the night before. The furniture was rearranged into small conversation groups typical of formal Chinese households. Under the embroidered tapestry, a camphorwood table gleamed beneath several lamps that had been turned on despite the sunlight that flooded through the windows and open veranda doors. At the terrace doors, hand-embroidered sheer draperies fluttered in the breeze.

In the center of the room, two Chinese art dealers Arisa recognized from the party sat on a K'eng chair. Nearby, Quentin was poised like a mechanical figure on the edge of a satin-upholstered bench. Behind him, Danny Ladera lounged against the door to the veranda. His gaze followed Arisa and Carter as they approached. On a straight-backed chair, old Kai Tang also watched, then looked away when Arisa glanced at him. The silence was strained as Arisa seated herself on a divan. Carter stood behind her, just out of sight, yet reassuringly close. She wondered how long the others had been there. She and Carter had responded immediately to Fung's summons, so the others must have been called first. The thought churned her fear that Lo Bat had not been receptive to David Fung's request that she be shown special consideration. She wondered if others were coming or if the ranks had thinned to these few. She glanced at Yue Hin and James Wu on the K'eng chair. Were they the only Hong Kong dealers still in the running? Kai Tang was probably working with Quentin as Carter had surmised: his refusal to meet her gaze confirmed his loyalty. His politeness at Maracudo's party had been superficial, nothing more.

In the depths of the house, the door chime sounded like a distant temple gong. All eyes went to the doorway as David Fung answered the summons and showed another man into the room. Arisa stared as she heard Carter's sharp intake of breath behind her. The man who entered ignored the others and went directly to a chair. He sat facing the door as the others watched curiously.

At first she thought she must be mistaken. It wasn't logical that this was the same man who'd accompanied Deline Armitage to her father's funeral, but neither was it illogical. She wondered who he was. No one else in the room had reacted to his arrival except Carter. She could feel his tension behind her. She didn't have long to consider the development. David Fung reappeared.

"We are ready to begin. Lo Bat has asked me to explain how the sale will be accomplished. He will display the jade so that each of you may view it, but he requests that you do not handle it. Each piece has been authenticated. You have my word they are genuine Chou dynasty pieces. Each will be identified with a numbered card, with one exception. Four small stones are considered a set. They are to be bid on collectively. We invite you to write out any bids, identifying the work by number. The sealed bids will be collected and studied. It is to your advantage to make your optimum offer the first time, since the highest bid will claim each piece. If there are no suitable bids, the piece will be withdrawn. Are there any questions?"

"If a piece is withdrawn, will it be reoffered?" Arisa asked.

"It will not," David Fung answered. He looked around the group and waited. When no one else spoke, he said, "We are ready to proceed then." He stepped back into the hall.

The tension in the room was palpable as he reappeared with Lo Bat, who was carrying a wooden chest. The peasant glanced around nervously, his eyes darting to each of the faces as he went behind the table. He opened the chest and unfolded a length of black velvet. Then with the air of a priest offering a holy sacrifice, he lifted the pieces of jade one by one from the box and laid them out. Quentin started from his seat, but David Fung's upheld hand stopped him. Lo Bat arranged the jade on the cloth, setting the pieces far enough apart so there was room for the numbered bits of cardboard David Fung distributed. When they finished, the two men stood behind the table.

"Gentlemen, Miss Travish, we are ready to begin. Please come to the table individually."

Everyone was straining for a look. Quentin was the first to move. He rushed to the table and bent to stare at the pieces of jade. Arisa wondered what he was thinking as he examined art work he knew nothing about. Just then, Kai Tang rose and joined him, glancing at David Fung for acceptance. Quentin stepped aside, then resumed his seat. His face was flushed.

One by one, the Chinese dealers from the K'eng chair went to the table. James Wu complained in Cantonese that they should be allowed to lift the pieces. This brought an angry negative from the distrustful Lo Bat.

When Wu moved on, Arisa glanced at Carter, then rose and crossed the room. She sensed him behind her though she could not hear his footfalls on the thick, lush carpet. His shoulder brushed hers as they bent to examine the jade. Arisa's breath caught as she studied the archaic dragon plaque, the first in the line. The mythical animal's head and tail curled toward the arched body, forming an aesthetically pleasing shape. It was carved with a pattern of spiral curls to resemble scales, and the large perforations through the neck and back suggested a beast in motion. The grayish-green nephrite was thicker and rough along the spine where the carving was unfinished. Still, it was a masterpiece and one of the finest examples of Chou work she had ever seen.

The chape was a simple elliptical shape flaring toward the base. It was unadorned except for a large hole at the top and two slanting perforations on either side channeled into it. It was the kind of piece a collector of antique weaponry would prize, but its intrinsic value as a display item would be limited.

The short, curved jade fish was more artistically worked, though simplistic in line detail and less ornamented than the dragon plaque. The flat form thinned at the head and tapered at the sides; shallow striations indicated fins and the outline of a circle the eye.

When she turned her attention to the grouping of four stones,

a thin sheen of sweat formed between her breasts. She immediately recognized the cicada form Professor Sun had shown
them in the snapshot. The pieces were not identical, though
all were generally the same. Four squat gleaming silvery white
insects, with folded wings so finely incised with veins that they
seemed to throb across the realistically rendered body. The
artist had used the coffee-colored markings of the stone to
create depth and life in the carving. A minute hole was drilled
through each nose for stringing as a pendant. She was hyp-
notized by their beauty, but at the same time a chill danced
along her spine. She closed her eyes a moment and let images
flash in her mind. Her father had told Professor Sun he'd seen
one of the Stones of Heaven. She had seen it too...
Where...? When?

Carter touched her arm and they moved away. The room was
very quiet, Instead of resuming her seat, Arisa stood by the terrace door with Carter. She turned her face to the hint of a breeze
that came around the curtain. Where...? When?

David Fung said, "Mr. Bok, do you not wish to view the
jade?"

The man who had arrived last walked toward the table. He
did not examine the jade as the others had but stood ramrod
stiff, staring at it. After a few seconds, he moved back to his
place.

Fung nodded. "Bid envelopes have been placed on the tables. If you will be so good..."

There was a flurry of motion. Quentin held a whispered
consultation with Kai Tang, who glanced at Ladera, who had
not moved from his post by the French doors.

"Which should we bid on?" Carter whispered.

"The Stones of Heaven." Her father had wanted them...

"Four pieces and the best in the lot. We could miss out."

"We've got to have them, they're exquisite. If they're all
inscribed on the back like the photo Sun showed us, they're
priceless."

"We've got to be realistic."

"Bid the entire two hundred thousand."

He looked at her searchingly. Did she know what she was
doing? There were high spots of color on her cheeks and her
eyes were deep amethyst pools. A bid of a hundred and fifty
thousand would almost surely take the dragon plaque. He hesitated. Arisa moistened her lips and watched him unswervingly.

They'd come this far . . . He reached for a card and pencil and quickly wrote out their bid. The corners of Arisa's mouth turned up in a nervous smile as he inserted the card in the envelope and carried it to the table. When he returned, Arisa leaned against the wall with her hands clenched tightly behind her.

The others filed to the table to submit their bids, all but Bok. When Fung looked at him questioningly, he shook his head. Quentin uttered a nervous sigh of relief at the lessened competition. The room was silent except for the faint whisper of rustling trees beyond the terrace. Somewhere in the distance, a child's high-pitched laugh drifted across the Peak.

David Fung began opening the envelopes. Every eye was on him. When he had extracted the bids, he arranged them like a poker hand.

"James Wu has bid two hundred thousand Hong Kong dollars for the scabbard chape. He is the only bidder. Mr. Wu." He nodded toward the dealer and the man hurried forward to lay out his money. Lo Bat scooped it up greedily as Fung wrapped the chape and slipped it into a leather pouch. Wu hurried back to his seat, his eyes glittering.

Fung laid the first card face down on the table. "There are two bids on the fish. Mr. Wu at two hundred and fifty thousand Hong Kong dollars and Yue Hin at three hundred thousand. Mr. Yue." The old man shuffled to the table to collect his prize.

The dragon plaque was withdrawn when Fung related that the single bid of four hundred thousand Hong Kong dollars, James Wu's, was not sufficiently high to entertain. Wu looked disappointed but said nothing.

Arisa's fingernails dug into her palms. Quentin and Kai Tang had not bid yet. They wanted the Stones of Heaven. She felt her brother staring at her. Her back was damp under her white cotton shirtwaist dress as she stood away from the wall.

David Fung cleared his throat and held out the last two bid cards. "Two bids on the four matched stones," he said slowly. "Travish-Montaigne bids two hundred thousand American, one million Hong Kong dollars. Kai Tang, bidding for Quentin Travish, exceeds this with a bid of two hundred and ten thousand American, one million fifty thousand Hong Kong." His glance at Arisa said he was sorry.

Quentin gave a victorious grunt and quickly took the envelope Danny Ladera passed to him. He strode to the table and spilled a stack of Hong Kong currency onto the gleaming wood. He gripped his hands together as David Fung wrapped the stones and put them into a leather pouch.

Arisa felt as if she'd been turned to cold, hard stone— drained and lifeless. She sank back against the wall and tears of frustration stung her eyelids. She should have listened to Carter. He'd warned her about Maracudo. She should have suspected that Maracudo would know how much she and Carter planned to bid. She bit her lip and swallowed the bitter taste of failure. Quentin shot her a triumphant glance as he went back to Ladera and Kai Tang.

"I'm sorry, Carter," she said when she finally found the courage to look at him. Anger and disappointment raged in his eyes. His mouth was a hard line as he watched Quentin gloat. "If I'd listened..." The dragon plaque would easily sell for double or triple the price offered. Instead, they had nothing. What would become of the plaque now that it had been withdrawn? If she could persuade David Fung to enter a second bid for them...

Wu and Yue Hin hurried out with their acquisitions. Fung was folding the display cloth while Lo Bat stuffed the piles of currency into the wooden chest. Arisa watched Kai Tang prepare to leave, his work done. He looked unhappy, and she wondered why he had not bid on anything for himself. As he neared the door, Bok said something to him in a low voice.

The dealer's face blanched and he cast a terrified glance back at Quentin and Ladera, then rushed out. A moment later, a car door slammed and tires screeched on the driveway. David Fung looked up and frowned.

"Let's go," Carter said curtly.

"Wait!" She restrained him with a hand at his arm. "I want to talk to Mr. Fung..."

Just as Quentin started through the doorway, Bok blocked his way. He gestured and said something in Cantonese, too fast and low for Arisa to make out. Quentin glared angrily and tried to push him out of the way. Behind him, Danny Ladera backed a step.

Bok spoke again, his English hard and brittle. "Give me the Stones."

Quentin blinked. Ladera growled, "Get out of the way, Chink. We bought them."

There was a blur of motion. Bok's hand slipped from his

pocket holding a knife. His arm thrust savagely and plunged the blade into Quentin's belly. Arisa screamed as her brother doubled in agony with a horrified grunt. Blood oozed through his fingers where he clutched the wound. Ladera shoved him aside as he reached under his coat. Bok struck like a snake. The knife slashed Ladera's arm before he could bring out his gun. Ladera cursed as the gun clattered to the floor. He crouched to retrieve it, but Bok kicked it away.

The room erupted. Arisa darted toward Quentin, only to be jerked back by Carter as Lo Bat ran for the terrace doors, the only other exit from the room. She just had time to see Bok raise the knife before Carter shoved her to the floor. The knife arced so close that she heard the soft whistling sound it made cutting through the air. It found a clean target in the running man's back. Lo Bat screamed. The wooden chest flew from his hands. He flung out his arms, as though embracing eternity, and then crashed face down onto the flagstones.

Carter tried to pull Arisa behind a sofa but she could not take her eyes off the scene in the doorway. Quentin had stumbled to the wall and was leaning on it heavily. His beige seersucker suit was covered with blood and his face was gray and twisted with pain. He kept staring at his middle as though he didn't believe what had happened. Arisa shook off Carter's arm and crawled toward Quentin.

The sound of the shot was like the Noonday Gun inside the confines of the room. Ladera crouched on the floor, breathing hard. Bok slammed against the wall as the bullet struck him in the shoulder. Ladera tried to steady his arm for a second shot, but Bok was too quick. His foot flashed like a hammer. Air whooshed from Ladera's lungs as the blow caught him in the chest. He tumbled backward without letting go of the gun. Bok advanced like a snarling cat, his body poised as his only weapon.

Quentin whimpered as Arisa tried to prop him up. Seeing it was hopeless, she eased him to a sitting position against the wall. He tried to talk but only gibbering sounds came out. She looked helplessly for something to staunch the flow of blood from his abdomen. If she could see how serious the wound was . . .

Behind them, Ladera fired again. The bullet went into the wall. Bok's foot came down heavily on Ladera's wrist. He screamed as his bones cracked and the gun slipped from his fingers. Bok was on him then, his powerful hands finding his throat and squeezing.

Carter moved silently and quickly around the perimeter of the room, his one thought being to get Arisa out of danger. David Fung slipped past in the other direction and disappeared through the terrace doors. Carter hoped to hell he was headed for help. When he reached Arisa, he jerked her to her feet.

"Get out of here!" He shoved her toward the door. For a moment, she resisted.

"Quent—"

"Run! Go!" He pressed the car keys into her hand and pushed her through the doorway but not before she had time to see Ladera go limp under the pressure of Bok's throttling grip. Bok saw Carter reach for the gun and whirled.

"Carter!"

Bok pounced and Carter was thrown from his feet. The two men tumbled and rolled, clawing at each other. The gun was lost under them. Stumbling, Arisa flung open the front door and rushed out. She looked frantically for help, but the Peak was wrapped in its isolated splendor. She started back into the house but knew there was no way she could help any of them by standing by watching. The only hope was to get assistance. Where was Fung? Where were the servants? She flew down the steps and pulled open the car door. As she fumbled the key into the ignition, she realized she was holding the leather pouch Quentin had somehow thrust on her. She flung it to the seat and turned the key. The powerful engine sprang to life, and she released the brake and put the car into gear. Blinded by tears, she maneuvered the car through the turn-around and careened down the drive.

Skidding through the gate, she spun onto the narrow road. She hunched across the wheel, one arm pressing the horn so that it blared a steady wailing warning. Dear God, was there no one else around? The tires screeched as she took the curves dangerously fast. Too late she remembered the sharp-angled turn before the final descent to the tram station. The Mercedes tried desperately to hug the road, but the outside wheels were over the pavement. A startled gardener looked down from a steep driveway where he was watering shrubbery, the hose in his hand forgotten as he saw the plunging vehicle. Water sprayed across the windshield and the car skidded on the wet pavement.

Arisa screamed and fought the sickening slew. She heard the crunch of metal against stone, felt the brief hesitation as the car hovered then plunged through the treetops and plummeted down the steep incline over the park. Through the windshield, the sun was a blinding ball of fire that exploded horribly as the car crashed onto Harlech Road.

15

She covered her face against the engulfing heat and screamed. "Daddy! Daddy!"

"Arisa! Get away from the windows!" Thick acrid smoke choked her as her father dragged her back from the litter of broken glass and flaming draperies. He slapped at a smouldering patch on the shoulder of her dress and dragged her away as another fire bomb crashed through the shattered pane, spilling its flaming destruction on the carpet.

"Elliot! What's happening? My God!"

"Hurry, Melisande, the back way!"

"My furniture—everything father gave us."

"Melisande, there's no time . . ." He clutched at her but she pushed away his hand.

"What have you done?" she screamed. "Why us? There's never been any trouble on the Peak."

"For God's sake, Melisande, we've got to get out of here. They'll burn us down with the house!"

"You brought them—filthy Chinese—your friends . . ." Hysterically, she beat at him when he tried to grab her again. Her nostrils flared and her eyes were wild. "Father warned you to stay away from them. But no—you were never satisfied! He gave you a job, made you a success—you could have had everything!"

The angry shouting outside was louder. The fire had crept across the carpet and was licking the edges of the chintz-covered sofa. Black smoke filled the room and dimmed the glare of the torches the rioters carried.

"I had nothing to do with the rioters, Melisande. Nothing."

Arisa crouched behind her father, burying her face in the rough comfort of his coat. She trembled as smoke filled her lungs and she struggled to breathe. The flames crackled and spit; her mother's voice rose above the din.

"You, you and *her*—your Chinese *whore!*"

"Be quiet, Melisande. You don't know what you're saying."

330

He put his hand over Arisa's ears as though to shield her from the venomous words her mother flung.

"Ohh, don't I! I never should have listened to your lies. Lies, all lies. You've found a way to see her, haven't you?!"

"She's gone, Melisande. Your father saw to that!"

"Her and that bastard son you forced me to raise. Don't think you fooled me for a minute. And now you've brought the rest of her kind here to the Peak—to my house."

The sofa burst into flames. A lamp cracked and shattered in the sudden explosion of heat. Arisa cried in terror and her father's hand tightened at her shoulder.

"Is it worth dying for, Melisande?" he demanded angrily. "I'm taking Arisa out of here—now." He grabbed Arisa's hand and rushed across the hall to his study.

"Stay here," he commanded. He hurried to the desk and began pulling out papers, delving for their passports, the little cash he had, and stuffing them into his daughter's hands. He yanked open the curio cabinet and took off his jacket. He scooped as many pieces of his collection as he could stuff into a makeshift bag and tied the arms of his coat over them. Then, thrusting the bundle at Arisa, he ran into the hall again and fumbled for coats in the entry closet. Melisande was outlined in the fiery glow of the parlor. He raced to her and grabbed her arm, dragging her out and ignoring her hysterical screams. He prodded Arisa ahead of them down the hall and through the kitchen. Melisande clutched the door in a last desperate attempt to go back, but Elliot struck her hand down and pulled her outside into the black night. Behind them, another window exploded and a steady, heavy thudding battered at the front door. It crashed in splinters and flying debris. The sudden gust of air billowed fire and smoke through the house. Within moments, the kitchen was in flames. Arisa felt her father boost her over the stone wall that separated them from the neighboring house. Then she was falling ... falling....

The fire seemed to be inside her. Her head ached with heat and her flesh stung. The noise was gone and she was suspended in darkness. She opened her eyes slowly.

The room was dim, but slivers of light crept around the drawn window shades. Hazy blue-gray shadows danced on the ceiling. She moved her fingers and encountered crisp linen.

Very slowly, she turned her head. A bottle hung on a metal standard; clear fluid dripped slowly into a plastic tube. Her gaze followed it to the white tape on her arm, which was bound to a flat board with adhesive.

In the shadows, a rustle of motion drew her gaze. Carter smiled as he came to the bed and peered at her.

"Hello . . . you're awake. . . ."

Her lips were parched and her tongue fuzzy.

"Don't try to talk now." He looked so worried she wanted to smile, but her muscle wouldn't respond to her brain's command. "You're going to be all right," he said gently. "Rest. I'll be right here."

He pulled a chair close and sat by the bedside, his hand holding hers. She closed her eyes and was swept back into the cool gray fog.

When she woke again, the pain had receded. She came out of a long tunnel into the brightness. The hospital room gleamed with a new day. The window was open and the curtains billowed in the warm breeze. The scent of roses filled the air. She flexed her muscles slowly. The padding and tube were gone from her arm. Her wrist was bandaged and she felt the pull of adhesive tape across her ribs. She turned her head and saw a bouquet on the bedside stand. Yellow roses . . . She squinted to read the small card that was tied to a stem with a gold cord.

"For now—Carter."

She smiled and reached out to touch a velvety yellow petal. The door opened and a starched, smiling nurse entered. "Good morning. How are we feeling?"

"We're feeling fine," Arisa said with a smile. "I seem to have slept a lot."

The nurse took her wrist and put a finger to her pulse, lifting her other arm to look at her watch. After a minute, she tucked Arisa's hand back on the spread. "Two nights and one day, not so much."

Arisa vaguely remembered Carter sitting by the bedside. The rest was a hazy dream. "Mr. Montaigne?"

"He'll be back. The doctor wouldn't let him stay all night, it's against hospital rules, you know." The twinkle in her eyes said Carter had argued. "I expect he'll be along shortly. We'll just freshen you up and have a bite of breakfast."

Arisa let herself be ministered to. When she protested that she was able to get up to use the bath, the nurse shook her head. "Not until the doctor gives permission. Hospital rules."

Bathed, combed, and fed, Arisa settled against the freshly made bed with an air of impatience. When the physician arrived, he pronounced her in excellent condition. "Those cracked ribs and bruises may give you a bit of pain for a while. Don't do any heavy exercise. We'll take the stitches out of that arm tomorrow."

Somehow she'd imagined it was a burn under the bandages. When she asked about the fire, he shook his head.

"No fire, young lady. Your car tore up the hillside and came to a stop against a tree, but it didn't flame up. Most cars don't, though you'd never suspect watching all those telly dramas." He patted her hand. "I suspect you'll be able to leave us tomorrow. I'll tell the matron you can sit up a while if you like. Don't overdo. Now I'll let that gentleman friend of yours in. He's been waiting impatiently."

Carter entered before the door swung shut behind the doctor. He looked relieved to see her propped up and smiling.

"Now that is decidedly better," he said, crossing to the bed and taking her hand. "How do you feel?"

"Fine. I've lost track of time. The nurse says this is my second day."

"It seems like an eternity," he said softly.

"A lost weekend." She sighed. "What happened, Carter? I remember seeing you grappling with Bok . . ." She shuddered and he pressed her hand.

"Don't think about it."

"I can't forget it. Tell me so I won't worry and wonder."

"All right, but only if you lie back and relax. I'll be blamed if you have a relapse."

She laughed, then winced as pain stabbed at her ribs.

"See?" he said. "Now behave yourself. There that's better. Okay. I managed to get the gun away from Bok and clouted him on the head with it. That's about it. Fung had called the police by then. Seems he'd let the servants off for the afternoon because Lo Bat wanted complete secrecy for his auction. Mrs. Fung was away, too. If any of us had suspected Bok . . ." He sighed and shook his head.

"He was in Los Angeles—at my father's funeral."

"I know. He's been in the shop several times. I thought he was a collector from Hong Kong, a friend of Deline's."

She was almost afraid to ask. "What about Quentin? Is he all right?"

"He's in another wing of the hospital. They operated. The knife didn't hit any vital organs. He lost a lot of blood, but he's going to be all right. Ladera is dead. Lo Bat, too."

She swallowed, remembering the ugly scene of carnage in Fung's reception room. She glanced out the window at the green vista rolling away toward the distant bay.

"Don't think about it," he said gently. "It's over, that's what matters."

"Another door to the past to seal shut? No, I realize now that it's better to face things than hide them and let them fester." The mist cleared from the hazy dreams in which she'd wandered the past thirty-six hours. Quietly, she told Carter the missing parts of the story that had been locked away so long. Her mother's accusations about Quentin, her hatred of the Chinese. "I don't know who the woman was," she said, "but my mother really never forgave him. I realize now she made his life a private hell. It was always what she and Grandfather Whitaker wanted, never what my father wanted. Hate is a terrible thing."

Carter looked at her compassionately. "We can't undo the past, Arisa. I think Elliot spent many years living with guilt." It explained a lot of things, especially Elliot's willingness to tolerate Quentin's coldness and demands for money. Expiation.

"Yes, I think you're right." And she knew something else she didn't put into words. The only explanation for her mother's hatred of Deline Armitage. She wondered if Quentin knew. She sighed and gave Carter a tremulous smile. "What about the Stones of Heaven? Quentin must have given them to me, I don't remember, but I had them in the car."

"They weren't there when we found you."

"Oh, Carter . . ."

"It doesn't matter. The police say Bok is a member of a Tong called the Crimson Hand. They're a pretty unsavory group, and they're dedicated to reclaiming the Stones of Heaven. Remember the legend you told me? Professor Sun's story?"

She nodded.

"Maybe there's something to it, At any rate, the Stones are gone. Bok may have had confederates around who managed to get them before the police arrived at the crash. If not, I feel sorry for the poor devil who picked them up thinking he'd found some easy money."

She shuddered. Carter brushed her cheek with his fingertips. "David Fung believes bad luck will follow those Stones wherever they are. He's giving Maracudo's money back to Quentin and is washing his hands of the whole thing. He's already donated the money Wu and Yue Hin paid for the other pieces to a benevolent society. He wants to give us the dragon plaque. He says he has no more right to it than we do. I refused, but we finally compromised and he'll let us buy it. His arrangement with Lo Bat was that he'd have the right to purchase any pieces that had to be withdrawn from the bidding."

"Face . . ."

"What?"

"He's kept his promise to my father. He saved face."

"Oh . . ." He grinned. "Old Chinese custom."

"Confucius said the entire social order was based on five human relationships: son to father, younger brother to older, wife to husband, subject to ruler, and friend to friend."

"Not business partner to business partner?" He made a wry face. "Well, I'll have to work on one of the others. Maybe wife to husband. Will you marry me?"

She looked at him, too surprised for a moment to speak. Thoughts dizzied her mind and her heartbeat quickened. Did she love him? What about Eduoard? Claire? The *galerie?* Travish-Montaigne?

He smiled gently. "That's an unfair question when you're weak and helpless. Take time to think about it. I'll ask it again soon." He bent and kissed her as though she were a rare and fragile porcelain doll. "And now, darling, I have to take care of a few things. I'll be back this afternoon. The nurse says you'll be sitting up and we can enjoy your veranda. I'll smuggle in a bottle of champagne." He brushed her lips once more and patted her hand. At the door, he turned.

"Just in case you still have any of those jealous little ideas floating around in your head, I'm on my way to tell Claire what she can do with her money and her games. Confucius say, no obligation old partner to old partner." He winked and blew her a kiss.

The smile lingered on her lips a long time after he'd gone. When an aide brought her lunch tray sometime later, she was still smiling.

"You look happy," the girl said cheerfully.

"I am," Arisa said. "I'm going home."

"Do you live in Hong Kong?"

"No . . . California." Hong Kong was the past, so was Paris. She was going home with Carter.

Epilogue

Arisa glanced around the crowded showroom with deep
satisfaction. Customers drawn by the Stones of Heaven lingered
to view the rest of the exhibits and many were making purchases
before leaving the store. The influx had begun before the sched-
uled time of the exhibit, with people waiting when the doors
opened at noon. She smiled at Professor Sun as she wandered
past the cluster around the Chou jade. The cabinet had been
specially designed to house the Stones of Heaven safely yet
allow everyone to see both sides of the exquisite carvings.
Professor Sun was eloquent in his description and history of
the pieces.

Carter excused himself from the two women he was talking
to and came toward her, smiling. "Your idea to have Professor
Sun was inspiration. He's as much of an attraction as the Stones
themselves."

"He seems to be enjoying himself."

"To say the least. He's ecstatic about having all five Stones.

I imagine his reputation will soar now that they're going to be in the museum."

She sighed. "It's where they belong. It's a shame that so much blood had to be spilled before they got there. I hope it's the end." She thought about the way the four stones that had disappeared after the auction at David Fung's house and its bloody aftermath turned up anonymously at the university. Professor Sun surmised that whoever had taken them had read the newspaper stories describing the stones and their history; it was enough to scare the culprit into getting rid of the "cursed" stones quickly. The fifth stone had come from her father's safety deposit box. There'd been a letter with it, a letter full of pain as he explained how he'd come into possession of the stone. He'd known nothing of its origins until he read Professor Sun's article. He told how he'd contacted the Professor and told him of his conviction that the Stones of Heaven had to be restored to the Chinese people. Antiquities of that importance should not belong to any one man, least of all to him, or even to the person who'd given it to him years ago.

The rest of the letter was a plea for forgiveness of his weaknesses. It was almost as though he anticipated never seeing his daughter again and wanted to clear the slate of the past. Forgive . . . It was she who needed his forgiveness, she thought. For her selfishness and blindness, for all the pain she'd unwittingly caused him. Somehow she knew that he understood.

She smiled at Carter. She knew he understood too. She squeezed his hand intimately as she glanced toward the door and saw Elbert Faus enter. The old man looked hesitantly at the crowd, then began a slow tour of the showroom.

Carter spotted him too. "Here's our number one customer now," he said softly. "I'll talk to him." He captured Arisa's gaze lovingly before he moved off.

"Good afternoon, Elbert. We're honored that you'd brave this mob to join us."

"One of the few pleasures left to me, Carter. Besides, I wanted to indulge myself in seeing so many people admire something that will soon be mine."

"We haven't closed the deal yet, Elbert."

Faus cackled softly. "But we will, my boy, we will. The dragon plaque is exquisite. My offer still stands to top any other offer you have on it."

Carter laughed. "It will help us atone for that fiasco on the Han bronze."

"I take it you got that straightened out?" His blue gaze was quizzical.

"Completely. The substitution was done by a man named Bok who's now in the hands of the Hong Kong police. He threatened and bribed the courier driver. I'm sorry to say that one of our people played an unwitting part in it, but she was being threatened, too."

"She?"

Carter studied the old man's face. He owed Faus at least a partial explanation. "Deline Armitage. Bok was really after the fifth Stone of Heaven that had vanished from Shanghai almost fifty years ago. He traced it to Elliot, then tried to get Deline to get it for him. The fake bronze was a warning that he was getting impatient."

"Why didn't she go to the police?"

"That's a long story, Elbert, one that's over now and would only hurt a lot of people if it came out." Confronted with the news of Bok's arrest, Deline had confessed her part in the scheme to secure the Stone of Heaven and her involvement with Bok and Quentin. Hesitantly, but determined to clear the slate of guilt, she told about the years she'd shared with Elliot during the war, the birth of their son, and her eventual exile from Hong Kong and everything she loved. The jade pendant she'd given Elliot was the only bond tying the two segments of her life together, and she never gave up hope that it would bring him back to her. Only after his death, when she learned the terms of his will, did she realize her self-imposed blindness. Quentin was weak and greedy. Elliot had never really been hers. The past was gone. Pale-faced, she'd begged Arisa's forgiveness.

Carter was surprised by Arisa's calm acceptance at learning that Quentin was Deline's son. It was almost as if she already knew and had made peace with it in her heart. She refused to listen to Deline's vow to leave the shop and the city. They had all looked back on the past, and now the door could be closed gently.

"I won't ask any questions then," Elbert Faus said decisively. "But I would like to have a look at those infamous Stones of Heaven everyone's gaggling about. You've created quite a stir in the art world, you know."

"They are magnificent, and they're finally going where they belong," Carter said. "They're in that case with the mob around it. And if you'd like another look at the dragon plaque, it's in that cabinet over there. Enjoy yourself, Elbert."

"I will, I will." Smiling, Faus walked away like an elder statesman.

"He's one hell of a guy," Tanner Holmes said.

Carter hadn't seen Tanner approach. "He certainly is," he agreed as he watched Faus make his way toward the group listening to Professor Sun.

"No repercussions from the bronze?"

"None. Anyone else would have brought the place down around our ears."

Tanner grinned. "Like Maracudo? I hear he's still fuming because you and Arisa wouldn't give him a crack at the jade. Arisa says he turned over Elliot's IOU to Justin Forbes."

"It'll be paid, but that's all Maracudo will get out of us."

"Unless, of course, he wants to pay Beverly Hills retail on Travish-Montaigne works of art. His money is as good as anyone eles's, Carter."

"Not in my book."

Tanner's grin broadened. "A man of principle. I think Elliot knew what he was doing when he took you on as a partner. You epitomize everything he always hoped to be. Too bad he didn't live long enough to see his dreams come true. I suspect he's smiling down on this little gathering right now. I think he'd even approve of Arisa and Deline telling Quentin to go fly a kite."

"Someone should have told him a long time ago," Carter said with a grunt.

"It probably won't do much good in the long run. Jokers like Quentin go through life weaseling out of one deal so they can plunge into another."

Carter shrugged. "He'll be lucky if he gets out of his current trouble with his neck intact. Manipulating stock accounts is dangerous business. If his client finds out before he can make good, Quentin could be finished in the brokerage business." Remembering Quentin's near-hysteria as he pleaded with them to let him sell Elliot's Stone of Heaven to Maracudo, Carter felt disgust and no sympathy for Elliot's son. He'd played too long on Elliot's guilt and Deline's misguided intervention on his behalf. He was on his own now.

Carter glanced around the crowded showroom. Deline was showing a set of carved ivory figurines to a blue-haired matron with a yard of mink across her shoulders. The woman was listening intently to Deline's explanation of the Chinese deities the carving represented. Deline's face was serene, and when her gaze met Carter's momentarily, a smile flickered at the corners of her mouth.

At the next counter, a middle-aged Oriental couple were examining a rare Ming porcelain Arisa had taken from the case. Her hands moved as gracefully as a flowing stream as she explained the workmanship and history of the piece. Carter wondered if she were speaking English or Cantonese. . . .

"You're a lucky man, Carter," Tanner said softly. "Do I hear wedding bells?"

Carter smiled. "I've asked, but the lady hasn't given me her answer yet."

"She's too beautiful to be in circulation very long. Better hurry or I might let the wolf out of my sheep's clothing." He looked at Arisa with deep affection. "She's quite a gal. I know Elliot's damned proud of her today." Sighing, he winked and tapped Carter's arm in a friendly gesture before he moved off.

Carter made his way to the rear of the shop as Arisa signaled a clerk to take care of the purchase the Oriental couple had decided on. He waited at the foot of the stairs for her to join him.

"Our receipts so far are fantastic," she said delightedly. "I bet every other shop in Beverly Hills is ready to close up for the interim! By tomorrow night we'll—"

"By tomorrow night we'll be dining in a very special place to celebrate," he said.

"Is that an invitation?" she teased.

"It is. Maybe we can make it a really special celebration." He captured her hand and held it firmly.

Her eyes danced. "What did you have in mind?"

"For starters, an answer to the question I asked you in the hospital in Hong Kong. Will you marry me?"

A smiled seemed to radiate from deep inside her. Her gaze was more lustrous than the most exotic jade. "Professor Sun says the Stones of Heaven exhibit at the university will be dedicated the end of October. October is a lovely month in Hong Kong. Lovely enough for a honeymoon," she said softly.

He smiled. "Would you mind stepping into my office, Miss

Travish? The kiss I have in mind would probably attract more attention than the Chou jade."

Still smiling, she slipped her arm through his as they went up the stairs together.

Also in Hamlyn Paperbacks

Judith Saxton

THE PRIDE

A powerful drama of courage and hardship in the years preceding the First World War.

At the heart of the rich cast of characters is the unforgettable Tina Rose, a Norfolk girl whose love for Edward Neyler sets a course of conflicting loyalties that will take her halfway across the world . . . Edward's brother Mark, whose marriage to a Chinese girl will bring him both ecstasy and despair . . . And Tina's family, infuriating and endearing by turns, but always surrounding her with warmth and protection.

This vivid panorama of passion and tragedy stretches from the vast dairy farms of New Zealand to America's booming oil towns . . . from the declining gold-fields of the Clutha to the thriving industrial cities of England. It is a superb and moving story of human love and endeavour.

FICTION

GENERAL

☐ The Patriarch	Chaim Bermant	£1.75
☐ The Free Fishers	John Buchan	£1.50
☐ Midwinter	John Buchan	£1.50
☐ A Prince of the Captivity	John Buchan	£1.50
☐ The Eve of Saint Venus	Anthony Burgess	£1.10
☐ Nothing Like the Sun	Anthony Burgess	£1.50
☐ The Wanting Seed	Anthony Burgess	£1.50
☐ The Other Woman	Colette	£1.50
☐ Retreat From Love	Colette	£1.60
☐ Prizzi's Honour	Richard Condon	£1.75
☐ The Whisper of the Axe	Richard Condon	£1.75
☐ King Hereafter	Dorothy Dunnett	£2.95
☐ Pope Joan	Lawrence Durrell	£1.35
☐ The Country of her Dreams	Janice Elliott	£1.35
☐ Secret Places	Janice Elliott	£1.35
☐ Letter to a Child Never Born	Oriana Fallaci	£1.00
☐ A Man	Oriana Fallaci	£1.95
☐ Rich Little Poor Girl	Terence Feely	£1.75
☐ Marital Rites	Margaret Forster	£1.50
☐ Grimalkin's Tales	Gardiner, Ronson, Whitelaw	£1.60
☐ Who Was Sylvia?	Judy Gardiner	£1.50
☐ Lost and Found	Julian Gloag	£1.95
☐ La Presidenta	Lois Gould	£1.75
☐ A Sea-Change	Lois Gould	£1.50
☐ Black Summer	Julian Hale	£1.75
☐ Duncton Wood	William Horwood	£2.50
☐ The Stonor Eagles	William Horwood	£2.95
☐ The Man Who Lived at the Ritz	A.E. Hotchner	£1.65
☐ The Fame Game	Rona Jaffe	£1.50